— PRAISE FOR *SIVULLIQ* —

"This is my favorite book of the year! Lily Tuzroyluke's debut novel *Sivulliq* is an instant Alaska classic. Gripping and raw, honest, and gut wrenchingly beautiful, this profound and heartbreaking story of resilience and love is as important as any modern tale ever told in the north. *Sivulliq* is unforgettable and haunting—a bold new work from a gifted writer sharing her talent and vital indigenous knowledge that can help us all become better human beings."

—Don Rearden, author of *The Raven's Gift*

SIVULLIQ

Ancestor

LILY H. TUZROYLUKE

Epicenter Press Inc.
Alaska Book Adventures™

Kenmore, WA

Alaska Book Adventures™

6524 NE 181st St., Suite 2, Kenmore, WA 98028

Epicenter Press is a regional press publishing nonfiction
books about the arts, history, environment, and diverse
cultures and lifestyles of Alaska and the Pacific Northwest.
For more information, visit www.EpicenterPress.com

Sivulliq: Ancestor
Copyright © 2023 by Lily H. Tuzroyluke

Cover illustration: Holly Nordlum
Cover design: Scott Book
Interior design: Melissa Vail Coffman

ISBN: 978-1-684920-41-9 (Trade Paperback)
ISBN: 978-1-684920-42-6 (eBook)

Library of Congress Control Number: 2022936026

Produced in the United States of America

For my children Ataŋauraq, Samaruna, and Nasugluk,
my parents Koo'teen and Kinavaq,
and two women who helped raise me—
my maternal grandmother Kaajasaadei,
and maternal auntie Kahs-gay.

For Indigenous leaders fighting for tribal sovereignty
and our ancient ways of life.

For Tikigaqmiut.

For our Ancestors, past, present, and future.

Contents

ACKNOWLEDGMENTS

TAIKUU SUUNA TO MY MOTHER SHIRLEY Koo'teen Tuzroyluke, parent, grandparent, leader, role model, teacher, master artist, matriarch, and mother to many. Taikuu suuna to my late father Emmanuel Kinavaq Tuzroyluke, hunter, whaler, harpooner, iron-worker, Vietnam veteran, and commercial crab fisherman. Taikuu for your love, patience, virtues, ideologies, and dedication as parents and grandparents.

Taikuu suuna to my kind-hearted, gentle, strong, and loving children—Ataŋauraq, Samaruna, and Nasugluk. You bless my life with joy and happiness. You make me laugh every day. You've directed me to this path as a writer. I pray you follow in the footsteps of our Ancestors—protect our subsistence way of life and tribal sovereignty, practice compassion for all-living things, and continue our cultural traditions. Value the bowhead whale over oil, giving over receiving, shared knowledge over self-interest, and public service over industry.

Taikuu suuna to the Tuzroyluke and Hank families of Tikigaq, my relatives, for always making me feel at home. Taikuu to my nieces and nephews, your auntie will love and support you.

Taikuu suuna to the Indigenous leaders who helped form my values, ideologies, life goals and objectives. I've witnessed my

Indigenous leaders fight oil and gas industries, rightfully question governmental authorities, dedicate their personal time, and tell their stories. I owe much gratitude to Rex Kayaliruk Tuzroyluk, Jr., late Jakie Koonuk, late Ray Koonuk, Sr., Caroline Cannon, Samarun Oviok, Sr., late Luke Koonook, and late Enoch Tooyak.

Taikuu to my writing mentor Bill Henderson who introduced me to the world of writing and dedicated many years to my craft, ability, and story ideas by sharing his knowledge, providing edits, and overseeing all minute logistics in the publishing process.

Taikuu suuna to my noble Ancestors. You survived genocide, wars, exploitation, land thefts, epidemics, assimilation, forced removals, residential schools, racism, and oppression. I will honor your resilience and fortitude to the best of my ability and pass your teachings to our descendants.

In the beginning of time, we lived as spirits. We wandered the earth, living in every rock, lichen tendril, wolf, caribou, whale, and beast. We soared in the heavens, winds, seasons, stars, and aurora. We spoke to the Creator about our love for earth.

Because of our love for earth, Creator granted us life. Creator granted eyes to see beauty, hands to guard, feet to walk, and a heart to love.

Man and woman opened their eyes. We looked at our hands. We are no longer just spirits, we said. We're Inupiaq. We're real human beings.

1 | EPIDEMIC

M Y SISTER QIVIU started dying A week ago.

"I can't breathe, I can't breathe," she says.

She vomits. Blisters grow over her entire body. On the third day, the blisters swell up with a thin, watery blood. I clean the watery blood through the day and through the night. She began smelling of old feces or rotting offal, I don't know.

In the morning, I woke to her body convulsing, her mouth foaming, and her hands gnarled and rigid. I inspect her body. Qiviu's body is worse than before.

"What happened?" She asks.

"A bad dream is all," I say.

"Is it bad?"

"No, no. You're getting better. Your legs are almost healed now,"

"My legs are itchy,"

"I'll make more ointment,"

I make a salve with rosehips, black spruce sap, and coltsfoot. Rosehips are to calm the skin lesions, sap for the inflammation, and coltsfoot to ease her pain. Last spring, I collected the rosehips and sap in a grove, between two murky rivers. I seep all the ingredients, adding seal oil, waiting until it's grey, heavy, green, and floral. I rub the salve over her body. She finally sleeps.

On the seventh day, her lips became white. I light the seal oil lamp, sit on the floor, and lay out my sewing. Our house is dark, but I see her rotting, white lips moving in the dark.

"Kayaliruk?" Her voice is hoarse.

"I'm here," I kneel next to her.

"Is it night?"

"It's midnight."

"What are you making?"

"A parka. A light parka for Samaruna. She will want to run."

"She's so fast. Going to be a fast runner like her aaka."

At dawn, I wake up. I don't hear her breathing. I know her bed is empty. I call her name, running outside to a grey and dull dawn. I find her body on the ridges, on a small slope of beach. She died not long ago. I close her eyes and position her hands over her body. I wrap her body in a caribou skin.

I call for my sons, Ebrulik and Nauraq. Ebrulik is twelve years old and Nauraq eight years old. They crawl out from the next house, my parent's house, and walk up the ridge together. I see them walking towards me, frail, tiny, and holding hands.

My sons. I hug them. I check their arms, necks, and faces. I check them both.

"We're good, Aaka. We're fine," they say.

My children haven't eaten enough. They've lost weight. My sons look for food every day. This is their chore. I heard them at night, while sitting with Qiviu; they walk up to the caches built in the hillocks, looking for whatever food is left, scavenging, searching, and scraping. Every morning, they set snares for ptarmigans and rabbits, then, they check the snares in the evening. My boys work so hard. We've eaten nothing but hope.

Last year, I'd sent the boys to the caches. Fat seal carcasses filled the entrance to the cache, round and frozen seals stacked on the northern side. We stored maktak, beluga, and caribou legs. Farther into the cellar, away from the light, we stored grass baskets filled with salmonberries, cranberries, blueberries, and crowberries. We'd string up dry fish: trout, whitefish, char, pike, smelts, and salmon. Nothing remains in the cellars except snow, growing taller in every corner, and solidifying into ice.

My children tell stories of the ancient world, the old world. They search for Little People on the tundra, little beings not taller than a human hand. They tell stories of strong men who stayed underwater for days. The strong men cupped their hands against the ocean floor, breathing with pockets of air made by their cupped hands. My children try to forget death by telling these old stories. They've carried dead bodies to the graveyard with their own youthful hands.

Seeing my sister, my sons cry, walking away at times, walking in a small circle and wiping their tears. I sing a grieving song. I don't know the meaning of the lyrics. The meaning of the song was lost generations ago, maybe centuries ago.

We carry Qiviu to the sled. We sit on the ridge, the wind gusting and whipping. I want to sleep, forget death, and remember life. I know we must take her body to the pyre. It is time to light the pyre. But I let them sit a while longer. I kiss my boys on their foreheads, above their perfect wide eyebrows, their defining and masculine eyebrows like their father's.

Aaka, are you listening? Show me how to comfort my children. I'm too young to bury all our people.

"Where is Samaruna?" I ask.

"She is awake," Ebrulik answers.

"Get the sled," I say.

My only daughter Samaruna is five years old. She is awake and sitting on the bed. I lift her up and kiss the top of her head. I check her face, wrists, and neck.

"Did you listen to your brothers?" I ask.

"Yes."

"Were you a good listener?"

"Yes. Can I see her now?"

"It is time to say farewell. Dress warm."

"Is she flying to the moon?"

"She is with the Creator now. Flying high behind the moon. Adii, my babies need to eat." She is too thin.

"Ebrulik got a rabbit!"

"He did? Was it good?"

"The rabbit was yummy! He taught me how to make a trap and I did."

"You're all so good. My babies are so good. Time to get dressed. Dress warm."

"I can't find my gloves."

"They're right here."

"Not those ones. I can't have those ones."

"Help me find them. Here, under these. These ones? Good."

The dogs pull our sled through our tattered, bloated village, waterlogged from the warm spring. I tried to keep all the homes in order, but death came again and again, and I left the homes to the ravens, foxes, and feral dogs. Soon nothing will be left except whalebones.

I braced myself for this day. It must be done. We'll burn the bodies of my husband, sister, mother, father, aunt, and uncle, covered in smallpox. We ride to the graveyard, carrying my sister under this gray dawn, and I notice every detail in the snow, every thick canopy of clouds, every yellow blade of grass sticking up from the snow. We'll burn their bodies and it'll be done.

We cross a field that grows tiny mosaics of sun-yellow poppies, purple saxifrage, sharp magenta cushion flowers, moss campion, and fluffy white cottongrass. Lichen covers the tundra rocks in smoky grey tendrils, blossoming outwards like flowers.

We carry Qiviu to our graveyard, an ancient graveyard, built centuries ago by our Ancestors.

I saw an ancient burial as a child.

Father knelt by a skeleton at a shoreline, exposed by the storm waves. Whoever buried her, removed her eyes and replaced them with jet-black stones. She stared at the sea with her round, black eyes. A long ivory spike pierced the skull down to the spine, keeping the skeleton intact. Talismans surrounded her body, made of jade and ivory. How strange and decorated.

"Why are her eyes black?" I asked.

"I don't know." Dad knelt, elbows to his knees.

"It looks scary."

"It's the old way. The meaning has been lost."

"What happened to her?"

"I don't know. Many people loved her. Look how they buried her. Look at the tusks. It's how we used to be. Our people will be strong like this again."

They buried her with walrus tusks, etched with elaborate scenes. Men throw spears at a mammoth herd. Women cut up belugas with their ulus while children run with slings. A large creature with an elongated neck and four flippers swims in the ocean while hunters throw harpoons from their umiaqs. A creature flies in the sky with massive wings, half-man and half-bird, chased by men with bows and arrows. I saw how our Ancestors lived in these carvings.

We carry Qiviu's body to a pyre. A dozen stiff and skinny corpses lay together, shoulder-to-shoulder, their jellied eyes sinking downwards. I look away from the faces. I don't want to remember their faces this way, drooping and distorting with death, mouths gaping open.

My boys stack the pyre. They work and say nothing. The day came faster, and the land turns blue and violet.

Smallpox began on the coast. The Yankee whalers breathe out the disease like dragons. The Yankees want their oil, so they sent death to feast upon our flesh. When will the Yankees be fulfilled?

The healers drained our old blood in the arms or back of the knee. They tattooed ancient symbols on our bodies, especially children. Tattoos protect our spirits.

On my oldest son, the healers tattooed a motif band found on fossilized ivory. The healer found a piece of ancient ivory on the beach after an autumn storm.

On my second son, the healers tattooed insignias of whalers. Whalers mark their tools with small symbols, a practice started by our Ancestors. The healer inherited age-old whaling tools from another healer. Before tattooing my son, she said the tools fell on the floor at her feet.

Far inland, on a river bluff, our Ancestors painted symbols on rocks. The healers tattooed bands around my children's wrists and ankles, including my youngest child, bands shown on the river bluff. My children braved hours of bloodletting and tattoos, how strong they are.

Our shamans said a person broke a taboo, bringing this sickness to our people. Did a hunter scrape a white-furred animal in the spring? Did a menstruating woman speak to another person? Did a woman give birth in another person's presence? Or maybe a person died inside their home and their family did not destroy the house. My father said it is best not to dwell on the origin.

I kneel at the pyre. I uncover my husband's face. His skin shriveled back in death, tightening against the skull, now a shadow of a man. His hair falls away. His body looks like a small child wearing his parka. This body is not how I remember him.

He doesn't look like a body should look, but then again, how are dead bodies supposed to look? I decide not to think about it any longer. Instead, I think of my husband hunting in the foothills surrounded by fog, walking on tawny rocks and smoky green lichen, like we did in our early days of marriage when we wandered in the country on our dog sled, unrushed, unhurried, filled, and content.

Where are you, husband? Is your spirit standing next to me? Do you hear my thoughts about you? You promised we'd grow old together. We'd have more children. We'd learn how to make sleds. We'd look for honeybees for honey. We'd be grandparents together.

My husband knew death was coming. He couldn't breathe from ulcers in his mouth. He shook and coughed, trying to get air into his lungs. He said it is his time. I begged him to stay a little longer, a moment longer. I woke the children and told them it was time to see him leaving. Ebrulik wanted to run after him. I held Ebrulik by his arms.

My husband trudged up the ridge, stumbling, but determined. My children and I watched him until he disappeared over the ridge, out of view, vanishing into the abyss. It wasn't an extraordinary day, not foggy, not stormy, or a bright day. It was grey and cloudy when a good man and a good father walked up to face death like our people have done for a millennia.

This is how our people face death. We walk to the tundra, underneath the sky, and we face death by ourselves. Even the Elders, old, feeble, and minds like children, somehow, they know when the time is near. I suppose I'll know when it is time.

My children and I waited all day for his return. Finally, I begged the boys to come back inside. It was getting dark and cold. I held them all. I covered them in furs, melted snow for fresh water, and searched for any food left in the caches. By night, the wind shrilled in short bursts. I waited for my children to fall asleep before finding his body.

"Time to say farewell," I tell them.

"I can't," Ebrulik says.

"I know it's hard, son. This isn't how he looked. You remember how he looked."

"I wanted to see him again." Now when Ebrulik speaks, he seems like a young man, not a twelve-year-old boy.

"So did I," I say.

Sam grabs my neck with her little arms. "We're going to light them on fire?"

"Yes. We're going to light their bodies on fire."

"Why?"

"They died from a bad sickness. A white man's sickness. It's what your aapa wanted."

"How will we see them?"

"We'll remember them. We'll come here and remember in our minds."

Each child says their farewell in their own way. I stand back. I don't eavesdrop. Ebrulik and Nauraq whisper in his ear, crying. Samaruna says she loves him. She wants him to visit her dreams.

When it's time to light the pyre, I don't have to say anything. The boys look at me and know it is time.

The boys start the pyre. From the base of the pyre, long serpents of smoke jet outwards, billowing up to the sky. We hear their fur clothing sizzling in the flames. Their hair scorches and their scalps turn black. Sinew cords pop. Wind pushes the pillar of smoke to the north, returning our people back to the sea.

"Step back," I tell them. We sit, hunched in the same position, wiping away tears. The fire smolders but our grief burns higher.

"Can he see me? Even if he doesn't have his eyes?"

"His spirit sees, even without his eyes,"

"All of them?"

"All of them,"

"Will he come home soon?"

"He won't come home,"

"He won't come home again. He's gone, Sam," Ebrulik cries.

"Ebrulik! She's still little. You don't talk to children this way," Ebrulik cries harder, curling downwards into his legs. I hug him. I kiss his head.

"Aaka, I'm hungry," Samaruna says.

"I know, love. It's whaling time. The crews will be on the ice," I tell them.

"Can we go?" Ebrulik asks.

"Yes, we can. We'll go north on the ice."

2 | ERYSICHTHON

— MAY 28, 1893 —

DEAR LORD,
    I'm sailing on arctic seas aboard a New Bedford whaling ship named the *Erysichthon*. We sail through the Bering Straits, between Alaska and Russia. Our destination is Herschel Island, in arctic Canada, where a small whalers' town is built.

We'll hunt whales in arctic seas for the next two months to hunt for the mighty bowhead whale. In two months, the ice will close. This is my first long sea voyage, and I am pleased to begin my chosen career as a whaler and harpooner.

Captain Richard Merihim scowls at the helm in the deckhouse, legs planted far apart. He looks at the sea with his seaglass, scribbling numbers in his notebook, repeating numbers over and over. He drinks coffee with the first mate Emilio, probably more whiskey than coffee. Captain Merihim is a man from New Bedford. Merihim is an angry man.

The captain and first mate spot a whaling ship ahead. It's a whaling bark mastered by an Englishman, a tall, lanky man. The whaling bark blows three columns of black smoke from their melting pots, evidence they've struck a whale, and now they melt blubber to oil.

Captain Merihim yells, "Lucky bastards! That could be us if we didn't drag our asses in the morning!"

God save me from Captain Merihim's anger. I avoid the captain at all times, especially while he's drinking. I keep my mouth shut and eyes down into my work. The captain's anger increased when he learned I went to school, a private school, no less. The Quakers' long-standing academy for the Betterment of Colored Children. I'm proof that the educated make bad life choices, he said.

I clean the deck everyday with the cabin boy Gerald. Every day, we clean the deck, recoil the whaling lines, and scrape ice using a scrubbing brush. We coil the whaling lines in perfect alignment, an assurance they'll pull out of the boats without incident.

Gerald stops scrubbing. I look at him. He's eavesdropping on the captain. "Captain says it's the Englishman. A mother and calf,"

"Boy. Let's finish this up," I tell him.

Gerald scrubs harder. Gerald is black, like me, but he's starting into the trade early. He's lucky. I'm twenty-seven and this is my first year. He's fifteen and will grow into the industry. He's lucky.

We work four hours on deck every day, working on a rotating schedule. I don't mind the days spent on deck. Below deck is suffocating, smelling of sweaty, spermy, unwashed armpits, unwashed groins, moldy wood, bilge water, and the green smell of algae, all congealed in thick streams. I've learned to sleep by breathing out of my mouth. On deck, we escape the bed bugs biting away at our skin, clicking cockroaches hiding in the shadows, and the rats gnawing away at every cask. I look forward to the cold sea air.

Fortunately, Merihim insists on a clean deck, not as a matter of hygiene, but of presentation. He yells at other ships docked in the bays, "You men live here? We are whalers! Not men of the grease!"

We pass the lucky whaling ship. The Englishman's crew hoists large blanket-sized pieces of whale flesh on deck, securing the mother and calf with chains and pulleys. Three men walk on the cutting stage, planks protruding above the water. The three men cut the whale with long spades. A few crewmen wave at our ship, including the English captain. To me, the Englishman seems a damn good honest man, if my opinion meant anything.

Merihim analyzes every detail of the Englishman's ship. He scrutinizes all whaling ships this way. "Ha!" He yells. "He's got the female on the chain. Is he insane? Why not bring up the calf first?"

"Beginner's mistake," Emilio says. The captain and first mate laugh. "Calves give more oil than any mother!"

"Better finer grade oil than any adult! He spits upon generations of whaling wisdom!"

Gerald stood. He looks at the Englishman's ship as we approach. No one wants to get whales more than Gerald, probably not even the captain. He's determined to get the extra purse for spotting a whale.

"What ya doing, boy?" Merihim asks.

"Nothing, sir!" Gerald collapses back down on the deck, probably bruising his knees in the rush. Gerald got no sense. He's only fifteen years old but I remember having more sense at fifteen years old.

A few days ago, Gerald smoked tobacco for the first time. We watched the ordeal in smiling silence: filling an old pipe with leafy tobacco, striking the match, a big inhale, and endless coughing fit. We laughed tears.

Later, I found Gerald lying on his bunk, facing the wall.

"Gerald. We all coughed at our first smoke," I said.

"Not in front of a crew," he said.

"True. That's true. You'll be fine, boy. Quit trying so hard to be like an officer. Be picky who you look up to."

Gerald and I sweep all the snow and ice overboard. We scrap fresh snow into our cups, melting down to a few gulps. I wish I could fill my hands with fresh arctic water for a long drink. Strange the things I wish for when on a ship.

We're done with the deck.

"Why do we have to clean the deck in the ark-teck?" Gerald asks.

"It's arctic. Arctic. Get some more schooling, son. You need more schooling. More reading," I say.

"I don't need any more schooling when I got a trade. My ma says. I'm lucky to get a trade."

"Your ma is right. You got a trade. Doesn't hurt to read a book? You want to be an officer? When you want to be an officer, you got to know how to read longitude and latitude, and north, west, south, and east."

We sit with Remigio, a skinny pockmarked Portuguese. We grab rope for splicing. We're splicing rope today. Yesterday we cleaned out the trypots, the pots for boiling whale blubber, dry as an old maid in heat, Remigio says. We're an unlucky ship with 452 barrels of whale oil, capable of carrying 2000 barrels. Even though we're in the thick of slow-moving, blubbery bowhead whales, we're not catching any beasts.

Remigio shares turtle meat in exchange for splicing rope. The turtle meat is from Galapagos Islands, lush green islands near the equator, a strange, beautiful place with sea iguanas, turtles, white sands, and clear azure waters.

At the Galapagos Islands, the cook wanted fresh wild pigs. He said we needed fresh meat to last until San Francisco. We tried. We heard pigs squealing on the island, running, large leaves moving as they ran underneath the foliage. Merihim said we've no time. So, we killed two large turtles, the biggest I've ever seen. The cook dried and cured the meat into jerky.

I wasn't keen on eating turtle meat, but everything goes stale on a ship. Water stales within a week. We clean the green, filmy slop forming on the water's surface, but a mildew taste remains. On most days, we eat salt horse and duff.

We fish every day, or try to fish every day, hoping to provide the cook with a few flounders, trout, or snappers. Remigio caught a king salmon last week and it was a treat.

"That was a fish you caught, Remigio," Gerald says.

"Oh, it was a fighter!" Remigio smiles. He's told the story many times although there's not much of a story. He went out at dusk, almost turned in for the night but tried his luck anyway on account of his ulcer, which causes excessive flatulence, he says. Best to stay on deck with his gaseous fits. He caught the fish on the first cast but fought a good quarter of an hour to get the monster on deck. He killed the fish, pulled it up by its gills, and presented the fish to the cook. We cheered. Fresh fish the next day. We smelled the fish cooking by breakfast.

"Ibai is right, Gerald. You can't be an officer if you can't read. Start training to be a captain. I've been on ships where the captain is training up to three other officers to be a captain. Three! That's how you get the best fleet. This is common sense. More than common sense. This is company strategies. Like them stock market boys who send people out to look for stock market traders. They search in colleges, can you imagine? Those boys are smart. What's taking so damn long? We should be through the strait. The captain should run the engines. There's more fuel at Port Clarence. Herschel. I would have seen us through the strait by now. If the captain asked me, I'd tell him. A good captain asks from his crew. When I'm captain, I'll ask my officers, what you think? You think it's time to run the engines? I'll be humble and ask their opinions. Not like these know-it-all captains. He just drinks with his best buddy, not talking and not training. I bring knowledge to the ship and ask nothing in return. It is god saintly to ask nothing in return."

"You have been here?" Gerald asks.

"Sure, sure. I harpooned a 40-footer."

"Will we get a whale soon? Today? Tomorrow?"

"You're too young to speak of whaling. Make sure the captain's chamber pot is clean."

"Done! Can I go now?" Gerald asks, blowing heat into his cupped hands. He shivers. Gerald splices rope faster than anyone. He's got wizard's hands, they say.

"Our shift is almost done. Sit with your back to the wind, Gerald," I say.

"Okay, alright," he says, moving.

We sit, side-by-side, splicing rope.

"Get another layer of clothing on the boy. He's got enough fat for two! I'm not one of you Gerald! I'm used to the cold," Remigio says.

"He's a child," I say. Gerald is a little too meaty for his age. The crew never lets up on his childhood fat. When you going to lose that baby fat, Gerald? Get to work and lose the baby fat, Gerald.

Me, I'm happy for the cold and happy to work in the north. No rats, snakes, crocodiles, or flesh-eating spiders. The land is clear, cold, and clean.

Gerald pulls a Sears Roebuck catalog from his pocket, shivering and flipping pages. "Can I afford this?"

He shows me a page of hats. Top hats.

"A hat? Boy. Save up your money for something good. Fashion comes and goes. Let me see, what's in here? Guns, alright, good. Stoves," I pause in the stove section.

"A stove?"

"I'm a grown man, Gerald. How is a grown man to heat his home? This one looks good."

"Ladies don't look at your stove and want to marry you for a damn stove."

I look to the Alaskan coast, at the dark sandy beaches, tide pools, caves, ice-locked lagoons, and rocky cliffs swarming with birds. The land is still covered in snow, even in late April, and I've heard the snow doesn't completely melt until June. I want a home in the wilderness, on a sandy riverbank where I'll fish for supper. I'm saving for an iron cooking stove, rifles, bullets, traps, pans, matches, tobacco, and flour. An axe, surely. I must start an inventory. I've accrued a debt to the company, but I plan on living in the west.

"Emilio. Take me down. Slow it down. Two knots," Merihim calls to Emilio.

The ship slows to two knots. Upon hearing the engines slow down, crewmembers emerge up on deck. Men crowd the stairs, one whaler holding a handful of cards.

Straight ahead, we see the thin line of ice. A succession of ships sail east towards Port Clarence, averting the sea ice. Port Clarence is a shallow port. The land naturally makes a good harbor, the spit curling around like a hook.

"What's happening?" A whaler asks.

"Port Clarence. Looks like ice," I say.

"Jesus, it's Grand Central Station. Yep. We're stopping in Port Clarence. We gotta hole up at the port. I'm telling you," Remigio says.

"How many?" Gerald asks.

"Damn. Can't say," I say.

"Will we go ashore? Ibai?" Gerald shakes my shoulder, excited for an answer.

"I don't know. Just wait."

Gerald and I are greenhorns, and we're black. We don't go ashore to any big ports for fear of abandonment. Gerald and I saw the Azore Islands, Talcahuano, Tumbez, San Francisco, and Nome from afar while the captain and officers rowed to shore for fresh food and fresh whalers. Even at Nome, not two days ago, Gerald and I watched the Alaskan town from the ship.

We saw Talcahuano at night, the town alive with lights and torches. We heard music across the water. People celebrated an event on shore. We thought it might be a wedding. We imagined walking the clay, brick roads, ordering crabs and clams near the sea, sampling the local exotic fruits and plants growing in their vibrant colors and prickly skins, and of course, seducing the dark-skinned indigenous women emanating macadamia oil, musk, and leafy air. Merihim laughed at our children's eyes and said to act like men, not like guttersnipes at a bakery window.

"We're going ashore! All the crew!" Merihim announces.

We cheer. Crewmembers yell the news below deck and we hear cheering from below. I suppose the captain doesn't fear we'll jump ship in Port Clarence. There is nothing but rolling tundra and sea.

"We'll stop in port. We're going ashore!" Gerald jumps like a little girl. He whoops and clutches my shoulder.

"Alright, Gerald. We're going. Jesus."

"For how long?"

"I don't know. Find a parka. We need a parka. Get your trading stuff," I say.

Gerald and I saved for trading with the natives. We'll get little more than a few dollars for our salary after they calculate accrued expenses like a mattress, dungarees, brogans, oilskins, utensils, knife, and such. Charging a parka onto our company account and we'd owe the company after landing. Better to trade with the eskimos ourselves to avoid owing the company and their inflated prices. Couldn't say we'd get the opportunity. After Gerald and I stayed on the ship at Nome, not two days ago, I wasn't sure if we'd get the opportunity.

I wish I had enough for the eskimo boots. Eskimo boots are better than heavy brogans but I don't think I have enough for trading.

Merihim rushes below deck. We rush after him. "Get the crates up on deck. Hurry. Move. I bet the good stuff is gone. Damn it. Damn it to hell! Where's the bags?"

Merihim and Emilio open the panels to the tween decks. It's a small storage area between decks. The crewmen form a line from tween deck to the deck. We haul up all the trading commodities for trading with the eskimos: flour, fabric, coffee, guns, knives, sewing needles, whiskey, ale, and the smallpox vaccinations. I've heard a person makes 600% profit trading in alcohol. Trading alcohol with the natives is illegal. We say nothing. The captain may only get a citation then we'll sail with a captain hell-bent on rowing you up Salt River.

We sail into the hook's eye, alongside steamers, schooners, barks, and brigs. Many of the vessels sailed beside our ship all the way from San Francisco.

"Sixteen ships, Ibai! Look at all the ships! Ibai! Eskimos!"

"Alright, Gerald. We'll see them soon."

The eskimos arrive in skin boats, mooring in the inlet. I count twenty boats. Other eskimos arrive by dog sled.

"I thought the women walk around with no shirts," Gerald says.

Sten and Lammert laugh. I shake my head. Sten and Lammert are two of the many Dutchmen on our crew and the strongest men I've ever met. The Dutchmen on our ship have whaled in every northern icy country: Greenland, Svalbard, Norway, and Iceland. They're frugal, unafraid to fully undress in front of the crew, and obsess about the weather. The captain is keen to listen to their weather predictions.

"Mind yourself. More than a few men will return to their captains with black eyes and empty pockets," Sten advises.

It is late afternoon when we anchor in port, and it is getting dark already. In preparation, we slick our hair, dress in our best flannel shirts, rinse our mouths from the stench of rotting teeth and velvety tongues, wipe our groins of vinegar-acrid piss, and fill our pockets with any trading items. We dress, prepare, and stand at our stations without complaint.

Emilio approaches Gerald and I, tossing water bladders. We catch the bags.

"Fill up the bags," he says.

"Yes, sir," we say.

"Damn!" Gerald says after Emilio leaves.

"We're going to shore. Be thankful. Let's haul ass to get water,"

"Alright. How long will we be here?"

"I don't know. Best to find our parkas first thing."

Our crew rows to shore in five whaling boats. The port is shallow, sandy, and gusty.

"Thank you, Lord Jesus!" I say as we row to shore.

"Amen," a few men say.

Port Clarence is in western Alaska, in the land of eskimos. Grey moraines cut through the soft, rounded hills. My impression of Port Clarence is an ancient place, untouched for centuries. The only evidence of modern influence are three wooden buildings, little bigger than shacks: a reindeer office, trading post, and gold office, all run by Americans, I later learned.

We land on shore, wet from recent rain showers. Farther up the beach is tundra covered in green moss, shrubs, lichen, and stunted alder trees.

Gerald jumps out before anyone, his legs submerged almost to the knee. He doesn't care. He smiles and hauls the boat up the shore. He bends down and lands on all fours, grabbing fistfuls of sand. I shake my head.

Hundreds of men walked the beach, a thousand men it seems, clumped together on this stretch of Alaskan coastline. I don't recognize all the nations of men. Northerners, Southerners, African

American, Irish, Dutch, Polish, Portuguese, Chinese, Chickasaw, British, Massachusetts Indians, and Maori. The whalers walk and move like a cloud of birds, no rhythm, no leaders, no followers, no headmen, no shouting men, instead migrating and flocking into streams and rivers. It is a strange feeling to see so many foreign men walking this ancient beach. It's surreal and unfathomable. Did they seek fortune? Did they seek adventure? Like others, I've believed the arctic is where I'd find my fortune, so I enlisted, planned, prepared, dreamed, fantasized, and prepared my mind. Dreams change. Dreams evolve.

Our crew spread out into the mobs while Gerald and I ask for the fresh water source. We aren't the only whalemen assigned to the task. After getting directions, we march south on the beach, feet sinking in the wet black sands and rounded stones. Merihim likes to assign extra chores to me, and to Gerald. I think there is a perverse enjoyment in choosing the same two poor greenhorns.

Further towards the tundra, a woman screams. It is a terrifying, high-pitched scream. We can't see her.

"Jesus," I say.

"What's happening?" Gerald asks.

"I don't know."

The screaming stops. We can't see the woman.

"Why was she screaming?" Gerald asks.

"I don't know. Pray for her,"

"I don't see her. You think there are any other women here?" Gerald asks.

"No,"

"How do you know?"

I'm sweating already. I'm rushing down the beach. "There's no women except for the captain's wives. And they're old women,"

"But there could be,"

"Let's get this over with. You're a growing boy and best to find a wife after you've reached manhood."

In Gerald's mind, he'll meet his future wife tonight on the edge of the world and they'll make promises to wed before we board. His older brother is a foot taller than I and he's wanted by every woman in the county. I imagine Gerald's going to inherit the same height and not have any troubles finding a sweet, loving wife. Yes, Gerald will continue on as a whaler. He's going to be a strong man like the Dutchmen and his older brother, and he'll advance up into the ranks on account of his strength and height and accommodating nature. He'll, no doubt, survive any hits, slumps, or dives in the whaling industry, staying loyal to the art of whaling.

Me, tonight I want to get drunk. If there are women, that'll be good, too.

We find a small creek in the south, where other whalers fill up barrels and bags. Up the creek a ways, whalers try their luck at fishing. Other whalers fish at a small slough, a thin slurry of water cutting through the tundra.

"You catching anything?" I ask.

"They were running earlier. Better than sitting around with these assholes," he says.

Gerald laughs.

We heft back to the boats, straps digging into our shoulders. I hear Merihim haggling with a translator, hand on the back of his neck. "Bullshit! Wolverine. I'm not interested in fox. No more red fox. Coffee, another pound of coffee, nothing more. Nothing more." He crosses his arms while waiting for an answer. "Good. That's good. You've made a good decision."

By the time we load the water bags into the boats, it's dark. Night comes fast in the arctic.

"We're done. Let's find our parkas,"

"C'mon, Ibai!" Gerald's smiling and jogging. He's ready for trouble.

At the first fire, a barber cuts hair while the man kneels in the sand. A few men wait in line for a haircut. Another man sells boiled potatoes wrapped in hemp sackcloth. He's got a few potatoes left, boiled, hot, and ready to eat. We shake our heads. Gerald is quick to find a bottle around the fire and he jumps in line. I stand next to Gerald.

"Good man, Gerald," I say. I swig the steel flask. It's whiskey, full, sweet, and burning. I want to take another swig but the next man snatches the flask from my hands. My cheeks burn and my heart relaxes. Gerald laughs.

We start off to the next bonfire. In the air, I smell good tobacco, resinous and woodsy. Remigio and the Dutchmen share vodka and smooth tobacco. The Dutchmen found some of their fellow countrymen.

A few men start singing a Confederate southern song about a belle and fighting the war. Some bullshit song.

"What the hell? No. No. No!" Lammert says. Lammert sings, almost yelling. They sing a song from their homeland, their fatherland, their motherland. The Confederates, not to be out-done, yell their song, which, in turn, causes both parties to sing louder. Gerald and I watch for a verse or two while taking a few shots of vodka. In the end, a fiddle starts playing Oh, Clementine, and hundreds of men start singing, successfully ending their singing competition.

"I heard the captain had to report how many barrels," Remigio says.

"Shit. What'd he do?" I ask.

"They babied him like he was a child. Said it happens to the best of them. Happens to all ships."

"Damn," I laugh.

"He said he doesn't want any pity. He'll butcher a thousand whales before going back to New Bedford with an empty ship. Not our fault he's not seeing those fish. He tells us where to go, so we go. Except we need the barrels. We need those casks."

Gerald and I continue down the beach.

Gerald staggers. "You got tobacco, Ibai?"

"No, I don't."

"Well, you should."

"I'll think about it."

"Tobacco is a man's habit. Dis-, distinguished gentlemen smoke tobacco."

"I suppose they do."

"Well?"

"Well, what?"

"You got tobacco?"

"Let's sit down for a while. Can we join you?"

We stop at a fire where a lone whaler sits on a grey log of driftwood. He's an older black gentleman with a peppered beard, heavy sodden clothes, and a Yankee army jacket. He's a decorated soldier but not wearing his medals. I see where his medals used to be in lightened, bright patches of wool. He breaks twigs with his hands, caretaking the fire.

"Have a seat, men. I'm not sure what this is. I think it's from the local berries, here. Where you from?" He offers a drink in a bladder bag.

"New Bedford."

"Born whalers of New Bedford."

"Yes, sir," Gerald says.

"He's starting early. This is my first year," I say.

"Never too late to start whaling. Or anything new, in my opinion. My pa started reading at sixty years old. You hear about that Borden girl?" When we left New Bedford, a Massachusetts woman was accused of killing her parents with an axe. 'Lizzie Borden took an axe, gave her mother forty whacks', as a song goes. We inquire about newspapers at every port.

"Yes, sir. Last we heard they're having the trial soon."

"Crazy woman. They found the axe in the basement, I heard."

"Yeah. We've been waiting for the news."

"Heard you folks have some hard luck this year."

"I suppose we're in hard luck."

"Yeah, I've been on ships with hard luck. You can't predict who's going to be heavy with fish. I sailed on a spanking new ship with a young pious captain and went home with a red ticket. Then I sailed with a one-eyed old man with gout and came back with a nice purse. You going to find another ship? Whalers come and go. Captains always need new men."

"Gerald and I got contracts. His mama lives not four blocks away from the company."

"You're in it then."

"Yep. We're in it."

"You'll have to tough it out to the end, then. At least you'll get experience. Skill gets a whaler through the season. Skill fills up casks."

"It's good advice, sir. Thank you, sir. How long you been whaling?"

"I can't say. I was probably his age when I first joined. Then, the war. Took me a couple years before I found a ship again."

Gerald shivers and holds his hands up to the fire.

"He gets cold a lot. He doesn't have the constitution for the cold," I say.

"You'll get used to it. Whaling is in our blood. Since black men and women come to America, we've been working the whaling ships. I heard Captain Healy is a black man. You seen him?"

Captain Michael Healy is more famous than the President of the United States. He's the captain of the Revenue Cutter, a policeman of the sea. Latest I heard, the mighty, famous sea captain Healy intends on introducing reindeer herding in an effort to save the eskimos. Fifty years of whaling took its toll on the people.

"No. Captain doesn't want an inspection. He's always avoiding an inspection," I say.

"I seen him. Captain Healy. He doesn't say he's a black man. I seen him and I know." He offers the bladder bag to Gerald again. "Oh, let him drink. He's doing man's work. The young drink for fun. The geriatric drink for their bowels."

I laugh with the gentleman. Gerald doesn't get the joke.

"He doesn't get it," I say.

"What, geriatric? It means I'm old, son!"

We both laugh again.

At this moment, a young whaler approaches our fire. He smiles, saying nothing, seducing with his smile and posture. Gerald looks at me, then back at the young man.

"I'm good. Thanks, though," the old man says.

The whaler leaves, finding an interested party down the beach.

"Why was he looking at me like that?" Gerald asks.

The old man laughs a high-pitched laugh, hitting Gerald on the shoulder.

"He's not been exposed to the world, yet," I laugh.

"Son. Whalers get lonely. Men find love where they can."

"What? Why you laughing?" Gerald sees the young man escort another man into the darkness. Gerald's appalled. "Oh my god! Why would he think I wanted that? I'm, I'm, I'm not that!"

We can't stop laughing at his naiveté.

"You drunk, Gerald?" I ask.

"What?"

"Gerald. Think you've had enough drink for now. I can't carry you back to the ship. No."

"I'm good, Ibai. Give me a minute."

"Oh, he's going to lose it. He's going to give it the ol' whaler's christening," the old man says.

Gerald scrambles up into some tall beach grass. I hear him vomiting, hurling, and the rush of liquid hitting the ground. I cringe. Good Lord, how much the boy drink?

Other whalers join the bonfire. The old man is well-known. Men offer their drink and shake his hand.

I warm my tired back against the bonfire, thawing out the chills in my bones.

I look up to the hills, shadowy contours against the starry sky. The hills call my name. The wind howls, lamenting, ululating like a siren calls men into the sea. I hear it clear as day.

I don't want to serve any man. I don't want to work shifts from dawn to dusk covered in soot and grease from industrial machinery or catch lung's disease at thirty years old from mining, or labor on a whaling ship hoping to advance a little more every few years. I want my own land. No captain, master, overseer, or boss. Free.

Can I not fight for freedom by being myself? Is this not a way to fight injustice? A Negro man living free in the great frontier, is this not fighting for a better world? I want to walk in the wild plains, taiga, tundra, fish for my dinners in the great arctic rivers, and live off the land. I'll brave the freezing arctic, wild animals, snow, and unpredictability. I'll brave it all. This is the part I'm meant to play to better this world. God knows.

Am I drunk? Maybe it's the drink after months at sea. Should I walk into the darkness, away from the ship, with the clothes on my back, away from drunken whalers and captains? I may not walk on land for months, nay, years.

Gerald's still in the grass somewhere. I hear him spitting and moaning about.

As I gaze into the dark land, an eskimo woman walks straight to me. She carries a child on her back. An older man follows close behind her, most likely her father. The baby sleeps underneath her parka. I see only a small head of black hair. Her chin and forehead are tattooed, not dark or bold but soft and delicate. Her hair braided and coiled into designs. She wears the skins of land animals. The eskimos do not mix sea and land animals, why, I do not know. She stands noble and Spartan.

She sees the trading items in my hands. I hold up flour, coffee, sugar, knife, and a pewter-tin timepiece I bought on the New Bedford pier, a timepiece covered in floral and leaf scrollwork. The timepiece hangs by a silver albert.

She looks through my bag with her hand and tests the knife against her thumb. She smells the coffee, biting into a coffee bean. She pinches a few sugar granules into her mouth. She holds the timepiece up into a shard of light from the bonfire. She listens to the timepiece against her ear, and then holds up the timepiece to her father's ear.

The old man hands over a parka. She bounces the child on her back, although I didn't see the baby stir. She waits.

I hold it up. It is a caribou parka with long walrus tusks designs. I notice the tusks first, long striations beginning on the shoulder and piercing downwards through the chest, about twelve inches long. I smile.

She gestures for me to see if it fits. I fumble putting on the parka. It's warm. There's fur on the inside, feels like deer fur but I'm not certain. I feel foolish with their eyes on me.

"It fits," I blurt, clapping my hands against my legs.

Gerald emerges from the beach grass, moaning. "Captain calls us back."

"He called already? Shit!" I'm looking for the woman. She's gone, disappeared into the crowds.

"You got a parka? From who?"

"She was here. A minute ago."

"Captain's calling. Ice is moving."

I see Emilio. He herds our crew back to the boats. The ice cleared. All hands are called to the ships. Crewmen extinguish the fires. Hordes of men walk solemnly to the ships, sharing their drink.

I look at the land. I hear the wind howling. A falling star shoots across the sky. There's time. There's still time. I'll live off the land. I'll walk to Nome and find work.

"Ibai! Get moving," Emilio growls. He stands behind me, scowling, threatening. He waits until I start walking towards the ships.

My opportunity is gone. Emilio and Merihim count the crew.

While we wait to load the boats, Gerald scrounges for a parka, stumbling, rambling, and drunk. He barters with an old woman. He puts on the parka. The parka fits. I can't believe it. What are the odds? Lucky bastard. We laugh.

"Gerald! That parka was made for you," I say.

"Look how grateful he is," the cooper Clayton says.

"That lucky bastard," Remigio adds.

"How did he do it?"

"Jesus, boy!"

The woman shows Gerald how to dance like an eskimo, which he attempts. He's smiling, stomping his foot and waving his hands in the air. He thanks the woman again.

Merihim recruited two eskimo men. We couldn't pronounce their names but eskimos aren't called by their names on any ship. Emilio named the two men.

"What should we call them? They need names. Look at this guy. Look at him." Emilio stood next to the eskimo. They are the same height. He looked at his legs. "I've never seen such stubby legs! Where's his ass end? Legs! Welcome aboard, Legs!"

Men laughed.

Emilio stood next to the younger eskimo. "He's got a face like a woman. Lips like a woman. I bet all the eskimo women talk of this one's pretty mouth. Berry! Lips as red as a berry, berry, berry!"

A few men cheered, "Berry, Berry, Berry!"

The eskimo men smiled, chuckling. They didn't understand.

Legs and Berry camped on deck. I've seen eskimos camping up on deck. It must be cold. I think I'd quite like camping on deck. Merihim also recruited two eskimo women, later discovering their names are Dorothy and Susan. Dorothy is the older woman. I don't know her age. Susan seems to be around twenty years old but she's lost most of her teeth so it's hard to tell.

"I sew. I sew parka and boots for you. Gold for new boots," Dorothy says to the crew.

"Gold!" Some whalers say.

"I'll trade you sugar. Remigio sugar," Remigio says, sucking two fingers while looking at the eskimo women. Whalers laugh.

Dorothy scrunches up her nose, holds two fingers close together, showing an inch. She snaps her head back in laughter.

"I'm more than that, little girl," he untucks his shirt and starts pulling down his trousers until the captain arrives. He tucks in his shirt with a scowl.

Dorothy and Susan board a whaling boat with Merihim and Emilio, laughing, drinking, and rocking their boat in the calm harbor.

"Captain said we need women to sew boots and pants," a whaler says.

"We need women for more than sewing," Remigio says.

"Not our business," a few say.

We row to the ship, my heart sinking deep into the black sands of Port Clarence.

Before loading up the boats on deck, Emilio approaches the crew. Emilio rubs his nose between his eyes with one hand. "Alright. Glen, Edgar, Ibai, Sten, Lammert, Remigio. We're sailing north to a village. You're going ashore. We leave at first light."

Why'd he call me? Captain doesn't like me at all. I'm called ashore to be a packhorse, the only reason he'd call me.

"You get to go? Can I go?" Gerald asks.

"Not my decision, Gerald."

"You get to go to shore! Will you get to trade, too? Bring my tobacco? Trade for a relic. I'll sell it when I get home."

I'm not looking forward to the trip. Emilio is a brute. I've seen Emilio and Merihim bring in new recruits, avoiding the landsharks for new whalers. Landsharks "cost more than a virgin whore slated for bigwigs", as Merihim and Emilio say. They disappear to the saloons, tenement houses, boarding houses, brothels, and opium houses, carrying back unconscious men. They dredge up men from every crevasse of society: jails, wanted criminals, fresh immigrants, men passed out at saloons, men drugged by whores. The new recruits don't wake until far at sea. We pity them. They wake in bunks.

After leaving San Francisco, Emilio stood in the forecastle doorway. He speaks to the new whalers they've "recruited". "How are these men today, then? Getting on fine? Cook makes a good breakfast. For the meager resources he's been given, he gets along well."

"Where am I? This is kidnapping! I'm a United States citizen! You'll be hanged!" A man yelled. We learned he was from Utah.

"I'm talking. Not polite to interrupt while a man is speaking," Emilio speaks like a schoolmistress. "As I was saying, before rudely interrupted, and what I am about to express in this culmination of a conversation, is you're now whalers aboard the *Erysichthon*."

"Whaling! This is kidnapping!"

Emilio punches the man. Emilio walks around the room before returning to the doorframe. He didn't speak again until leaning against the doorframe. "You've been blessed, brothers. Blessed into a brotherhood. Whaling is an ancient profession, as old as whoring. Every swimming creature is a fortune if it can be boiled down to oil. We travel to all the ports in the world. London, New York, Australia, Bangkok. This is your grand adventure. This is the greatest adventure of your life, brothers!"

"Scoundrel! Police! I'll report you to the police! I'm a United States citizen! I could die! I might die at sea! I'm not a sailor!"

"Do you have no manners, son? I don't have any patience for a man with no manners!" He kicks Utah until he loses consciousness.

They locked him in the storeroom with a bucket. We heard Utah cry through the night. "I can't breathe in here! Please! I'm not a whaler! I'm not a sailor! Please Lord Jesus!"

A day later, Utah walked up on deck, clothes wet from sweating, smelling of vomit and shit. Emilio sat, watched him throw his shit bucket and wash his clothes in seawater. This naked, sweaty man washing his clothes on deck is a vision I won't forget.

We asked Utah, "What were you doing when they got you? At the saloon? Playing cards?"

"They nabbed him while fucking a whore in the alley. His white ass showing to the moon," someone said.

I tried not to laugh. Damn. That's tough.

I get to sleep as soon as our shift ends. I'm dreading the morning.

I missed my opportunity to jump ship. God has a plan. If I trust in anything, it is that God has a plan. I think of the native woman, the faint lines of her tattoos. This was the first time I met a native woman.

God has a plan.

3 | Our Birthing Place

WE CHASE THE HUSKIES FOR MOST of the morning. It's tiring and useless. We've got no food to bribe the dogs into the harness. A few dogs bolt away at the last moment, grinning and trotting away. They've run loose all winter, running up on the ridges, even dad's lead dog Kikku. I recognize her crying from the hillocks.

We need more dogs, at least ten. Maybe twelve. The leader would be best, but I'd be grateful for any of them, even our straw yellow MacKenzie River dogs who've proven idiotic but the strongest sled dogs of them all.

In the night, I'd hear the dogs fight and howl for food, and I shut out their crying. They're emaciated, matted, and rank. Over the winter, two females gave birth to litters, but the mothers ate most of the puppies themselves. Another guilt, another regret. Sorrow doesn't resurrect the dead.

I don't like to see my father's dogs running loose on the ridges. He walked dogs every day, especially as pups, sometimes lashing a light travois of long saplings to the pup, not heavy enough to ruin the dogs' hips but heavy enough to teach them to listen, sprint, veer left, veer right, take a sharp turn, and stop.

"Quit spooking the dogs, Sam!"

"I'm not spooking! They like me more than you."

Samaruna distracts the dogs with her running. The boys attempt corralling the dogs, clapping their hands, whistling, and whooping. Nothing works. Then, Samaruna's distracting attempts make the chore more exhausting.

"I'm so hungry. Don't fight. Help me load up the sleds, Sam. Find your toys. You don't want to leave behind your toys, do you?"

"Awwww," she puts on an exaggerated frown, shoulders sagging in resignation.

"Look for your puppy, Samaruna. He's around here somewhere. Maybe his Aaka will come for him."

"What about those other dogs?" A group of wild dogs grew over the winter. We hear them at night, howling and fighting over scraps.

"Those dogs might be feral. Take dad's rifle with you."

"No, we're alright. We'll get Kikku."

The boys grab sticks and rocks. They're so brave.

Dad left his Winchester rifle. He kept the rifle oiled, clean, and wrapped in a sealskin scabbard. Aaka made him a bullet bag made of bearded sealskin lined with waterproof intestines. I hadn't looked at the rifle for a few months. Not since dad died. Rust grows on the handle. I wasn't watching these last months. I'll try to oil the rifle. I can't let the rifle get any more rust. We need the rifle.

My sons want to go hunting. We've prepared them since birth. My husband made them bows and arrows, slings, bolas, and spears. They've practiced. They've competed against each other, as brothers do. They check the weather each morning, like old men, examining the clouds, wind, smell, and stars in the sky. My sons have strong bones and sturdy feet.

My children know the Prayer Story by memory:

Long ago, a little boy went out to trap squirrels for his aaka. His aaka loved the squirrel parka. He went out at dawn, setting his traps. He waited all morning, all day, and into the night. The squirrels ran across the tundra by the hundreds, and he didn't catch one.

The second day, he set his traps again. He prayed, "Thank you for giving your life to me. Thank you for your gift."

After his prayer, his body looked like mist, his traps looked like mist.

He caught many squirrels. With each squirrel he said, "Thank you for the gift."

This is how hunters pray before they hunt.

Now I must take them caribou hunting by myself. Are you listening, husband? When I imagine their first caribou hunt, I hear the thundering of ten thousand caribou hooves, a deep hollow trembling of the earth. I see our boys aiming their bows and arrows and running with spears. I see you kneeling on one knee with the rifle against your shoulder, taking the final shots to injured caribou.

I'd watch the hunt, waiting in mother's worry and agony, watching her boys in the streams of never-ending caribou, but also yelling my cheers. A wonderful mother's dream dreamt since the beginning of time.

I scrape the ice from the sleds. Then I line the baskets with smoked moose-hide.

When I smell smoked moose-hide, I think of my mother. She said the Koyukon people smell like smoke and earth. It's how they cure their moose-hides, she said. They scrape off any meat, flesh, and hair, stretch out the hides, soak in water and moose brains for two days, and then smoke with spruce and birch branches. The process makes the moose-hide much softer and preserves the rich, dense, smokey fragrance into the hide.

I lead Sam down the pathway. I hear her playing with her two dolls. One doll wants to play inside the house; the other doll wants to drive a dog sled.

I lead her to my aunt and uncle's house at the end of our village. We need sharp tools, cups, rope, and sinew. My uncle made the best knives. He harvested flint, jade, and slate in the hills. He harvested cedar driftwood from the beach and fresh spruce from the interior. I recognize his knives when we travel to Messenger Feasts, when the people cut their food.

I start in their entryway. I climb down into the doorway and look at the wall in the light. Uncle organized his tools with hooks and shelves. I search through seal nets and fish nets, spears and cutting tools, bows and arrows, seal skin buoys, jigging hooks, retrieving hooks, dog harnesses and packs, flensing knives of all lengths, and waterproof gear made of intestines. I choose the best spears and knives he owned.

"Are we going?" Sam sat in the doorway.

"Yes. We are going to see my uncle."

"Where is he?"

"He is north. A little ways north."

"How far is it?"

"It will take a couple days."

"I'm hungry."

"I know, love. We will fish at the river tonight. We might get trout and whitefish."

"Will I fish, too?"

"Anything you want."

"Will we come back?"

"Yes, we will."

"Is it rude to dig around in his stuff?"

"Your ataata won't mind. He gave everything to us now."

"Even his house?"

"Even his house. Wasn't it thoughtful?"

"I can live in his house?"

"Wouldn't you get lonely without your aaka?"

"What about when I'm grown up?"

"When you're grown up, you'll live in this house with your husband and children. I'll live in my house and be a grandma."

"You can't be a grandma. You don't have white hair."

"I'll have white hair one day."

"But you have to be old. Really, really old to have white hair."

"Start a pile for me. Grab this. Good job. You are very strong."

"Can I play now?"

"I want to look inside, too."

"Awww. Alright."

We make our way down into the house, crawling at times, going through three doorways made of whalebones. I start a fire in the main room, in a square fire pit lined by blackened stones, the smoke rising to an opening in the roof. The house froze over the months, but it's in order. It seems bottled in time, suspended. My aunt kept the floors clean and uncluttered, all objects in a designated place.

My great-grandmother Ag'niin lived her last years in this house. Dad and uncle moved her from the old village, an ancient village built near the pointed end of the peninsula. They transported her in an umiaq, swaddling her like an infant. She said, "Stop babying me." She sat tall and proud in the umiaq, carried away by her strong grown grandsons.

She died in the year of plentiful rabbits, before the white man's sickness. She lived to be over a hundred years old, no one knows for sure. Ag'niin remembers white men, even in her youth. White men traveled to the arctic for hundreds of years, all for different reasons. They traveled to study plants, to study animals, to search for routes, to search for metals, to search for precious stones.

Ag'niin was a tiny woman. People feared her, especially children, because of enormous scars on her face. Every morning, she swept the floors with an owl's wing. From the ceiling, she hung herbs, plants, flowers, mashu bulbs, stalks, stuffed birds, and bags filled with jade, quartz, ivory, pyrite, amazite, geodes, and flint. She lost her eyesight in her last years but continued picking plants by their smell.

She kept the fire fragrant, burning sticks dipped in soot. She peeled long stalks of plants, thorny on the ends. She made clay pots made from seal blood, down feathers, and a powdery-white clay found on the north side of the peninsula. I remember her hands most of all, her calloused fingertips, her blue veins meandering over her bones, and her tanned brown skin. She'd sit in the sunlight, dust particles floating the still sunny air, wetting her hands before molding the clay, water dripping on the tiles.

I remember talking to her after I married. She spoke like a young woman, not slow, tired, milky, or decrepit. She spoke like a woman of twenty years old, sharp, idealistic, and bursting with ideas.

"Do you love him, your husband?" She asked.

"I do."

"You're lucky. I've had three husbands. Two I didn't like. The first husband went beluga hunting. I knew he'd die on the ice. I dreamt of his death a week before it happened. Even though I didn't like him. He was mean. Irritable. I didn't want him dead. What would I do after his death? I said I've got a bad feeling. They found nothing of him except his boots. I don't know why he left his boots. The second husband was tiny man. How I going to love a tiny man? I want big sons, tall sons! I left him and he married another woman, one of those women with big hands and loud voice. She bossed him around like a puppy."

She made me laugh.

I start in the cooking area. I look through the utensils, cups, and stone bowls. I like the sheep horn cups. The cups are light and tough.

"Aaka, look!" Samaruna wants to bring all her toys. Balloons made of duck feet, dolls with ivory faces, a miniature wooden boat with geometrical markings, scraps of fur, a toy sled with fuzzy dogs attached to a gang line, and a sling.

"We're going to have to leave some toys at home."

"Awww, Aaka."

"We'll be back soon. Take the sling. You can practice. One doll."

"Awww. This balloon? Can I? Oh please?"

"Alright, alright. Put this stuff in the bag, too. And these. And this."

"Aaka!"

"You've got big muscles. You're strong. You got it?"

"Yes."

"Are you certain?"

"Yes. I'm certain. Bye!"

I stand at the bedroom, staring at the black and heavy shadows. The bed frames built against the walls, usually covered in caribou skins, now naked and skeletal.

Strange things happened in this house during my aunt's final days. She held on longer than anyone. Food went sour. Cups tipped over. Flames danced on the floor, away from the fire pit and burning coals. Flies crowded outside her home, yet did not enter. Even now, I hear the buzzing flies, heavy as bees.

I feel a pinch on my arm. A mosquito? A spider? No bite to be found. My hair seems to stand sideways, floating in all directions. My body fills with static.

I can't stay in this house another minute. I smell the drying mashu stalks and I need to get out of this house.

I finish pawing through the parkas on the walls, and brush through the hats and mittens. I extinguish the fire. I grab all the cups in my arms, the gloves, the hats, the sharp knives. I shut the window. I close the door, crawling in the darkness.

Crawling through the entrance, I tell myself not to think of scary stories, but I can't stop my mind. Caribou Man, no, don't think of the Caribou Man. He is half-man and half-caribou with glowing red eyes. Don't think of the demons jumping from shadow to shadow, bodies like a black fog, whispering incantations and curses. Don't think of the wide-mouth baby smiling from ear-to-ear and mouth filled with shark-like teeth.

Darkness seeps downwards into the earth, like water, like a growing creature. I hear everything. I hear the water dripping somewhere in the tundra. I hear the mice scratching in their burrows. I hold tighter to the cups in my arms, trying to squeeze courage out of them.

In the last leg of the tunnel, I hear Sam in the corner. I don't want her to know how scared I am.

"Hello? Samaruna?" I ask the shadows. The huskies whine outside.

I pause in the dark, let my eyes adjust. I hear a little scratching in the corner, and see iridescent eyes, pearlescent blue like the scales of a deep-water fish. The eyes blink. Dust and dirt and feathers swirl around the room, the wind beating like a heart. I can do nothing but hold up my arms to guard my face. I fall down, dropping everything.

Silky white feathers escape the tunnel. I see scaly talons curled backwards. I listen to the bird's powerful wings flying away, my heart beating and thumping.

I sit, my back against the permafrost, looking up at the sky. The dogs stopped whining.

Samaruna appears. I can't see her face. Her black hair falls downward, hiding her round face. "Did you see that?! Aaka! Did you see that?!"

"I did! What was that?!"

"It was an owl. That was the biggest bird I've ever seen!"

"Yes, it was."

"Did it scare you?"

"It scared me."

"Aaka, you're more scared than me when I saw the mouse. Even more scared than me when the mouse crawled into our house. Mice aren't my friends. Dogs are my friends, not mice. Aaka! They found my puppy! There he is!"

"Thank your brothers. Say thank you."

I crawl outside and brush myself off. An owl. I felt the air from its wings on my face. Sam talks about her puppy, but I am thinking of the owl, its glowing eyes and massive wings. I search the meaning and symbols of everything, my husband said. I don't like the growing, dark feeling in my belly. My heart flops in my chest, not racing but beating hard.

"All of the puppies died except this one. Look how fat he is," Nauraq hands over the puppy to Sam.

"His mother is up there," Ebrulik adds.

"She will follow us. Don't worry. Are we ready? We're ready." I look at my children. They're sad to leave home.

"I don't want to go. I want to sleep in aaka's bed," Nauraq says.

"I don't want to go either," Ebrulik says.

We could stay here. We could rebuild our homes. We'd start by cleaning out the caches, throwing out the baskets chewed up by the mice. We'd shave down the old, smelly ice building up in the corners, and then air out the houses from the stale air and collect rainwater. I'd repack sod and grass on the roofs. I'd throw all our old clothing onto a bonfire, not even give the clothing to the dogs. I'd start everything fresh and new.

But my children are hungry. We must find food. We must find

my uncle Ataŋauraq.

"I have your aaka's tent. The one she made two years ago. How about we go to the river and fish for the night?" I hug the boys and we walk toward the sled. They sigh.

"Fishing will be alright," Ebrulik says.

"You are good boys."

The boys circle the sleds, securing each section, pulling the ropes taut, inspecting, a ceremony of hunters before traveling. Will the dogs make it?

We unhook the dogs and head out through the main roadway, leaving behind empty and crumbling houses, passed a decorated graveyard fluttering with pools of ashes. We depart our village into silvery, white tundra.

My mother chose this ancient place. She had no memories here. When she saw the low tide, the lack of jellyfish to scare away fish, and wandering baby seals on the beach, she knew this is home. She carried fresh water in a clay pot and watered the earth. The land is porous, cold, solid, sturdy, by a dry stony meadow away from insect-infested marshes.

Mother and father explored this land, like my husband and I explored this land. Before bearing children, my husband and I roamed, explored, and memorized every curve of the land, every hill, every creek, finding ores of flint or hematite, finding agate crystals up on cliffs, and a rock shaped like a walrus. We camped in the sacred spots, places known for ghosts, a cliff where a man hung himself over the loss of his wife, a mountain to find a wealth of marmots, a waterfall surrounded by sea bird eggs, a creek filled with king salmon, a cave where our people hid from the Natuaqmiut after a long chase, and a hill called Iluitsuq meaning 'Many People Killed'. We explored these places, like my parents explored these places.

My mother didn't know the history of the cove. Tikigaqmiut, Nunamiut, Qikiktarmiut, and Tannik people told mother the stories, she told me, and I tell my children.

In ancient times, at this shallow cove, the Koyukon attacked our people. The women fought alongside the men, running half-naked from their homes to show their courage. The Elders took the children into their umiaqs, fleeing to the sea. The Elders shielded the children's eyes but could not shield their ears, and land went silent. The Elders and children buried the Inupiaq and Koyukon people side-by-side on the stilts of the whalebone, then they journeyed north to begin again.

In ancient times, when the world was cold, prosperous, and flourishing, it was a birthing place for our people. Newly married couples traveled to the cove, spending their first days as husband and wife. It is where love began.

"It's a north wind. Good to bring up the animals of the sea," I say, smiling at the wind.

4 | BRACKEN RIVER

W E ARRIVE AT THE RIVER IN midday, faster than I thought. We traveled along the beach until reaching the cliffs. We went around the cliffs by going inland, using a gentle and worn trail. The dogs fared well. A few dogs look close to death. Survive a little longer, I pray. Please, dogs. A little longer. We'll feed you fish, dogs. Are you here, mother? Help me feed my children. Help me feed our dogs.

I hope the dogs see the journey ahead and know we're getting fish. They grin at the open lands and I'm grateful for their strength to continue.

I cry before reaching the river. I hide my tears from my children. Last year, we traveled to this tributary with three healthy dog teams. Today, our dogs are starving and near-death.

"Aaka?" Sam nestled in the sled, surrounded by hides and furs.

"Yes."

"I see his mother."

"The puppy's aaka is following?"

"The dogs are following."

"Good." I look back. The wild dogs follow our trail. This gives me hope. The dogs may be still teachable. The dogs may be tame.

We love this bracken river filled with trout, whitefish, tomcod, pike, char, graylings, dolly vardens, and salmon. We begin our journeys at this tributary, traveling on the icy river like a road into the vast hills of tundra.

I call for the dogs to stop and throw out the brake. The boys help the dogs stop by running ahead, ensuring they don't tangle or jerk. We stop the dogs at Aaka and dad's drying rack. The boys find tracks of wolves, polar bears, and fox, but no human footprints. Next to the drying racks, they find an ulu, scraping tool, shreds of a tarp made from seal intestines, and a broken weir.

I stand on the riverbank, looking out to the sea, now covered in ice. Open ocean is miles away. Sam plays with her puppy.

"Do you remember being here last year? You and your dad went far down the beach for the crab. I raced with your auntie on this riverbank. She could jump farther than anyone I knew."

My girl did not hear. She chases the puppy down the riverbank, the dog sniffing and peeing.

On an idyllic summer day, we walked through the meadows and hillsides, sitting in circles, laughing and filling sacks cottongrass, salmonberries, crowberries, cranberries, mountain alder, northern golden rod, and rose hip roots. We collected cloudberry tea and Labrador tea, and wild celery. The Elders walked together, laughing, talking of the old days when they would travel to the Messenger Feasts, across the channel to Siberia, or south to trade in Qikiqtaġruk. We'd mix a dessert of fresh berries and lard, whipping and whipping the lard until fluffy.

My sons are good fishermen. They collect an axe, fishing lines, and hooks. They walk to the ice, checking their steps with the staff, pressing and checking. They find a good spot, wiping away fresh snow. Ebrulik swings the axe, chipping away at the ice. I'm so proud of my boys. Sam follows her brothers out onto the ice. I yell. "Follow their steps. Careful! Walk only in their steps! Boys! She's the youngest! Let her fish!"

This tributary is a good nest of driftwood. The currents circle where the river spills into the sea, a spiraling swirl of freshwater and seawater catching cedar and alder driftwood. Rough seas send up good amounts of driftwood. I start a fire near the root of a large cedar.

I'm exhausted. I want to sit in the sled, rest, but my children are working hard, my young boys working hard as men. So, I continue.

I unpack the tent, rolling it onto the ground. Sam grows impatient waiting for the fishing hole, and joins me, helping with the tent, getting in the way more than helping, but I praise for her efforts. Getting up the tent is slow work. I tire too quickly. My husband put up the tents. Last summer, I fished with the little ones on the ice, jigging and hooking for trout and tomcods, and then we'd return to a warm tent on the riverbank.

My hands are cold and dry, wrinkled and peeling like an old woman's. I inherited my mother's hands, her large knuckles, like a fighter, yet still slender and feminine. I rub my hands, remembering mother covered in boils, her mouth spurting blood, why must I suffer this way? I miss my gentle and kind mother who taught my children how to ice fish. She'd cook all day, filling our bellies, bodies, bones, hearts, and eyes, saturating our spirits with joy. How can I raise my children like my mother?

I sit in tears. Sam grabs my neck.

"Aaka. Are you crying?"

"Yes, love. I was thinking of your aaka. I miss your aaka."

"Aaka. It's alright."

"Thanks, baby. She was the most special woman, your aaka." I stand up. I can't give up. I wipe my tears and blow out my sadness. The boys got the fishing hole open. "Sam, they're fishing now."

"Don't start without me!" She's running and yelling.

"Hurry up. They're starting."

I put up the tent, first by dusk, then by firelight. Winds picked up, whistling and shrilling. I see snow flurries stirring over the snow, shimmering under opal moonlight. We hear wolves in the hillocks. We look east. I prop dad's rifle up near the fire. My children aren't afraid. They left all their fears back in our village.

When the tent is up, fire going strong, I join my children on the ice.

Ebrulik holds the fishing line with a rod, about four feet long, while Nauraq clears away ice from the fishing hole with a cup. Nauraq and Samaruna look down into the water.

"A trout. I can see fish. Trout maybe. Big ones," Nauraq says.

Ebrulik looks, and then sits back into fishing position. "Let me see. Pikes. They are going down to the sea. They spend the winters in the rivers."

"Will we get pikes?" Nauraq asks me.

"Yes. The spirits watch over us," I tell him.

"How do you know?" He asks.

"It's what our people believe. Aaka and aapa watch over us, too. The Sea Goddess Sedna will send us food. Aaka and aapa are probably talking to her now."

"They are talking to Sedna?"

"They walked to Sedna by walking on the ocean floor. They climbed huge reefs and swam with whales and seals to find Her."

"Alright. Where are we going?"

"We are going to find Ataŋauraq." Ataŋauraq is my uncle, my dad's brother. My dad and his brother looked alike, both strong and happy. Both wore ivory labrets, piercing both sides of their mouths, piercing through the cheek to mouth. Not all men pierce with labrets. But dad and uncle are more traditional. They like stories of the old days.

"Can I be on his whaling crew?"

"Yes."

"Can I paddle after the whale?"

"You won't paddle for a few more years. You will both grow up to be whaling captains with your own whaling crews. Look at all the stars. A beautiful night."

"What is over the horizon?"

"The Siberians."

"It's not on fire?"

"No. Over the horizon are the Siberians and the Chukchi people."

"Can we visit them?"

"Our people and their people haven't been friends. Maybe one day we'll be friends."

"Is it far?"

"Not far. People see Siberians during whaling sometimes."

Ebrulik pulls the rod up higher, looks into the fishing hole. I hold my breath. He pulls up the line. It's a whitefish, a big whitefish curling up and flexing its gills. We smile and forget the cold. I cut open the stomach, scrape away the guts, pour water to rinse the meat, and cut square pieces.

"Aaka, you're the fastest cutter I've ever seen. Even faster than dad, aaka, and aapa," Sam says.

We eat the entire fish on the ice. The fish is soft and briny, warming and filling. While we eat, Ebrulik catches a trout. I kiss them all on the cheeks and cook the trout by the fire. By the end of the night, they get whitefish, trout, grayling, and pike. They did not want to stop, free from the cold, free from hunger. They fish and wrap the morsels in an intestine tarp. I call them and they pack up their fishing gear and fish.

I serve steaming layers of baked trout. The outer skin is crispy and blackened. The fish filled our bellies, we felt warm, complete, pleasant and dreamy. We cut blocks of frozen fish for the dogs. The dogs sense a meal, whining and pacing.

"Aaka! Aaka! I got a whitefish! He's big! He's the biggest white-fish!" Sam smiles.

"Good, baby girl!"

"Maybe we can go hunting for the people. I'll go caribou hunt-ing," Ebrulik says.

"That is a kind thought," I clean out bones from Sam's fish. "You are good fishermen. The dogs get their meal. We can go whaling with uncle, that'll be fun."

"Can we go home after?" Nauraq asks.

"If you want. Anything you want."

"I want to go home. Will Ataŋauraq live with us at home?"

"He has his whaling crew."

"We'll be his whaling crew."

"We made it this far. We are doing good. You'll see your friends during whaling. Lots of maktak to take home. I'll trap fox for more bullets. Did we bring our traps? No matter. We'll ask my uncle to borrow his traps. We'll barter for bullets."

"Aaka, we'll get squirrels for new parkas," Nauraq says.

"Good! Yes! I'll make new parkas."

"I'll help get ptarmigans!" Sam says.

"Yes! Ptarmigans are delicious. Good idea, love. Enough for tonight. Feed the dogs. Take a steam and put on clean clothes."

The boys feed the dogs, throwing out blocks of frozen fish mixed with offal. Over the months, we've fed the dogs ptarmigan droppings but little more. Our Elders said to eat ptarmigan droppings if we're starving so the boys searched for the droppings every day.

I set up a small steam tent, placing fiery river rocks into the tent. I make them steam and throw their old clothes. I put them to bed, cocoon them in fawn skins, caribou furs, and kamiks filled with dry yellow grass.

"Aaka?" Sam asks.

"Yes."

"I got five fish."

"Five! That's one, two, three, four, five." I count with my fingers and make her count with me.

"Can I fish more?"

"You're tired, love."

"Did they get more than me?"

"No. You got five."

"Alright."

We'll travel up to Tikigaq and join my uncle's whaling crew. With maktak, caribou, ducks, geese, fish, and the smaller ptarmigans and rabbits, we'll eat well. Ebrulik must prepare his tools. I'll ration our food. We'll eat more fish than usual. Our dogs will eat more fish than usual. We'll travel to the Kukpuuk River where I'll fish the river while the boys scout for caribou. This is the best plan I've got.

I could have brought them inland; I repeat the thought over and over. Inland, near the denning bears and thick clouds of insects, in the marshes full of copulating mosquitoes, squirming worms, and maggots, but away from the Yankee whaling ships carrying their plague, whiskey, and greedy men, where the sickness grew like a mold, spreading, flowering, blossoming, killing everything.

I kiss my children and I pray. I want to dream good dreams. I want to sleep through the night without waking up to check my children's skin for boils or breakage of the skin. I want my children to sleep through the night without sweating and crying. I want to dream of running along the riverbanks, far inland where the streams are covered in petrified wood, the amber stones holding slivers of tree branches and cadavers of insects who lived in ancient times. I want to dream of running through the stone ruins with faint, blackened hearths of our Ancestors who hunted mammoth herds. I dream my teeth fall out in my hands. I look at my bloody palms, at my teeth shaped like snowy owls. The owls flutter, cutting my palms with their tiny talons, and fly away into an opaque, hazy nothingness.

5 | RAT KING

‸

"**S**HIT. THIS IS THE PLACE. REMEMBER this place?" Merihim's eyes are heavy.

"This is the place. We're here, sir," Emilio says.

"Call for anchor. I'm gathering up my things. Get the shit ready. Get the boats ready." He holds the rails as he slips down below.

We anchor near the ice. I see a thin line of land in the east.

I follow Emilio to the tween decks along with Sten, Lammert, and Remigio. We follow him into the shadows. He doesn't use a lamp or match. He laughs when I stumble. I follow the smell of his smoking pipe. He finally lights a lamp, and we uninstall the panel to tween deck. Boxes, casks, and bags of flour line up in the deck. He hands heavy sacks to me, which I carry up to the boat.

The captain took over an hour. The cook sent coffee. By then, we've stocked the boats with trading goods. Merihim emerges on deck, smiling, relaxed, staggering.

We lower the boats and head to shore.

I look into the blue deep. I like the drawing of Charles Darwin's depictions of the sea floor. He traveled to Galapagos Islands, too. I'd draw crabs, clams, mollusks, and clams crawling in the murk, seals dancing with schools of trout. I'd add columns of ice growing

outwards like a spider web. When I have my own house, I'll buy
dark pencils and paper. When I look up, Merihim lights his pipe.
He's staring.

"What are you looking for, boy? Mermaids and giant squid?"
The men laugh with the captain.

"No, sir," I say.

"Is this your first time ashore in Alaska?"

"No, sir. At Port Clarence."

"There is nothing in this frozen wasteland except oil. No
human should live in this hell hole. The eskimos live underneath
the dirt. A few good men get a mind to live in the wilderness.
Drive themselves mad and die. Is that the life you want, darkie?
God does not live here."

The whalers stare at me with pity in their eyes.

I keep my eyes down. I worry what to say next. Or what not
to say. He is a white man and the captain. I don't care. I don't care
what he thinks. I don't care what the others think, but I do. Other
men respond with quick wit, dignity, diplomacy, even humor. I
wish I had a fast, cunning wit. I made my decision. I'm jumping
ship. I'm jumping ship at the first chance. I missed my chance in
Port Clarence. I won't miss another chance.

I met his wife twice before. The company sent me to his home
to deliver an amended contract. His wife received me at the door. A
young woman, barely in her twenties, dressed in lavender velvet and
gold. She stood back as if disgusted by a smell. "Could you not have
used the service door? A proper employee would know such things."

"I apologize, ma'am."

"You are here, now. No use in wasting time going to the side
door. He's in his study." I followed her inside. The entrance led to a
grand staircase, splitting into two directions like a forked road. She
pointed up the staircase and walked away, her footsteps echoing
in a large mahogany hallway. He's got gas lighting in every room.

He lives in a manor with a cobbled lane. The parlor is lavender
and gold, like the wife's dress. All the tables are topped in marble. A
portrait of the captain and his wife is the centerpiece of the room.
It is the tallest portrait I've ever seen, taller than a man. She perches

on a settee carved in grape motifs, wearing a white gown while he stood beside her in a black suit with puffy maroon scarf on his chest. Both are not smiling.

The study door was open. He saw me. He stood at his dark, heavy desk speaking to an older sharp-nosed woman in frilly lace. I stood in the doorway, then the hallway. I didn't mean to eavesdrop on his conversation. His mother or mother-in-law spoke with him, I don't know which.

They hung Currier and Ives prints in the hallway, framed in gold flowery motifs. I studied each print, trying to appear like I'm not listening even though there is no one to witness my manner.

"Let me conduct this business. We'll discuss this later," he said.

"This is urgent. Make your man wait."

"Jesus, woman! After I get my business completed, we'll have this discussion!"

"Business can wait. Let her adopt a child."

"We've discussed this matter and both me and Anne agreed no adoption."

"Find the right child and she will agree. This is a family you're starting. Understand? A family. She'll need help when the baby comes. Help from a sibling. Not a servant. Or an absent father. It's been a year. She goes to the grave every day. This isn't healthy."

"Anne is fully healed. There is no reason we can't have our own children. Can we speak more this evening? After supper?"

"A young girl could help Anne when the babies come."

"A girl?"

"While you're absent for years at a time, who will help your wife?"

"I'm a whaler and this is what I do."

"Many children need a Christian home. It has been the topic of our church assembly. We've spent hours raising funds and holding drives, and why not make the commitment? Have you seen the cities? Foreigners are taking over this country. The children have nothing and no one. A little girl could be a good helper for a son."

"I don't give a damn what the church is doing these days. Next year, you'll be raising funds for lions in Africa. Am I supposed to bend to every will of your god damn church?"

"Do not take the Lord's name in vain! This is Anne's church, as well!" She signed a cross over her body and kissed her silver crucifix hanging around her lace-covered neck, dangling to her waist. She left, not looking at me. I saw the child's grave underneath an alder tree at the west end of their estate. A stone angel looked upwards, a cherub with stone curls, reaching upwards towards heaven. Fresh, picturesque roses sat in a marble vase.

I visited his home again before our journey to Alaska. Emilio sent me to retrieve his personal effects. I loaded his trunks on to the cart. He handed me his coats, gloves, jacket, trunks, canvas bags, and chests. Meanwhile his wife chased him around the house, yelling, screaming. The mother stood between the husband and wife. She cleared her throat, saying their names, weak as a wounded bird. He shoved things into my hands then slammed the door, hoping to hide as much of the argument as possible.

The captain hired a strict mistress to govern his wife. He found an older woman of their church with no children or family and paid an obscene amount of money. I heard glass thrown and furniture screeching across the floor. Their servants scurried out of the rooms.

"I'll kill you!"

"These are the words of a lady! Does it not say in the Scriptures to obey your husband? Her husband, her bound partner in the eyes of the Lord."

"Don't quote Scriptures to me! You drunk! You scoundrel! Running to your whores every other day with your officers! Instead of a wife, I've become a slave. A prisoner. Quit looking at me, you old hag! Get her out of my sight!"

"It is for your own protection. Do you not care about your reputation? None of the other wives mind a mistress. You will not make a mockery of this marriage. It's done. She's hired."

"I manage myself! Why become your wife when I cannot make any decisions in this household!"

"Manage? You do nothing but socialize at parties and spend money! Yet you think you can run this house?"

"I will never have children with you! I'm not giving birth to your children! Never!"

He yelled at the mother. "For God's sake, talk to her! Tell her she'll make no fool of me! I'll do more than hire a chaperone! I'll hire a man to watch your door every moment of the day!"

"I'm the legal wife and the legal owner! I'll fire her! I'll call the authorities!"

He laughed. "You'll never be the legal owner of any my property! You're my property in the eyes of the law. You cheat on me, you lie to me, you leave me, and you get nothing! Nothing!"

"Enough! Both of you! Please! I beg of you! Salvage this day. Salvage this moment. You'll both regret it. For months, you'll both regret it."

I waited on the dray. No use taking a half-filled cart to the port. At last, he arrived with another crate and sent me off. He said nothing.

I wonder if he looked for a child to adopt. Homeless kids are everywhere. In the cities, they swarm you, smelling of damp earth and factory grease. The cities built stone orphanages on the rivers, where the orphans beg for food and money.

We got to the ice, navigating through bergs and slush ice. Ice is complicated. A layer of ice covers the sea, fusing on land, a never-ending belt of ice. Boulders and bergs litter the ice, heavy with fat snow. Clear blue lakes sit on the ice, glimmering glacial-blue ponds. Cracks in the ice are frequent, rivers of seawater gurgling, fracturing, and cutting the ice. In some parts, circles of ice float together in the sea, like large lily pads floating in the currents. It is treacherous and beautiful.

"Get the boats up. Jesus, it is bright," Merihim says.

We're assigned packs to carry into the village. I'm given flour. I'd say sixty pounds I'm carrying.

The captain walks towards land and we fall in line behind him. I'm staggering at first. He walks faster than the rest of the crew. When he does work, he works harder than the rest. The only thing I admire about the man.

About a mile in, he sends Glen and Edgar to get fresh water.

"You two. You're going this way. North. We're going straight east. Meet us back here."

Our ship needs fresh water. A few barrels of fresh water got contaminated by rats. We opened the casks, slimy water and bloated dead rats. Rats chew through everything. Fresh water goes bad fast anyway.

I worked as a rat collector for a season. In 1885, New Bedford was infested with rats. No one knows where the rats came from. We debated about which ship might carry rats. Did the rats migrate on a frigate, brig, bark, schooner, sloop, fishing boat, or tug? Were the rats from London, Australia, New Zealand, Azure Islands, or San Francisco? Maybe the rats migrated from New York or Boston on some rat-infested train car.

A person couldn't walk down the street without seeing rats scurry down the sewers. The rats were so populous they weren't afraid of humans, as if we were the inferior species. They ate all the shrews. Sickness fell on every neighbor, from the manors to shantytowns, from the wealthy to poor. We heard of plague and illness from Massachusetts to South Carolina.

Rat collection is horrid, grotesque work. We wore gauze masks and leather gloves up to our elbows. I pulled a handcart with three other men and delivered the dead rats to an empty brick warehouse on the outskirts of New Bedford for exhumation. I think it used to be a loom factory.

We collected rats by the hundreds, especially in the old, abandoned buildings in crowded neighborhoods, where the rats built their nests. Rats are smart. They built nests underneath concrete, where the exterminators have to chip away at the sidewalks in order to find their nests.

We worked in the graveyard for a week. The rats burrowed down into fresh graves while horrified mourners demanded the mayor step up their efforts. He declared a health crisis in the city and hired exterminators, collectors, and rat squads. The rats bit children and babies while they slept. Many residents trained their dogs to kill rats and sleep at the floor of their children's beds. We even collected a dead dog, trained to attack rats, then killed by rats.

About twenty rats got their tails tangled in a giant rat king, squealing and tumbling in a dark alley. We heard the rat king from a block away. The citizens, a small crowd of appalled women and men, called our collection squad.

"Kill it! You must kill it!" They said.

"We're rat collectors. Not exterminators," we said.

"You work for the City Mayor. It's your job," they said.

We killed half of the rat king with sticks until the exterminators arrived with clubs. They clubbed the rats with terrible squeals, crunched skulls, and wet splats, like stepping on a large beetle, first crunch, and then squishy innards.

At home, I got a few handfuls of the rat poison and Dad and I poured the powder down their burrows around the house. Eventually, we had to hang all our food up in sacks, hanging from the beams like the Indians in the old days.

One night, I woke to papa stomping on the floor. He spattered rat blood across the floor. Another rat ran frantically around the room until it caught its foot in a floorboard, screaming as loud as a woman, screeching and flopping. He kicked it against the wall and the screeching ended.

"Damn rats!" He yelled and plopped back onto his little bed, his wool blanket landing on his body like a winged creature opening its wings and capturing the wind. For the life of me, I couldn't stop laughing for days, the look on his face and the furious stomping, my morbid humor.

I'm grateful for this land where it's too cold for rats. I still dream of squealing and screeching rats, like the cries of monkeys. I dream of their fleshy long tails knotted together in a giant rat king. It may be years until I no longer dream of rats.

We finally reach the beach. From this distance, I know the village is empty. I see no people. The captain walks faster. I don't see his face, but his tenseness rises.

The village is subterranean, hidden under the hilly tundra. Their homes are not like the Indians in the south. Their homes are made of sod and earth like African homes, reminds me of something ancient, earthy, thriving. They live on the beach, like me and dad.

"Damn it to hell," Merihim spit.

"Is this the place, sir?"

"Yeah. This is the place," Merihim slides his pack to the ground with a thump.

"Looks abandoned, sir."

We release our packs to the ground and broke away from the captain. If he's going to erupt, we don't want to be near him. I walk with Remigio.

"I thought they made their houses of ice?" I ask.

"Not these kind. Those are the Inuit. In Canada and Greenland. Not in Alaska. Look at that. There," Remigio points.

"What are they? Wolves?" I ask.

"Those are dogs."

"That means eskimos are here?"

"The eskimos wouldn't leave their dogs, but no one is here. Don't make sense."

The captain walks towards the dogs, pistol in his hand, loading the gun with bullets. "They are off hunting and merry making, making babies they can't feed. Devil mutts!" He shoots his pistol and the dogs run off. He finds a doorway. "C'mon!" He yells.

The doorway is a hole down into the earth. We drop down a few feet. I held my hand against the wall. Permafrost. I follow the men downwards, stooping, sometimes crawling, away from the light, I hear the men moving downwards and sideways. I see nothing except flashes of wooden steps by scant sunlight. The tunnel smells of earth and whale oil, like the baleen drying yards of New Bedford. I smell furs, the aging smell of furs when stored too long, dusty and gamey.

My head hit a ceiling beam. "Shit!"

The men laugh.

I finally see a doorway. It feels warmer here. Not enough to remove clothing but we are out of the wind, which is enough to raise the temperature.

The captain whacks at the wall with an axe, snow and dirt crash in from the surface. Dust flies up. For a moment, we stand looking around the room. A primitive home, covered in furs, stones, wood, and sea animal intestines. At the apex of the home, there is a window made by animal intestines stretched over a frame. The floor made of rock tiles, smoothed, fit together like a puzzle and cemented in the cracks. I press my fingernail in the crack.

The far wall is plump with fur clothing, gear, and tools. Merihim smiles. "Women lived here. Many women, maybe. God bless them. God bless them! The women kept busy. Here. Here. A wolverine. Look at it. The size of it. What a hunt. One day I'm going to hunt these creatures. Nasty creatures. They can kill you in one swipe. Put everything here. See this? It's a whaling spear. They won't trade some of these items for any price. Look at this adze. Look how big it is. Nothing compares to the adze of an eskimo. Turn all the boards. Yes. Yes. Bring these up. Put the ivory work on the table. Careful! I want them in perfect condition. This is a men's necklace. They all have one. For hunting. Jade. Jade is rare this north. You see jade more in the south but here it is good. The men carve animals for protection. See this? A chain made of ivory links. All that ivory to get these links together. Imagine the time. This one. This one is the winner. It's a storytelling piece. Lovely. Exquisite. These are used for gambling. To count their wins and losses. See the craftsmanship. Its centuries old, I'm told. See the aging? The dark color like this? Its mammoth tusks. They use this mask for ceremonies, I'm sure of it. There is an old man in New Bedford. He collects weapons and talismans of ancient civilizations to protect himself from the devil. The devil!"

"The older the piece, the better. Museums and art lovers want age. They want ancient. Pieces tied to the supernatural. Tell a scary story of the origin and it can be sold for twice its worth. Is it a witch transforming, from the icy hell on earth? A demon crawling out from the underworld? Is this a protection spirit?"

"What if we hadn't come here today? This mask here. Who would know this was a dance mask by the eskimo, if not for captain of the *Erysichthon*, delivering from a mud hut to an expert and educated curator, who will catalog and record its significance? By golly, we are fulfilling God's duty, God's will. We are a lucky ship. Instead of these precious artifacts withering away in the ice, it can be fully restored in a museum, by a professional curator. Take as much as you can. It's human history. A worthy artist can record the artifacts. By God, we are going to save the culture of these people. Their ways will not be forgotten or erased."

Merihim sat at the native's hearth. He sat for the next hour while we searched the remaining houses.

I know stories like this eskimo village. It's an ancient story, the white man plundering the villages of tribal people. I saw Merihim toss aside a necklace of teeth. I recognize the teeth. I own a book of ancient creatures illustrated with skeleton diagrams of saber tooth, mammoth, cave bear, and cave lions. These teeth are unmistakable. Feline teeth are feline teeth, from the house cat, lynx, to saber tooth. I didn't see the long canines, but they might be here in their house.

Merihim doesn't know the value of this necklace except as a string of teeth. I imagined the necklace passed from father to son, father to son, father to son, until smallpox, and returned to the earth by the ignorance of a plundering white man. He tossed grass baskets woven tight enough to hold oil. In a hundred years, who would know the story of the saber-tooth necklace except by the white men who put together the native history in theories, thesis, and hypothesis, all from a white man's imagination.

We ransacked all the homes, pillaging everything. We packed up snow knives, fishing lures, detachable spear heads, parkas, ivory and baleen necklaces, dolls with ivory faces, destined to museums and curio stands, whoever would buy at the highest price. We pack everything except the necklace, which I bury under a loose tile.

Flies buzz through the bedroom, through the shadows and sun-rays, glimmers and pearls of purple iridescence. I walk in, through dusty sunlight and buzzing flies, acoustics in the rooms sounding my footsteps. All the beds stripped.

"What happened here?" I ask Sten.

"'Pox.'"

"Damn." I stand back. I look around the room. Beds stripped. Shiny, oily bowls at the bedside, probably oily from their home-made antidotes. Surreal. This is something which happens in the

Old World, not in America, not in an American territory, certainly not in 1893.

The city of New Bedford built pesthouses to vaccinate every citizen. Dad and I woke to sheriffs and policemen pounding at every door. We stood in line for the doctor and nurses, dressed nice and clean. This was the city's campaign for investors to look at our shining cities, free of infections, and Old-World plagues replaced with modern medicine. All citizens must carry a Certification of Smallpox Vaccination.

I'd have a mind to boil my shirt after today.

"You'll be landed if you catch the sickness. You'll have to find your own way home. Don't want to get stuck up here, lad. You'll be landed in the arctic and have to pay your own way home," Sten says. He signs the cross over his body and prays out loud, "St. Joseph, patron of departing souls, blessed Mother, and Jesus Christ, Thy son. Hear our prayer."

The way Sten prays, the way he stands, reminds me of my father.

"Dad? Dad?"

"I can hear you," Dad said, napping. It's August but hot.

"I got some lamb. Coffee. A few pieces of peach tart. The tart is from Ms. Earlsmith. She asked about you."

"That's kind. Very kind."

"She still in love with you?"

"She's sentimental. I can't bring myself to love any woman who is not pragmatic."

"She would bring you good company, old man."

My dad laughed, coughed, and sat up. I lit the candles, fire, and oil lamp, lit everything until our little house was warm and light, and I read him the Sunday psalms and prayers. Dad was lonely.

Once a week, we attended church and visited the spice factory. Father loves the spice factory. We purchased coffee beans, orange tea, and a premixed spice rub, which was on sale, and usually a sweet candy treat for dad's sweet tooth. If I could, I'd buy him the peppermint, taffy, and cubes of sugar for his tea. What else can he enjoy in his old age, although, the doctor says sugar is not good for his bones.

The owners asked if we'd like to sample their new white lily tea. We sit and sip. Quakers buy little more than what is needed in life, nothing garish or extravagant, nothing for show or pride. We love our coffee, tea, and spices. For this, the spice factory is filled with Quakers on any given day. The owners learned to cherish their dedicated customers, and we are treated well when we walk into the door.

Papa and I also went to the market every other week for vegetables, fruit, flour, and sweets if we could afford it. We didn't buy much. The market trips were for dad, those everyday activities, which he enjoyed more and more as he got older. He always thanked me after shopping. "Thanks for the trip, my boy," he'd say.

In his last months, I carried him on my back to church and the spice factory, walking the beach as we always had, he got light as a child. Our walk home from the wharf was a relatively short walk. We hopped off the docks to the beach, crossed a black rocky beach covered in shiny mussel shells and barnacles crackling under our feet, passing the brick spice factory, whale oil refinery, two canneries, and a small thatch of trees. Our preferred route home, since it avoided the roads and paths covered in horse manure and the cannery workers hurrying to their shift.

We gather everything in the village worth a penny. The captain finds a hand sled and we tow a full sled out of the village. He drinks and smokes and promises a round of drinks for everyone, the perks of our employment.

We reach the ice.

"Holy shit! It's a fucking eskimo!" Remigio yells.

We stop. Glen tows a young native. She couldn't be more than five years old. Glen plops the water bladders on the ice. He paces like a sentry dog in heat, all-overish, all-possessed, holding a rifle in both hands.

No sign of Edgar. I don't like Edgar. Edgar's family lost their fortune in the war. "Niggers robbed us blind of house and home after the war. All the kindness we showed the no-good darkies who didn't deserve a doghouse," he said. His family were slave owners in New Orleans until the "Declaration Proclamation bankrupted their Bill of rights and sent them into the lowest gutter of society."

"Where's your mate?" Merihim asks.

"Acknowledge the corn there, Glen!" Remigio demands.

"Cold as a wagon tire. A damn eskimo shot his face off! I nearly got shot myself. Asshole damn got himself shot." He rants, pacing back and forth.

"Gimme the gun, Glen. Jesus!" Lammert says.

"Put down that gun before you shoot me," Merihim orders.

"Right, right oh," he hands the gun to another and continues pacing, wiping his nose. His hair is spiky and sweaty. "They shot his damn face off! I could be a damn ghost right now! Hell isn't ready for me yet! I'm going to church! Forgive my sins. Almost dragged by the demons of Hell, but Lord got other plans for this asshole! I'm reading the Good Book, as Lord is my witness. Jesus is Savior! I need a drink. No. Got to get right with the Lord. I'm getting right. The eskimo killed Edgar."

"What for? What'd he do?" I ask.

"What'd you accusing me for?"

"Like an ambush?"

"That's it! An ambush."

"What you bring this child for? Jesus, Glen!" Remigio asks. He laughs in disbelief.

"What were you thinking? Why'd you bring the child?" Lammert says.

"How was I going to get back safe? I needed the girl! They'd kill me if I didn't!"

"Balderdash!"

"Dash!"

"Should we get Edgar?" Remigio asks.

"I'd caution you before getting Edgar's body! A bee of eskimos is that way."

"Haul him across miles of ice?" Merihim made up his mind already. We're not retrieving his body. "Is it a girl? Where are your parents?" Merihim kneels. He finds a soda biscuit and holds it out. The girl fell limp. "We can't leave you here in the middle of nowhere, can we?"

"Women are bad luck on a ship," I say. He's thinking of taking the girl.

"Maybe he's right, Captain. Kids don't fare well on ships," Lammert says.

Remigio saw an opportunity to support the captain. He takes every opportunity to side with the captain, no matter how immoral. "She's a guttersnipe. The humane right thing to do is give her a new home. She can't survive out here alone. Her family died from the 'pox."

"They did. That they did. Look at those eyes. Eyes like a Romanian gypsy."

6 | NALUAGMIUT (WHITE MEN)

THE BOYS STARTED HUNTING GEESE AND DUCKS AT DAWN.
They shook me awake and asked to use the rifle. I slept
a while after they left. I'm waking up. The sun shines bright
through the tent door. I hear Sam's footsteps outside the tent.
"Samaruna?"

"Yeah?"

"What you doing?"

"Nothing. I'm playing!"

"Alright, just checking on you. Did you eat?"

"No."

"Let's eat. Where are the boys?"

"They are up there. Getting ducks."

"Alright, good."

"Aaka. My dog is running away."

"Where? You'll get him. He can't be far."

"He's running towards home."

"He'll come back."

"Aaka! I want to get him. Help me."

"Wait until the boys are ready. They'll go with you."

"Aaka! He's running far! We have to catch him!"

"Sam, wait until your brothers are done and they'll help you. Let me get dressed and I'll get your brothers to help." I sit up and rub my eyes. My back is sore between the shoulder blades. The ducks and geese fly overhead, somewhere far away, but I hear them. The dogs are quiet. They must have slept good, too.

I boil water for tea. I cut fresh fish for my children. I start packing up the tent. It'll be a sunny day. Wisps of striated clouds stretch high in the sky, far down into the horizon. I smell sea air from a south wind and I wonder if the whaling crews prepare on the ice.

I drink tea but still my body is heavy. I design clothes in my mind: a parka trim of triangular designs, dyed with ochre, crowberries, or soot. I design gloves made of wolf faces, the nose dried and stiff. I design a tunic of bleached fawn skin, a supple white tunic with fringes longer than my hand. I design clothing to distract my mind.

Last year, I didn't need to distract my mind. My husband and I wanted another child. We discussed sled-making, learning how to choose the right spruce trees, and making fresh sinew from beluga. We planned trips inland to search for flint and chert, gifts for our family and the Messenger Feasts. How preoccupied and happy my mind was, yet, how foolish and ignorant.

I'm not sure how long I've stared at the tent and our bedding. I wipe my tears and finish packing. Afterwards, I call for the boys. "Boys! Boys!"

They don't hear me. Or pretend they don't hear me. After all their whining about not leaving home, they don't want to stop hunting. Children. It's hard to get them started on any activity but once they're involved, they're involved. The boys sit high on a ridge with their bow and arrows. I climb the ridge. They caught an eider and two geese.

"Look! I caught this one, and Ebrulik caught the others," Nauraq says.

"I see. Good ones. Fat. I'll cook a breast but we'll save the rest for later, yeah? Better to use the sunlight for the trail."

"A little longer?"

"Alright, a little longer." They're hooked. I picked up the eider and geese. They are heavy and limp. I hold them up. "Help me pluck them."

"Ewwww." They both say.

I laugh. I knew they didn't want to pluck them. "Get your sister's dog, then. She can't get him."

"Aaka! She's way over there."

"Get her please."

"They're way over there."

I look. She chases the dog on the beach, by the ice. "Adii. Go get her before the dog gets too far. That's too far. Go get her."

The boys went down the ridge and onto the beach.

I pull up my sleeves to pluck feathers, even in the cold wind. Birds have lice, sometimes with long bodies like a worm, sometimes circular and fat like an ant. The bugs are small but fast. I toss the feathers and check my sleeves for any bugs. Already, I imagine bugs crawling up my arms. I left this chore to my Aaka. Even when I was married, she spoiled me. She plucked them for me.

I hear something. I'm kneeling on this berm, sleeves up to the elbows. What is that? I stand up. What was it? Faint yelling. No, Nauraq shouts my name!

Nauraq yells. He screams for me.

"What! Boys! Sam!" Earlier I propped the rifle up on a snow brick, like hunters during whaling. I grab the rifle. I'm running and checking the rifle.

I see Nauraq waving his arms. Where's Ebrulik? Where's Sam? Is it a wolverine? A wolf? A polar bear? I wasn't watching. She got too far.

He shakes. He points down the beach. "Naluagmiut (white men)."

We run. What do they want with my children? Leave them alone! Leave my babies alone. My body seems so heavy. I toss my parka aside and run. Anything! I'll do anything. No! Not happening! They wouldn't take a child! A woman, yes, but not a child! This is a misunderstanding.

I see my children in a little eddy down the beach. Two large men, tall as trees, harangue my children. Ebrulik guards his sister. He's crying. Samaruna cries. The white men dressed in blue and brown wool, bob up and down, knees bent, laughing, blocking their escape. It is like a game to the Nalaugmiut.

"Stay here!" I yell to Nauraq.

I aim my gun.

The two Naluagmiut stop laughing and stand up straight. They speak in their ugly, choppy Yankee tongue.

The shorter man, the closest man steps forward. He smiles like a wolf, gleaming white teeth. He speaks in long sentences. He circles me, talking and talking. He asks questions. I know by the fluctuations in his voice. The other Naluagmiut laughs.

"Away! Get back! Back!" I yell. He copies, exaggerating the word. They both laugh. My babies cry. I jerk forward with the gun, but he continues forward. He doesn't stop. I smell his musty clothes. His breath smells like a decaying animal.

He lunges forward. He's not smiling anymore. He slaps my rifle to the side.

I correct my aim. He tries slapping the rifle again.

I pull the trigger. His head flies backward. I see flashes of skull, bone, and blood spray upwards. He falls backwards onto the ground, his face blown off into mush. He twitches on the snow, hands and feet quivering.

Behind me, the boys yell.

He's got her. He's got his hand around Sam's neck, practically lifting her from the ground. He could break her neck. She's up on her toes, choking, trying to breathe. He spits. He's yelling and holding her neck.

"Stop! Stop! Please!" I yell.

Ebrulik stands behind me, gripping my tunic. My babies cry. Both cry for their Aaka.

I put the gun on the snow. He's stopped. He's not choking her.

I put down the gun. I kick the rifle across the ground. "I'm not here to hurt you. I won't hurt you."

He loosens his grip. She's coughing but she's breathing. He yells in his ugly tongue. I've never seen a pointier nose.

He inches towards the rifle. Ebrulik and I back away. I hold up my hand to Sam. I offer my hand to my daughter.

I'm blinded. I can't see. I can't see anything. My face burns. My head burns. I taste blood. My children cry. "What happened?" I spit. Blood fills up my mouth. The boys wipe my face.

"Aaka! Aaka!" They cry.

"Yes? I'm here."

"Aaka!" Ebrulik presses his hand on my forehead.

"Don't cry. What happened?"

"The white man took her!"

"What white man?"

"The white man took Samaruna!"

"What white man? Where?" I don't remember. I don't remember. I lie down.

"Stop! Aaka!" Ebrulik cries and holds my forehead. "He's taking her. He's going down to the ice."

"What happened to me?"

"A white man hit your head with the gun."

I feel my head. I feel flesh. The Naluagmiut split my forehead clear open. I feel every draft of wind down to the skull. "It's fine. Wrap it. Wrap it up. Bandage it! Take my sleeve." They rip off the sleeve but it's too short. I hear them ripping the sleeve into another piece and they wrap it around my head. "Where is she? Samaruna? Sam? Sam! Is she far? Let's go! C'mon."

"They're going to the water. To the ocean!"

"Take me. Let's go." I stumble. Blood gushes on the snow from my head. They both hold me up and run with me. How strong my boys are!

Blood blurs my eyesight. I feel the cut on my forehead now, throbbing, the skin moving as I run. We're running on the ice now. Blood gushes with every footstep. I hear my own heartbeat beating in my forehead. I feel blood pumping through the exposed blood vessel. Every beat of my heart and blood drips down. Don't faint. One more step.

"Aaka, your head!"

"Don't look. I'm good. Is she close? Do you see her? Do you see her?"

"There's a ship! I see a Naluagmiut ship in the water."

"Are they going towards the ship?"

"Yes!"

I slump down to the ice. "It's fine. Let me lie here. Boys. Get the sled. How far is the sled?"

"It's close."

"Alright, get the sled."

"Aaka!"

"I'll be fine. I promise."

"Aaka!"

"Go, go now."

My scalp is split open like a dark blossoming flower, blooming, curling back, opening its petals. Am I blossoming into death? The slash radiates, pulsates, and chants. The side of my face droops downwards while my scalp slips upwards. It is eerie and disorienting.

I spit upwards, spraying blood upwards on my face like a whale's spout. Blood. A bleeding organ? No. The blood isn't internal. The blood runs from my scalp into my mouth. This is good. Bleeding from the organs is never good.

I feel little more than a helpless orphaned cub, debilitated, left exposed on the ice. I scream out loud. I scream and scream into my hands. Are you there? My husband. My dear one. My love. I lost her. I don't know how I lost her. I lost our baby. Help me find her. Help me. I'm swaying and swaying. Is the ice moving? Or is it the sky? Is this death? Or a mockery of life?

I gasp awake. I dozed off. Stay awake. Tell a story. Make up a story. Siberians attacked a woman's village. A Siberian split her head apart with a club. As she lay dying, a spirit approached her. He wanted to marry her. She asked him, what about my mother? She will miss me. With a piece of her flesh, he bloomed a field of violets. She felt the petals with her fingertips, and she felt veins. He said, when your mother sees these flowers every spring, she will think of you. Even today, a millennia later, the petals and leaves of violets have veins because they were created from a woman's flesh.

I'm lying on good, solid ice. The sheet of ice is a hundred years old, maybe older. I see all the signs of a sturdy ice shelf. I remember finding a fossil in the ice, a tiny insect creature solidified into a black fossil. Dad chopped it out of the ice for me. I hear the ice moving, water sloshing upwards in small lulling waves. Not strong. Steady. I taste salt in the air.

I know ice. I started whaling at eleven years old.

After the whale is harpooned, the crews race out to the whale. I've seen a dozen umiaqs race out to a bellied-up whale, because the first eight whaling crews get the best sections. They mark their place in line by touching the whale with an oar. Whalers follow ancient hunting rules.

As the whale is towed to the ice, we wait on ice edge, readying the ropes, tackle, and pulley. The crews pull up their umiaqs. Dozens of whalers are needed to pull up a whale.

The first cut of the whale is near the middle of the back, even as the whale floats in the sea, even before the whale is pulled up to the ice. Whalers walk on the whale's back, cutting a rectangular piece of black skin and pink blubber.

The captain's wife prepares the first cut, boiling the skin, cutting it down to pieces smaller than ptarmigan eggs, and serves steaming, warm, and soft whale skin to all the whalers, boyers, cooks, and helpers, a whale dish soft enough to bite through with bare teeth.

The Elders stand nearby to oversee the entire process, resolute, guiding, commanding, and cautioning. The Elders stand through day and dark night, even as the cold rises into their legs, at times, spending days away from land. They continue, they persevere from the whale pulled up on the ice until nothing remains on the ice except currant-bloody ice and skull. The bowhead skull is gifted back to the ocean, sent with prayers, sent with thanksgiving, sent with the promise to honor the spirits and to provide for our families.

We harvest all the whale. The successful whaling crew, the crew which harpooned the whale, get the whale's flippers, tail, stomach, tongue, kidneys, and heart, but not to keep. Much of these parts are given during the whaling festival, given in order according to tradition.

It is a great honor to gift the whale. Captain and wife stand together at the whaling feast, holding slices of flipper, calling the names of the people. Three days of giving, dancing, singing, and blanket toss. Each clan sings and dances their songs. Gifts of arctic fox, red fox, silver fox, wolf, and wolverine skins are tossed to the elder women. Whale meat and skin delivered to each house.

I hear little footsteps. I can't sit up. I move my eyes, trying to see. I yell, "Sam? Sam! Oh. Oh!"

It's her little pup, panting, smiling. He collapses by my side. I know what to call her puppy. Pairuk. Stays behind. He stays behind.

I cry. I'm shaking. My baby. My baby girl! My little one! Why did he take my little girl? What will he do with her? I try not to think of horror stories. Murder, no! Rape, no! Kidnapping, no! He'll leave her. What use is a little girl to him? Why did he take her?

I hear my sons arriving with the sled. They yell for me. I hold up my hand to let them know I'm alive. My poor boys. Why must they see their mother this way?

"Help me up." The boys help me to the sled. I hobble over the ice and collapse into the sled. "I'm fine. Go, go!"

We didn't get far on the sled.

There's a crack in the ice.

"Can we get the sled over?" I ask.

"No. No."

"Can we jump over?"

"Yes."

"Help me up." I see a little now. The crack in the ice is a few feet wide. I'm trying not to drag my feet. I'm trying to hold my limp head up.

"Aaka! Hold my hand."

"It's alright. I got it. Jump over." I hurl my body over the crack. I see the ship now. It seems so far. "Do you see her?"

"Aaka, I see her!"

"Where is she?"

"There are boats! White man boats!"

I hear something. I hear a ship. I hear the evil hum of an engine. They're taking my girl. My baby. My baby. I can't see her, but I hear her crying. Her cry stings my ears, pulls at my tendons, sinew, and arteries of my heart. I fall to my knees.

She loves this ugly doll with cranberry-colored beads for eyes. She loves the little yellow buttercups in the hill valleys and the strong bitter perfumes of cranberries, burdocks, and iris. What do I do?

"Boys. Help me to the sled. The ship follows the whales. We'll follow the ship." I can't see, but I hear the evil hum vibrating in the ocean, a low and constant tone. The evil hum drives away, dying, swallowed up by the sound of sea birds and ocean waves.

7 | CUTTING IN

⌄

THE CAPTAIN CARRIES THE GIRL KICKING AND BITING. She makes a scene, reaching outward, begging anyone to save her from boarding the ship.

I think we all had the same reaction, the same expression. We can't say anything to the captain. He's the damn captain in this mess. Who would have thought the captain has a liking to fatherhood?

The crew shakes their heads. They argue about the girl.

"Jesus damn Christ. Are we going to have to live with that?" A whaler says.

"It's only a child. Not the devil," I say.

"This is a whaling ship. We're not pleasure sailing through the bay," another whaler says.

"It's the captain's business."

"None of our business."

"Say nothing."

"Don't ask questions."

"I'm invested in this ship, invested!"

"We've got to cross three oceans, four oceans with a child on board?"

"Make the best of it. A man finds happiness in different places."

"Keep your shit packed. Make friends with all the other captains. Just in case."

"Really? You think he'll be caught?"

"Quit your worrying. It's done all the time. No one cares."

Eskimos are contraband. Ships are confiscated for contraband. The US Revenue Cutter arrest captains, confiscate ships, and leaves the crew to scrounge for another ship.

Other whalemen report contraband. Whalemen don't like competition. We're up against the US Revenue Cutter and other whalemen. Bad news all around.

The captain makes himself a fine display of the goods, spreading the eskimo artifacts across the deck.

He organizes a theatre of goods. In the percussions, he lays all the furs and parkas. Utah knows furs. Maybe cause he's from the West. In the bass section, he plants the tools, spears, harpoons, and flensing tools. In the viola and violin section, he displays his treasures, ivory, jade, baleen jewelry, gambling sticks, and storytelling tusks. He sits in the violin section, in the high octave of his haul.

How infantile he looks. You'd think he conquered Europe. He squats, moves, rearranges, and reexamines his artifacts. I hate him. I pity him. He speaks to his crew. "See this? We're splitting the profits for this."

They are a few smiles, but we know we'll get a mere fraction of the profits, after paying our outstanding debts to the company.

Remigio stares and whistles. He squats next to the captain. "What a find! And a beautiful child. Is she to be presented to your wife?"

"For my wife, yes."

The eskimo women giggle and laugh like they've fallen into wealth themselves. They explain the proper uses of the tools through pantomime, digging through the artifacts, bending over at the waist, proud of themselves with this little bit of authority. The young one Susan would be pretty if she wasn't drunk all the time. The older woman Dorothy tries on a parka, but Merihim yanks it off her head. She's pouting and stomping about, like he'd notice.

She scowls. She sees the girl. "Girl too skinny. Me and you, have pretty girl. Loooooots of money. Half-breed girls prettiest ones!"

The eskimo women are convinced they'll find husbands on board. It is not unheard of. Whalers find eskimo wives. Even if Merihim brought them to the states, he'll dump them at the last port before New Bedford.

I head below deck. My next shift doesn't begin for another four hours.

"Ibai. Take the girl below." Merihim doesn't look at me.

"Me, sir? Yes, captain. Where?"

"Keep her in your sight."

I look at the girl. She cries. Oh Lord. Jesus, my Savior. I bend down. I've studied lithographs of eskimo children, elongated eyes, chubby faces, and rounded limbs, like Oriental cherubs dressed in furs. She is nothing like the lithographs. She cries, gasping in air, whimpering. She looks to the ice. The ship's engine rumbles, she looks down at the deck, and cries harder. Oh Lord. I pick her up and she faints. I'm holding her limp body. What does he want me to do? She's lost her family to smallpox. I yell to Merihim, over the rumble of the engine. "Captain! What about the vaccine? A smallpox vaccine for the child?"

"You're right. Good thinking. Jurek. Give the little one a vaccination, will you?"

"Yes, sir." Jurek rises and follows me below deck.

"I think she's unconscious," I state.

"She's alive. She's fine."

"What do I do with her?"

"Damn if I know."

"Shit."

"You're a mistress. Congratulations."

"Screw you." I put her down on my bunk. Jurek gets the vaccination. Others crowd around.

"Drop that thing off first chance we get," a whaler says.

"Jesus. She's a child," I say.

"What's wrong with her?"

"Passed out. Fainted."

"Didn't I tell you? The planet Venus is dominant in the sky. Bad luck. I told you. Bad luck was coming," he said.

"Enough of your witchcraft."

"It's not witchcraft, it's science. Stargazing is older than Jesus."

"What am I supposed to do? We can't squeeze into one bunk every night." The men laugh.

"You journeyed to the top of the world! Crossed the Atlantic, the Pacific, the Bering Sea, and became a governess!"

"You've been promoted."

"Gerald. You've got more room. Let her sleep next to you." I raise my voice to Gerald across the room.

"You're skinnier than me. Captain'll give you shit."

"You're shorter. You're a kid. She's a kid."

"Nope."

Damn. Shit. Merihim will give me shit if she's not with me at all times.

Jurek administered the vaccine, and she didn't wake. I let her sleep at the bottom of my bunk, her head by my feet. I can't move. But she sleeps. I sleep. I feel her moving as she dreams.

In the morning, she sits in the galley. The cook drops her a tin plate of chicken and cornbread while we ate salt horse and hard biscuits. We stare at her. She stares at the food.

"She's got tattoos around her wrists. Can you believe it?"

"They tattoo kids this young?"

"She won't eat it."

"Trade me for the cornbread." Jurek offers a hard biscuit.

"Leave the kid alone. Captain wants her to eat American food. No more eskimo, ya hear?" The cook yells, tilts his head, and squints an eye.

"She's seasick," I say. She's sweating. Maybe she understood me. A second later, she leans forward, stomach against the table, and vomits on the table. We stand up and move backwards. "Damn. It's alright. I threw up, too and I'm a grown man."

I clean up her vomit. Then we went on deck for my shift.

For two hours, she sat against the bow. She vomits overboard. Merihim offers water but she won't look at him. When he offers the cup, she flinches backward. I pretend not to notice.

"What is that?" Gerald asks. Gerald gags, pinches his nostrils.

The captain and first mate looked north with their scopes. In unison, Remigio, Gerald, and I stood and look north with the captain.

"That's the smell of money, boy! The smell is walrus piss," Remigio says. He held up his own tiny scope, hands the scope to Gerald. "We'd get a barrel of oil for each walrus! By God. We're in luck. And the ivory!"

My nostrils burn. It is a strong acidic stench. After the smell, we hear their grunts and barking. The walnut-colored babies cry to their mothers like lambs. The adolescent males croon their mating calls, too immature in age for the females to notice. A scarred, ruddy old bull barked at the males. It is a concert, an allegro of walrus calls.

They sunbathe and scratch at crawling pests on their skin. In the water, the creature swims like a seal, dancing and swaying in the current, searching the sea floor for cockles, crabs, and sea worms. The four-ton animal is thick with fat, five inches of fat, meaning a cask of oil from each walrus. Casks equal money.

The company office displays walrus tusks on the walls, in the office on the wharf near 4th and Guinness. It is a wall of hunting expedition photographs topped with a lion, elk, zebra, and walrus tusks. In the photos, unsmiling and bearded faces stand proud with their rifles, dressed in fur hats and moccasins. They hunt walrus, fur seals, narwhales, belugas, and ringed seals. They pull up right whale, bowhead whale, and the nearly extinct sperm whale onto famous whaling brigs which sailed the seas for over a hundred years.

For the last two years, no whaling ships are walrusing. Killing walrus is not illegal or banned. American churches and societies asked the whaling industry to stop killing walrus on behalf of the eskimo villages who depend upon the animals for food. These recent years, scientists and botanists traveled to the arctic, bringing back tales of slaughter, mass killings, and exterminations of walrus herds, inciting the churches to start a campaign to protect arctic walrus. The church leaders wrote letters to the newspapers, social societies, and universities, describing walrusing as garish and inhumane practice.

Returning with an empty ship is worse than death, a whaler's greatest dishonor. We don't dream of returning to New Bedford with an empty ship. The mere thought sends whalers into agonizing fits. New Bedford depends upon successful ships and the entire city watches the ships in earnest. No whale oil means no candles, lipsticks, lotions, potions, or women's corsets. In 1850, the *Patriot* returned with an empty ship, the captain telling tales of mutiny, sea monsters, and wrecked whaleboats. In 1864, the *Inquistr* returned with a mere 60 casks after a two-year voyage to the southern seas. Their failures are legendary, so-called unlucky ships and unlucky captains.

"Fresh fat for the pots. That's a barrel per walrus, sir. Yes, sir. Easy oil. You'll be smart to get those animals now. No one going to look down at you for that decision. They don't know our company. We know our company, and our company wants oil," Remigio says to the captain.

"Will we get to go?" Gerald asks, almost prancing around. Gerald can't go. He's a cabin boy. He's a shipkeeper. While we row after whales, he stays on the ship with the cooper, blacksmith, cook, and carpenter. Gerald also doesn't have experience shooting a gun. I doubt the captain'll trust him to kill a rabbit.

"Stop the engines," Captain shouts. "Remigio. Jurek. Alastor. Xaphan. Sten. Lammert."

Remigio hurries below with the officers.

"You are going?" Gerald asks Remigio. "Will I get to go?"

"You're a shipkeeper, boy."

"Sten will go. He is the strongest," Gerald whispers.

We ready the boats, packing repeating rifles, single shot rifles and take down rifles. Emilio distributes military cartridges, military-grade bullets manufactured for the army and navy. We lower the two whaling boats into the water from port side. The men climb into the boats, stoic, ready to hunt. Remigio kisses the cross around his neck, as if going into battle, as if for glory and honor. Gerald admires it all.

The whalers cross the water, pushing away ice with their oars, and then climb the ice. We watch the scene by Remigio's scope, passing the scope down the line of whalers. Gerald crowds his way into the line. He holds the scope, mouth open and eye squinting.

"Watch Sten and Lammert. They've walrused before." A Dutchman says to Gerald. Sten and Lammert walked on ice with their perfect physiques, prancing and leaping across floes. They are liked by everyone, they love everyone. Even as they speak in their native tongue, they laugh and can't stop laughing. I sit with them at times, I don't understand their words, but I feel their good energy, their goodness permeating everything.

"By Goll. That'll be me," Gerald says.

"Enough, Gerald," I say. Gerald looks up to all strong men, whether misguided or not. I tell the boy to think for himself, make up your own mind. That's what God gave you. He doesn't listen.

All this time, the girl stays by my side. She watches the herd of walrus and the whalers.

The walrus bark and snort, alarmed by the smell of whalers. The walrus escape into the water, crashing, swimming away in a dark cloud, heads bobbing in the water. Herded into the ocean like cattle, they trample the younger adolescents, smaller females, and babies.

It is a slow scene. The men spread out on the ice, walking north and holding up their rifles. I see the captain. I hear the first shots and I cringe. The gunshots are like firecrackers, pops and pops, a hollow sound.

Meat flies into the air. The guns make a mess of animal. At close range, they blow holes in the animal. The walrus barely scoots along, four tons of fat inching along, bellowing and barking.

I can't move. My stomach is a hard fleshy knot, my skin is covered in goosebumps, and yet, I cannot move or look away.

I remember the voices of my people, my church family, the Quakers singing in the spring sun. My preacher Mathias, a tall old black man with a peppered beard, belting in his bass voice. An old woman screeching the words with her eyes closed and hand clutching her heart. How could I have been so naïve? All my life, I've believed whaling is a noble quest for a better world, a more civilized world.

For my preacher Mathias, whaling is God's errand and whales are God's creatures.

Mathias bid farewell to me as we cast off the moorings in New Bedford. Factory smoke started up for the day. Fishermen and whalers walked the pier and docks. The navy held port for the day.

"Your father and mother would've been proud of this day. It is what it is. God bless your journey. Whaling is God's errand," Mathias said.

"I'll remember. Thank you, sir."

"My wife sent these." He handed me a cloth filled with two peaches, two apples, and a small satchel of coffee.

"Thank you for everything."

"You've become a fine man. A good man." He shook his head and laughed. The laughter wasn't from humor in the situation, it's his nature, his way of communicating his joy, his love. I'm going to miss the old man.

"I'll send you letters. I'll write."

"Learn what you can. Stay warm."

I walked to the ship, my belongings on my back, carrying the cloth under my coat. Mathias waved farewell with his hat in a wide arc.

I saw Gerald's mother and siblings. She hugged and kissed him. She cried; how proud she is of her grown boy. The Dutch family was the largest, an entire group of men, women, and children. The men of their family are strong, like the acrobats who dance on the high wire, throwing each other about in the sky, fearless, smiling, and unafraid. Their women hugged them but didn't shed tears like the other women. They stood brave and proud on the pier. Anthony, the Romanian cook, held up his sobbing wife, a bright folk scarf covering her head. He comforted her and scolded her. When we left the pier, she fell to her knees and people rushed to her aid. She wailed and he hushed her, even when she couldn't hear him. He wiped away a few tears.

No one came to bid farewell to Emilio. "We don't have all day. What a shit show," he said.

The shooting stopped. The waves calm. Emilio and Sten row to the ship.

"We cut in now." Sten climbs to the deck.

"Will I go?" Gerald asks.

"Get ready."

"Yaaahoooo!" Gerald runs below ship for his parka, eager as a puppy.

We cross the sea to the ice, along with nearly all the crew, armed with lancing tools. Even the eskimo women join our cutting in duties. The girl stays on the ship, standing at the helm with the cooper. I look down into the abyss, into the glassy layers of arctic waters, the colors of azure, sapphire, tanzanite, aquamarine, lapis lazuli, and jade green.

The air smells of gunpowder.

Emilio gives instructions. "Cut the tusks. Then the fat. Get it aboard."

We climb the ice and group together in three or four men. Sten asks me to join them with a sort of elbow pointing. I follow Sten and Lammert. Gerald runs off, lancing tools clinking.

The shots were not fatal, more of a disembowelment. A handful of walrus gurgle and choke, scooting along the ice with gaping yellow holes, dragging their blown intestines behind them. It is a slow death.

"Jesus. They aren't dead," I say.

"It's in pain, son. Put it out of its misery," he says. Lammert hands me an axe.

"How? Where?" I ask, shaking my head.

Lammert turns his head. I hear the animal's heartbeat, faint and rapid. Its chest caved in, the ribs broken on both sides from the bullets. The animal looks in my eyes. I'll try the esophagus, less fat at the esophagus.

It took more than one attempt. I'm not sure what I'm striking for, jugular vein? Artery? Throat? Spinal cord? Trachea? The animal goes into shock. Blood and fluid surge from the animal, filling a puddle, and it goes limp, a flopping backwards further opening the axe's laceration. I step away from the growing puddle.

"I'm sorry, brother. The poor guy was in pain. You did a good thing, brother. Let's get busy with this one before they send you to put down another." Sten pats my shoulder.

"Faster we work, faster we will be done," Lammert adds.

Food rises in my throat. My mouth fills with saliva, a watery precursor, and I vomit an acidic soup of fleshy chunks and pale biscuits. I burp and my esophagus burns and my nose burns. I continue vomiting, trying to block the noise of cutting in.

When I looked up, the Dutchmen hack away at the esophagus, a bulbous sac hanging from the throat. I vomit again.

"We'll peel away the skin with the hook!" He says loud. I vomit again. They laugh. "You'll get used to it."

Everywhere I turn, men hack away at the carcasses using axes, lances, and knives. Organs fall onto the bloody ice. I look to the horizon. I want to return to the ship. I think of my list: coffee, flour, skillet, matches, cooking stove, and tobacco. I don't smoke but I can use tobacco for trading. In the wilderness, I'll wake in morning, throw fresh wood in the cooking stove and brew fresh coffee. Once a week, I'll make bread. Real bread, not the biscuits made for sailors and whalemen.

I've hunted elk in the northern forests with the Indians. It was a mix of Indians: Pequots, Massachusetts, and Mohican. The hunting was a lot of waiting and patience. Do not chase, wait until he comes, they said. We waited in one spot for hours while one hunter circled ahead with an antler. He scraped the antler against the trees, imitating a doe in heat. The Indians gifted me a hindquarter, liver, and leg. I did little to deserve so much of the meat. I didn't want to refuse. I'll hunt caribou like I hunted the elk. Approach the herd, wait, do not chase.

"C'mon, Ibai. Let's get started." Sten hands me a staffed hook. I hook into the skin and lean backward while they try a saw. The saw can't pierce the skin. Walrus hide is tough. Next, they use a lance that looks like the long-curved spear of a Roman pike. The lance works. The animal moves with each slice, the fat bouncing and jiggling. It's strange. I shiver. The movement makes the animal seem alive in a way. The intestines spill out and the ice is greasy, a broth of blood, fat, and water. We'll cut blanket pieces, pieces as wide and large as a man's bed. Hence the name blanket pieces. Afterwards, we'll drag the pieces to the boats.

The other walruses are put to death. The baby walrus scream and their mothers' cry and bellow from the water, weak and horrid screams. I've read of walrus hunts of stranded explorers and sailors fighting for survival on icy seas. How I cheered for the men in these great stories, using their ingenuity and will to survive. Today is nothing like the great stories.

I remember all the sad speeches at the Grand Regatta, Fourth of July celebrations, and Christmas events. I believed it all. Mayor Charles Ashley spoke to the whaling captains, whaling companies, and New Bedford residents in his booming voice. He'd stand at podiums decorated in fluttering red, white, and blue ribbons. The women adorned in matching ribbons around their waists. I'd smile and clap.

"We are proud to employ men of all races, from the proud European Americans, Irish Americans, and African Americans. With our growing industry, we've sponsored scholarships at the most distinguished universities in these United States, our young men and women attend universities with the most lavish, accomplished pupils in the nation. With our proceeds, we've expanded our great scholarship to include two more students this year."

I smiled at the men and women around me. We raised our glasses. I believed it all. When the whaling ships suffered loss, I suffered loss. I prayed for men's safety and successful catches. I sat in church, praying among the pious, the faithful, and we prayed for ships and their crews.

I celebrated when ships returned home with 2000 casks of oil. I'd rush in to announce the news to my father, how the ship returns, and the piers filled with families and politicians and newspaper writers. Cameras flashed and we threw our hats into the air.

What did the ships do to fill up their casks? How many whales and walruses? How many tusks stored in their holds? Whaling is nothing but filling the banks of rich white men who already own the world.

I hate myself.

Gerald runs, announcing to all the crew. "The captain wants them all beheaded. Beheaded!"

"Jesus, Gerald," Sten and Lammert laugh.

I held the tusks while Sten and Lammert sawed away at the face. I put my feet up against the walrus torso and lean back. We work for two hours.

Sten and Lammert finally stop for a break. All the tense weeks of looking for whales, they seemed relieved for work.

The captain comes around. The captain smokes his pipe, stands with a stiff back. He stands there for a moment. I don't look at his face.

"Good work, lads," Merihim says.

"Quite a good catch today," Sten says.

"Yes, sir. Every cask counts," Lammert says.

I think Merihim attempts to strike fear in the Dutchmen with his presence, his silence, his scrutiny, but the Dutchmen aren't roused or intimidated. They answer his questions but do not contradict.

"What you think of today, Ibai?"

He never says my name. It's the Dutchmen's presence which makes him more respectful. "A fine day, sir. Fifty casks will help."

"You see? Our crew knows the value in filling casks one at a time. I'm not too humble to get what we can, when it counts."

A whaler calls for the captain. He raises his pipe at Sten and Lammert and walks away.

"He's a tiny dog with a loud bark. My papa worked under a man like this. For years. Too long. I asked him, why you work for this man? He's no good. He said men like him are everywhere. Can't avoid these little men. Whatever you say to them, you'll lose. They'll find a sneaky little way to defeat you. Say little as possible. Little dogs don't get far in life," Lammert says.

I see their defiance and I admire them.

"Have you seen something like this before? Hunting like this?" I ask.

"I've been sealing before. Now that's shit work. The babies get stranded on the ice. We club them. Bashing in the heads of baby seals with their cute faces," Sten says.

"Cute! Jesus Christ!" Lammert smokes from his pipe, laughing.

"I'm not kidding. Have you seen one? The babies are fluffy and wide-eyed and looks like it's smiling."

"Shit!" We laugh. Sten and Lammert are good men.

"Lord. Let's see what the others are up to," Lammert says.

Dorothy and Susan cut up walrus, as well. They work, sleeves pushed up, hands and forearms bloody. Dorothy pulls out the heart, kidneys, stomach, and intestines. She pulls out a long line of intestines.

We walk together. All the walrus are faceless, their bodies intact, but faceless. The captain collects the ivory tusks, laying them up, side-by-side, snouts and whiskers attached to the tusks. We walk along the line of tusks.

Emilio drinks a cup of warm blood, donning a cannibalistic smile, blood on the corners of his mouth. "You must try. It is the pure essence of the animal."

"You sick bastard," the Captain spit.

"It's good for you. Blood is full of iron. The Massachusetts Indians drink the blood and eat the heart while it is still warm. While the heart still beats," Emilio's voice is heavy and syrupy, reeking of his opium hangover.

"Sixty casks, and the ivory," Sten says.

"Ivory is a good price because of the ban," Lammert adds.

"Sixty casks closer to home."

The bell rang on the ship. We look to the ship. The captain looks with his seaglass. The ship turns west, away from the ice, away from our boats. I don't know what is happening.

"It's coming in. Fuck! Fuck!" Merihim runs.

All the men run. The ship's bell is ringing. The men run.

"Move! Ibai!" Sten yells. We run to our walrus.

"What?"

"The ice is coming!"

We run. Sea ice is unpredictable, feared, and a living creature. The ice will crush this entire field and we'll be swallowed by the sea. Sten and Lammert carry our walrus head by the tusks, each holding a tusk, blood dripping on the ice between them. They gallop with their long legs. They try to drag other walrus heads but it's too late. We can't get them all. They know the dangers of ice. I run with the lancing tools.

If men get left behind, it'll be me and Gerald.

"Move your ass, boy! They'll leave us if they must," I yell at Gerald. He's carrying a walrus snout. Gerald pulls foot for the boat.

I arrive the edge of the ice and I see the ice field coming. Slow? Fast? I can't tell.

They throw walrus heads into the boats in this dull splat, squishing, splattering, the boat rocking in the waves.

Gerald threw a snout, but it was too heavy, and it clunks in the water. He pauses a moment, looking at the captain. "More, Gerald! Another! Get it all in! Get the tools! Toss those in! Move, move, move! Get it in the boats! Gerald. We're leaving! Gerald!"

We pull foot away from the ice. I'm sweating. The captain grinds his teeth in this strange sideways position. We pause to look back. The ice closes.

The ice is as large as a football field. From this distance, the ice looks harmless. But it groans. We hear a tremendous smashing and pushing of ice, pushing up a grey waterlogged ridge. The carcasses bob up with the ice, then slide down between the slush in great splashes.

"You fuckers. You damn fuckers. Curse you, devil," Merihim curses.

I row. Merihim isn't cursed by the devil. He is cursed by God.

8 | My Scalp

MY SCALP. A LITTLE MORE TO THE RIGHT, and he'd cut my artery. I hold my scalp together with my hand to keep it from slipping backwards, upwards, away from my forehead.

"Get a needle and thread from the sled. From my pack, and water," I tell the boys.

They run.

I don't remember anything. This bothers me most of all. I don't remember waking up this morning. I remember fishing last night. I remember nothing of this morning. Blood drips into my eyes. The sky turns pink. I press snow to my eyes and see a little better.

"We brought water." The boys kneel.

"Good boys. Smartest boys. Help me, Ebrulik. Help me get the bandage off, son." My hands shake. I remove the bandage from my head. The boys start crying. "Don't look. When I say, pour the water. A little at a time. Ready. Pour it."

I close my eyes. The water burns. The water scalds, boils, freezes, I don't know. I scream into my fists, again, like before, knuckles pressed against my mouth.

A puddle underneath me grows. My blood mixes with meltwater. At first, my blood spreads like a pink flower blossoming and unfolding in rosy tendrils, swirling, curling, then, the blood transforms to ruby tentacles grabbing, reaching, clutching for prey.

"Aaka!" Their faces whiten.

My boys. I can't stop now. My hands shake. "We're almost done. It's almost over. Is it clean? Make sure it's clean."

"It is," they say.

"Pour some water over my eyes. I can't see." They pour water and wipe my eyes. They look away from my scalp. I see now. "We're almost done. Nauraq, you're alright. Let me see the thread. Peel it a little more. It's a little too thick. You two are so brave."

It is caribou sinew, made from the caribou's tendons, transparent and tacky. Aaka helped me dry, cure, and peel down the sinew for sewing thread. The sinew darkened a little with age, but it's still strong and pliable. Except the thread is too thick. My skin would get big scars from this thickness. He peels the sinew down, hands trembling. I thread the needle.

"Ebrulik. You're going to stitch me."

"Aaka! I can't."

"Shush, shush, shush. Hand me the needle. Hold the skin together. That's all. Don't look. Pinch the skin." I might faint. I might throw up. I can't stop now. He squeezes his eyes closed and pinches my forehead together.

"I'll sew it, Aaka," Nauraq says.

"Can you?"

"Yes."

My little boy. The eight-year-old. His hands shake, but he does it. I feel the cold tip of the needle, piercing, pushing, and a pop through the skin. Pain arrives like a pack of wolves. I've felt birthing pains, hunger pains, the despair of losing my husband. I taste liver-flavored pain. I cry and shake. He pulls the thread and I feel every bump of the sinew. As I suffer, my sons suffer.

The stitch is working. I feel the tension. My children mend my skin like they mend my heart. "You did it, son. How many more?"

"Three. Four."

"We'll do four. Can you do it?"

"Yes."

My children know how to stitch. They've watched the old women stitch up umiaqs and qayaqs. They know the waterproof stitches for our boats, stitches which keep our men between life and death, between floating and sinking. My children know stitches.

Ebrulik holds my hand, looking away. I feel a shadow over my eyes. Looking up, I thought I'd see my husband standing above, obscured by the sunlight, but it is a falcon, swirling in the sky in a large circle.

Four more burning pierces, but we do it. My sons do it. My scalp is together. We sit a moment, in relief, and in despair, and in gratefulness, amazed at our accomplishment. I notice how quiet the day is. I listen for the ship's engine. I hear nothing.

"Can you knot it?" I ask.

"Yes."

"Cover it with fish skin. Ebrulik, some fish skin."

"What kind? Pike?"

"Yes, pike." I don't know what kind of fish skin, but pike will do.

"You did it, son. I'm proud of you." Nauraq holds my hand. He stopped crying. He wipes his tears.

The boys bandage my head with fish skin and leather. I touch it. The bandage is tight. "Help me up." My eyesight goes white sitting up. "Are we ready? Alright."

We walk to the sled. The boys carry me most of the way although I'm walking better than before.

"Your eye is red. Bloody." Ebrulik looks at my right eye.

"The white part looks red?"

"Yes."

"I've seen it before. The eye will heal. I'll make salve." What is the name of the plant? Pink. Fuchsia. I see it but can't name it. Budding plant marking the start of winter. Fireweed. Boil water with budding petals. Not old, dry, or fully bloomed. Fresh and budding. Boil it down. Boil it down. Seep until potent and fragrant. Soak cotton flowers in the salve. Put it over your eye at night, I heard mother say. Let it sit. Let it sit. Mother, are you watching?

"Aaka. I'll steer," Ebrulik says.

"I'll run," Nauraq says.

"Thank you." I climb in the sled. I remember holding my breath and telling myself to stay strong. I must have fainted. I wake up and the river is far behind.

"Son? Where are we?" I ask Ebrulik. His eyes water from the wind and sunlight. We spent the winter months curled in our home, hibernating like those bottom-feeding fish, existing like ancient eel creatures living in the ocean ravines with bulging filmy eyes and translucent teeth. We spoke little, ate little, moved little, and slept for days hoping to dream of my beloved husband, their father, how we prayed to see him in our dreams.

"We see the ships."

"Can you?"

"The ships are there."

"Good." I sit up higher in the sled. The trail is bumpy. I feel my head. Blood runs down my face, but the stitches hold in place. My forehead felt deadened, now reawakened with pain.

We slide up into soft snows and the boys stop the sled. They lead the dogs back to the trail snow. The dogs jerk the line, yelping and jumping. The dogs need water soon.

"The dogs don't listen, Aaka," Ebrulik says, pushing the sled.

"They haven't learned to run together, son. Be patient."

I pray for my sons. I pray to my Ancestors. I pray to my husband, "how could you leave me?" I pray to my parents and grandparents, great-grandparents, my great uncle who died from old age who we found on the tundra lying on his back, arms up, hands behind his head like he watched the clouds passing by as he died. I prayed to my mother's siblings who died from starvation, years and years ago when a famine struck the entire coast. I pray to our Ancestors whose names and stories are forgotten. Are you watching me now? Do you see my little sons pushing these starving dogs along the coastline after their sister? Do you see me, a mother, alone, starving, wanting to die, wanting to live, wanting to forget and remember? Do you see?

"It is a person!" Ebrulik yells.

"Is it Ataŋauraq?" I place my hand over my heart. Is it my uncle? My prayers are answered!

"I don't know."

"How many?"

"One."

The person stopped on a long stretch of beach, a spit separating the sea and freshwater lakes. I recognize this beach. There are no hills or cliffs nearby, flat lands for miles. It is always windy, white caps on the ocean at every moment of the day. The beach littered with entire trees of driftwood. I love this beach. It is ethereal and peaceful.

It's an older woman in her fifties. Her dogs bark at our arrival. It hurts to hear the dogs barking. The sun hurts my eyes. Everything hurts my head.

She takes off her gloves and ties the gloves behind her back in the hunter's style. She grabs our dogs' gang line and helps the dogs stop.

She offers water to my sons, then to me. She sees the bandage. "What happened? You need help?"

"We are following a ship," I say.

"A ship?" She asks. She looks towards open water. Her entire neck is puckered in scars, like tiny spruce needles and tealeaves.

I shake my head. We don't have time. "Is Ataŋauraq with you? My uncle?"

"There is no one."

"My daughter is on the ship. We must follow the ship. Thank you. We must go."

"At least let me feed your children and dogs while you're here." She saw the state of our dogs. She's polite. She doesn't stare.

"Yes. Alright."

"Your boys?" She walks to her sled.

"Yes."

"Boys, eat. There's food." She hurries. She waves at the boys. The boys follow her to her sled. She gives caribou meat, maktak, dry fish, and dried blueberries to the boys, then to me. She fetches blocks of caribou meat and threw out blocks to our dogs. We're hungry.

"I'll ride with you."

I don't know what to say. I nod. Feels better, safer, with another person.

We left, going north. Not long after, she appears behind our team.

I fall asleep again. Or fall unconscious. When I wake, the boys are breathing hard, their hair heavy with hoarfrost crystals.

"Stop for a while, sons. Take a break."

"Are you sure?"

"Yes. Give the dogs some water."

The boys stop the dogs. The woman pulled her sled next to ours. I stay seated in the sled. I can't get up.

"More food for your boys," She says. She unstraps a pack in her sled, pulling off the twine. "Come, boys. Feed your Aaka."

She gives more maktak, caribou, and dried caribou. The boys eat in silence. I pull my food into small pieces.

Her dogs are healthy. She wears a new caribou parka. She is like a demigod, shining and strong. Whoever she is, I'm thankful.

"Did you know dogs follow you?" She asks.

"The dogs are all that's left of our home." I see the dogs in the south.

She stands near me, saying nothing. She leans against our sled. "Here. Have a look." She gives me a seaglass, a white man's seaglass to see far away. I look at it a second, then look to open water. We're closer to open water than before. Because the winds are high, the ice forms narrow here.

I've heard great accounts of the Yankee ships, grandiose, wide berths, filled with gifts and trinkets, how generous and unique they are. Men and women stocked their furs for trading, sitting on the ice for passing ships. But the ships are a manmade thing, devoid of life, a patchwork of timber topped with a spider web of ropes.

There is a ship going north. It's too far north to see anything distinctive about the ship. There are two more ships coming from the south.

"I see it! I see her ship! Boys! Is this hers? Is it her ship?" I place my hand over my heart, how my heart hurts.

Ebrulik looks. "It's hers!"

"Are you sure?"

"Yes," they say. "The same creature in the front."

"Here, boys. Feed my dogs, too." She hands them blocks of frozen caribou meat. The boys walk to her sled. "They took your daughter?"

"Yes. Yankees. I don't remember. They took my memory, too."

"Can she find her way off the ship?"

"She's five."

"Five years old?" She almost yells. She shakes her head, peering at the ship with her looking glass. "We can't climb on their ship. No. Getting onto their ship is no good. Not good at all."

"What do I do?" I'm crying. The crying hurts. Talking hurts.

"I know a white man. He's kind. He may know how to help."

"I don't know."

"The white man is a holy man. We can ask him."

"Will he help her?"

"I don't know. Our people do not return from the ships. They go south and are gone forever. You'll have to draw them off the ship. You know the cape ahead. They have to pass the cape ahead. A tight turn in the sea. It's a chance to get their attention."

"The Yankees?"

"Yes. You can't climb their ship. No. You'll have to draw them off."

"Me? How do I get them off the ship?"

"Fresh meat. That is how we get them off the ship. Alright. Boys. We're riding up to the cape ahead. You'll have to unload your sled. Get it light. Take a pair of clothes. Your hunting pack. Nothing more. We're riding hard. Fast as we can."

The boys look ahead to the cape.

"What will happen to our things? Our dad's tools?" Nauraq asks. He helps her unload the sled.

"He'll forgive you. Nothing is more important than a child's life. Make him proud."

"We will," they say.

Together, they throw everything from our sled. Nothing is left, not even a good seat cover. We each pack a hunter's pack which carries spearheads, arrowheads, cutting tools, flint, cottongrass, water bladder, and rope. We also pack one extra parka each and a small tent. Now we are traveling like hunters.

She unloaded her sled, as well. We saw fresh-made tools, fishing net, harpoon heads, buoy, caribou antlers, and two pelts of caribou.

She offered her pelts of caribou, and we throw our old bedding. We left a huge pile on the beach, along with her belongings.

The woman gets on the foot rail on her sled. "Boys. Your Aaka will ride with me. We're following the ship. Your mother needs rest. Can you make it to the cape by yourselves?"

"We'll run the sled by ourselves?"

"All on your own."

"We can do it!"

"Good boys."

Beside me, she tied down a new, polished rifle. "Go ahead. Rest. I slept well last night and it's not evening yet."

"I'm Kayaliruk. My sons are Ebrulik and Nauraq."

"I'm Nasauyaaq. Or Nasau some call me." She kicks off the sled and we head north to the cape, following Samaruna's ship.

The boys smile for the first few minutes. With little weight, the sled goes faster. They each stand on a foot rail, sharing the handles. I'm so proud to see my boys running a sled together, side by side.

"Are you sure they haven't passed the cape yet?" I ask her.

"They're looking for whales. They like to hunt whales by our villages. They know it's the best places to get whales. It doesn't hurt to pray."

I finished eating the maktak and caribou, and then covered myself with the extra parkas. For the first time in months, a person watched over my boys, and I felt safe enough to sleep. I slept a heavy dreamless sleep and when I wake, I see the tall dark shadow of the cape.

We travel to this cape every year for fresh eggs. The birds lay their eggs on the cliffs. My husband wasn't afraid of heights. I'd watch him from the boat, climbing far up the cliff side, climbing through the convulsing clouds of birds. I'd scold him for climbing so high. What if he fell into the water? The waters below are treacherous. The ocean currents churn and circle. Men fall in the currents and don't resurface.

We spent a summer day in a hidden beach within the cape, reached only by umiaq or qayaq. The beach is in a crevasse, surrounded by black shale cliffs on both sides, the sun beating down with no winds. The cliffs are covered in reindeer lichen, rock tripe, sunburst lichen, and jewel lichen, yellow orbs and coral rings mixing with grey reindeer lichen. We watched colonies of murres diving for arctic cod, capelin, and sculpins, diving in a splash. The black and white seabird flies far out to sea for food, flapping with their little wings. At the peaks, groups of caribou climb the green plateaus for lichen through outcrops of serpentine. I wonder how many of our Ancestors walked on this beach? Did they bathe in the sunshine with their families, wondering, wandering, watching the synchronized flights of birds?

Tonight, on this black night, the cliffs are a void on the horizon, obsidian lines against the starry sky. This time of year, we only get a few hours of night. Even though it is night, we must go hunting now, before her ship reaches the cape. I pray the white men stopped and took rest for the night.

I get up and help stake down the dogs.

"We'll leave them here. They'll be safer here. Those wild dogs stopped up there. They're probably resting for the night," Nasau says.

"Is there anyone left alive?" I don't know why I ask this question. It feels so long since I've spoken to an adult.

"A lot of people went inland," she says.

"I thought of this, too. I should have brought us inland."

"It's no use. The people inland got sick, too. The only thing helping is the vaccination."

"What is that?"

"A medicine to keep you from getting sick. You can get the vaccination from the holy man in Tikigaq. The white man."

"There is a cure?"

"Not a cure. It keeps you from getting sick."

"A medicine to keep you from getting sick. A medicine. A white man's medicine. Maybe I could have taken my family north. A few months ago. I said we need to go north. I asked my husband to take us north. I asked my Aaka. What if we went? I could have gone myself. I'd learn of the medicine. And brought the whole family. My husband. My children. My Aaka and dad. Everyone. They'd be alive. They'd be alive." I'm walking in the dark. The boys hug my waist. I can't breathe.

"There's no time for this, young lady. Boys, get the net from my sled. Unload it," she whispers. I hear love in her voice. "This is a white man's illness. Think of it later. Your boys are watching. Think of your daughter."

She's right. I repeat these words, she's right. Still, I feel the anxiety rising like a hill. She's right. I help them with the net.

"What are we doing?" Nauraq asks.

"We're trying to get the white men off their ship," Nasau says.

"How?"

"Food."

"Will they bring Sam off the ship?"

"That's what we hope."

"Are we fishing?"

"No, young man. We're sealing tonight."

"In the dark?"

"In the dark."

"Aaka! We're sealing tonight."

"I heard, son."

"We're netting seals. The fastest way to get seals is netting. We need as many as possible by morning. It is dangerous at night like this. I've heard of strong men netting twenty seals in one night. See my net? A beauty, isn't it? I traded with an old man on the north side." The threads of the net are still tacky from its freshness, as if the sinew had been peeled and braided the night before. We help her pack up the net and other tools.

"It's my first seal," Nauraq says.

"It's his first seal. I caught my first seal a few years ago," Ebrulik says.

"You'll get your first seal by morning," she says.

"Aaka. I'm going to get my first."

"You are son. You'll be a hunter by morning," I barely say the words. I'm exhausted.

"His first seal won't be given to an Elder. Won't it be bad luck?" Ebrulik asks.

"I'm an Elder. He can give it to me."

"You're an Elder?"

"Aren't your boys sweet? I'm old enough to be your grandmother. This hunt is to help get your sister back. Creator will forgive you. You'll be a lucky hunter all your life."

"Where did you get the gun?" Ebrulik asks.

"I traded for it."

"With white men?"

"Yes."

We rolled up the seal net into a long line and hoisted the net over our shoulders. We walk in pure darkness, tethered together by holding the net. The white snow beneath our feet is little more than dark indigo. No aurora, stars, or moon to guide our way. Not even a faint twilight.

I hear Nasauyaaq pressing the ice, checking for weaknesses. I shuffle at first. I reach with my arm, grasping, grabbing, as if something could help my balance.

In springtime, our whalers break trail to open water. We travel the same trail throughout whaling season. We stick to the trail to avoid falling in hidden cracks, openings in the ice, and fields of slush. We grew up with stories of Ancestors who fell into the water, not able to swim back up. Ice is to be feared and respected.

We didn't map a trail. We didn't see the ice in daylight. Our next step, we may fall into water. Will it sustain our weight? I imagine myself falling through the ice, stunned by the icy cold, unable to swim, unable to fight for life, stuck underneath the ice.

It is not a level walk. We climb up snowbanks up to our thighs with deep snow, slide down snowbanks, landing on gritty, crystallized snow, old snow, or snow made on a cold, wet day. Nasau hit a few frozen puddles, cracking the fresh new ice with her stick. She led around the puddles, some large as ponds. The dogs' whining gets quieter and quieter as we leave the shoreline.

My foot sinks in soft snow and I gasp. "Sorry, sorry," I say. I don't want the boys to know how scared I am.

Nasau pauses, then keeps walking. If she is afraid, I cannot sense it. "It's not too much farther," she says.

I hear a slurry of water running nearby, like a river. In the north, there is a crack in the ice. A current weakens the ice, cutting, buckling, and uncoupling with its stream.

"Wait here."

We sit while she works in the dark. I'm not sure what she does. She walks to open water, then walks away. Then ran. Is she mad?

"Aaka? What is she doing?" Nauraq leans against me.

"I don't know, sweetie. Don't be rude. Listen to her."

Nauraq leans against me. I touch his cheek to check his temperature, like I did when he was a child, like I've done with all my children.

"Alapaa! Your hands are cold," he says.

"Sorry, my boy." I kiss him on the forehead.

Nasau calls my name. We pick up the net and tools. "Kaya. Over here. I had to test the length. I needed to know how long the seal could hold its breath from the water. We'll make a hole here. The net will hang downwards, not sideways."

We hammer into the ice, taking turns, chipping away until the hole darkens with sea water, the ocean sloshing and laving upwards. I'm exhausted. A few times, I nearly missed my foot. My hands blister between my thumb and pointer finger. My shoulder burns. It seems like hours. We chip away until the hole can fit a seal's body. We chip two smaller holes on both sides. We'll thread the net lines through the smaller holes.

"We aren't making too much noise?" I ask.

"Seals are curious." She answers.

We lay out the net, check the rope, lower the net, then secure the rope lines with blocks of ice. Ebrulik and Nasau shoulder most of the work.

We line up at the seal hole. We'll pull the seals up together.

Closest to the seal hole is Nasau, then me, then Ebrulik.

"What's your younger one's name? Nauraq? Nauraq. Use this. Call them up." She gives him a seal claw.

"I won't help pull them up?"

"You'll spear them when they come up. Can you do it?"

"Yes. Aaka, I'll spear the seals!" I hear his smile in the dark.

"I heard, son. Watch your step. Tell me if you get too cold."

He walks with a staff, stops, and kneels. He scratches at the ice with a seal claw.

We're quiet. I lean back on my son.

"I love you, Aaka." Ebrulik says.

"I love you, son. Are you tired?"

"A little bit."

"You want to sleep a little? Lean against me."

"After you sleep, Aaka."

"Thank you, son. I love you."

My boys are so strong. They've got strength to live life. They look forward to the future. I'm ashamed of my weak thoughts. Please do not let me wander into those dark thoughts again. Not like I have. My husband said his dark thoughts were like a ravine made of brittle and fractured stone, endless, bottomless, an abyss of the unseen world. When he gets himself into the ravine, he doesn't know how to get out.

This is how I've lived my life these past months. In the void of the ravine, breathing prickly air. In the ravine, I have a black heart, a vengeful heart. Afterwards, I'm water heavy with guilt. I fall into the ravine again.

I fall asleep hearing Nauraq scratching at the ice with the seal claw. I dream of stars and the Creator flying to the moon.

"Aaka! Pull!" I hear Ebrulik whisper.

The rope jerks forward and I'm awake. I'm standing up with the rope in my hands. We fight the line. My hands can't grip the rope because of my blisters. I push with my feet against the ice.

"Boy. Nauraq. Get on the end of the rope." Nasau tells Nauraq.

We're fighting the seal. The woman does most of the work. I'm the weakest. Yes, I'm the weakest. How will I save Samaruna when

I'm the weakest? I pull, shutting my eyes, tearing my scalp apart with each pull.

Pull. Slack. Pull. Slack. The rope burns my hands, even though my mittens. I reposition my feet. Ebrulik repositions his feet. We gain an inch and another. Its final fight ends with whipping and splashing but it's on the ice.

Nauraq pierces the seal with a spear. Another flex of its body and its dead. I fall on the ice, relieved. The boys want to see the seal. It's smaller than I think. Maybe I'm tired. Maybe I'm weak. I don't know. I don't care because we got one. We untangle the seal. It's a female.

"She was tough one, huh?" Nasau says.

"Aaka, we got it."

"We did, son. Your first seal."

Nauraq gives water to the seal, honoring the catch. "Water for your journey, seal. Thank you for your gift. Nasauyaaq. I give this seal to you."

"Thank you, Nauraq."

"You did good, son." I hug him with one arm.

He turns away, back to scratching at the ice with the claw, carrying the spear. My poor boy. Nothing is like the old days. If he hunted with his father, he'd get a bite of the heart. He'd give the seal to an Elder and the Elder would feed him, bless him, and give little ivory trinkets. But this is not the old world. This is a new broken world. There are few Elders. There are few hunters to teach my son. My son doesn't have a father. Instead of blessings and trinkets, he retreats to the ice with a seal claw.

In a moment, he runs to me. "Aaka? Will you pray for me?"

I try not to cry. "Creator, watch over this new hunter. Help him learn the weather. Help him learn our ways. Bless his days with animals. May he provide for our people his entire life."

I look up. Wind blew away the clouds. The stars are in full theatre, casting their luminescence across the horizon. I see dewy shades of opal, quartz, and lavender phosphoresce bleeding together, mixing, and fusing. With the starlight we see the ice, open water, and cliffs. So bright it seems now, compared to our long blind walk across the ice.

We repeat the same actions all night. We feel a seal caught in the net, we pull and pull the thrashing seal, the seal is pierced, and we've caught another. By morning, we've caught eight seals. We drag the seals to open water. We make two trips.

At dawn, we heard the bear.

"You hear it? It smells the blood. Load up your rifle." She said.

I load up the rifle and follow her up into a hill. The boys follow. She scans the ice. I listen. I hear it. It's a polar bear. The boys stand together. They hear it, too.

"You see it?" She whispered. She unsleeves her rifle.

I rub my tired eyes. I see it. The bear sniffs the air, dripping salt water. He's as tall as my sons. It's an old bear. 20 years old, maybe. I see how he walks and juts and sways with old hips. He presses his nose to the ice, pawing. He's searching for a scent.

"The Yankees won't be able to pass up a bear. We must get it."

She's right. We need the bear. If the Yankees see a polar bear, they'll come to the ice. They won't leave a polar bear.

"Let it come closer. Closer." She says.

We all know stories of the polar bear. Fickle creatures. No one knows how a polar bear will react. He might run away. He might charge. He might descend into the waters. When I was young, I saw a polar bear swipe at a dog as it ran. The dog dragged its back legs on the ground, yelping, half of its body ripping away as it ran. The dog collapsed. My father jumped onto his dog sled, strapping on his weapons, following the bear for three days until it finally slowed.

I hoist the rifle. Aim high. Adjust for wind. Tight against the shoulder.

I shoot first. Nasau directly after.

The bear clambers up, stumbles, and fell again. He falls to his side, all fours facing towards the ice edge.

He flinches and we all jump back. Nasau reloads but he shudders his last breath. A few days ago, I wouldn't have been able to kill a bear. I'd be too frightened. I've killed caribou, seals, not a polar bear. He smells like the ocean. Salty seaweed. Fresh air. He warms the air around him.

He's old, but white and brilliant. Some bears get yellowing fur with age, scarred, or diseased, but he's pristine. It's a good omen. Sedna knows which bear to send.

"Aaka. Aaka! You got him. You shot a polar bear. You got the first shot." Nauraq says.

I nod my head. My mouth's dry. I can't swallow. My tongue's dry as sand. This is how hunters claim the whales. Whoever harpoons the whale, claims the whale. Doesn't matter if the whale is just injured in the first throw. First throw gets the whale. Same with animals. Whoever get the first shot, gets the animal.

"My first bear. I give this bear to you, Nasauyaaq."

"Good. I've gotten many gifts this dawn. I've not received so many gifts in one day. You've got some aim. Deadly aim."

"My husband said the same."

"Let's see if we can drag him a little." She looks at the bear from the side.

"Drag him?" I ask.

"No, you're right. He's too heavy. Let's clear the view for them to see. Get the axes."

I throw up. The woman and boys pretend not to notice. I pour fresh water into the bear's mouth. "For your journey. You gave your life for my daughter. I will tell her."

"Was this your first bear, Nasau?" Ebrulik asks.

"My first polar bear this year." She smiles at him.

We chip away ice and watch the sea. It is dawn. The ships must be sailing again. It doesn't take long before the ice is clear.

"Me and you will wait by the water. Your boys. Your boys will wait farther to shore." Nasau says.

"Aaka? Can I wait by you?" Nauraq doesn't want to go. He hugs my waist.

"It's safer this way. Please listen. I must see if they bring your sister. Can you do this for me?"

"Yes."

His eyes are so big. I love my boys. "You're a good boy. My hunter. We're not far away."

The boys walk towards land, as they were instructed, peering back, resistant, hesitant. But they listen.

It'll be a sunny, cloudless day.

"You can sleep. I'll watch for the ship."

"Aren't you tired?"

"I slept some. Don't worry. I've had sleepless days. Are you certain you can do this?"

"Yes. I'm certain."

We're killing the men who climb the ice. Nasau and I agreed. While the boys busied themselves with dragging the seals to open water, we spoke.

"These men kidnapped your child."

"I know what I have to do. Thank you for being here."

We stack snow up, like a hunting blind, and we burrow behind a snowy ridge. She is at my back. I feel the warmth and I can't help but fall asleep. I hear the running water of the ocean. The dripping of water from the ice, drip, drip. drip. I fall asleep to the groan of ice beneath me.

I wake. Who is she? What am I doing? I blink. I'm confused. I connect all my memories. I remember. I remember Samaruna and the ship.

"They're here. This is the ship?" She hands me the scope.

"Yes." I say. My heart beats.

"You're sure?"

"Yes."

"Shoot your gun. Then use this. Run like hell." She hands me the axe. She holds the spear.

I wedge the rifle in the ice. My hands shake. I succumb to adrenaline. Fear streams through my veins, corrosive, caustic, and venomous.

She grabs my hand. "You're afraid. Good. Fear gives you strength. Fear sharpens your senses."

"Maybe some of them are good men."

"Good men wouldn't allow a child to be stolen."

I agree. I nod, and swallow. Yes, she's right. Kidnappers of children. I disown my feelings of remorse. I sever my feelings of remorse. Think as a mother. Sever. Disconnect.

I hear the ship. They've stopped. The ship sputters coalsmoke into the pristine sea air. A boat lowers to the water. Four men row to the ice. I wish they could drown in the ocean. Flounder. I see them. I see them all. Clear. I see them: tiny figurines of men; kidnappers; carriers of disease; plunderers taking what they want.

There is no time. How easily they pull up the wooden vessel. They climb the ice. They trot across the ice with long legs, like moose. There is no time.

I recognize the tall, skinny man. I grab her seaglass and look again. Foggy memories of the tall man—the pointy nose, his height and build, the brown wool. I recognize him.

"The tall man. He took my baby." I whisper.

"The man with the hat?"

"Yes."

"He's yours."

She fires. I fire after. I shoot the man walking next to tall-man.

Tall-man spins around in wonderment, in confusion, arms flailing around him like strings. He doesn't hear my footsteps. No time to speak. No time to scream. No time to squawk a sound. He opens his eyes wide, mouth wide, and I swing the axe into his skull. I hit bone. The axe vibrates from hitting skullbone, straightened spine, and body. He falls to his knees, eyes looking at each other.

Icy splinters spring up everywhere. Gunshots from the ship. They're shooting.

"Your rifle! Come with me!"

I'm running through shards of ice stinging against my cheek, like hot embers piercing my skin. I can't keep my eyes open. I can't see. I hold my arm up to shield my face.

I stagger and crash to my knees. Nasau grabs my sleeve and yanks me up to my feet. Nasau yells. "Get up! I got you!"

She holds me up and we're running. We run towards pools of water on the ice, towards the sun's glare.

It is over. It is over. We found the boys. Nauraq covers his ears from the gunfire. I want to hold my babies. My boys.

"Did you get the count?" Nasau asks Ebrulik, out of breath, watching the ship.

"Twenty-four." Ebrulik says.

"Twenty-four, plus the four dead men?"

"Twenty-eight, four dead."

"How many guns did you count?"

"Four."

"Good lad. You did good."

"What if there are more?"

"They work with as few men as possible. Keeps their caches full."

I hug my little boy. Nauraq tightens his hands around his ears. He cries. I hold my boy. I kiss his forehead and apologize to him.

"It's over. My son, it's over. I killed the man who took your sister. Instead of dying alone with courage, he died like a serpent in the presence of others. He died a coward's death. His spirit will haunt the others." I tell Nauraq. He says nothing.

Nasau and Ebrulik watch the ship with the scope. The ship sent two more vessels to collect the dead bodies. They sent a dozen men on the ice, armed with rifles. They stack up the seals in their vessels. A few sentinels looked out onto the ice with their scopes.

To get the bear, they sail their ship as close to the ice as possible. Using chains and pulley, they dragged the bear on board by two legs. All the crew went on deck to see the bear. This took time. After chaining up the bear, they left quickly, starting their engine and going north.

I didn't see Samaruna. Not once did I see my baby.

"What do we do next?" Ebrulik asks.

"Next. We go to Tikigaq. To the white man. It's another day to get to him. Half a day if we do not rest. Let's go."

I'm heaving up what little is in my stomach. I'm coughing, throwing up, and holding my tight stomach. Nauraq grabs my hand, pulling me to the sled. He doesn't talk. But he smiles when I help him into the sled and tuck him under a parka. I kiss his forehead again.

Ebrulik climbs the back of the sled. He needs sleep. Both of my boys need sleep. "Sleep, Ebrulik. I'll run for a while. I'm fine. I got sleep."

Ebrulik climbs into Nasau's sled, covers himself in furs. We push off. It is sunny and windy. Nasau and I run the dog sleds.

After some time of running on the shoreline, I'm hallucinating.

Nasau and her sled move in a blur. Nasau speaks, her mouth moving, but I don't hear her voice. I hear dragging, like a body dragging over grainy snow.

I feel my husband running behind me, see his shadow, I can't see him, but I know he is there, running, breathing on my cheek. I want to turn and see him, why can't I see you?

I taste the salt water of the sea, splashing in my face. I taste the blood and I know it's the blood of the men I killed.

Within a few feet of my sled, the ship sails up onto land, sailing over ice, so close I smell coal burning. Faceless men work on deck, twitching, jerking, dressed in wool and brass. Blood spills from their decks. They pull at ropes and look onto land with scopes and rifles. They shoot harpoons like cannons.

Their ropes branch outwards, grabbing everything and bringing on deck, swallowing up everything, seals, polar bears, the ropes grip onto a whale, the ropes squeeze the whale until it bursts.

I woke in a scream. I brush away bad spirits. Nasau grabs my shoulder. The boys sleep in the sleds.

"What happened?"

"It's the lack of sleep. You hallucinated. Time to move. We're a few hours away from Tikigaq."

9 | FRESH MEAT

"IBAI! OUR LUCK IS CHANGING. FRESH FLIPPERS." Merihim says. "Oh Jesus! Jesus! Look at it! It's a monster."

I'm at the helm with the captain. It is a sunny morning, but cold. I see seals, a stack of them. Seal meat is good eating. I'm surprised how similar the animal looks to the Atlantic seals. I see a polar bear. It is big, bigger than I imagined.

"Fresh meat for days." Emilio smiles.

"Call for anchor."

"Anchor! Anchor!"

The engine stops. Emilio picks the men, and they lower to the water.

It's a short walk to the seals and polar bear, less than fifty yards from the ice edge. The seals laid by a crack in the ice, a river of water funneling through the ice.

I jump at the first gunshot. Merihim looks out with his scope and Emilio runs below deck.

The bell rings.

I'm sitting behind the bow with Gerald.

"What happened?"

"Stay down, boy! They've got guns!"

"Who?"

"I don't know! Stay down."

Emilio emerges with rifles, and they begin shooting. They stop and cuss.

"Damn!"

"Damn it to hell."

"Fucking savages!"

"What the hell was that?"

Four dead men on the ice, pools of blood growing and staining the ice. One drags himself across the ice, before falling limp, cheek against the ice.

"These son of a whore bitches don't know a cunt from an asshole! Smallpox is God's punishment for their evil ways. America is better off without their sins. Let them die! Inbred savages." Merihim yells.

"Get the bodies. Pack up the meat. Do not let their deaths go to waste. We'll bury them at sea." Emilio orders.

10 | REVEREND JOHN BEACH DRIGGS, MD

To His Holiness, Archdeacon of New York,
        Episcopal Diocese of New York,
    I deliver troubling news of my station, hearing firsthand accounts of a child abduction of the Tigara indigenous population near Point Hope, Alaska. Be assured, I've written urgent letters to the United States Revenue Cutter Service, to the notable Captain Michael Healy of the cutter Lacina.

    As I write, Capt. Healy administers the law to nearly 300 whaling ships in arctic waters, and in vast and unforgiving seas. Healy, I'm sure you are aware of his presence in the arctic given his popularity in American newspapers, in the Senate, and with the Presidents, is in the arctic seas, currently sailing alongside the Alaskan coastline.

    His ship monitors the remote arctic, the Aleutian Islands, and the Alaskan northwest coast near Canada, and I do not know his current location. Healy inspects ships for any violation of tariff codes, laws, and regulations, shielding the eskimo populations from the denigrating whaling presence, ferrying reindeer herds from the Asian coast to Alaska, securing experienced reindeer herders from the Asian coast, assisting shipwrecked whalers, even mapping tides, reefs, meteorological, and cultural events, while delivering vaccines, mail, and supplies to outlying communities. Given his tremendous responsibilities, he is a difficult man to contact. He is a good man, who I appreciate as an ally and good friend to the Church.

For the Church's archives, and if the matter is brought to a United States court, I write as much detail of the situation for the child's health and safety; and, in the event the perpetrators are brought before a United States Court since the parties in question are United States citizens.

A five-year-old eskimo child has been kidnapped by American whalers, whereas the mother was injured in the kidnapping. The mother is healing, and received the smallpox inoculation, and states two white men grabbed her child. In the kidnapping, a white man was killed, an unfortunate necessity as the mother defended herself and her children.

The child was taken aboard a ship, although I have no name of the offending vessel, they gave a vague description of its front carving, a serpent of sorts. This crime is not uncommon in the lawless north. In 1892, the USRC discovered five eskimo youths on a whaling ship, none over the age of thirteen. The Lacina arrested the perpetrator and brought the criminal to a Seattle court.

I'm troubled by this news. I've heard of child abductions, women taken as slaves, and tricky contracts with eskimos, which obliges individuals to years of hard labor and little pay. God knows what horrors the children endure on such vessels.

Today's news was delivered by my two eskimo friends, Elise and Raymond, an older couple with grown children and many grand-children. Since the start of smallpox, they walk the surrounding lands, searching for those in need, informing their people of the smallpox vaccination, which I administer under the Episcopal Church's funding.

Smallpox continues to spread, especially at the most remote locations, although I've administered vaccinations year-round. The eskimo population is in decline, decimated by waves of smallpox, tuberculosis, influenza, syphilis, among many other sicknesses brought with the contact of white men. Tigara, around 1800 AD, was a booming village of 2,000 villagers. Now, the village is 250 eskimos, six American whalers, and one reverend. The arctic wilderness is like the Black Plague when people screamed about the End of Days, when mass graves were dug and filled, when houses were marked and quarantined, stories I read in primary school. It is not events we witness with our own eyes. I briefly reviewed the census before departing New York, though not in detail, and now regret this nagging question, how much of the eskimo population has died from sickness?

Relationships with the eskimo are complex. They've experienced horrendous treatment from the explorers, fur traders, and now the whalemen, who pollute our volatile relationship by stealing, trading alcohol at inflated costs, and violating their women.

Despite the whalemen, I plan great measures to solidify our relationship by befriending their leaders, steadily providing education to the young, and vaccinating as many as possible. I'm planning a trip to the Noatak River, a few hundred miles south of Tigara, to further inoculate and provide necessary medical assistance.

My own relationship with the eskimo started with contentious emotions.

I landed on the beach, left with several crates of supplies. The Tigara eskimos wouldn't allow me to leave the beach. I attempted communication with several men.

Even though white men were stationed near Point Hope, a few miles south, in a whaling station they called Jabbertown (named for the numerous languages spoken), they won't permit white men to enter Tigara. It rained for the first two days and all I could do was build a meager shelter under my crates, a sort of canopy between crates.

This is when Healy arrived. By this time of year, the ocean was free of ice, and I clearly saw his ship not far from shore.

He came ashore, his men rowing him ashore while he sat stately and rigid.

"Do not worry, Reverend." He said. "I know the Tigara natives, and I'll relay your intentions to the natives."

I thanked him, over and over.

He crossed over the berm, walking in long confident strides up into the village, and soon arrived again with native men.

"I let them know you're a trustworthy man."

"Thank you kindly, sir." I nodded my head to the eskimos.

"I told them you're a Holy Man. A spiritual man."

"And a doctor. Please let them know I'm also a physician. I've brought medical supplies funded by the Church."

"A doctor! A good fortune for the arctic. I'll remember you're here, Reverend. I may need you before the season is over."

"Yes. A surgeon, to be exact."

"We're damn lucky. Oh, excuse me Father."

"Reverend. Reverend Driggs."

"Reverend."

I set up a tent not far from the beach, not wanting to further irritate the people. They said nothing. There were no more confrontations, but people didn't welcome me either.

I built a small house with the assistance of local eskimos. They've seen white men's housing at Jabbertown and had a sense of what I wanted to build. I showed them pictures in a magazine. They paged through the magazine together.

I continue my duties as a physician. This took time, as I stated, the Tigara eskimos do not trust white men. Before winter, a young girl broke her finger. I heard her crying and running, crying for her mother. I knocked on their door with my medical bag. I injected the site with morphine. They were quite surprised when she stopped crying. How could she not feel the broken bone? I told them, the best way I could, the bone is set. Except the medicine would wear off soon and I'd be back with more morphine.

It took another two months before I inoculated the first patient against smallpox. I cannot fully illustrate how difficult it is to explain a medicine which stops a sickness before it begins. I drew pictographs, rudimentary sketches showing a sick person with bumps on their skin. Then showed them the glass bottles of medicine, and the signs for 'no more', 'no more sickness'.

The mother of the young girl with the broken finger was the first patient. Then the young girl.

As a physician, I vaccinate against smallpox, attend to grippe, examine pregnant women, among other concerns. Besides smallpox, there is nothing out of the ordinary, maybe a lung infection or viral infection. Nothing which can't be cured with attention and comfort.

Elise and Raymond brought in the small family during school. I couldn't be prouder of our school. When I first arrived, I failed to communicate any concepts or stories to the people, not knowing any of the eskimo language. The eskimo dictionary I brought proved useless. The answer came in the form of a brave little boy named Kinavaq, who knocked at my door. After he looked around in my house, quite freely I may add, and I fed him pancakes, the answer arrived. First, the people learn English. Then, learn of the Lord Jesus. I came to preach and became a teacher.

Elise is my dearest friend in Tigara. She knocked on my door one afternoon. I offered her tea and biscuits. This was our ritual. Every few days she arrived for tea and biscuits, sometimes bringing a piece of sewing. I learned her name and she learned mine. I wonder what her husband thinks of our visits, but I think he senses I'm quite harmless, especially towards female relationships.

As I said, I'm proud of the school. I stand looking at the school every afternoon as I walk home. I look at its small paned windows, even planks, and perfect angles of the roof. It is a modest size, 30 feet by 56 feet.

The Episcopal Church granted funds for a humble school structure. I procured the building material from San Francisco by chartering a vessel. This is a common method. Dr. Sheldon Jackson, an educator, is now building new schools across Alaska, and raising funds from the government. Because of Dr. Jackson's reports to the Education Commission, the Episcopal Missionary Society is now rewarded with government contracts.

I hear now, Dr. Jackson and Healy work on introducing reindeer herds for the impoverished eskimo population. The whalers and Russian fur traders slaughtered whales, walrus, seals, and sea otters for so many decades, I'm afraid the animals will be extinct in a few generations if actions aren't taken now. Dr. Jackson and Healy raise funds to purchase reindeer herds in Siberian and instruct Alaskan eskimos how to raise reindeer. This is an impressive mission.

Healy and his men helped erect the school building. Healy found every able carpenter in the vicinity, from his ship and another ship. Good, strong American men built this school, with much help from the eskimos. We did good. The school is not painted, but I've ordered paint. I need the paint by the end of the summer. I don't want to go another winter without paint.

Every morning, a girl or boy raises the American flag, as the instructions of Alaskan public schools. As a missionary school, we are not obliged to follow the same protocol. but I thought it's a good practice for our schoolchildren.

I've developed a curriculum for the Tigara School, working from the first years, the alphabet, naming of animals, arithmetic, currency, formal greetings, and Lord Jesus Christ Our Savior. A few learned pupils are writing their names, parent's names, and basic introductions. So much progress in so little time. Much to my surprise, the alphabet song I've created traveled hundreds of miles away, attested by a traveler from another village. He arrived Tigara, sang the song with no mistakes.

Our lessons for today are: alphabet song, lunch with tea and biscuits, the story of Hansel and Gretel, and games of checkers, which is the children's favorite. The children are smart. They created their own checkerboards with drawings on sealskins.

Now, the eskimo will communicate with the outside world. I see their minds open to new ideas, traveling, adopting new technology. Would they further their education by attending a secondary school, a university? There is new hope in the last frontier in the hearts and minds of children.

Easter was a special day for Point Hope. I baked a cake, to the best of my ability. I used the last of my sugar. It was a simple cake. No frosting. I topped it with frozen berries. The children and I made paper flowers from old sheet music. The sheet music was ruined on the voyage up to Alaska, and having no musical instruments, I put the sheet music to another use. All the students joined in, including the parents. It was quite festive.

We now have fifty students at our school. Although the numbers haven't surpassed some of the other schools of southeast Alaska because of their larger city populations, in villages of similar numbers, we've achieved a great many accomplishments.

Adults join the school, even the Elderly, sitting at the back of the room, their backs against the wall. I welcome them all. The people arrive on time, even on stormy days, they arrive precisely on schedule. They listen and do not interrupt. Any crying babies are bounced and coo-ed. I don't remember any children, even in my childhood, who behaved so well and eager to learn.

I teach. I write curriculum. I attend to patients. I hold a small church service every Sunday. There is peace in my humble duties.

If only I thought ahead and brought more books. I've got bibles, Book of Psalms, an eskimo dictionary, John Muir's Travels in Alaska, Robert Louis Stevenson's Treasure Island, complete works of Edgar Allan Poe, an encyclopedia of animals, and a Sears Roebuck catalog. I've collected a few newspapers and magazines with each year, left by travelers and whalers. The Sears Roebuck catalog is a great sensation. The women look through the fashion, women in corsets and flowing dresses escorted by men in tuxedos. The women memorized the costs of rifles and handguns. I believe the women drive the prices in their society. A local carver studies the jewelry and creates a perfect replica of a woman's brooch but carved in ivory, exquisite and painstaking work with plenty of details.

The most surprising result is I'm learning their language. I'm more than a rudimentary speaker. I converse with Elise and Raymond about plants, hunting, and their ancient stories.

I started drinking the local stinkweed tea, it is quite nourishing, reminds me of dandelion tea. I wonder what the locals think: me, a tall white man leaned over, picking stinkweed tea in the marshes. It is quite a maze in the boggy tundra. A person must dredge through feet of water, feet sinking into mossy tundra. I'm reminded of the mossy forests of Delaware, every inch covered in wet moss.

On a winter day, I felt my throat closing, my muscles tightening, surely, I'm getting grippe, I thought. Elise served stinkweed tea and dried fish. By morning, the grippe was effectively fended off. I faithfully drink the tea every few days and haven't felt the least sick, even in the coldest winter months.

I also picked berries, much to the people's delight, in autumn. I stored cloudberries, crowberries, and cranberries, enough to sweeten my breads every Sabbath. Of all the animals of the area, my favorite is caribou. It is like deer of the southern states, but rich with gamey tastes.

I've learned a lot about Eskimos, more than I expected, their history, enemies, and ancient ways of hunting. I've documented some of their stories. Ancient Tigara is magnificent. I've seen the outlines of old houses, the sod houses, where their Ancestors dwelled. There are graves exposed by the shoreline, where the old Tigara people buried their dead. I've escorted many historians and scientists to this old Tigara, where they diagram, sketch, and dig for artifacts.

Old Tigara is of great interest to the Smithsonian Institute. Already they've awarded scientists for their discoveries. They request Healy and any visiting scientists to document the area and procure ancient relics. Artifacts are in abundance in Tigara, the people digging themselves to trade for modern conveniences.

I'm acquainted with Nasauyaaq, the woman who delivered the young family to Tigara. Nasauyaaq joins the same Tigara whaling crew each spring. It is a great honor for a woman to paddle after the whale, at least this is my interpretation since I don't see many other women paddling after the whale. She is capable of lifting more weight than some men. She is welcome by all men and women, young and old. I see the change in others when she enters their homes. Her voice is regal. She meets your eyes and will not turn away. I'd guess she is fifty-five, but I'd dare not ask her age, like all women, she may be insulted by the question. She is elusive, as well, and tends to spend much time in isolation. Even if I was an eskimo man, I believe it would take time to gain her trust.

Every year, I attend the whaling festivities, from breaking trail, preparing the boats, camping on the ice, pulling up the whale, and the related whaling festivals. It is a joyous occasion every season, a treat I'm blessed to witness and participate.

Because I have no knowledge of the ice, or of whaling, some of the young boys have more rank than I. Upon my first visits on the ice, the whaling captain said I'd follow a young lad, 11 years old, and take orders from the young lad. Laughter followed.

I spent my first year serving tea, chopping ice, feeding the dogs, among other menial tasks. However, this type of learning, taught for generations, is effective. I learned to move fast when ice approaches, how to discern dangerous ice fields, and steer a dog sledge.

I met Nasau last year when I administered her vaccination. She sat on the bench, back straight, polite, and strong. I administered the inoculation, in the presence of Elise and Raymond, and she wandered my house, looking at each article, observing but not touching. My belongings are few. A photo of my parents, a photo of my parent's home in Delaware, my surgeon's degree from New York Medical School in a glass and wooden frame, a brass cross, a lithograph of Jesus and the Last Supper, and an advertisement of the New York Opera Company signed by the feature opera performers, where I traveled as their doctor for a time. Since her visit, I've heard rumors of her travels. As a writer, and with my growing understanding of the eskimo language, I'd like to document her history and her travels, if she would permit.

My advertisement of the New York Opera Company is a prized possession.

I miss opening nights. The men dress in tuxedos and women dress in flowing dresses with lavish, long trains. Champagne is served. Three stories of opera boxes fill with millionaires, dukes and duchesses, visiting emissaries, visiting diplomats, the wealthiest names represented in those gilded ornate boxes, the women fanning themselves with silky, feathery fans. The boxes engraved with garlands and emblems, rows of delicate and painstaking details. Statues of the muses greet operagoers at the grand staircases.

We traveled to Philadelphia, Boston, Massachusetts, and Virginia. We traveled by train, riverboat, pleasure ships, and carriage.

I was the physician for opera singers, including Jubilee.

"Who is this, then?" Jubilee sneered.

"Driggs. Our new doctor. You'll like him, Jubilee."

He goes by the name Jubilee although I never knew why. His eyes glazed over, and he says nothing. He sits stiff and bored. I look him over. I don't explain anything. He was tense.

He's a prima donna, a former protégé of some famous singer in La Scala. I don't have a memory for names.

I first saw him perform in Faust. He overtook the stage with his straight, dancer-like steps, pointed toes, outstretched arms, and his face overwrought with emotion. He wore wigs with dark, long tresses. He sang of a magical elixir for youth in order to find love. I wept. I yelled Bravo! Bravo! enough for my voice to get hoarse for three days.

I witnessed his voice recorded on wax. They allowed a few people to sit in the recording. He sang into the recorder, a dark cone shaped like a brass tulip. He started with his eyes closed. He sang with his entire body, swaying with each note. Where do singers keep all this breath, all this pressure, all this power in their lungs? It is as if they keep a river of breath in their body, such a vast array of notes from the lowest G to the highest F note.

He spoke of a La Scala opera, which was performed under the night sky, in a stone theatre like the Roman arenas. The stage troupe lit the grounds with oil lamps and torches, the musical ensemble hidden beyond a levels of stone seats.

He swears by this story, although many question its validity. As he closed the final scene, as he sung the last note, hands stretched outwards, violinists, viols, cellists, and percussion holding the final note, a cloud of starlings flew overhead, a swinging cloud, obscuring the moon and stars. He ended, without observing the starlings, naturally, stood still. The theatre erupted in applause, screaming Bravo! talking excitedly, wondering how did they stage the birds to perform at that moment? Was it divine intervention? Was it the Hand of God?

Whether the story is true or not, on nights I know I'll not be disturbed, I listen to his record, to his voice, close my eyes and imagine the night opera, under an Italian blue moon, stage lit orange and yellow by firelight, soloist singing the final notes while a massive cloud of starlings, wisps across the moonlit sky.

My mother writes regularly. She updates me on the family. She tells me of my father, brothers, and certain single women in society. She knows better.

When she learned I'd leave my medical practice to join the church, she fell ill for weeks. Father wrote about her dying, shallow breaths, her very will to live. An act she's perfected over decades of practice.

She couldn't tolerate her doctor surgeon son moving to the Territory of Alaska, where I'd forego her hopes of becoming an outstanding, upright, award-winning surgeon, staving off illness and death to famous and important people in society.

When she didn't convince me to remain in medical practice, suddenly I'm the heroic, heartfelt, unthinking, caring, selfless son who's changing the fate of helpless natives of the world. I can't imagine how she paints me to her friends in society.

The people refer to Nasauyaaq in a term I don't understand. Maybe the word cannot be translated. They call her a word, which can mean the old ways, the old way, or dying away. My intuition, when they attempt translation, is she is strong like the people in the old days, or she is the last of her kind. Somehow, in my gut, I feel I must record her history for their future generations, the church, or for God himself. Who knows why men feel these callings?

Nasauyaaq arrived during school late in the day. Seeing the urgency in Elise and Nasauyaaq, I closed the school day with the children reciting formal introductions in English.

I arrive at my home and the family waits. Elise lit the room. She tells me what happens in English.

"Are they Nasau's relatives?" I ask.

"Not Nasau's. Ataŋauraq's niece. They are Tigara traders, south of here. They live in a small village." Elise answers. The small family lives in a remote, outlying camp, a small group of families who consider themselves Tigara.

I'm a friend of their uncle Ataŋauraq. He is a whaling captain of Tigara with a grown son. He is a formidable man, a few hundred pounds of muscle. The young mother sits on the long bench in my kitchen. I speak in Eskimo, as well as I can.

"What happened here?" I lay out my bag. They're surprised I speak their tongue. I unpack my medical supplies. It is better to allow the patients to see all the instruments: syringe, glass bottle, small file, rubber tubing, stethoscope, mirror, and measuring device, tongue depressor, thermometer, scissors, and tweezers. I have a surgical bag, but it would certainly frighten the young family since it consists of several large, sharp knives, one specifically for cutting bone.

"Hit by a white man." She says. She is a petite young woman, in her twenties. Two boys sit by her.

"Your sons?"

"Yes." She smiles. She doesn't trust me. She smiles and she's polite, but she doesn't trust me. Her boys stare, as well. I smile at them.

I approach the mother with my stethoscope. Her sons look at the instrument. I show how I listen to my own heart. They understand. She permits me to listen to her heart.

Eskimo kids are always curious about my beard. Eskimos do not grow full beards. Eskimo men grow moustaches and a little hair on their chins but nothing more. A common trait among eskimos and Indians of the south.

"Heart is good. Breathing is good, too. I'll look at her head now. I'll rebandage it afterwards." I show her scissors and motion I'll cut the bandage from her head. She nods. The boys stand and watch.

I see dried blood in her hair. Her face is half bruised. I cut the bandage away.

"Does she know his name? The white man?" I ask.

"It is worse. Bad. They hit her head with a gun. Took her daughter."

"Took her daughter! Where is the white man now?"

"She doesn't know. They're on a ship."

"A whaling ship?"

"Yes. For whaling."

All the filthy whalemen and traders! Jesus, Mary, and Joseph. I'm writing Healy about this incident. It must be reported! I remain calm. My years working at the New York Immigrant Hospital taught me to always remain calm, repressing any alarm, as not to further agitate the patients.

The laceration is five to six inches long, cut along the occipital frontalis and orbicularis oculi. Skull intact. No debris seemingly left in the wound. I press gently, feeling for any grit, dirt, or rocks. I'd say she suffered a skull laceration without focal or mass lesion.

They've sewn the wound together with sinew, such a thick thread to sew together the skin. The scar will pucker. But the stitches are strong and good. I could cut the stitches and restitch, but it would hurt. At the very least, I can inject morphine around the wound.

I check her pupils and facial muscles. Pupils aren't enlarged. No paralysis on one side of her body. No signs of cranial bleeding. Bleeding may be happening. Bleeding can happen in the days following a brain injury, when the patient and doctors believe the danger has passed. There is nothing I can do about the bleeding, if it is occurring.

"I know your uncle. Ataŋauraq is a stubborn man, he is. He is delivering vaccines. He's probably at Kali by now, or Utqiaġvik. These are good stitches. I know stitches. I work on people's organs, their insides. Stitch them back up. These are good." How do I explain the duties of a surgeon?

There is another Ataŋauraq, her uncle's namesake, who was killed by his own people. It was the first I've heard of eskimos killing other eskimos, at least within their own community.

The story of the other Ataŋauraq is a sad tale. The other Ataŋauraq fell into alcohol, multiple wives, listening to white men. He tried to exert authority over Tigara villages. Sheer force of authority doesn't fare well with Tigara eskimos.

"The little one stitched her up." Elise says.

"You don't say? My Lord. You are a brave young man. Stitching people up is not easy. Some doctors work years to stitch as good as this. Can she describe him to me? Can she describe the white man to me?" I ask Elise.

Elise interprets. "She doesn't remember. She remembers last night, but nothing about seeing the white man. Her boys remember."

"This is common of head injuries. Her memory of the white man may never return. I think it's best to stay for a week, so I can monitor her. Head injuries are sneaky. Her brain could swell. You could fall into a coma."

"They can't stay. They need to find the ship." She interprets.

"I know a captain who can look for your daughter. His name is Healy. I will write to him right away. This captain, he is good, a great umaalik of his people. Healy is a resourceful man. Righteous. He will arrest these men for their crimes. I know where they are headed. To Canada. To an island where the whalers built a white man's town called Herschel Island."

"She wants to know where it is. Is it far?"

"It is far. I'll show you. I've got a map. Let me finish. The stitches are good. I'll inject morphine around the cut. It'll take some discomfort away."

I've mapped the general area of Tigara with the help of local hunters, a passion of mine. The hunters retain great detail of the land. With each turn of the shore, they tell stories of their Ancestors. I hear of a lizard-like monster which lives in the ocean, a massive creature, and capable of eating a person whole from shore, almost like a snake emerging from the ocean, grabbing the victim in its jaws, then returning to the ocean. The people say the ocean is deep near Cape Lisbourne and why the creature lives by this shoreline. I hoped Nasau would add more detail to my maps, but I'll wait after this more pressing issue.

I lay the map on the table. The young mother and Nasauyaaq stand next to me. The young boys crowd the map, saying nothing.

The arctic coast of Alaska is hundreds of miles long. They'd pass six large eskimo communities and countless camps. The coastline goes northeast until reaching the top of the world, then east to Canada. "We are here. They go all along this coastline, northeast, following the whale. They leave the territory of Alaska. Into Canada. Their destination is Herschel Island. This is the farthest north they'll go. They turn around, go back south. When ships go south, they'll cross the ocean to the Siberian coastline, not the Alaska coastline, following the whale migration."

"They will go to Herschel?"

"Yes. All whaling ships go to Herschel, so I'm told. All whaling ships travel the Siberian coastline. So, you know where the ship will travel in two places. Herschel and Siberia."

In my journey north, Herschel Island was a point of great excitement for whalers since all whaling crews go ashore. Captains do not worry about whalers abandoning ship since Herschel Island, is, well, in the arctic. There is nowhere for whalers to escape or run, unlike cities, towns, and ports where whalers jump ship, especially those whalers who've been recruited involuntarily. Herschel is where whalers anchor, rest, trade, look for new recruits, among other needs and wants of whalers which I cannot imagine. Herschel Island now boasts a church, although, knowing whalers, I'd imagine their nightly activities are not condoned by the church.

"Will the ship, will the captain take her to shore? Before Herschel." They ask.

"I don't know. I honestly don't know."

"They ask how fast a ship goes in the water?"

"Hmmm, I don't know. I'm sorry. I don't know."

"Herschel Island? Siberia. You know this for certain? You know?"

"Yes. Yes." I look at the mother. I look in her eyes. "Yes. This is where they will go."

They talk back and forth, urgently, forcibly, pointing at the map. The mother shakes her head. She holds in tears with her fingertips. She points at the map with an upturned hand. She drinks water, wipes her mouth. Her sons hug her sides. She can't speak.

Nasauyaaq proposes a straight route across land, traveling a river. They'd cut many miles if they traveled over land. The mother doesn't want to leave the coastline. She hopes the captain will come to shore and they can see her daughter then.

"You can't paddle after a ship. They have steam engines. I'll write Healy. Can you tell them? I'll write to Healy, he's a captain. Healy will bring the girl home if he finds her. Whalers spend two months in the arctic before going back south. Can they make it to the island in a month?" I ask Elise.

"Strong men travel this way in a month."

Nasauyaaq volunteers, this I understand. With two sleds, they'll make it to the island in less than a month. She kisses the boys on their heads. The mother agrees and there is peace in the room again.

"She says to write to this captain. They'll go to the island and Siberia. Both places. Nasau will take them."

"Very good. Good. They'll have two chances to see the girl. I'll write to Healy. But they must get vaccine first, yes? Get the medicine ready."

I vaccinate the mother first. She is comfortable now. I don't know if she trusts me yet. She is, no doubt, in a difficult state with the loss of her child.

I look at her sons. The boys are malnourished. I do not ask about their father, but I imagine he perished from smallpox. God knows what they've witnessed during this smallpox outbreak. "I'll give you the needle then. Both of you look like strong young lads, you'll do just fine." They do not fear the needle. They've already been tattooed in many places, around the wrist and ankles. They're interested in the glass vials, syringe, and rubber tubing, looking but not touching. I let them hold the rubber tubing, which brings smiles. They've never felt anything like rubber.

Tigara children are resilient. Even in these dark, tumultuous times, the children make jokes. One summer day, a group of children laughed at me. I turned around. A young boy followed me, imitating my walk and posture. He walked with clumsy long strides, straight arms, and furrowed brow. They've taught me not to worry so much about life and take small moments to laugh.

Nasauyaaq walks around my house, freely as she did before. She noticed my new photograph. It arrived a few months ago. It is the New York Immigrant Hospital, where I worked as a surgeon. I'm proud of this photo. It reminds me of my accomplishments, my knowledge, and my education. Yet, it seems a lifetime ago, another life. Colleagues, appointments, meetings, contacts, company dinners, fundraising efforts, drives to help the poor, and working with the people, what a dizzy, noisy life it was.

I stand with other doctors. We stand on a manicured lawn, wearing our best suits. It was a sunny day. I wanted to squint but the photographer kept telling our group to keep still, open our eyes, smile.

She spots me. I'm clean-shaven, wearing my spectacles, a navy suit, and loafers. She points and smiles. I nod.

"That's me."

She stops at the Last Supper. "This is white men? Eating together? They dress like this?"

"How my people dressed a long, long time ago. Where it is warm. There are deserts. Vast deserts."

"We have a desert here. South. Past three rivers."

"A desert! Close to here?"

"Yes."

"Takes a couple weeks." She points along the Alaskan coastline going south, past three major rivers, farther, past two sounds. My Lord, she's traveled far. How long did it take?

"You know this man?" She points at Jesus. Every inch of her upper arm is tattooed. Lines, half-circles upon the lines, rounding motifs, little men in bands. I see scars, burns, and slashes, even through the tattoos. I first noticed the scars on her neck, which, I'm sure most people notice first.

"He died. They buried him in a cave, a tomb. When they returned three days later, the door was open. He appeared to the people and rose to heaven."

"Heaven?"

"Paradise."

"Paradise?"

"The afterlife. Food is plenty. There is no sickness. We're reunited with our family. We are with the Lord."

"Is there good hunting in paradise?"

"Yes. Good hunting every day."

"Good. Good. Where do the whaling ships come from?"

"From many places. From the south. From a city called San Francisco. Another city called New Bedford."

She tries to pronounce San Francisco and New Bedford.

I have a newspaper from San Francisco. An old newspaper featuring the growing gold rush to Alaska, a large fire claiming a few buildings, the bridge, coming and goings of ships, land for sale, and advertisements for medicine. I offer the newspaper which she lifts. She speaks to Elise.

"She wants to know how we stop them from coming to our lands?"

"I don't know. If I think of an answer, I'll let you know."

"Why do they take so many animals when soon the animals will be gone?"

"I write to them about stopping for a season. I know it is not enough. Not nearly enough."

She smiles and folds the newspaper. She smiles at my little effort, and I feel inadequate.

I play music from the opera. I wind up the recorder. Adjust the volume. Place the needle on the record. She puts her ear up to the gramophone. She smiles and shakes her head.

I show her the poster. She points at the man. I nod my head.

"He's got long hair."

"Oh yes. It's a wig. Yes, I mean. Long hair for the opera. This is in New York City."

"New York City."

"Tigara is my home now." She laughs, not in rude way. I show her the encyclopedia of animals. "I was born in Cuba. Leaves big as a drum. Flamingo birds. Pink. Parakeet bird. Green like grass. Turtles, large ones. Lizards. Bugs are so loud. All day and all night. Buzzing."

I remember bits and pieces of Cuba. Feelings. Holding a stick bug in my hand, colorful birds flying overhead, canopies of trees, and the sound of the rain drumming against the leaves. I'm forgetting the names of places. I'm forgetting the language. There is no one to speak Spanish.

"What did you eat?" She asks.

"White man food." We both laugh. "Can you tell me of your travels?"

"Me?"

"Please do."

She spoke of a village of Inupiaq people who live on cliffsides. They build their homes on the cliffs, using stilts to support the homes. Cliff-dwellers, she calls them. What a wondrous sight, it must be. She talks of Inupiaq who live in the mountains, the Nunamiut, which means inland peoples.

I spent the evening listening to Nasauyaaq about her adventures, Siberia, Canada, interior Alaska, Messenger Feasts, shamans and witches, and old Tigara. The arctic is a mysterious place. I told her of my own encounter with a strange creature.

When I first moved here, I saw a strange, dark being. I went outside to smoke my pipe. It was a winter night. The entire land lit up by the bright moon, every shining ray of moonlight against the snowy land. A black figure walked in the darkness, underneath the moon. It was tall, slow, and menacing. Even from a far distance, I saw it was a tall figure. Long legs. At first, I thought it to be a caribou or a moose. But the way it walked I saw it had but two legs. It couldn't be a human, not with its height. My heart beat fast. I held onto my cross. I prayed.

I ran inside, shoved the bench in front of the door, and loaded my rifle. I'm not a gun person. I'm not an expert gun shooter, but I can shoot a rifle. I lit my fire. I prayed. I repeated the Lord's prayer over and over.

I didn't want the evening with Nasauyaaq to end, but alas, she's traveling with the small family and must rest. I understand why the people respect her, this effigy of the ancients. I see the strength of their people in one woman.

The next morning, Nasauyaaq donated her net and tools to the Tigara villagers, a generous act I am grateful to witness. She described the beach where she left tools and hunting weapons, which she also gifted. This act caused quite a sensation.

The boys gave a few of their dogs to an old woman, even though the dogs are skinny, she said she'd love companions for berry-picking.

I bid Nasauyaaq and the family farewell. I shake her hand and give her an Episcopal coin necklace amulet, nothing of great value but sturdy and symbolic of the church's good will and blessing in their venture. I advise Nasauyaaq to travel easy within the next few days. Take it slow. Let the young mother heal. I hold the Bible and read a passage while she prays with me.

There is a word used in opera, sprezzatura, a nature, a way of performing in the opera, when art is so beautiful, when art is touched by God it is called sprezzatura. Nasau is like sprezzatura. She is beyond description, a woman with such strength, she is beyond words.

I've sent correspondence to the US Revenue Cutter Service in the states and to Captain Healy. I've provided modern medicine to all family members and information about the whaling stations.

I ask our church to pray for the eskimos searching for a child among 300 whaling ships and thousands of whalemen. They journey across the arctic, crossing 750 miles, fighting the wild and its unimaginable obstacles, and the whaling industry who brought human evils to a most beautiful, untouched land and its occupants.

O Mother, Virgin of virgins, I beseech you to grant your grace upon this family. With our prayers and the help of God, they will recover their stolen child. God Bless the Diocese, Episcopal Church, the people of Tigara, and this small eskimo family as they begin their perilous journey.

Humbly, your servant, Reverend John Beach Driggs MD

11 | THE ESKIMO CHILD

THE CAPTAIN DRANK ON DECK. I'M AT THE HELM.

Emilio oversaw the cleaning of the walrus tusks. They scrub the tusks, purifying the ivory of any meat, blood, or whiskers. The crew doesn't speak either, except to give directions.

Emilio sat with the captain, sharing a flask of whiskey. By this time, the captain feels tipsy and euphoric. I stand at the helm again, by the captain's side. I'm not rising in the ranks, the captain demands I stand at his side at all times.

"The men haven't been watching. They need to watch at all times. Am I sending blind men up? Spot those fish! The eskimo women, send them up on deck! They are better for something other than a good hand job. We need more eyes on deck. We're in the thick of the damn fishes."

"It is the beginning of the season yet, captain." Emilio drinks.

"We will have to compensate by trading more this year." Merihim says.

"Of course. We must think of the shareholders, of the investors, sir."

"We'll bring my wife's bibles."

"It is a good deed to bring the bibles."

"I will bring my wife next year."

"She'll be a good motivation."

"I want two ships by next year. She needs a bigger cabin. She will come next year. She fears the cold waters."

"She will find her courage."

"I'll look for a ship in Nantucket. The ships are surplus. The cargo companies are getting ships for nearly nothing. Who wants to go by ship anymore when there is a railroad from New York to San Francisco?"

"The industry will regain traction. America needs oil. How would the factories run their machines?"

"America's headed for a damn recession. Whalers are needed. Fucking politicians. Did you see the new regulations? Some coal miners die in God knows where, die on their job, and we are hit with a shitload of regulations across the board. It's the bleeding-heart Christians. They call themselves Americans! If they gave me an audience with our lawmakers, I could fix this industry. We could bring the tax preparers, the accountants. Those old men are a disaster. The laws are a mess. What a mess of laws! Emilio, you are a good man. It's hard to find good men in this world. You're a damn good man. Stronger than most whalers. Your mind is as strong as the most intelligent man. Maybe even more. A warrior. We are warriors to fight for a better world. A civilized world. Every ounce of oil we bring back, an inventor or scientist is able to push mankind farther into peaceful times."

"You are a fine orator, sir. Fine. You belong in the lyceums, running for Governor."

"That's what I'll do. Governor. My stomach. It's the damn food. Whatever I ate isn't sitting in my stomach right. The cook is trying to kill me with all this fowl. Nothing but birds every night. I need red meat."

"Governor and captain. You are needed in politics. These politicians don't know."

"They don't shit. They mull over hundreds of pages of regulations, for what? No one ever fucking reads the regulations. Who reads them? I could write the regulations. They say we take advantage of the eskimos here. The politicians live thousands of miles away. They've never set foot on a ship. They use the oil to light their homes and run their machinery. Yet, they say we take advantage of the eskimos. Spit on us, every step of the way. The ignorance of Washington. The eskimos are criminals. They steal every chance they get. Is the eskimo man or woman more important than American citizens? We all make sacrifices. I've not heard any complaints. Let them come, greedy bastards. All these damn new recruits. They come and come for the money."

"Most of them sign up for the money. What's not to love about the sea?"

"And this is what a lot of these men don't get. They work for a purse. You and I, Emilio, look at me. You and I Emilio, we aim for a cause."

"Damn right."

"It isn't about the money. Screw the money. We got money. It's the cause. It's the adventure. It's mastering the high seas as adventurers have ventured for, who knows, centuries? I'm damned."

"Damned is a harsh word. Still the start of the season."

"I should have brought the woman. She would put sense into me. She would reason with me."

"Women confuse the senses."

"At least I wouldn't have to worry about the damn church boys sticking their nose in her ass. Sniffing where they don't belong. She says they got manners. I got manners, don't I? At least acknowledge I'm there. She offers drinks to all the congregation. Let them wives get the men drinks! Instead, my wife acting like a damn slave to every man in the Lord's house. Obliging, she says. Her mom says she raised her right, and to serve all the people of the Lord! Oblige your husband, I said. Her mom said I made a scene. Woman, the scene here is my wife acting a slave to all the menfolk except her husband."

My shift is over. I don't say anything as the next shift comes on deck. Better to let the captain brood by himself and his beloved best friend Emilio.

It's been a week now since the girl's been on board. The ship sails away from land, into open seas, closer to the Asian coastline.

Apparently, we'll be in the thick of the feeding grounds where the whale stops to feed. In a few days, we'll continue east to Herschel Island.

The girl was seasick for three days. Every day, the captain asked if she got through yet. When I said no, he'd retreat to his cabin.

For a little girl, she threw up a lot. She vomits as much as a grown man.

"Jesus! Where is she storing all this?" Remigio said.

"Damn it!" A whaler said.

"Give the girl some laudanum! Anyone got laudanum?" Another whaler said.

"We're not giving the girl laudanum. That'll make it worse. Best to let her get through it." I said. I offer her dry fish, the only thing she'd eat.

"C'mon. Lunch time." I say to the girl. I don't have to force her to follow me anywhere. She listens. The only time I lose sight of the girl is when I use the head, then she waits in the hallway. We go to the galley where my crew is lining up to eat.

Anthony is the cook. He is Romanian, hairy, and smells of cabbage. Despite his vulgar appearance, he's a master chef. We give him fresh fish, squid, octopus, and seaweed, and he creates tasteful and savory dishes. He's also got the nose of a hound dog. He smells everything. He knows where everything is stored, even in the dark. Millet, rye, corn flour, spices. He complains of people's odor: feet, armpits, teeth, breath, groins, and ass. How does he smell it all? A gift or curse?

He is an ogre, scowling every moment of the day. In all my born days, I've never known someone so grumpy. When I pass him on the ship, he grumbles. He is a hairy, burly, pudgy man. He reminds me of the German tales of hairy creatures with elongated fingers who eat children wandering in the forest. He broke his arm once in a factory. He bore a huge scar on his forearm, a fracture from factory machinery. I don't know what kind of factory, but the scar is old and glossy. His only enjoyment is current news. Whalers ask him what's happening in Washington and he always groans. Those assholes! America is going down a shithole. Reconstruction, my ass. Foreign aid! We're saving other countries from their messes when we can't even clean up our own messes. More free food. More free clinics. What are they doing with my taxes?

He works in a little cubby, a little bigger than a closet, wide enough to fit a wide iron stove. He opens the window while cooking, a wooden shade pulled upwards and latched. I see the grey sea through the foggy window. We stand at the doorway. I show the little girl my frown and she put on a frown. He scowls. He grabs our plates from our hands, turns away, slops our meals, and returns our plates.

"What's wrong with you?" He asks the girl.

"It's the food," I say.

"The hell with you, Ibai. She's a little thief. I saw her take it again."

"Leave the girl alone. You never use it anyway."

The girl loves a large ladle from the kitchen. When Anthony's not in the kitchen, she takes it. I see her sneak into the kitchen when Anthony leaves. I say nothing. I see the ladle disappear from the counter, her little hand appearing. The girl collects strange things: ladle, a footstool, a broken end of a broom, and pieces of twine she braids and braids. When I was a child, I collected things from the sea. Like other children, I liked collecting shells and rocks from the beach.

Some days Anthony doesn't notice the missing ladle for hours. Then he's yelling my name and about the ladle. "Ibai! The kid's got it again! Ibai! Get it back! Ibai! Damn kid!"

She likes to braid twine. I noticed her collecting little bits of thread and twine, then braiding together. When I daub the ends of rope with tar, she watches for bits of rope. Poor kid. She doesn't have dolls, toys, not even her own bed. I wonder if there is anything else she can do to pass the time?

She anchors the end of her twine on a rusty nail on the wall. She tests the strength of her twine. She braids, and then pulls. She ensures the twine is strong.

"Planning your escape?" I asked. I point at the rope. She looks up, wondering if I would take her string. Seeing I wouldn't, she went back to braiding. She keeps the rope coiled in her sleeve.

I showed her how to tie a bowline knot. She failed the first few attempts, handing me the cord. She got it and went off running. She asks for more knots. No words. She hands me the cord and I show her another knot. This knot-learning keeps our time occupied.

She's made friends with a few crewmen, Sten, Lammert, Gerald, even Remigio occasionally shows a soft heart towards the girl. They offer her dried fish. Sten sang a Norse song to the girl one evening. He dropped a spool of darning thread, which rolled across the forecastle floor. She retrieved it for him. He sang a song of his people. When she smiled, he clapped once, and all the men laughed in happiness. She ran back to her seat, my plunder chest, smiling. I asked him later, what do the words mean? He said he doesn't know. Love, he thought.

Maybe we all feel sorrow for the girl.

She learned whaling is monotony, the same routine day in and day out. She knows the routine. Clean decks, clean equipment, and watch the seas for whales. She stays by my side at all times. This girl is quiet, never a peep. She understands English words although I've never heard her speak English. I see in her eyes an understanding. Captain. Eat. Ice. These words affect the child.

I want to guide the ship closer to the ice. Not enough to damage the ship, close enough so she could land safely onto the ice. The girl is better off with her people. I wonder if she has family. Smallpox hit every village on the coastline. How would I find her family even if I could? Where are the eskimos? Besides Port Clarence, I have not seen any settlement of natives. Maybe smallpox killed them all and she is truly an orphan. Besides, what is the worst that can happen to me? Marooned in the arctic?

One afternoon, the captain climbed on deck and read my mind about letting her jump ship. The girl and I looked down at the ice together.

He screeched, "What the fuck do you think you're doing? Lose the girl and I throw you off the ship! Mutiny! I'll imprison you for mutiny!" The captain would imprison me for mutiny. He can conjure any story he wanted and the company would believe his story. He's the captain and he's white. He would conjure all the crew as witnesses and my black ass would be in prison for life.

12 | You'll Carry This Axe Now

WE START OUR JOURNEY AT SULUKPAURAQTUUQ, the tributary of the Kukpuuk River. The clouds sulk over the entire
land, dense, mute, wispy at their underbelly where snow cascades
down to the land. We sled to the east, plowing through soft snows,
where the river branches outwards like roots of a tree. We'll follow
the thickest root, as far it goes.

I'm grateful for the winds and snow. In the cold, the river
remains reliable, sturdy, and strong as iron. We need the river to
stay frozen. Faster for traveling. I want to be far inland before the
ice breaks. For now, we don't have to worry about melting ice.

We follow the hunter's way of traveling. A hunter steers the sled
while the other hunters run alongside the sled. No one rides in the
sled. Better for the dogs to pull an empty sled without the burden
of extra weight. The runners break trail, lead the dogs, and make
sure the dogs don't get tangled. I volunteer to run as much as I can.
To my shame, I ride in the basket more than the boys combined.

Dogsledding on the river is the fastest route in winter. Like
a well-ridden trail in an endless basin. At Sulukpauraqtuuq, the
tributary, the river embankments carve into flat tundra. As we

get farther into the hills, the riverbanks grow tall as cliffs, bluffs made of clay, slate, sod or fans of alluvium sands crumbling into the waters.

We camp underneath cornices on the river bluffs, seeking shelter from the snow, away from the wind, the river rocks clacking beneath our feet. We find blackened rocks, charred driftwood, wind blinds, bird blinds, cairns, and ochre-hued markings on the rocky bluffs. We rested at Aaquagzaiyaak, where two women froze to death, and transformed into stones, one on the north side, the other on the south side. The women traveled to the Qagruq feast but froze on their journey. Along this long river, we rested at Uqaq, a place to find fields of blackberries, at Qatsi, a flat long cliff, at Auksaakiaq, a place to find masu roots, at Kayyaaq, a river junction with good fishing and masu roots, and at Iŋaluzat, a hill resembling intestines. My husband and I camped at many of these places.

My father said these hills were seamounts, mountains under the sea. He collected rocks shaped like large insects, sea creatures, or shells. How long ago did this creature live on our lands to be solidified into the rock? Now the seamounts are nubs, monadnocks eroded by wind.

We pass by abandoned homes, all in souring ruins, filled with the acidic taste of death, searching for signs of life, or survivors, I don't know anymore.

We know there are no survivors long before reaching their homes. No smoke, no barking dogs begging to be fed, no children hunting ground squirrels which will soon awaken by the hundreds. We look anyway. Out of ritual? Out of pity? No, we search out of hope. I hope we find a survivor, any survivor, maybe an infant escaping the awful fate of the parents or a child sitting amongst the dead, waiting, unknowing what to do. There is no one except the ravens, onyx-oiled, cawing from afar, cawing their messages of death.

Most corpses are mummified by the dry arid air, leathery, parched, skin taut against their bones, and balding. Other times the corpses are puffed, blackened, worm-eaten, fuzzy with mold and no longer look human, more like skin and fur molded into death effigies. The fetid odor clings to our skin, our clothes, lining our nostrils, like crab juice soaking its way into your fingernails, the fishy smell staying for days. When I lift food into my mouth or wipe my brow with my forearm, I smell death on my skin, hands, and hair.

We can't stop to bury the dead. Losing a day would be disastrous. The boys know, Nasau knows, and I know. So, we mourn for the dead in silent prayers, pushing our sleds along the river.

"After we get your sister, we'll help these people. Afterwards," I say.

At a camp, inside a limp tent, I pulled back the tent door to a swarm of flies escaping. A dead woman lay in a twisted position, belly exposed. Her belly moved in ripples, crawling, moving from inside her body, underneath her skin. I retched in the snow while Nasau told the boys to stay back, stay away, don't look. She lit the tent from all sides, throwing in any tinder or dry wood she could find.

"Aaka, look!" Nauraq says.

I drink water to cleanse my mouth. I run over.

A dog lay on its side, snarling, showing her teeth, but she didn't move.

"She's alive. She's a mother," I say.

She snarled again, the last noise she could muster, a sputtering into death. She birthed not long ago, her nipples red and engorged.

Nauraq found a puppy alive. "Look at him."

We crowd around the little pup. The pup licks Nauraq's face with vigor, wagging his tail so hard he almost falls out of Nauraq's hands.

The boys try not to show their tears. They laugh and dote on the dog. We left the camp with smiles, accomplishment, and new hope. Days of searching, days of disappointment.

I 'm not proud of my thoughts in the first days. I was exhausted. I wanted to quit, surrender to the circumstances, resign to live alone with the boys, bargaining with myself. How could a good mother think of quitting? We'd rest for moments, mere moments, then Nasau yells to move on, and I hate her, and I love her.

I decant these thoughts. I decant the outpouring thoughts to yield, submit, accept that she's lost for eternity. I pierce these thoughts, delimb, disjoint, amputate, lacerate, and bury the thoughts. I remind myself that I've killed grown men to protect my children, to fight for my children. I am Tikigaqmiut, I am Tagiagmiut, remember where you are from.

The winds are cold, waspish, and numbing. The cold starts with my hands, wrists, moving its way into my arms, nose, and ears. Our hair whitens with frost, opalescent and lustrous cobwebs clinging around our faces. In a forceful gust of wind, I tuck my face into my hood, how the skin burns from the cold. By dark, the boys look like old men.

Dogsledding is laborious. I want to scream every time they get tangled. Every time they fight or run our sled up the riverbank. Nasau stops, walks over, untangles them. She says nothing. She is patient.

This morning, two dogs chewed through their harnesses and ran away. The boys ran up to the hilltop, scanning the hilly country.

"The snow is deep. Too deep. Can we move on without them? Perhaps they'll follow?" I ask.

"No. We need the dogs."

I cry without a sound. She's right. We need the dogs. I join the boys up on the hilltop. We spread out. Nasau boiled tea, cut up fresh caribou, and fed the dogs while we walked the hilltops.

"There! East! They're going east!" Ebrulik yells.

"At least they're heading the right direction," Nasau says.

We load up the sleds following the dogs. They didn't stop or slow down, running until dark.

We stop for the night, feeding the dogs again. The two runaways scamper back to the gang line, ashamed, heads bowed down, begging for scraps. Nauraq and I harness the runaways and feed them.

"Aaka, they're good dogs," Nauraq says.

"Yes, they're good dogs. All dogs are good. I'm worried about your sister, is all."

"I'll teach them to stay."

"You're thoughtful, my son."

This morning, we found two dogs stuck together. A female got loose and mated with another dog.

"We'll get pups, but she won't be able to run soon. Then, again, after she births. We'll have to trade her. She's valuable to someone. We'll trade her for another runner," Nasau suggests.

My body is not the same after childbirth. Urine soaks my pants, not a steady stream but a drip, drip, drip. Worse, my tailbone twisted from my last pregnancy, forcing the pelvic bones to grind together at times, a dull pain radiating outwards. I know when the pain is coming. First, my hips and groin go numb. Then a dull pain spreads down my legs. Soon, my groin is throbbing and piercing. I waddle.

"Are you well enough to run?" Nasau asks.

"My tailbone is out of place. Ebrulik knows how to pop it back." I lie on my back and Ebrulik places his foot on my chest, grabs an ankle, jerks upwards, twisting at the same time. I feel my spine pop, from tailbone to between the shoulder blades.

"Better?" He asks.

"Yeah." My leg moves without pain. The sharp pain disappears. Later in the evening, I change my clothes and wear the tundra moss for woman's blood. I'm finally comfortable and dry.

Our Elders didn't have time for pain. My father knew a pregnant woman who traveled with her family. The family pulled an umiaq up on shore. She bent down, squatted, and gave birth. When she stood, she tucked the child into her parka and continued pulling the umiaq up onto shore. I'm not like the Elders. I can't run. I can't run with this tailbone twisting and contorting my spinal cord.

When I run, when I steer the sled, I think of my daughter on the ashen sea. I think how quickly she was born, not like my sons who refused to be born. I walked during her birth, unworried, unafraid, and when her head peaked, I pushed three times, screaming with every fiber, and there she was, born with black hair and faded-blue birthmarks covering her ankles, wrists, and back, like the tattoos she'd get as a child. I think of her fishing, the little fishing rod and fishing line in her hands, cheering and jumping at each fish. I think of her standing over me while I butchered a seal, she'd look at its organs, saying "Aaka! That's disgusting!"

What are they doing to my child? Is she fed? Is she well-clothed? Is she trapped, defiled, tortured, bruised, or chained? Is she treated as a slave, as inferior, or put to work? I don't know, I don't know, and this lack of knowing gnaws at me until I'm aching, crying, writhing, and then stiff with torment.

I haven't seen the captain's face. I'm haunted by his face, the man's non-face, the blank face. He's only a figure in the distance wearing drabby wool, staring at me with his scope. I don't know the color of his hair, eyes, or skin. I want to see his cannibalistic face, the brutish face filled with self-importance, ignorance, and entitlement.

I'm not like those other women, those pious women who forgive others and pray for their enemies. I want to bash in his skull. I want to hear him shriek loud as magpies. I want to cut off any finger that touched my child and throw him into the ocean for the eels, crabs, and scavengers where he will face Her, Sedna, the Sea Goddess. She will make him answer for his slavery, kidnapping, thievery, and crimes against my children.

Hatred takes all my being, soaks up every fiber, sinew, and porous bone. So, I wait until the last moments of wakefulness. I wait until my eyes are heavy, and then I descend into the dark ravine of rage, a place devoid of light, only blacks and darker blacks, every shaky step I think of his blank face. I flop downwards into this ravine, a limp body, cracking, breaking on the edges of the ravine, sharp as knives, my body cut open with each fall. I thump at the bottom. Every night, I live in this ravine.

Tonight, we stay at Savikmin's house. Savikmin was a friend to my parents, a man with four daughters. He sought four husbands for his four daughters. He spoke everyday of being a grandfather. His straw-colored sod house is built on the river above a small, rounded palisade where he keeps his drying rack and umiaq.

We know he isn't home. We stake down the dogs. I throw open his white-man's door, hurrying inside.

"Savik? Savikmin?" I yell. I know he isn't here. His daughters aren't here. His house is empty and dusty, but the house is clean. No signs of sickness.

Last year, he spoke of marrying a daughter to a Koyukon man. Did they make it? His daughters started a collection of ground squirrels for fancy parkas, to wear for their weddings. The ground squirrel furs aren't here. This is a good sign. I'm out of breath.

"Four daughters," Nasau says.

"Yes. He was anxious to marry them. He wanted to go to Koyukon lands. Then circle up north. I don't know. I don't know."

"This valley is good for caribou and wolves. He must have trapped a lot of wolves in this area. Good wolf area." Nasau looks through his glass-pane window, peeling, rattling, and fading grey. She knocks against the glass pane.

He installed a white man's window in his east wall and a white man's door to the front entrance. He found them in the forest, in the south, while trading for muskrats and beaver skins. A white man's riverboat sputtered upriver, wide, clunky, and spewing up black smoke. They stopped by a thatch of black spruce. He waited and watched. They emptied the door and window on the riverbank, along with empty tin cans, and an empty wooden box. He waited until they left and packed up the discarded things.

"They didn't want it. Must have been lightening up their boat, who knows?" Savikmin said.

The white men painted the door brilliant purple, like the thistles of wild onion, or octopus tentacles. He extended his entrance until it was tall enough to fit the door, which totaled a few more strides. He needed the room anyway, to store food all his grandchildren, he said. What if each of my daughters has two children? That's eight grandchildren. What if each had three? That's twelve! When I die, I'll be surrounded by grandchildren! Blessed with four daughters, this man!

My husband liked the door. Easier to use, he thought.

Savikmin displayed the tin cans on a shelf, empty, paper curling backwards.

"What kind of food?" Nasau looks at the picture, cradling the tin can in her palm. The boys crowd around her.

"Yellow dots?" Nauraq asks. Yellow dots, bright as dandelions.

"Seeds?" Ebrulik asks.

"I don't know. Green balls in this one. Green balls!" She shows me the tin can although I've seen it before. Her and the boys laugh.

Savikmin left the cans behind. He left behind dry fish, dried caribou, dried blueberries, honey, masu, and a full bladder-bag of seal oil. Nothing scraped clean like our cache. They aren't starving.

Yes. He is alive. I see the cans and dry food and I know he planned his journey. He didn't leave in a hurry. Nothing is in disorder. He took fresh food, squirrel parkas, and his daughters. Thank you, Creator.

"He took his family south. They're safe," I tell the boys. The boys busy themselves with bringing in food, bedding, and ice for water. "He took all the squirrel parkies for his daughters."

"Yes. I agree. Everything looks in order," Nasau assures me.

"I hoped he'd be here. He would have volunteered. He would have taken the journey up to Herschel."

I'm relieved to sleep at Savik's house, even if he isn't here. The tent is cold, damp, and wind makes its way into the tent. I check the boys several times a night. The preacher says we don't have to worry about smallpox, but I do. Perhaps I'll worry about smallpox into old age.

I light a fire in the fire pit. It is the same routine every night. I feed the boys. The boys feed the dogs. We check the dogs for chafing or injuries. Tonight, we sleep in a house, so I hang our clothing to dry. Then I hang our tent to dry. His house is big, at least fifteen paces across, enough for his daughters to sleep side-by-side without squeezing together.

I tell the boys to wash themselves with a hot rag. They eat and talk with Nasauyaaq.

"Far in the south, Inupiaq people live on cliffs. They build their homes on the cliff sides, using long poles to hold up their houses," she says.

"You've seen them?" Ebrulik asks.

"I have. It's amazing. Their entire village on a cliff side."

"How do they sleep? Won't they fall over into the water?"

"They have walls made of walrus skins."

I raise my voice. "Boys. Wash while the water is hot."

The boys stand behind the tent, throwing aside their clothes, water drips and splashes.

Their knees are bruised. Their elbows are bruised, purple blue circles.

"Ouch, son. Your knees. My poor boy. They hurt?"

"Aaka. It doesn't hurt. I promise," Nauraq says.

"And your elbows. Let me see."

"No. It doesn't hurt. My hand, though. See? Blisters. This one is the biggest one I've ever seen."

"Let me see!" My heart is racing. Not blisters! Nauraq holds his hand over the hanging tent. I yank his hand towards the light. His fingers are blistered, at the crook of the fingers, the middle and fourth fingers, where they grip the sled handrail. I hug him. My heart takes time to slow down.

"Aaka!"

"Sorry. We may have to pop these blisters." I squeeze them a little, he gasps through his teeth. "I'll wrap your fingers in the morning. Holding the sled will be easier."

At morning, Nasau teaches me how to use the axe.

"How will you defend yourself against white men if you can barely lift it? It's a part of you, now. No excuses. You'll run with this axe. Don't be jealous, boys. I'll make you better knives. Make belts to carry a knife, huh? Start working on making a belt. Hunters must always carry a knife."

"I don't know. Is this too dangerous for them?" I ask.

"Aaka!" they whine.

"Alright. Alright," I say.

"Boys learn at this age, Kaya."

I carry the axe, heavy and whacking between my shoulder blades at times. It is made of clear flint, tied with bearded sealskin sinew. It is lighter than other axes, I suppose, but I'm not used to carrying any weapon except a small cutting knife.

She demonstrated how to throw the axe. I practice every time we stop, hurling the axe. At first, I tossed the axe a few feet. Now I propel. I'm not as strong as I was. I want to launch this axe. I'm determined. I will.

13 | DINING IN
CAPTAIN'S QUARTERS

Besides my regular duties, I must watch the girl at all times, even when she dines with the captain and first mate in the captain's quarters. I don't know why he insists I sit with them. I think it's a meager show of authority by making my ass watch them eat.

The captain and first mate are crass and vulgar, ruffians in fine officers' clothing. But they dine as gentlemen. Each night the two eat a similar meal with slight variations: clam or oyster broth, preserved olives or cucumbers, seasoned nuts, a main course topped in marmalade, and a dessert, all the while drinking the anti-fogmatics strong enough to scorch a man's throat. After a few drinks, they're all-fired. I don't care a bean for whiskey, rum, or ale. Besides their spirits, they sometimes drink a tonic of cocaine, heroin, or hemp, a mixture for their nerves. They complain of life, their sorrows, the price of oil and kerosene, and paying taxes. Captain wants a Concord buggy. Emilio wants a Brett carriage.

I sit against the wall, away from their dining table, on a bench covered in a long, tattered cushion. His bed is barely visible, hidden behind a half wall of sorts. It is a backwards room, suffocating and cramped. He tries to father her. He tries to win her over in sweets. Tonight, he serves mackerel in a wine sauce, seasoned beans, and marbled jelly, a swirl of custard and jelly bouncing on her plate. She dents the jelly with her finger and wipes her finger against the table.

"Do not wipe your hands on the table. Use a napkin. My wife will teach you proper manners. Not these savage ways. Sit straight. Use your utensils. You'll eat with the First Families of Virginia. Fork in the left hand."

She sits, looking around the room with her big eyes.

The eskimo women, Dorothy and Susan, join the table. They sit with straight backs, napkins in one hand, hair tied back in buns which they must have seen in a magazine. They drink at the same pace as the men, no more. No doubt, they've tried drinking more than the men but were quickly punished. When Merihim or Emilio empty their cups, Dorothy or Susan rush to fill glasses.

Dorothy nurses a black eye. Every night usually ends with fighting between the officers and women.

"Too spoiled. Daughter of a rich man. I'm a hard worker. Like you. I give you little half breed girl," Dorothy says.

He makes Dorothy stay in his room most of the time. He doesn't want any other man looking at her. She cried about staying in the room all the time but then he made her stay outside all day with him while he sat in the crow's nest. She didn't complain again.

Last night, Dorothy laughed too hard, too long, too enthusiastically at a joke about captain's lovesickness. All of them were drunk. His fist flew across the table, knocking her backwards against the wall. Plates shot outwards and drinks spilled across the floorboards. She covered her nose with her hands, blood gushing everywhere.

"Jesus Christ! Quit bleeding on my floor! You spilled my drink. Do you know how expensive this is? Of course, you don't! Stupid fucking, eskimo, dumb shit!" He yelled. We didn't move. Emilio scrunched his face, disgusted at her blood gushing down her hands. Merihim punched her repeatedly, over and over. I stood up. He rushed to my face. "What you looking at, boy? Got something to say? Got anything to say to your captain? No-account coon! C'mon boy!"

"No, sir," I said.

"You going to fight me, boy?"

"No, sir. Not by a jugful."

Another night, Sten gave the evening report over their dinner table. After Sten left, the captain grabbed Dorothy's finger, pushed her finger backward. She smiled at first. She didn't know what was happening. Then, a look of pain. She cried out, trying to pry his hand away.

"Did you smile at him?" He asked. His face twisted, sneering.

She cried out and shook her head. Her eyes closed tight. She knelt on the floor, elbow on the table. He let go. She collapsed on the floor. Emilio left. I motioned for the girl to follow me, too.

Tonight, the two men laugh. They're feeling their liquor now. It is a strange energy.

"Once she sees the modern world, she'll be happy to leave this frozen wasteland. Where we live, it is warm. No need for fur clothes. We eat at a table with chairs. With utensils. There are trains to take to other cities."

"She'll learn. Anne is a good teacher, no doubt. No doubt." Emilio eats his marbled jelly with a silver spoon, legs crossed.

"Eyes will pop out of that little skull when you see the candy store. Bins filled with candy canes, buttermints, and lollipops. Enough to rot baby teeth. Where we are going, it's warm every day of the summer. No more parkas. Not like summer here in this shithole. Tell her, tell her I'm taking her to where it is warm every day."

"She said she's going home to her mother," Dorothy interprets.

"Enough of this fantasy. Did you tell her that her mother is dead? Your mom is rotting away somewhere with the rest of them. You would be rotting away with your mother's body somewhere if it wasn't for me."

"She said her mother is alive and will find her."

"Devil of a witch." He coughs on his drink. He pounds his chest to loosen up some liquor in his chest. He laughs. Emilio laughs.

"Poor child. She's an orphan. It'll take time, captain. Give her time," Emilio says.

"Your mother, your new mother is the most beautiful woman you've ever seen. She's an angel. Angelic. Tell her, woman," he says. Dorothy glares at him. He doesn't notice.

"She says the same thing," Dorothy says.

"How? As a ghost? Your mother's name is Anne."

"She said her mother's name is Kayaliruk."

"Nonsense. We saw the village ourselves. This is a photo of my wife. We'll get your photo in Pauline Cove and mail it to my wife. Every week, we eat oysters on the wharf. Steamed oysters and fat sweet butter. My wife will have a baptism for you." He shows a photo of his wife, a straight-faced angelic woman dressed in white lace.

"She wants to know why we go north?"

"Not a child's business."

"She wants to know who is the man in blue. I told her."

"The man in blue, eh? The man in blue is your new father."

"She said her mama is coming for her. She'll jump far."

"Your mama is dead." He offers the spoon to her mouth, but she covers her mouth. "The little thing will not be convinced until she's seen her dead body. It would be inhumane for the girl to see a dead body. Inhumane and unacceptable. You must accept your mother's death. Death is a part of life. You want to remain here in the wilderness as an orphan? Tell her, she is an orphan."

"I told her. She is ruined. My children listened. This one doesn't listen. Bad, bad, bad."

"Your mother's name is Anne. I've had enough of this talk from a girl knee high to a rabbit. Your new mother is the most beautiful woman in the world. She is an angel,"

"Beautiful wife." Emilio adds.

"She is like a silky butterfly. Or a dove fluttering away in the sunshine."

"A dove!" Emilio laughs.

"She is also one heartless bitch! She's got the devil's horns! I've never known a more ruthless, heartless, ungrateful woman. What am I doing, Emilio? Of all the young virgins, I picked the snotty, ruthless bitch of the litter! Why is she in here? Here?" He points at his temple and pounds his chest with a fist. "Lord sent me a demon in the form of an angelic cherub woman. A muse! I've got a ship under my command. I own a damn manor, and investments. What does it mean to her? Nothing! She wants a fucking, churchgoing, son of a bitch with lily-white hands and an inheritance. Shit, Emilio!"

"Women are the devil, sir. She's got you. She's got you good."

"Fuck her!"

"Aww, c'mon sir. It's the liquor talking now. She'll come around. Think of the child." Emilio speaks of the eskimo child.

"You. You little shit angel. You're going to have a new mother. She'll love you. What woman wouldn't love you? She'll make dresses for you in every color. In silk and fluffy fluttering taffeta or some damn shit."

"Satin. Velvet."

"Right! Velvet in every color to match our home! Women. Women and their clothes. Their fantasy minds. All fiery passions and fantasies in their heads. How can a whaler fulfill these unrealistic fantasies? I wasn't born into wealth. Not like pansy church boy! What do women see in men like him? My hands worked. Don't women want bravery? Adventure? No, no! They want silky, velvety shit-faced cowards who wouldn't know how to navigate a skiff! Her brain is, what it is? What would be the word?"

"Confused?"

"Confused! A child's fantasy confused. Grow up, girl! Strong men don't grow up in wealthy mansions riding a white horse. We come from the dirt. From the mud. From the damn gutter. And we work. We crawl like lizards from penny to penny and we hold those pennies as if they are $100 dollar bills, a treasure, proud of every cent. Then she falls in love with the church boy born with servants."

"Women do not think like a man. They don't know right from wrong."

"What would you do, Emilio? Am I wrong? Tell me, am I wrong?"

"No, sir."

"What would you do?"

"A delicate question. If I had a wife, not your wife, but a woman like her. I'd force her to see the light. She needs it. I'd make her see."

"What husband and wife are married for fifty years who were in deep passionate love? No such thing!"

"Nope."

"Marriage is built on trust! On honesty! Women! They want passion. They want Romeo and Juliet who fucking killed themselves! How is that for passion?"

"Honey! I love you!" Emilio made a motion indicating slicing of the neck. They burst out laughing again, until tears rolled from their eyes.

"Happily, ever after!"

"Oh shit!"

The eskimo women smile. Me and the girl watch in silence.

They wiped tears from their eyes, tears from laughter.

"Eat. I can't eat. Cook is trying to kill me with all this bird meat. Stomach is not right again until I've eaten red meat. Jesus! We need deer meat. Even moose meat would settle my stomach. Show the girl it's a good meal. This little one doesn't know a good meal like my wife doesn't know a good man. What is wrong with all the women around me? I'm surrounded by ungrateful females." He lit a pipe, blew a cloud upwards. "I knew a gypsy dame named Elizabeta, Polish woman, I think. She lived in a green caravan. I saw her dancing at a gypsy wedding, under a full moon. They played drums. Hundreds of little silver bells playing and an accordion. The fiddle. She arrived dressed in coins and scarves. Always wearing red flowers. What an enchanting woman. You've met a girl like that before, Emilio?" He finishes his bourbon in one drink, waits for Susan to pour another. He eats a few bites, swipes his mouth with a linen napkin. "Do you know the eskimo language, Ibai? Of course, you don't. Your first voyage anywhere besides the devil's ass of a town. The eskimo women here learn faster than you. Tell her, woman. Tell the girl her name is Elizabeta."

"She said her name is Sam."

"Sam? Elizabeta. Pretty, is it not?"

The girl says no in English.

"Bully for you, girl! She speak American? I'll be damned. You teach her to speak American, boy?" He asks me.

"A few words. A few moments ago." I shake my head.

"What words?"

"Yes. No. Whale."

"Whale," she says.

"No savage food for you. You eat American food. Civilized. Dine as a civilized citizen. Understand. Tell her." He points at the girl.

"She said she'll jump far away. Far away from the ship."

"Nonsense. You'll stop this. Get her to bed. Ibai. To bed with you!"

She stands before I stand. She knows my name. She and I have been through this routine for the last week. The girl follows me back to the forecastle. She sits on the floor. All the men from my shift are sleeping. I sit next to her and show her my book called African Kingdoms. "This is where I'm from. She was a great queen in 500 BC, one of the richest kingdoms and eras of human history. You see? She lived in a pyramid and her people lived in peace. She owned many animals. This is an elephant. I saw two in a circus. They came by train."

She looks through every page until finally going to bed.

14 | ANCIENT MONOLITH

EBRULIK LEADS THE DOG SLEDS NOW. A few weeks ago, they were skeletons. I saw their ribcages, collarbones, their bulging knees. Now they smile at me. I see them gliding, running the sled, strong as men. They turn, wave, and smile. I wave back.

I haven't healed as fast as them. My body still droops, fades, and drains as the day goes by, as if I drag the dog teams down with my weight. The fatigue dissipates, at times, when I've eaten, sleep, and recovered. I'm no longer chilled at every gust of wind. Nasau is not the best cook, but she feeds us well. We wake up, work hard, run, and run more. Thirty miles in a day.

Nasau teaches my boys how to take care of a dog team, which my husband did, but good hunters continue learning. Their questions are never-ending. The boys want to start their own dog team and I'm happy for the distraction. They need hope, something to look forward to. She knows a lot about dogs.

"A dog's heart is big, bigger than a wolf. A dog's lungs are bigger, too. If you think they're getting exhausted, believe me, they can run farther than you and me combined. Your dog team is an extension of yourself. Listen to the dogs. Talk to them. Know all their names. You must know them all. Never hit or whip dogs.

Dogs keep us alive. Dogs will turn their faces towards you if they are in pain, or uncomfortable. Pay attention. Sometimes it's their harness and not fatigue. Dogs eat twice as much when running. Equip your sled with dog food. Cut their nails, check their pads. Check underneath their harnesses every afternoon and evening. They chafe underneath their legs. Look at their form when they are pulling. Curled tail means the dog isn't pulling his weight. A hunter must be the alpha dog of the team. There'll be a day when you're running after your own dog team because they got spooked or you fell off the foot runner."

"I pick dogs that are kind and gentle. A small, gentle dog is the best sled dog. Once, I thought this male dog could be my leader. He pulled weight. He tolerated puppies. Listened to my commands, but he bullied when he couldn't get his way. Leaders must be tolerant. It takes time to pick out a leader. You can't tell when they are puppies. It takes years to get your lead dog trained. I've seen lead dogs traded for ivory, furs, flint. Lead dogs are hard to find."

"Get a puppy. Raise her in the harness. Walk her every day with a leash. Teach her to stay, and learn the word no. By the time she's a year old, you'll know where to put her in the gang line."

"Dogs know what will happen before you. Once, I couldn't get the dogs to stop. It was winter and getting late. They ran me up a steep riverbank. The sled flipped over. A pack of caribou weakened the river ice. Dogs must have heard the ice breaking because they drove me up onto land. Dogs know what will happen before we do."

"Tie down your dog food really well. I got scared, really scared once. I ran far inland and dropped my dog food along the trail. We went to bed hungry. I waited a week in that spot until I found a small frozen creek. I fished enough smelts to get home. Another time, a pup bit open a tarp of dog food. I left a trail of dog food. I circled back and picked up what I could. Learn from my mistakes."

Nasau and the boys caught a caribou this morning. A small group of caribou ate lichen up on hills. Ebrulik shot the caribou through the neck. We butcher, cure, cook, and eat. In better times, I'd boil the bones for broth, but we've got no time. So, we strip as much as possible from the bones and throw bones to the dogs. We stop for half a day. I'm frustrated at the time but its needed.

Nasau shares a long-hidden secret with the boys: where to find an ore of clear flint. Her ore is a clear vein, hidden in hills lining from east to west. The flint can be chipped into arrowheads, spearheads, knives, and can be bartered. We look down at the clear vein hidden in a fissure, some parts clear as water, some parts cloudy and translucent. The flint is sharp.

"Can you remember this place?" Nasau asks the boys. They nod. "When you have children, when you get married, get flint from this ore, but not more than you need. We'll get some now. I like black obsidian, but clear flint is my favorite. Gives weapons a certain beauty, doesn't it? I'll show you how to make spearheads, and arrows. This is the best way to learn. When you make your own arrows, you begin to value each arrow, each spearhead. We'll make narrow arrowheads for birds. Wide arrows for caribou and moose. You two boys will also learn an old art. An ancient art not practiced for at least a generation. Not since I was young. You'll learn how to make arrows to kill men. Do you understand?" She studies their faces. Did they understand the seriousness of the moment?

"Yes," they say.

She leaves dry seal meat as an offering to our Creator and our Ancestors. The boys cut pieces of their hair and lay them upon the ground. "You boys have the sweetest hearts. You see the mountains?"

"Yes."

"Shall we try and reach them today?"

"Yes! How much farther until we reach the sea?" Nauraq asks.

"Another mountain. A mountain pass after that."

"Alright."

"We are good. We are doing good. We'll make the river."

Sunlight frays the sheet of snow over the lands. Underneath the snows, willow, alder, burdock, stinkweed tea, cloudberries, tundra moss, Labrador tea and all the foliage wakens, feeling the warmth of the sun, now in a crusade to overcome the snow. A fresh, nervy green aroma is in the air. I see signs of spring: curls of bright-green leaves, a strong fresh rosebud, sprouts rising from the snow, and stalks of tea fighting to stand upright. For once, I pray for cold fresh snows. We need hard traveling snow.

We make our way around great marshlands, cushioned with peat moss, mushroom moss, wool moss, and garnet moss. The marsh ponds are filled with thick cranberry-colored roots, water plants, matted weeds, decaying grasses, all weaved together in meadow blankets, quaking with each step, and laden in plankton-filled water. While we travel near the marshes, I pick willow, marsh cinquefoil, and iris. Not in great quantity, but enough to last the next few weeks.

Flocks of birds burst across the sky, geese, ducks, cranes, swans, cygnets, herons, sandpipers, redpoll, and thrush, soaring, diving, swarming, darting, hopping, and dancing their mating dances. We hear the flocks from hills away. Foxes and bears wait at the marsh outskirts, filling themselves with birds. We pick eggs in the morning, eating them raw, or boiling for our travels.

"Where do they go in the south?" The boys ask.

"The birds? To warm lakes in the south, across the sea. Farther than I've ever been," she says.

Ground squirrels poke their heads from their burrows. When we stop to eat, the boys follow the hawks and ravens hunting squirrels, and then use their slings to catch ground squirrels. Or set little snares.

We hear wolves howling at night. This is wolf and bear country. We see the lean wolves wandering up on the hills, looking down, and watching our camp. We know stories of wolf attacks. Even the boys know the stories. We don't speak of the accounts, not in the country. Speaking of tragedy attracts tragedy. It's a mixture of fear, taboo, superstition, and respect for the animals. Our guns and the dogs keep us safe from intruders. We keep the fire going into the night, as a precaution.

After visiting the ore of flint, they've practiced making spear-heads. She shows them how to make a pronged spearhead for hunting birds, curved and pronged like an eagle talon clutching for its prey. They're building their hunting bags with chert, lures, and arrowheads.

Today, we reach a legendary mountain, an ancient monolith surrounded by lowlands. People hunt sheep on this mountain and look for caribou. They climb up, looking in all directions, searching for migrating caribou.

"It's like a herd of sheep," Nauraq says. We look up together.

Rams, sheep, and ewes eat grass and lichen on the jagged peaks. I climbed the south side of this mountain. Not high enough to see the sheep but high enough to find tufts and cobwebs of their wool strands. My husband carried a ram across his shoulders, kicking up dirt and gravel as he descended a sheep trail. He climbed too high, ran down too fast, how my heart leapt with every step. I scolded you, husband. That was too fast going down.

We'll sleep at the foot of the mountain. We set up our camp.

"Ebrulik's in love," Nauraq says.

I look to Ebrulik. He looks away. He hurries with the tent.

"Are you? Who is she, son?" I hug him to my side. I kiss his forehead. "I want you to marry her. After we get your sister, we'll find her. All of us."

"Really?"

"Yes."

"She is from Qikiqtaġruk. I saw her at the festival. She is pretty."

"I'll love her as my own daughter. We'll find her and ask her parents."

"How long before we can marry?"

I count the number of years. Is it time already? It is time. Husband, I wanted you to be here. "Ten years."

"Ten years is forever."

"It'll be your wedding day before you know it. You must learn to hunt. You must learn how to build your own house. So, you can provide a good life, huh?"

"She'll wear the wolf ruff, and wolverine. We'll see her soon?"

"Yes. We'll try to find her soon. You must be respectful to her parents. Be polite and generous. They'll watch to see how you'll treat their daughter."

"Before winter?"

Before winter? I can't think. Time moves slow, time moves fast. How long has she been gone? How long have we traveled? I don't know. Can we find Samaruna and travel south before winter? "Yes. I think we can. We'll try."

Nauraq pokes my shoulder. "Aaka. Can we go up the mountain?" Nauraq interrupts.

"Tonight? It's getting dark already."

"Oh please? We won't go far."

"Alright. Help us feed the dogs first. Don't go too far. Stay where I can see you."

The fire is going high, the dogs are fed, and the boys want to go up. They need to save their strength, but boys are curious.

We watch them climb up a hill of silt fanned out against the tundra floor, ankle-deep in sediment and silt, pushing a small cloud of dust behind them. They smile and wave.

"It's nice to see them happy," she says.

Nasau throws more wood on the fire. We set up the tent and eat caribou meat. She lights her pipe and blows out skinny clouds of smoke.

I'm not a friendly woman who makes friends right away. My mother knew how to talk to people. My husband, too. I don't know how to be close to people.

I know little of Nasau, the woman helping my family. She had a husband once. He lived in the interior. She likes to stay in the same routine. Wake early in the morning, drink coffee, smoke her pipe, check the dogs, checks her rifle, and sharpen her knives. She works from early morning until night, drinking coffee all day long.

I sense a great sadness in the woman. I sense guilt and remorse. I sense these things within people. I believe she'll die with secrets. I don't have the heart to ask her. She also doesn't trust people. She arms herself at every encampment. If she worries about a place, camp, or unknown turn, she keeps her rifle within reach, hidden underneath a tarp.

She doesn't tire of my stories. The boys remember my stories, the polar bear and his wife, the wide-mouth baby, the Caribou Man, the mouse wandering from his field, the worm which traveled months on a porcupine, among many others. She listens to them all. She doesn't interrupt.

One night as the boys snared squirrels, she told me of a place called hell, a place she learned from the religious white men. Fires, sulfur lakes, demons, and eternal suffering. She fears this place. She held the cross around her neck for some time.

I thank her. "I want to thank you for helping us, for helping my daughter, my family. Where were you before this? Before the sickness?"

"I was up north. I was in Kali for a while. I went home. What used to be my home. Where my parents are from." She has long tattoos on her arms, long motifs curling on her forearms. She saw me looking at them. "A Siberian woman gave me these tattoos."

I'm rocking and she notices, I notice. I stop rocking. I'm a mess. She doesn't know what to say. I'm the same way. I don't know what to say when people are hurting. My Aaka did. She was good at comforting.

"I talk to my husband. In my mind." I admit.

She nods, smokes her pipe. "I talked to my husband, too. I left our home. The home we built. I took nothing. Hooked up the dogs and left. I didn't go back for a number of years. I was determined to kill myself because I thought I was going mad. Better to end it now, I thought, but I had my dogs. I had my health. One day, I ran into an old couple. They had no food in their caches. I hunted for them for a season until their cache was full. I found a purpose. It'll be the same for you, I'm certain. You'll get your daughter. Then your sons will need wives."

"I've not mourned him. He wouldn't have let this happen." I'm crying again. I'm weeping. It seems so far away. I've not mourned my husband. He died only a few months ago and I've not mourned him. I can't breathe. What is Samaruna doing now? What is the captain doing with my baby now? Is she locked up in the ship, in the belly of the beast, locked in a room with no food or water? Is she locked up with a man in the ship? Do they soil my little child with their evil? A mother could drive herself mad with these thoughts. I'm dying. I can't breathe.

"You think it's a mistake? That he is dead? And you're alive?"

"At times."

"Your boys said you did everything you could. What if it was your husband and not you? They probably would have killed him. Without thinking. Then what? Your children would be orphans."

"My husband is gone, and I don't know if I'll ever feel whole again. I'm with my children and why do I feel so alone? Can't a woman live with her children and feel whole?"

"I've taken care of myself all these years. You will, too."

I'm calming down. I wipe my eyes. I wipe my nose. "We haven't seen any people."

"It's hard times now, but they are out there. In the country. Your sons say you're a storyteller."

"I was."

"But you're not anymore?"

"I see places. A creek or river, a cliff, and stories come. Nothing comes to me anymore."

"What of this mountain?"

"I see my husband." It is hard to look up, my eyes sting and burn. I see him carrying the sheep down the mountain. He was a strong man, but gentle-spirited like Nauraq. I pull off my kamiks. "I'm going to kill him. This captain. I will kill him."

"I understand."

"He might take more children. I must."

"I'd do the same."

"It's the right thing, isn't it?"

"Do not accept the Yankee abuses. Do not accept the way we've been treated."

"How? How do I get him? What am I supposed to do? Attack the ship at night?"

"Yes. They've lost five men."

"What about this other captain? He, Hea, Healy?" I don't know how to pronounce Healy.

"What if we can't find Healy? You heard the reverend. Three hundred ships this year. We'll find this ship. Your sons are almost here. Let's agree we'll kill this captain."

"How? How?"

"Remember this. You've killed three men. Three. You're strong enough to see this through. You're not done yet. Understand? Here's the boys."

"Aaka! Aaka! We saw their tracks. They've got their babies now. Signs of sheep everywhere!" They found a sheep horn. Nauraq hands it to me.

"This will be a good cup. Let's pour water in it, see if they're any holes."

Ebrulik sits, smiling, out of breath. "Lots of sheep."

"You want to come back next year?" I ask.

"Yeah, it was fun."

I wash the horn, pouring in water. "Your father got a ram. Way up on the top. Ebrulik was a baby. Long ago, a woman couldn't bear any children. Her husband left her because she didn't give him any children. She trekked here in the middle of winter. She climbed the mountain and prayed for children. When she reached the bottom, she was meet by a group of hunters where she met her new husband. She gave him many children. Women still travel here to pray for children. Your father hunted for sheep, I made a fire and prayed for another child. I got two more, Nauraq and Samaruna. Your aaka said this mountain is medicine. Look, Nauraq. It doesn't leak. Put it away. We'll work on it tomorrow."

15 | THE STONE PEOPLES

MY HUSBAND, MY LOVE, WE'RE FARTHER than I've ever been. We've reached the stone homes. There are three stone homes, built in a col, a low pass between two summits. The stone homes don't have roofs, just four walls. The floors grow high with moss and dirt, higher in the corners. Sod and moss fill the cracks in the rock walls, spotted with muted lichen.

"Have you been here before?" Ebrulik asks Nasau.

"Not for many years. Some say these are Koyukon homes. Or Gwich'in. Others say it is our Ancestors. The Stone people. Go through the mountain pass, south, and you'll find the Koyukons. We live on the north of the mountains. They live on the south. Far into the east are the Gwich'in. We see them hunting sheep sometimes. Up on the mountains."

"You've talked to them?"

"Yes. We invite them to our Messenger Feasts."

"I didn't see any Koyukons at the feasts."

"They'll be there. They go to muskrat camps in the spring. They're probably there now, in the south, hunting muskrats together. I hunted caribou with the Koyukon. They rub fat on the nose of the caribou. Like we give animals water at death. They rub fat on the nose. We'll stay here tonight. Feed the dogs."

Before bed, after we've fed the dogs and built a fire, they search the dirt floors for treasures.

Every night, the boys ask Nasau about her life. This is their nightly ritual. Her late husband is from these mountains. He lived near the tree line, where the caribou eat.

At the beginning of our travels, I couldn't listen. I was too exhausted. I lie, paralyzed in sleep, stuck in that place between awake and asleep, a terrorizing and paralyzing darkness surrounded by piercing high-pitch tones interlaced with whispers. Now I'm strong enough to listen.

"Do you know this place?" They ask.

"I've seen this place before, but I've not camped here before," she says.

"What do they say about this place?"

"I asked my husband about these houses. He was from this area, and he didn't know. Maybe no one knows. We visit this place to think of our Ancestors, about their lives, where they hunted, what they hunted. We'll never know their names or the names of their loved ones,"

"Aaka knows," Nauraq says.

"Do you? Do you know who built these houses?" Nasau asks me.

I see the people arriving, building, birthing, dying, and finally leaving, in flashes, in still memories, like watching a mushroom grow from birth to death, compressed into one breath. "It was summer all year long. This whole valley was green with ferns, bright as the aurora. A thick layer of moss grew everywhere, on every tree branch, on every rock. Every step, you walked on green moss, green as a budding leaf. Lots of trees, lots of large greying trees with rippling bark. A clear river ran this way. The sky rained for days and days on end. Even on sunny days, a mist stayed in the air, like floating rain.

"There was a lake, not far from here, in the next saddle, the little valley over this hill. The water was so clear and calm, when you rowed over the water it felt like flying.

"The people chewed this root. The root of a sapling. Something medicinal. They lived long lives, over a hundred years old, because of this sapling root. They wore shells around their neck, metallic shells, like fish scales all around the shell. This shrew lived in the forest, big as a hare."

"Like a mouse? Big as a hare?" Nasau asks.

"A shrew with upright ears." I show them with cupped hands, ears on top of my head. The boys laugh. "They feared a large carrion bird, so large it didn't fly, it ran across the land."

"Ran?" Nasau asks.

"It ran. The men kept their spears together, on each side of the valley, looking out for the large bird and saber tooth. They built these houses to protect against the giant bird and saber tooth.

"But the cold started. The trees withered away. The forest died and they couldn't find their sapling roots or fruits or plants. They couldn't live here. They died, slowly, over a few generations because they didn't like the cold. They didn't know how to survive. Stronger men and women migrated here. Like me and you. They loved the winter, the cold lands."

"The people came with the mammoth. This entire valley, this slope, I see alive with lights, light from their hearths. On the ridge, they bury their dead, up on the stilts like we do. A reminder to honor their Ancestors.

They were like whalers. They hunted in their own crews, with their own captains. This is how we learned to divide the whale between the hunting crews. We learned from our Ancestors who hunted the mammoth."

"Every year, they hold a festival for the mammoth. They dance a strange dance. They gamble and trade. They lived generations and generations in this place, until the mammoth died away. A man stood on the ridge, up there, looking down at everyone. They didn't get any mammoth that year. He spoke to them, his voice echoing and echoing. He speaks of finding another paradise. He told his people it was time to leave the valley, leave the lands. They'd go north to the sea, to hunt seals, where they'd learn how to hunt the bowhead and beluga. He tells them to be brave and think of their children. He says to pack all they have and go to the sea. It's a caravan of people, even the Elders, and they leave the valley forever." I end the story and they are quiet for a moment.

"Beautiful. You have a gift, Kaya. A true gift. Where do you get these stories?"

"I don't know. They come," I say.

"Aaka is the best storyteller ever," Ebrulik says. "They ask for Aaka to tell stories at the feasts. Have you been to a lot of feasts?"

"I used to go. When I was young. I met legendary runners. Atnaqchiaq. Kinavaq. Kakianaaq. This man from Kali, I forgot his name now. I've never seen men and women run so fast. They are all muscle. Not a pinch of fat on their bodies. I didn't run but I competed in the umiaq races with a Kali team. It is fun. Some people don't know how to row in a boat, but they compete anyway. It is all laughs."

"Were there a lot of people?"

"In Utqiaġvik, there were more tents than the eye could see. The beaches lined with umiaqs. A gathering like you've never seen. We danced and sang, and the earth moved. I bought a bracelet from the Inuit. Dried seaweed from Siberia. People planned marriages and trips. There were no Yankee whalers, riverboats, or Hell. I saw a shaman at Utqiaġvik. We gathered in a dark tent. He sang. He danced. People say he knows the tongues of animals by carrying tongues in a bag around his neck. They say if a dying animal lands in your trail, it's offering its tongue to you. Cut it out. Let it dry. Carry the tongue and you'll know the animal's language. That's what happened to him. Dying animals landed at his feet and he received their tongues. At the feast, I saw him dance. Blood came from his mouth. His eyes went back. He spoke of my past. I don't know if I imagined what happened or fell asleep. I don't know how he could have known the things he knew. Raspberry baby. It was a joke between me and my husband. I've got a birthmark that looks like a raspberry. The shaman whispered raspberry baby, raspberry baby, and other words I couldn't understand. Maybe I fell asleep. I dreamt the shaman and I walked through a storm together. The wind was so strong we had to walk backwards. He looked at me, as we walked backwards against the wind. I saw his face, clear as I see you now. I thought, I must be asleep. I must have fallen asleep. I heard our footsteps in the snow and the wind howling. When he said raspberry baby, it was like his voice was near my ear, but he was walking. What does this mean? Walking in a storm with a shaman by my side? I think about this dream of his."

"Will they have it again? The feasts? The shaman dance?"

She didn't answer. She wonders how many people are alive. The boys knew what she was thinking and ask, "How many of our people are alive?"

"I don't know, but we're alive. We've got the vaccine in our bodies. Trust there are others, too. Time to sleep, time to dream of our Ancestors. Pray the Ancestors tell their stories in our dreams."

16 | US Revenue Cutter Lacina

IN EARLY MORNING, THE CAPTAIN SPOTS the US Revenue Cutter *Lacina*. As soon as the *Lacina* is spotted, Emilio races below deck, towing the girl, keys jingling. The *Lacina* inspects another ship, the bark *Leon Kay*.

"Ibai. At the helm. Slow down to 2 knots. Cut the engine. Slow us down. Don't make it obvious." The captain says. He dreads an inspection. Every turn in the sea, he speaks of avoiding the authorities.

A skiff flags our ship.

"Damn, my luck! First the seals, now this! Fucken shit bastards. Call for anchor! You're not to leave my side, boy. I heard this captain might be a nigger. Can you believe that! The US put Alaska territory in the hands of a nigger. Remigio, get Gerald."

A few men in matching dull blue uniforms row over in the skiff. A man yells up. "Inspections, sir. Have papers ready. Captain'll board." The skiff rows away back to the cutter.

Gerald and I stood at the helm while the captain retreats to his cabin for a fresh shirt.

The cutter is a frigate, narrow and sheathed in iron, one of the legendary naval ships. Their deck is bright and varnished, their canvas new and unpatched, dauby painted upon the cables. The *Lacina* is a vision, representing everything Merihim wanted. The frigate sailed in the Civil War, carrying Yankee men from New Hampshire down to the Carolinas.

"The girl didn't want to sit with Dorothy. Emilio said he'd break every one of her little fingers," Gerald says.

"The shit he didn't?"

"That's what he said."

"Said she'd spend the rest of her life with mangled hands."

I'm so angry, I can't respond. The captain would have his back for it, or would he? Emilio and the captain are like brothers.

Dorothy and Susan know what to do for an inspection. They'll busy themselves with sewing while Dorothy pretends to be the girl's mother. For a lay person, this is a good plan. But what if Healy knows the eskimo language? He does enough work in the villages to know the language.

The captain hides any contraband deep in the tween decks, behind stacks of plywood used to make casks.

"Gerald. Don't say anything to the officers. Yes, sir. No, sir. That's it," I tell him. He nods.

I saw the *Lacina* in New Bedford, two years ago. Healy had just begun mastering the ship. To receive the *Lacina* cutter, New Bedford planned a Grand Regatta lasting three days. The city, yacht club, oil companies, and whaling companies united to sponsor a parade, grand reception, whaling boat races, ball, and a picnic after Sabbath services. I watched papa walk with the veterans in the parade at Union and Purchase Streets, standing in the thick of the parade crowds. I waved my hat and cheered for him. New Bedford denizens are proud Americans and proud whalers.

For a week, I worked for the Elder Captain Stuart Frestrain and his wife, who entertained relatives and visitors from Connecticut, Delaware, and Rhode Island. My father crafted harpoons and nets for the Elder captain. They worked together for decades.

I spent most of the week securing fresh foods: oysters, crab, lobster, clams, shrimp, freshwater fish, seawater fish, root vegetables, and fruit. I had to travel to an outlying farm for the strawberries and apples since the markets ran out of fruit. Mrs. Frestrain frenzied over the shortage of fruit and resorted to purchasing fruit preserves for garnishing dishes.

If I wasn't getting foods, I was ferrying the visitors to all the events. They traveled by Concord to all the events, making a show of their arrival. The Frestrains are a prominent family.

The grown son of Elder Frestrain won the whaling boat races, a race he dedicated to his father. The Elder smiled, shook his son's hand, and they received the first-place ribbon together on the docks. It was a triumphant moment for the old man.

Societies are a foreign place, alien, surreal. I drove the old captain and his guests to galas at the New Bedford Whaling Society balls, banquets, and picnics. Every place donned columns of roses, peonies, daffodils, and tulips, towers of special dark chocolate truffles, clinking white china, and silver utensils. I'd return home with a plate of food for the old man, to our rickety shack on the beach, lit by a gas lamp, a little blue flame burning until I return home. I'd tell him of the events.

Merihim emerges, freshly shaven and combed hair. Merihim, Emilio, Gerald and I wait at the helm for over an hour.

"America is going to hell, and they send us a darkie to police whalers," Emilio tsks.

"Check the log. Sign every page," Merihim says. He hands the logbook to Emilio.

"All this wasted time. I'm not made of coal. People treat him like the damn pope! Why yes, sir. I'll get that paperwork ready. Over-glorified police officer who knows how to string up rigging? He's a cabin boy with a badge. He is a darkie. I've heard it over and over. We heard it. They say his mother was a slave! Can you believe it? A slave."

Healy departs the *Leon Kay*, shaking hands with the crew. He makes his way down to the skiff. *Leon Kay* starts their engine, blowing up smoke.

"Jesus, Hell, and Christ. It's about time."

Healy rows over, a proud Johnathan wearing blue and bronze, triumphant, smiling. Merihim snickers.

I stand on deck with the other whalers, ready to greet Healy. A few years ago, at Point Barrow, three vessels shipwrecked in the waters, and he rescued 160 men from drowning in arctic seas. He is admired, respected, feared, and known by all. Our crew whispers about Point Barrow as he makes his way up.

He boards with three men dressed in kamiks and wool, their chests decorated with emblems of accomplishments.

"Fine day, sir! Fine day," Healy says. Healy shakes Merihim's hand, Emilio's, then a few whalers. Healy's men follow his footsteps. None of Healy's men smile.

"Healy. I'm Merihim. My first mate Emilio. A fine day for whaling. Welcome," Merihim says.

Healy's officer steps forward. "Captain. We must conduct an official inspection and search of your vessel and verify said vessel abides tariff laws set by the United States government. Any contraband, alcohol, unlicensed firearms will be confiscated. Any unpaid servicemen, indigenous natives will be freed. You've read the current regulations?" This is a practiced speech, which he says with a grin. Healy eyes everyone.

"Of course. Yes, sir." Merihim follows.

Merihim hands his paperwork to Healy. Healy walks, looking around the deck. He reads through the *Erysichthon* correspondence.

"From New Bedford? San Francisco? The company is moving their port?"

"They are."

"Any passengers aboard?" Healy asks.

"Seamen only. Exclusively a whaling ship."

"I must review the logbook. A matter of protocol."

"Yes, yes."

"Your vessel has stayed well. No repairs. No renovations?"

"Good ol' fashioned English oak."

"Oak? I'd guess its pine. Australian pine, is it not?"

"Oak. I'd bet my best brandy."

"Another day perhaps. Duty calls. We don't want to delay your day any longer than we must. My men here will inspect the cargo, supplies, steerage, what have you."

"Please. I'll have Emilio take you aboard."

"No need. They know their way around a ship. Yes, let's begin. Paperwork. You and I will review the paperwork while they conduct the inspection."

"Please sit then. Fresh coffee?" The two captains stand by the helm. Chairs are brought up on deck. They sit. I stand with Gerald.

I listen for the hurried footsteps of his men going up on deck, but they walk around in steady footsteps. Emilio stands on the cabin stairs, one foot on the stairs, one foot on deck. He listens for any commotion within the ship.

"Thank you kindly. As I was saying, any passengers?"

"No passengers."

"Any mail? Postage?"

"We did carry postage near Unalaska, but it was safely delivered to its vessel."

"Are these your orders? Registered in New Bedford?"

"Of course. Proud to be from New Bedford. Finest whaling town in the world. We've heard about the *Ophelia*. A tragedy."

"It was lost with all hands aboard. The wreckage confirmed."

"And the *Winnie*, in Unalaska! $60,000 worth of oil and bone, sunken in the deep blue. Devastating year for whaling. Whalers need better maps in the area. What is the Revenue Service doing for better maps? It'll save lives, sir!"

"Better maps, it is true. But Winnie was caught in a lee shore. We are piecing the information together with the ship's log, and the survivors. A few of the survivors are headed south for surgery. Frostbite. Probably lose some limbs."

"God rest the dearly departed. I hope the remaining whaling season is peaceful for the Revenue."

"Most of the deaths in the arctic are due to crime, poachers, rum-runners, illegal trading with the natives. Already we've confiscated more ships than last year. Not two months into the season. Two ships are headed for auction. We've spotted Russian poachers in the Priboloffs. We stationed a few men on the islands to protect the dying seal populations, and the walrusing! The amount of visibility of walrusing and still, ships continue to walrus. Exflunticating the walrus is exfluncticating the eskimos. There's degradation on the frontier. Fortunately, the church answered the call to send more missionaries. It is an uphill battle, but we are making progress."

"Progress?"

"Yes. Piracy has no business in today's world when there are honest men trying to make a living. We confiscated a booze boat from California. Little tugboat, a little more than a sloop. Some men are desperate for money."

"You don't say? Mexicans should find an honest living. Dangerous and unholy men, is my thought."

"They were Americans all."

"Americans! Well, I'll be damned."

"All the barrels of liquor we dumped into the water. Liquor has no business in the wild frontier."

"Of course, it is a sin to Moses. I must report, sir, quite urgently, belatedly, we were attacked by the eskimos. I lost five men in one day.

"You've suffered casualties? Five? God rest their souls." He turns the pages of the logbook, back and forth through two pages.

"I feel the same sir. God rest their poor souls. You'll see in my logbook, the coordinates. T'was not far south from our current location. I want to launch a full report. A full investigation into this incident. The natives attacked in full daylight. It was a massacre. I thought of writing the newspapers. Other ships must be warned of this danger."

"Of course, I must file a report. I see the date. Coordinates. What time of day?"

"Will this take a significant amount of time? Can we not fill the paperwork upon our return? I'd prefer getting north before night."

"It is crucial to file reports as they occur. While your memory is fresh. Paperwork is part of our duty. If you'd like to protect your fellow whalers from danger, as you've stated, it is best we complete a full description of the event. I'll require basic information, date, time, description of assailants. I found the date here in your log. What time?"

"Let's see. It was in the late afternoon. Ibai! What time would you say the eskimos attacked? Afternoon?"

"Yes, sir. Afternoon, before dinner, sir. About 5:00, I'd say. Sir." I stand. I look to the horizon.

"Yes. Sounds about right. 5:00 in the pm. Ibai. Retrieve my map. We were on the ice."

"On the ice, you say? What was the purpose of landing?"

"Searching for fresh water. Fresh water. You'll see at the top right corner. Fresh water. We ran low, far too low in the previous days. Suffered a few banian days ourselves."

"Far deficient in water supply."

"We planned on resupplying more fresh water from Port Clarence but saw an opportunity to move north, which I didn't want to miss."

"Was there a disagreement on the ice? An altercation?"

"No sir, none at all. My men were attacked from afar, like wild deer. Shot by rifles. No speaking at all. The shots came out of nowhere. You can read it in my log."

"I'm reading. It is our policy to conduct the proper interviews and examine the bodies, if appropriate. Did you collect the bodies? A formality."

"Gladly, however, the deceased gave permission to be buried at sea. We have their contracts, if you need to examine."

"It is our standard procedure. I'll interview the witnesses."

"Emilio, can you?" He asks Emilio. Emilio leaves for the contracts and witnesses.

"How many natives did you count?"

"We didn't get an accurate count, per se. They shot from afar, as I said."

"You are positive they were natives?"

"Yes, sir! I've got witnesses. Emilio was on deck. I was in the crow's nest, looking for them fishes. Is there a problem? It was eskimos."

"I understand the emotion. It is a hard to overcome losing men on a ship."

"I'd like a full investigation! Can you not examine the area?"

"Given the incident occurred on the ice, I'd be unable to examine the location, but I'll file a report, post haste."

"A report! Whalers' lives are in danger, sir! It was a massacre! We got no warning."

"Our resources are limited. It isn't the Cutter Service alone whose been affected by lack of funding. All of America is short funded. You want to file a report? Your company may require a report."

"My company requires a report. I'm disappointed more cannot be employed. Sir."

"How many assailants?"

"I can't say. They were yards away. A hundred yards away. A few of our men got a glimpse of the assailants."

"How many eskimos?"

"How many? We don't know how many because they shot from a distance like cowards."

"If you were to make a guess?"

"I'd say half a dozen. Eight. Yes, not more than eight. They couldn't have moved that many men so fast after cleaving down two of my men."

"Cleave? I thought they were shot. Were they shot, then stabbed? Help me understand."

"Shot. Yes. Yes. Two of them were shot and two were cleaved. Bled like hogs."

"Did any of your men fire weapons?"

"We did. But the assailants got far out of range to return fire."

"How can I search for the assailants without a description? Young? Old? Tattoos?"

"They shot from a distance. They're savages. I'm glad the missionaries are doing their work."

Healy scratches his pen. He's quiet, another minute goes by.

"How will you proceed?" Merihim asks.

"Without an accurate description, the best I can offer is a report. The report will be filed to my superiors. I'll alert other agencies. I'll inquire with other whaling companies if they've experienced similar incidents."

"No presence? I ask no odds. None at all, except to conduct a proper investigation. Can you not send for more ships? Losing my men is a great loss. Finding replacements is a challenge. We've lost capital."

"I'll send the report. Posthaste. I'd also recommend diplomacy in dealing with the natives. We are in their indigenous lands, let's not forget."

"Diplomacy. That's what I've been telling young Ibai, isn't it? Working on our relationship with the indigenous culture, aren't we? They're living in the dark ages as far as I'm concerned. Inferior culture. They are animals. No art or culture."

"To the contrary, they do possess art and culture."

"Culture? What culture? They do not have operas or symphonies."

"You and I possess a different definition of culture. If you are dissatisfied with my proposed actions, I encourage you to write to the Cutter Service."

"I intend to."

"I look forward to furthering this conversation."

"What do you think of amalgamation in the Cutter Service? Mixing whites and blacks on the service? I opine the mixing of whites with blacks is stepping backwards from Cutter progress. I've heard officers of a certain lineage getting up in the ranks of the Revenue service."

"The Revenue fought for the North. The winning side, I may add. It must have come as quite a blow when the south ceded. Persons of color are welcome in the service, as we've seen in the War. Men of all colors contribute under the American flag. You must be a historian with this much knowledge of the revenue service."

"Not at all. No."

"I'd like to continue this discussion greatly, if I had the leisure. I'm a meager man of the service, with my duties. Your papers, sir. I'll get to my paperwork so you can be on your way."

Merihim sits back. Healy opens a leather-bound notebook. Healy writes another ten minutes, another fifteen minutes. Merihim says nothing.

I'm reveling in this moment. I keep a straight face but I'm reveling. How intimidated the captain is. We wait, the good part of a half an hour while Healy and his men search the ship and interview the witnesses. His men asked questions, searched rooms, and filled his instructions.

Healy finally spoke to the captain again.

"Any sick on board?" Healy asks.

"No, none sick. Are there illnesses in the territory?"

"Smallpox. An outbreak of smallpox. All your men have their papers?"

"Yes, sir. Every single one."

"I'll need to inspect the cargo."

"Your men don't conduct the inspection?"

"Not of the cargo. I prefer inspecting with my own eyes. A formality."

"I'll bring you about, sir." Merihim stands.

"No need. Young man?" Healy addresses me.

"Yes, sir."

"Please lead the way."

I catch a glimpse of Merihim. He glares. If the contraband is discovered, if the girl is discovered as a captive, captain will make sure I'm imprisoned. He'll blame this on me.

I lead Healy down below. His men search every room. They look through the galley while Anthony frowns. Most of our crew sits in the forecastle, watching the men inspect the room and bunks. I light a lamp and lead him to cargo. He walks with sharp, crisp steps.

"Young man, what is your name?"

"Ibai, sir."

"Ibai. Interesting. What kind of name is Ibai? African? Israeli?"

"Basque."

"You don't say! Destined to be a whaler! I don't think I've ever met a person with a Basque name before."

"My parents worked for the industry my entire life." The Basque whalers are extinct. The Basque pioneered whaling in 700 A.D. or some ancient time, I don't know exactly.

"How is your season, young man?"

"It is my first year, sir. I've got no other seasons for comparison."

"It is a fine trade. Like Douglass said, a man must have pragmatic skills. Congratulations on your new career."

"Thank you, sir."

"How do you like your vocation?"

"There is much to learn. I love the ocean. I hope to see more of Alaska, sir."

"I felt the same way when I started."

"Thank you, sir."

"Did you see the incident with the natives?"

"I was on deck."

"Did you see the wounds?"

"Yes. Two gunshots and two stabbings."

"Ibai. Let's acknowledge the corn. Was it eskimos?"

"I saw eskimos, sir. From afar." It was true. I saw parkas running. I know nothing more.

"What did you see?"

"I saw men in parkas, running, and our men dying on the ice."

"Very well. Very well. I'll submit the report. Take me to the hold. Lead the way, Ibai."

I lit a lantern and led him down. I take him down the main stairs, down the steep, dark stairway. I hear his men talking in the forecastle.

We walk to the rear of the ship, passed the tween decks. I hold my breath. He didn't say anything about the tween decks. My heart is jumping in my chest. I've already accrued a debt to the company. Will I end up in prison? Sent to Seattle or San Francisco? It can't be as bad as serving on this ship. Who knows how long I'll be in prison? What kind of work can I get once released from jail? All these months lost? I'll have to start again.

The hold is dark. I hear the creaking of the ship and dripping of water somewhere. The hold is empty, save for the 452 casks we filled in the Pacific. We walk in the dark with a lamp, walking past casks of oil, casks of dry food, and unmade casks. He knows ships. He searches every corner. He knocks against the walls with his fists. He slides his hands against the wall.

"Okay, young man. To the tween decks."

"Yes, sir." Damn! Damn it!

We climb the stairs. He helps remove the panels from the tween decks. Tween decks are narrow. Tween decks store unmade casks, metal sheathings, canvas, rope, and tar. The hidden room is built against the far wall. Any walrus tusks are hidden in the far wall.

I hear a noise from the hidden room, groan of wood. He looks in the direction of the room. I drop the lantern.

"Excuse me, sir. Pardon me, sir. I apologize." I examine his face. He smiles, a sort of smile to say it's fine and we'll move on.

"No problem, young man. We're done. Let's close this up."

"Yes, sir."

As we pass the galley, he stops. Dorothy and Susan sew parkas and boots on the table. Did they conjure up these parkas and boots? Or have they truly worked on these?

"Fine work, ladies. Beautiful."

"You buy?" Dorothy asks.

"How much?"

"$35.00 for coat. $17.00 for boots."

"Keep it up. Don't let whalers cheat you. This is fine work, young lady."

"Woman. Mature woman."

"That's correct. I apologize. Mature woman. Who is this?" Healy spots the girl sitting on the floor beside Dorothy.

"My helper. She's my helper."

"Your daughter?"

"My daughter now."

He speaks in eskimo. I don't know what he says. He leans down and gives the girl a nickel. The little girl refuses and says a few eskimo words. He looks confused. Asks Dorothy a question in eskimo.

Dorothy holds out her hand for the nickel. Healy stands up. He hands her nickel without smiling. Then Healy smiles down at the girl. He says something in eskimo, waving his hand.

We get up on deck, the captain glaring at me. Healy reviews paperwork and talks to his men. Healy whispers with his men.

Healy approaches Merihim. "Captain. There are a few citations but nothing of great concern. You've got an admirable crew. My best wishes as you sail north. Your company will receive the report within the next coming weeks. Good day to you, sir."

"Thank you."

"Good day, gentlemen. Good luck this season. Fine sailing!"

Healy departed. He is a fine man, dignified, well-spoken and educated.

I stand at the helm and the captain scowls, clutching the citations. He goes through the citations. "I didn't like him. Ibai, run the engines!"

17 | STORM FROM THE SOUTH

O N THE TWENTY-FIRST DAY OF LEAVING THE COAST, we're stuck in soft snows. We push, using all our weight and muscle to get our sleds through the mush. We navigate up on the mountainside, tilting. It takes more muscle to keep the sled steady but we do it. We can't lose a day, please. I pray.

"Do you feel it? No wind this morning," Nasau asks.

"Yes."

There is stillness everywhere. No wind or birds calling. The air is void.

Within the hour, haze covers the lands. Halos surround the sun in bright prisms. A storm is coming. It will be here by nightfall.

"A storm from the south. We'll shelter against the mesa and give us a little windbreak. Hurry. We've got a ways ahead."

At first, tiny eddies of snow blow across the land. The wind shrills in short bursts. Misty clouds cover the horizon.

By the time we reach the mesa, hard crystals blast from the south. Violent gusts of wind roar over the land, like a great river. Ravens ride high in the storm. The sun will disappear soon.

I fight a long, straight current of wind then get whipped around in a swirling, pulsing gust. The snow is blinding, wetting every surface of exposed skin. My eyes burn. My damp skin burns with cold.

We shelter against the mesa, a gentle slope going up to a plateau top.

I yell at the boys to start on the tent, but they can't hear me. I wave and they understand.

Nasau and I turn the sleds on their sides, forming a circle of sorts. We stake the dogs in between the sleds and cover them completely in a tarp. We pack snow around the dogs' shelter, insulating with snow and ice.

Nasau yells. "Help the boys. I'll finish this!" By now, I only see wisps and flashes of her in the snowstorm.

The boys burrowed a cradle in the snow, spiked in the center stake, and worked on one side of the tent. I made Nauraq sit on the tent flap while we stake the side. We insulated the tent, using our hands to pack snow. I tell the boys to get into the tent while I get the bedding. I climb in the dog shelter for the bedding. The ropes around the sled are frozen together and it takes time to untie and retie again. When I arrive with the bedding, the boys had packed more snow against the walls.

The tent is so small that I must crawl. I lay down a polar bear fur on the ground. Nauraq lies in the middle. We can't build a fire, not in this wind. What if the tent catches fire? We cram together, submerged in snow, the wind strumming and thundering outside. Please Creator, protect my children from the wind and cold. Protect Nasauyaaq from the wind and cold. Protect our dogs from the wind and cold. We can't lose a day, Creator.

Nasau arrives with two dogs, their eyes crusted over with snow. They shake themselves of snow, lie down next to the boys, and cover their noses with their furry tails.

"I'm staying with the dogs!" Nasau yells.

"Are you sure? No!"

"You watch your babies! I'll watch mine! I'll be back in a bit to switch out these dogs!" She's gone, packing snow around the tent door.

It is difficult to breathe. The storm whisks away the air, robbing our lungs. I use a caribou hide to cover our heads, trapping breathable air. I feed the boys. I wrap scarves around their necks to keep wind from entering their parkas. I check their skin.

"Aaka! Your hands are so cold!" Nauraq says.

"Are you alright, son?"

"It's hard to breathe."

"It'll get easier."

"What about the dogs?"

"Dogs are stronger than men. Can you get some sleep?"

"Yes."

Before long, the storm helped seal our tent in snow. Although more than once, I thought the wind would pry the tent off the ground. I secured the tent flaps and I see glimpses of the storm outside. It is still daylight. The snow blasts sideways.

In a while, Nasau switches out the dogs, by now, the two dogs lying at our feet are free from snow and ice.

"Everything good?" I ask.

"We're good. You?"

I nod my head. The dogs are switched and she comes every few hours.

In the night, I woke in the dark, wind whistling above, and I didn't fear. Huddled in a small tent, packed under snow, I didn't fear. This surprised me, this lack of fear. I've got my two sleeping sons, warm and well-fed. I've got my axe within reach to punch through the snow. Fresh air trickles into our tent. This absence of fear gives me hope.

I drift off to sleep with this newfound hope. Until I start dreaming. I dreamt I traveled on the Nuataam Kuuŋa with my sister and parents. We row on a smoky jade green river surrounded by lush green alders and birch. My parents are young, smiling, and proud of their daughters.

The captain whispers in my ear, in a raspy, hoarse voice, breath smelling of rotting flesh. I can't move. I'm stuck in this sitting position. I can't move my head. I can't lift my arms or legs. He whispers in Yankee, and I don't understand any of the words except the words drive deep into my bones, into my spirit, and my ear seems to freeze over in frost. My parents don't hear the captain. They smile at me. They talk, row with paddles, and offer food. I sit, paralyzed, listening to the raspy Yankee whispers. I'm trying to scream to my mother, sister, and father, he's in the boat, he's in the boat! Instead, I wake myself up with moaning.

In the morning, I wake to no winds. No sounds outside. We punch through the snow with the axe.

Nasau is awake. She's checking the dogs. She's built a small fire and boils water.

I look north. I shake my head. I can't believe it. I can't believe it. Nasau smiles, hugs my side with one arm. We smile together. The land is white for miles and miles, covered in good, hard, traveling snow.

"Getting to the river will be easy. We'll ride hard today."

"Yes. Yes!" I say.

The boys wander to the top of the mesa while we fix food and feed the dogs. They saw the hearths of mammoth hunters. The hunters lived at the top of the mesa, a flat plateau, where they could spot the herds of mammoth. The boys explored and wandered until we called them to the sleds, and we rode faster and stronger than we've ever run.

18 | THERE SHE BLOWS!

AT 10 A.M., WE HEARD THE yell, There she blackskins! There she blows! Every whaler rushes on deck and we start untying the whaleboats. We've gone through this routine many times. We've practiced. We've chased whales and lost whales.

We row four whaling boats out to sea, spreading out in a circle.

I leave the girl with Gerald when we chase whales. She stands on deck, watching with her big eyes. She listens to Gerald more than anyone. Is it because he's the youngest on board? Maybe. He's also got the softest gentlest demeanor like a kitten. She doesn't smile or laugh. But she doesn't cry or outburst around him either, which is the best I could ask for.

This day, we pray, kiss our talismans and crosses, repeat the Lord's Prayer, pray to Saints and archangels.

We sit in the water, waiting for the mighty beast to rise again. It dove deep under the surface. Ten minutes go by.

The whale emerges by Remigio's boat. He stands at the bow. Remigio shoots his shoulder gun, a gun equipped with explosives. It's a low blast. Rope coils out of the boat. The whale pulls the rope out so fast we see smoke rising from the coil. Jurek douses the rope with water.

We're yelling, "Throw the rope! Throw in more rope!"

We row to the whale, ready to chase.

They attach another line of rope, now extending the rope to 300 fathoms.

"Christ! Christ!" A whaler says.

The whale pulls the rope tight and now pulls the boat along in a sleigh ride, called the Nantucket sleigh ride, their whaleboat bouncing and skipping on the waves. The men hold onto their boat as they skip along. The whale drags the boat farther out to sea then circles back towards land. We're not far behind.

"Not too close! Not too close!"

We don't want to get in range of the tail.

"Watch the line!" A whaler says.

The captain is in a frenzy with teeth clenched, squeezing his oar with both hands.

When the captain gets a shot, he shoots the whale again. This time, the whale stops, and floats belly up.

We yell. We cheer. Remigio holds the shoulder gun up in the air.

It is a bull whale. He is nearly fifty feet long and fifty tons.

We slice a hole in the whale's lip, hook the lip, and start towing the whale to the ship. The ship comes around, where we board and prepare the staging. It takes an hour securing the beast to the ship before we cut in. We unload all the lancing tools, cutting tools, winches, block and tackles. The cooper builds his casks for oil. We light the tryout pots. We're ready.

Captain puts me on the front winch, where I'll turn the winch for the tackle, each turn pulling up the chain a little more. When I tighten the large winch, we gain another foot of whale flesh.

The girl sits at my side. I think the captain would have put me in the cutting stage if I didn't have the girl to watch. For once, I'm grateful. Instead of standing on the stage all day, I'm on deck.

We skin the beast in layers, first in blanket size pieces. We cut the blanket pieces smaller and smaller until reaching book-sized pieces called bible leaves.

Up on deck, the tryworks boil down the bible leaves into oil. It is a process. We are a floating oil factory. A funnel starts from the tryworks, a copper funnel which looks like a bowl up on deck. The funnel goes into a canvas pipe, snaking down into the ship where the cooper makes casks, fills casks, and stores casks of oil. Whaling ships don't need to tow in whales to shore. We pull up the oil, meat, bones, and baleen, and it is boiled, cut, and stored.

When I get the chance, I fed the girl some whale skin. This is the eskimo's favorite part of the whale. They eat the black skin with an equal amount of blubber.

The girl knows to hide the whale food. She hides the prize in her hand and waits until she can safely eat. Later, other men brought her the black skin. Gerald, Lammert, Sten, and even Remigio brought her black skin. Remigio whispers, don't be telling anyone I gave you that. I nod at him. He's a nasty old man with the women, but it was a kind thing to give to the child.

We spent the next fifteen hours on deck. I got to eat, sleep for an hour, and take a crap. Other than that, we spent the day on deck.

"Better than being down below, isn't it? I think so," I said to the girl. Did she understand?

The captain's got the fever for whaling now. Before we're even done cutting up the whale, he's up in the crow's nest searching the sea with his glass.

I want to go home. I'll work in the factories. I'll work the railroad. I'll work in the mines. At this point, I'll do anything to get my home in the wilderness, everything except stay on this ship.

19 | River Break-up

To the east, birds fly up in the sky all at once. Birds fly to the sky in droves, screeching and cawing. The dogs jump, bark, and yank at the gang line. We pause. We sense disaster. Or movement.

"Aaka?" The boys ask.

"Get off the ice! Off the ice!" Nasau yells.

We rush the sleds up the riverbank, shoving the sleds upwards. We've traveled close to the riverbank, waiting for this day.

Bellowing. Trembling. Rattling. Creaking from the ice drives our dogs up higher on the riverbank. Ice pulls away from the riverbanks, yanking away wind-toppled trees, driftwood, and yellow grass, leaving sod edges like jagged wolf teeth.

Murky water rushes to the east, downstream, a deluge gushing to the ocean. Ice collects, folds, swirls forward like an icy wave, tumbling upon itself. Ice chisels at the river's edge, burrowing, collecting, dragging, boring its way to the east, then north to the sea. Deposits of ice strand up on shore, a moraine of ice accumulated like a ridgeline, soon to melt under the sun or be pulled back into the river.

"That was amazing!" Nauraq yells.

"Time to find a boat. We find people and we'll find a boat," Nasau says.

On the river, we've seen camps and boat frames. No covers on the boats. It's no use looking for skins to cover the boats. It takes skilled hands to cover an umiaq. The skins must soak in saltwater for three days, then be sewn by skilled Elders. Even my mother was too scared to try the stitches, and she was an experienced seamstress. One weak stitch and the umiaq could sink.

"This is a good time to pack the dogs. Faster if we walk," Nasau says.

"Already? No. Yes. You are right." I shake my head. She is right. Yesterday, the sleds were a hard push. It is time to abandon the sleds. The snow is mush. We've heaved the sleds these past days. I'm disappointed.

"I thought we'd find a boat by now. Where are all the people? Where are the camps?"

"We'll find someone soon. Whether they left the umiaq behind or are willing to trade for one. We'll find someone."

"Are you certain there is no faster way?"

"The river knows the fastest way to the ocean."

She's right. The Kuukpik river is well-travelled by the coastal people as well as the inland people.

Each dog gets a little pack, strapped against their backs. From this point on, we won't be carrying much of a tent. The tent is now scraps, enough to cover our bodies from rain.

She speaks to the boys as we work on the dog packs. "These rivers originate from an ancient sea. A thousand years ago, this land was covered in a sea. My mother said when your spirit is troubled, seek a river. Rivers take our messages to the other world, the spirit world."

In the next seven days, we arrive to groves of conifers, evergreens, spruce, and birch on the river. We travel through tall shrubs, some thorny, sticky, and fragrant. The river is free of ice, ambling, singing, and filled with trout. We see fox, mountain sheep, brown bears, wolves, and even wild dogs.

By the tenth day, we reach large spruce forests. Now we must navigate through thick deadwood decaying on the forest floor. We avoid swampy morass, taking the sturdy terrain near the river-banks. If needed, we walk up to the foothill slopes, a short relief from the insects, or to bathe in the small mountain ponds, refreshing, invigorating, and rippling with wind. Other days we walk along tall river bluffs, sandy, hot, and overflowing with fine silt and alluvial fans.

I tell them woodland stories like the old woman with an elf-like little man, tall as my waist, from a home among the moss and bogs. She fed and sheltered the creature and the creature helped her live a long life. Like the two-headed serpent with long tentacles and green eyes that snatches children wandering on the river, or the one about a giant wolf with webbed feet living in a blackwater lake.

We're not used to the forest. We find a glade or a moor, for our overnight camps, if we can, to see more of our surroundings. We listen to the sough of the forest, rustling and calming.

Tonight, we found a small glade near the river with a stream flowing to a small pond. Shoals surround the river and streams where fish may get caught for easy fishing. I shear down the fur on our parkas with a sharp flint blade. Our parkas are heavy for winter. I shave the fur down to half-length, making our parkas lighter in weight and lighter in color. We look like hunters.

Nasauyaaq collects a mushroom-looking fungus from the trees, hard as wood, fan-like, and growing high on trees.

"The Koyukon call this smutch. You burn it to keep away the bugs. Start cinders on the side and it'll burn through the night."

"Smutch?" Ebrulik asks.

"Smutch. It works."

"I'll get some on our way home. For my future wife. She will not get bitten up."

"You are thoughtful. You'll be a thoughtful husband. Near here, my husband found a huge, long skeleton buried in stone. A body larger than a grizzly, but the head shaped like a duck."

"A duck?" Nauraq asks. The boys laugh.

"A duck."

"What kind of creature?"

"I don't know. The skeleton buried in stone. Must have lived hundreds of years ago."

"I want to see it," Nauraq says.

"Me, too. I want to see all these lands." Ebrulik waves his hand in an arc, covering the land.

I want my boys to see all the lands, as well, where they'll be at peace, content, and fulfilled with all the land offers, a mother's dream.

This morning, on a hilltop near the river, we see people. They gather around a fire. They stop, stand up.

"Do they have an umiaq?"

"I can't tell. Looks like children. I don't think there's an adult among them," Nasau says.

"Children?" I ask. "Still, they might know where to find a boat," I say.

"Yes. I'll go over first. I'll ask."

We sit and drink water. She walks over. It is children. We stay by the river until Nasau waves. They are a small Nunamiut party, the inland people. They are three teenage boys, a group of small children, and one old man. The old man sits on the hill, plucking birds. They hunt geese with a net. They live in a tent. Their people migrate after the caribou and live in yurts. I think they are Tulugaqmiut, people of Raven Lake.

I don't know who is frailer, the old man or the children. All of them looked at the edge of death. Or the edge of life. The children look cadaverous, anemic, and pallid. They smile, laugh, and ask questions, but emaciation shows through their clothing. The old man, as well, seems crippled by anemia. None showed the signs of smallpox, although two survived the affliction, scratching at the healing scars over their faces and necks.

There is a Koyukon boy. My sons stare. He is a young man, maybe 15 or 16 years old. He dresses in moosehide and caribou, his longhair pulled back in a braid.

"Don't stare," I whisper.

"You've got the vaccine?" Nasau asks the children.

"Yes," they say.

"Did you see men come through here?"

"Yes."

"Ataŋauraq? Their uncle?" She points at me.

"I don't know," they say.

"When was this? A few days?"

"Not a few days ago. Farther back."

"A few weeks?"

The teenagers nod their heads. Nasau spoke to the young man in Koyukon. He listens and speaks in his language. She knows the Koyukon language!

My boys talk to the teenagers.

"I'm going to have a whaling crew someday. Do you want to be on my whaling crew?" Ebrulik asks.

"Yes," they say.

The young children crowd around me. They are all girls, from five to ten years old, I'd say.

"Are they your sons?" one asks.

"Yes."

"You are pretty. Our Aaka is pretty too."

I don't want to ask about their mother. The answer, no doubt, will break my heart. "Did you help get the birds?" I ask.

"Yes. We chased them. Cousin used the net, too. Where are you going?"

"To the river. Then to the sea."

"Can you stay for a while?"

"I'd like to, but we are looking for my daughter. She is five years old and alone."

"Is she lost?"

"Not lost. Stolen away. Stolen away by bad men. Otherwise, I'd love to stay and eat geese with the prettiest girls in the country." I want to travel everywhere and find children like them.

"We're getting ready for caribou. They're coming."

"They'll come soon. You got family around here? Uncles? Aunts? The caribou will come soon, and the people will follow the herd."

"We know where they will go. Up into the mountains. Into the mountain's spine."

"Good." I walk up to the hillside where the old man plucks birds. I sit by him. He doesn't speak. We sit on the hilltop together, the hillside to our backs.

They've caught a dozen snow geese, laid side-by-side. He puts a few geese aside for parkas. Geese parkas are warm and waterproof.

I yank and pull. I don't like the old man plucking these geese by himself. A little girl helps collect the down.

My mother dusted away bugs with a handful of long beach grass or leafy branch. She'd say, you need to learn how. One day, I won't be here to help you.

As I sit with the old man, I wonder, did I learn enough? I'm the last adult left in my family. Did I ask enough questions? How will I teach my boys to become whalers? I can't help the tears. The old man hears my crying. He pats my knee without looking and goes back to his defeathering. In a second, I'm recovered. I breathe deep. I hide my tears.

The old man and I finished plucking the birds, and I join Nasau by the dogs.

"I traded my dogs for the boat."

"Your entire team? A boat?" I shake my head in disbelief. Her entire team? Not her entire team?

"No arguments. It is done. The river is not far from here. Half a day away." She leans, kneels. She pats a dog on the ribs, scratching its ears.

The boys give the dog Tumi to the little girls. They hand the leash over.

"I get to keep him?" A girl asks.

"You get to keep him," Ebrulik says.

"He's strong," Nauraq says.

"Keep him well fed. Especially when he's running. They eat twice as much when running on the sled," Ebrulik says. My children echo Nasau's teachings to the young girls.

"I will!"

"We will!"

We stake the dogs to the ground, tie them off.

"They've got their boat near the bluff. We must leave now," Nasau says.

We say our farewells to the old man and children. The young girls already play with the young dog, Tumi. Their family is given another chance at life, as well as ours. Nasau saved two families today.

The teenage boys are good runners. They lead us on worn trails, down into creek beds, up onto hilltops marked with bones and inuksuks.

We run north towards ridges of rock, lines of bedrock, drumlins uprooting themselves from the tundra. We run in a dry creek bed made of rounded cobbles. I see poppies, cottongrass, fireweed, dandelions, and rosehips. I smell the floral aroma of buttercups and rosehips in the air.

Long ago, our people camped along this creek, living in tents made of camel and mammoth. The women raised their children on their own, away from the men. They played with their children in eddies, now this dry creek bed. Are they watching me now, running by their ancient encampments, running with my boys as they did? Or do I imagine old stories, which don't exist?

Nauraq slows down after nearly an hour of running. I hang back with him. There is no shortcut. He is too heavy to carry.

"I'm tired," he says.

"It's alright, son. Rest. We'll catch up. They will ready the boat." I wave at Ebrulik who runs ahead with Nasau. He knows, without words, that I'll wait behind with Nauraq. They press ahead.

I hold Nauraq. We sit on the riverbank. I kiss his forehead while he rests. I love my son so much. He tries hard and works hard. At his age, I played with my friends. I competed in games and ran in races. He runs across the entire country after his sister. I give him water and dried fish.

It wasn't long before he regained his strength. We ran north at a steady, slow pace.

We run to a conjunction where three rivers join into a mighty river. We stand in a great braided floodplain made of silty and sandy channels. The river shores remind me of the sea, with sandy, spiked salty goose-tongue grass, and flocks of birds.

We reach bluffs and outcrops of stone, striped in long striations.

The group stopped. The boys pulled an umiaq towards the water, stored on a rack, underneath a high bluff.

The boat is fresh and strong.

"I hope she is found," one boy says.

"Me too," the other says.

"Thank you," I say. My boys give their bird spearheads to the young men. I'm so proud of my boys.

We leave the young men behind on the riverbank. They stand until we've disappeared down the river, away from the bluff. Before the sickness, I would've called them boys, but now I call them men.

We're going north to the sea. We row north, like warriors, like seamen, like whalers. We'll soon to be reunited with the sea.

20 | MAN OVERBOARD!

THE BELL RANG ON THE SHIP. I almost drop the captain's steam-ing fresh coffee as I walk up on deck. We look up at the crow's nest. Lammert yells, "Man overboard! Man overboard!"

The captain rushes to the bow. His face transforms from curios-ity to anger.

We rush after. I see the girl. She jumped ship, landing in a crop of floes not far from the ship.

"Oh shit!" I say.

"Call anchor!" Merihim yells.

"Not in this ice, captain!" Emilio says.

All morning, we've crushed through a field of ice, going at a slow 2 knots. The ice delayed our progress. Now, we can't turn around, and we can't stop. We don't want to lose any momentum once we're sailing through ice. The ship's got another 100 yards of ice until open water.

"Damn it! Keep an eye on her! Don't let her out of your sight!" He yells.

I stand with other whalers, watching, ready to lower the boats. We've got our little sea glasses, watching the girl, our backs safely to the captain.

She jumps into a pool of floes. She teeters on a little ice floe, rocking back and forth. She waits until the rocking stops and starts paddling.

"Jesus!" Sten says.

"Look at that!" Remigio says.

"What's she doing?"

"Is she paddling? She's paddling."

"With her hands?"

"No. It's a ladle. A kitchen ladle," I say. I shake my head. I'd laugh if the captain weren't so near.

"Holy shit," Remigio says.

We stifle our laughter with coughs. Sten clears the corners of his eyes with one hand, smiling in his palm. I'm smiling and drinking the captain's coffee.

The girl carries an ice hook. It's a small hook kept next to the stairwell, used for hooking freshwater ice. As she jumps, she hooks the ice at her feet, steadying herself. A dangerous maneuver. She does it. Damn smart girl. The first waves come from our ship, curls and hills of water. She's rocking up and down but doesn't teeter.

She jumps and jumps again until clearing broken ice. On her last jump, she fell on her stomach, but she gets up. She runs.

It's another fifteen minutes before we clear the ice.

"Damn it! Stop the engines! Get a boat down! Ibai! Lower the boats! For shit sake! Stop the engines! Get the boats in the water!"

The two whaleboats reach the meadow of ice floes, but the girl is a dot on the skyline.

We wait on deck, watching with our scopes. We laugh in disbelief, joy, and triumph. She wins and we all win. Clever girl, we said. I don't know how we'll compose ourselves when the captain returns.

"What happened?" Remigio asks.

"Captain sent me for coffee. Insisted the girl stay with him on deck. She jumped. Not my fault."

The captain and men didn't return until nightfall. They got the girl.

Later, we fetch Susan to translate. Susan plops her ass on a cask, sighing. She translates in a flat voice. We sit at our bunks, listening to the girl's story. We quiet down. We don't want the captain to hear our questions to the girl.

"What happened? Ask the girl what happened?" We say to Susan.

"She made it to the beach. She built a windbreak with snow. She dreamt of her mother."

"She made rope. What did she use the rope for?" I ask.

"To keep her hook and the little scooper from falling in the water."

"To keep her tools from falling? Smart." Was I this brave at her age? Maybe I was and I don't remember.

Captain found her tools. On one end, she tied the ice hook. On the other end, she tied the ladle. Then carried the strap over her shoulders. With the rope, she wouldn't lose her precious getaway tools. When the captain found her, he picked up the roped instruments, held them up in the air. He cut the rope with his knife, threw it away. He kept the ladle and ice hook.

We laugh and give the girl little trophies: string, rope, dried fish, even a few red Russian beads. She walks around the room, collecting her little gifts.

21 | CLIMBING HER SHIP

I WOKE TO THE SOUND OF SEA gulls, recognizing their unmistakable cries. I close my eyes and thank the Creator. We're close. We see fields of rounded stones, meadows of dry tundra. We've left behind the great marshes and tall mountains. The northern coast is more like home.

Terns, kittiwakes, and seagulls sing their songs, mating calls and displays of dominance, and I'm up, starting the fire, warming up water, and cutting fish. Nasau rises not long after, then the boys.

I pack. We rush downriver, the boys yawning and snacking on fish.

I watch for the coastline, eagerly, at every turn, at every bend of the river. How much longer? Dear Creator, my husband, how much longer? It mustn't be another day, is it?

The river moves fast. We get downriver with little work, except to navigate. We sway and jerk along a clear and fast river. The river is green and fresh. Alders and willows grow on the river, leaning towards fresh water, drooping, reaching.

On the thirtieth day of leaving our coastline, we arrive at the sea. I thought the boys would be happy to be on the sea. They aren't. They're afraid.

We went gushing out into the ocean, passed the breakers, and shoreline, out to the sea. Ice recedes far out to sea. Whaling ships pass by. We see seals bobbing in the water. It is a bright, yellow day.

"Which way are the ships headed? Are they headed back home?"

"No. No! They're headed towards Herschel. We'll still get our chance to see her on Hershel."

"Aaka! Aaka!"

"Yes?"

"Look."

A ship sails behind our umiaq. It's gaining speed. The ship runs its engine.

"What do we do?"

"I don't know. Nasau?"

"Hold on." She looks out with her sea glass. "It's not her ship. Definitely not."

"Is this safe?"

"Let's row closer to shore."

We avoid the ship, the ship overcoming our umiaq not long after.

The men didn't acknowledge our boat. They didn't move. They didn't look out with a sea glass. They turned their heads towards our direction but nothing more.

"I don't think they care what we're doing, unless we've got items to trade."

The next ship was the same. The whalers turned their heads but continued with their work.

"Let's stay out of their way. If it looks like her ship, we'll land."

"Alright. Alright."

We rowed as far as we could, spending hours rowing along the coastline. It'll be a week before we reach Herschel Island. From the numbers of ships going to Herschel, I've guessed their annual hunting hasn't peaked.

"This ship anchored for the night. Maybe we should land, too."

"Yes. Alright."

On the fifth day at sea, as Nasau looks at the approaching ship, she stops. She looks up in the sea glass again. "Kaya. Kaya?"

"What? What? Is it hers? Is it?"

I look in the west. My heart beats. I tear up. "Oh! Oh!" I cry, the oar resting across my knees. I cradle the oar in my arms like a baby. I shake.

"Let's land. Hurry. I don't want them to see us."

We hurried, my heart jumping. I watch the ship. It's getting closer. I see the serpent clear and true. We approach the surf in such a hurry we dip far down in the front, almost falling forward, but Nasau stables the umiaq with her oar. We're rushing.

We drag the umiaq up on the beach. The ship will be able to see me with their sea glass soon. I put up my hood.

She stands with her back to the ship. The boys look.

"It's alright, boys. It's alright if the ship sees you. Make it look like we're a family out hunting. That's all."

I'm behind the umiaq. There are a few men on deck. The captain and men walk around the deck, nothing more. The ship continues into the east.

"What do we do?"

"It'll be dark for at least an hour tonight. We'll shave down their numbers again. We'll whittle down their numbers. Are you ready?"

"I'm ready."

Nasau and I have planned this day. Nasau and I will board the ship while the boys keep the umiaq. The boys must row away once we're on board. Then, row back when we're ready. I hope Samaruna camps on deck. Some Inupiaq peoples work on the ships and camp on deck. Will she be on deck?

Nasau stressed I cannot go down below. Too many men, she says. We don't know what the ship looks like down below. They have guns and more men. We search the deck. Kill any men in our way.

"Aaka. What will you do once you're on board? Will you get her?" Ebrulik asks.

"If I can."

"Will you kill the white men?"

"If I have to."

"What if they're armed? Aaka? I'll go for you."

"No. I'm trying to do what your father would do. Alright?"

"Alright," they say.

"Ebrulik, watch your brother. Row away as fast as possible. Make no sound. You hear me? My life depends on you. Do you hear me? How will I escape if you aren't here to get me? Come and get me. If anything happens, you follow the ship to Herschel."

"Aaka."

"Follow the ship to Herschel. Find a way to get her off the ship."

"Aaka."

"You're both good. The best sons I could've asked for. I'm proud of you both."

We cry and weep. My poor boys, they've grown so much but still have the hearts of children.

I braid my hair tight, up and away from my face. Nasau paints my forehead grey with soot, from my forehead to nose. I paint the boys' faces. They're not afraid. Not yet. Nauraq smiles showing his white teeth against a grey painted face. Protect my boys, Creator. Protect them. Keep them hidden in the darkness. I kiss both their ashen foreheads.

Would it be better to leave my boys on shore? Alone, waiting for their mother to return? Husband? Are you listening? Where are they safe?

All I know is I can't leave them any longer than necessary. I can't leave them watching me from shore, rowing away, thinking this is the last time they'll see their mother. If I die, I'd rather they know. I'd rather they have my body to bury. Or know my body is resting in the sea. It is better this way, isn't it?

We leave everything on shore, which isn't much. We row fast as we can. In the precious moments we're on deck, the boys must row by themselves. I don't want them to labor any more than they need. It might save their lives. We throw and leave it all except the weapons Nasau and I will carry on deck.

I carry the axe on my back. Nasau gives me a polar bear club, made of the bear's femur, strong enough to break rock, which I'll carry by hand.

We wait until nightfall, then dusk. This time of year, we get a sliver of night, a mere hour of darkness. We must wait until the darkest of the night, when we can board the ship without notice.

We launch out to the ocean to where the ship anchored for the night. Her ship is two miles ahead, on the horizon. The water is black, rolling, and quiet. I smell the ship, even though they've shut the engines, I smell the coal smoke on the water. My hands shake.

The orange glow of their lamp spreads in perfect circle around the ship. Nasau looks through her scope. She whispers. "One high up on the ship. You know where I mean? Up the ropes and in a basket? Two men at the front, one at the back."

Every paddle of the oar, I watch the Yankees. Do they hear? Do they know we're here in the dark?

We steady our hands against the ship, preventing the umiaq from knocking against the ship. I jump, the umiaq dipping a little in the water, but Ebrulik pushes the umiaq away at the same time. They're clear. I see my boys watching me in the darkness, full white pleading eyes, but they row away.

We climb the ladder. Is she behind this wall? Is she in a room on deck? My heart beats hard. My hands sweat.

We're on deck, ducking in shadows. The men talk by the helm in quiet voices. Ropes tied off everywhere, swaying with the ship. Wood creaks.

No one camps on deck. She's not on deck.

Somewhere, deep inside the vessel, a man coughs. I see a dim light underneath my feet. I see downstairs. At the bottom of the stairs, at the left, there is a room, ropes and canvas totes against the wall. I see nothing else.

Nasau points up, and then climbs upwards alone. I nod. I kneel in the shadows. I sit in the shadows while she climbs. The climb is slow and laborious. Every gust of wind and I think the man will jump up from the basket and yell below. He doesn't. She pauses at the top. The man gasps, thumping. She climbs down alone.

She joins me, out of breath. She points to the helm.

We start walking to the helm. I can't breathe.

A man holds cards in his hands. The other man stands at the helm. They turn in shock. Half a scream. I cave in his face, breaking the bones. His eyes look at each other. I hit again between the ribs, caving in his chest. He's a strange pile of limbs. He looks up with his crossed eyes.

Nasau threw her spear with such force the man flies backwards against the ship's bow. He's staked against the ship. I follow her down the stairs, down to the ladder, to the water.

A young boy reached the deck before I climb down into the umiaq. He is young like Ebrulik, maybe a year or two older. He is too scared to move, so he stands and stares.

We slide into the vessel, rowing away into the darkness. Lanterns ran back and forth on deck. A bell rings while we row north, away from the ship.

22 | TAKE A GREENHORN!

MERIHIM AND EMILIO PACE WITH THEIR rifles, looking out onto the water. Sten carries Lammert down from the crow's nest. We wrap the three bodies in canvas.

Gerald is in shock. Merihim and Emilio question him.

"What happened?" Emilio demanded of Gerald.

"Three men are dead," the captain hisses.

"Tell me what happened," Emilio asks.

"Savages on the ship. On the *Erysichthon*, sir. I think they were women," Gerald says.

"Women?"

"Two eskimo women," Gerald thinks, trying to remember the details.

"It's Henry. Lammert."

"Why weren't they armed? Take a whaleman! Take a greenhorn! Instead, they killed one of my damn harpooners! All officers will be armed. Blacksmith. Cooper. Harpooners. Will be armed."

"Damn travesty. We'll hold funerals in the morning," Emilio says.

The captain retires to his cabin cursing and screaming.

We gather around Gerald in the forecastle.

"Tell us what you saw, boy. You saw the savages."

"They were eskimo women."

"Women!"

"The boy doesn't know what he saw!"

"I know a woman when I see one. She was a woman."

"How old? A girl? My age? Remigio's age?" I ask.

"I don't know! She was at least ten years older than me."

"A young woman, then?" I ask. Can they not see? It is the girl's mother!

23 | HERSCHEL ISLAND

⌄

HERSCHEL ISLAND IS A WHALERS' SETTLEMENT, built on a sandy island shaped like a bird's head, the beak facing east. Ships dock at the neck. Smoke curls up into the sky from the buildings and tents.

Herschel Island was established a few years ago. There are a few permanent buildings, a common house, church, and enclosed drying shacks for baleen which are sheds with wide vents at the roof to circulate air, freeze-drying the baleen of sea vermin and excess blubber. The rest of the town is shanties, lean-tos, tents, and eskimo tents, built between each other, shoved together from scraps of metal and wood, mismatched, slanted, and greying from wear.

No one looks at the shanties like our shantytowns. The captains revered these "humble" creations. White men build shanties and they are resourceful and creative. A black man or immigrant builds a shanty and they are lazy and criminal. What a sideways world we live in.

In the town, even as it crumbled and barely stood, we yearned to see every inch like explorers. The eskimo women giggle together. They're excited as whalers to see Herschel.

"You gonna find your husband, girly?" Remigio asks.

"No husband. Captain my husband," Dorothy says.

We sail into Pauline Cove, on this bright and clear day, standing at our stations, the captain standing proud, like Napoleon entering port with his naval ships.

I count twenty-seven other ships, either anchored or sailing nearby. Brigs, barks, whaling boats, even a small sailing schooner later said to carry scientists and botanists for some European university, and skin boats filled with natives rowed into the harbor.

"The Norwegian ship is wintering over, and the little schooner," Emilio says.

Men prepare to winter in the cove, insulating the roofs of their ships with sod. Herschel was built for whalers who'd winter over in the arctic. Herschel created a location for a stockpile of supplies. Companies save money when whalers stay and guard their supplies and stockpiles. They save in travel expenses.

There is also a sense of security for whalers, knowing these stockpiles exist. There are five-year stockpiles in Point Barrow and Herschel in the event of a shipwreck.

The newspapers publicize all the grueling and shocking details of whaling incidents, accidents, shipwrecks, cannibalism, starvation, and frostbitten hands and feet. They describe the dead bodies of whalers and explorers, how they're abandoned in the arctic, never to be buried in the Christian manner. They print the gory details, death by death, a kind of morbid entertainment for the masses like Jack the Ripper and Lizzie Borden.

Gerald looks at the town with his little scope, talking out loud, announcing everything he sees. "I smell fresh bread. Can you smell it?"

"Corn bread," I say.

"No. It's sourdough."

"Are you crazy? I know corn bread when I smell it." Somewhere on a ship nearby, someone is baking bread.

We are all on deck. Gerald and I stood with Sten, Remigio, Jurek, Tytus, and Anthony.

"You're going to have to wheelbarrow me back to shore. I plan on not remembering tonight. I want whiskey. Real whiskey.

Not this corn crap we've been drinking. Tonight, we drink to Lammert! Our fellow countryman. A brave and honorable man. To Lammert!" Sten says.

"To Lammert!" We yell.

We buried Lammert and the whalemen at dawn, our first duty of the day. The deck is clean of blood and bone, any evidence of bloodshed.

"All the fuss about this shit town! There better be drink!" Jurek says.

"Ibai. What will you do, Ibai? Are there girls?" Gerald asks.

"Girls!" We laugh.

"Women?" He asks.

"Quit trying to sound like a man, Gerald," Remigio says.

"We pooled money for Gerald to bust his cherry," Jurek says.

"Get 'em, Gerald. You find the ladies and let us know," Sten says.

"Where? I don't see any women. Not even eskimo women," Gerald says.

"Follow the whiskey. You'll find them," Remigio laughs. "Listen to Remigio, lad. You'll never forget your first time bedding a woman. Don't be picky. As long as she is drunk, but if you can, find a soft, large woman."

We laugh.

Sten grabs Gerald's shoulders and looks him in the eyes. "Boy. Behave yourself. Be a gentleman. Take off your hat. Say, excuse me madam, how much are you offering? Then, let her take the lead."

The captain calls for anchor and we cheer.

A skiff approaches our ship. He climbs the ladder, hanging to the bow without climbing aboard. He hands Emilio a stiff invitation, scribed in calligraphy. On the back, a red waxed insignia. "Captain. We request your presence for dinner at the main hall. The wives are holding a dinner. It's a fancy dress event."

"A dinner." Merihim stares at the invitation without opening.

"Yes, sir."

"Supper?"

"It's a formal event. Please wear your best dress."

"Formal event?"

"Yes, sir."

"Good Lord. All right. Thank your captain."

"They don't have enough serving plates, so bring yours."

"Our plates?"

"Plates." The man looks annoyed with the captain. He's probably the first mate of a more tenured ship, a more experienced ship. He doesn't have to be polite. He doesn't need to grovel to men like Merihim. He left without saying another word.

"Women. Civilization is thousands of miles away and they want a fancy dress party. Where's my powdered wig and brocade jacket?" Merihim laughs.

"Of course," Emilio says.

"A formal dinner!"

"We're in the arctic, not Washington!"

"A dinner? With music? Will there be girls?" Gerald asks.

Emilio walks to the crew. We shut up. "This is a dinner with the captains. Behave yourself. Don't be embarrassing our captain with any rowdiness. Best manners. The captain will be watching you. Each man must cut firewood. See the stockpile? All crews cut wood on entering Herschel. Don't embarrass your captain." He left below deck.

We saw the stockpile of firewood. Another crew worked at chopping wood, gathering driftwood on their backs, and stacking up cut wood.

"All the slave work and they make us attend a fucking gala."

"Jesus Christ in a bottle!"

"The work doesn't end."

"God damnit, son of a whore!"

"There is no rest for the wicked."

We set out to shore, dressed in our best shirts, stuffing our pockets with whatever trading items we could, coin, razors, and trinkets. It's forty degrees and a sunny day, warm enough to leave my parka behind. I've acclimated to the weather.

Eskimo women sit on the beach with baskets filled with trout, char, and some type of minnow fish, fresh and bright with life. Anthony inspects the fish, scowling, using his hand to look in the baskets. He buys a basket of fish, mostly trout. A few women held out artifacts and curios.

We got to the woodpile. Gerald rushes off to the beach to get driftwood, working faster than any whaler. Emilio also left to town.

"He'll be back," Sten says.

We're all irritated with the task. Emilio will make sure that we've contributed.

"I need a dentist. You think there's a dentist?" Jurek asks.

"Maybe not a dentist. Healer, maybe," Sten says.

"Shit, I'll settle for a damn shaman at this point. These two teeth need out. Rotten."

"I'm getting drunk. I'm drinking for my mate. I need to send a letter to his family."

"He is at peace." I say.

"What do I write? He was killed by savages? Knocked into the ocean by a beast? Or gone down in a shipwreck thinking bravely of his family? Not killed by a woman."

"We're not soldiers, for Christ's sake. He knew the dangers. His family knew the dangers. Honesty is best."

It is an hour before we got our leave. We walk into town, following the stream of whalers going towards the largest building.

The dinner is arranged at the biggest structure in the town, the main hall, a gathering place. Outside the men stood in groups, drinking ale, and whiskey. A few men even climbed up on the roof. On the inside, the building is larger than it appears; the ceiling is twenty feet high. I imagine a company sent the materials for this purpose, it is made of all the same lumber. It is well-built, like a Viking longhouse with beams and pillars of wood. There are matching windows, one door in the front, and one door in the back. The doors are wide open. The floors lined with planks, salvaged from an abandoned ship after hitting a shallow reef. There is little seating. The hall is filled with crude benches made of ship remnants and driftwood.

The tables set up in a square for the captains to dine together, facing one another. The tables are covered in colorful linens embroidered in pansies, peonies, daffodils, and milk thistles. There is a mix of serving platters, plates, and dinnerware in silver, silver-plated, and brass. There are two slender vases stuffed with wildflowers.

Crews sit behind the officers, at tables and benches. Twenty-seven crews tried to cram into the hall with not enough tables or seats.

"C'mon Gerald." I see an empty bench, where a few men stood up and turned to leave. Me, Gerald, and a few of our crew fight our way through the crowd, cramming passed a hundred men. I can't believe we got a bench this close to the captains. We're squished together while the walls are lined with standing men, holding their plates. "We'll get more food sitting in front."

A whaler plays a fiddle in the center; a whaler wearing a fresh black jacket over tattered whaling clothes.

We sat by the crew of scientists and botanists, sent by a university and funded by the US Navy. They asked the captains about the terrain, natives, and proposed Northwest Passage until captains grew impatient.

Merihim and Emilio are well known, we discovered, as the night pressed on. Every captain shook Merihim and Emilio's hands.

"Emilio, chap! How the hell are you?" An old whaler asked, dressed in a fresh suit. He's drinking, heavy-lidded, and smiling. His wife stands at his side, holding a tray with ginger ale.

Emilio stood, shook his hand with both hands. "We're good sir, thank you. Your wife is more beautiful than ever," Emilio says.

"You are a scoundrel! When will you marry, young Emilio? I know a few beautiful ladies," The old wife says.

Her husband clicked his tongue. "Darling. Leave the young man. Let him see the world."

"My husband thinks I speak my mind, but he wouldn't be a captain without his wife."

"True, that is true. "

"How is your season," The old man asks.

"We had bad luck this year with the eskimos. The captain handles himself well, quite well."

"Savages. It's the same around the world. In the '80's, we suffered the most vicious attacks in the Pacific Islands. Loads of whales. Great hunting grounds, but brutal relations with the natives. It was horrendous. I barely survived the '80's. Next year, my lad, you'll rebound all your losses."

"Next year?" Emilio asks, drinking ale.

"Of course, of course. Level out your losses over the next year. You'll see. Take some photographs for your company. Shareholders will love seeing your fine work. A fine memory."

A photographer flashed a few pictures of the captains. Merihim and Emilio joined the photographs, not smiling. It wasn't long before the captains' wives complained of the smoke from the camera. "I'll take photographs outside, ladies," he told them.

We watched the whole ordeal from our bench.

"The photos cost a fortune," I say.

"I can't afford a photograph," Jurek says.

"I'll be lucky to make a dollar," I say.

A white-collared priest stood in the middle of the room, holding a bible in one hand and calming the room with the other hand. The room quiets. The preacher's wife stood at his side.

"Gentlemen and ladies. I will bless the wonderful food. Please remove your hats."

We stand and remove our hats. We stand all at once, chair legs scraping and screeching against the floor. I close my eyes. I always close my eyes during prayer. I clasp my hands together.

"Lord, Jesus Christ, our Savior in Heaven. We've come together for a special occasion this evening, together in brotherhood, in thanks for good food. We ask you bless this food prepared by wonderful and faithful women who've followed their husbands to the treacherous north, in service to the whaling tradition, in service of our great American country. We pray for all the men and women affected by the fire in Chicago. For our American brethren in New Jersey as they confront laws overseeing the industries. In the name of the Son, the Father, and the Holy Spirit, bless this food about to enter our bodies. We pray these men and women go forth in peace. Amen."

"Amen."

The captains tell the latest news, a show of their authority. They tell of the riots, labor marches, and fires with great pride. I hear there was a great fire in Chicago. A shame. The damn Irishmen rioting in New Jersey. What do they have to riot about? They're rioting to steal our jobs, they say.

None of the crews interrupt the captains. Not even Remigio dares to interrupt the captains. The captains would be embarrassed with an interruption from their crew, and the punishment would be harsher for this embarrassment. We knew to shut up. We spoke in hushed tones, a little more than a whisper, like school children passing notes and secrets but our whispers more sinister. When the wives arrived with their serving trays, we removed our hats, stood, and thanked them.

We listened to the women talking, not out of interest, but of proximity. We pretend not to overhear their conversation, but we are squished up by the wives. There are six whaling wives and the preacher's wife.

"I wanted dinner rolls. We couldn't find a handful of wheat flour. But corn flour! We found corn flour. Cornbread is perfect, Emilia."

"I had so much help. Ida wanted to make dinner rolls for the officers, but no!"

"Oh no!"

"Bad taste to feed them better food than their crew. In their cabins, yes, but in front of all the crew, no. This would've brought envy. Not good for our officers."

"Not suitable for Christian dining, absolutely not."

"All the lovely dishes! Pork! I haven't had pork in weeks."

"We certainly had to cook duck. Of course, ducks are everywhere here."

"You are so resourceful, Portia."

"But the tenderizing took days, and the spices. Almost all the spices used up for the duck."

"It's a meaty bird."

"It is."

"Even the fish. I'm not accustomed to the fish. How to describe the fish here?"

"More oils? I've got the same taste as you. I prefer salmon from the Atlantic."

"Same as I."

"Or Pacific tuna."

"Who brought the tapioca? What a divine treat!"

"That was the German ship. I don't know the name."

"I can't pronounce the name. My German needs practice. An incredible thoughtful accompaniment to our dinner."

"And ginger ale. I love getting ginger ale whenever I can. I'm hopeless."

"That's from Mrs. Hibbard."

The women shushed. They sat up straight. They whispered.

"We've overheard the worse news."

"It is horrid."

"Too horrid to repeat."

"Tell me. Tell me!"

"She beats her servants."

"No!"

"She beats them."

"What about her husband? Doesn't he do something?"

"That's only part of the story. Her husband! It's too disgusting to say."

"I can't imagine."

"It's awful!"

"He loves schoolgirls. Not even women. Pubescent girls. He lusts after them in every city."

"No!"

"Lord!"

"She's given him ten children! Strong boys and girls. Their children have children. He's a grandfather! She's a grandmother!"

"She must report him to the authorities! It's immoral!"

"And shame herself! No. She'd be ruined."

"Their children would be ruined. Who'd want to marry their child with such a father?"

"I heard, you won't believe, it's difficult to believe. In Hawaii, the authorities caught him with a twelve-year-old girl. Twelve years old!"

"It's a child."

"Poor child."

"Unimaginable."

"Today, I boarded her ship for the almond meal and ginger ale. I overheard her scolding the cook. You ruined this perfectly good flour into this mushy mess? You must think I'm made of money. She accused the cooks of trying to kill her. Then she saw me. I was terrified. She is awful. I'm not associating myself with this monster. An Elder she may be, but she is a monster. I'm not respecting a woman who treats human beings in this manner."

"I, as well."

"Hear, hear."

"You are a shining light, dear. This is a great example for all."

A few of the captains approached, holding out their arms for their dear wives. They all rose and joined their husbands, smiling, picking up trays and platters.

We sigh.

"Jesus! I thought the captains were bad," Sten said.

"That is some craziness. Gerald said there's a tavern on the end of town."

"Good lad! Gerald, get over here, boy!"

"A tavern, you said?"

"Yes. There is ale and women!"

"How much?"

"I don't care how much. I'm spending all I have for some drink and a good woman."

"The price is robbery! Inflation," I say to Gerald. The women here are expensive because men are desperate. It's either pay the high price or wait months for another opportunity. That's years away.

"But can I afford it, Ibai? Can I?"

"Don't worry, boy. Jesus! Wait until this is done. Get us another cup of ginger ale, or whiskey."

Gerald squeezes his way through the crowd. He's happy. He's smiling.

Drinks are served, including ale, the ale won't last. I didn't get any jello but did get a slice of rhubarb pie.

"A thank you! To our wonderful wives. To the wonderful wives here who provided this fine meal, and for your sacrifice to travel the world with your loving husbands!"

Everyone claps. Men whistle. The wives smile and curtsy. They smile with their trays, their servitude evidence of their dedication to their husbands and the whaling industry.

"And to the captains! To our whaling fleet! We wish all the best of luck in this whaling season! Although we all know who'll bring home the prize for largest haul in!"

Everyone screams out the names of their ships. It ends in laughter.

"Desserts and drink for all!"

"Look at Gerald, little cunt."

He approaches the old wives, removes his hat, and bends forward, stiff and awkward. They offer another dessert. "You are a growing boy, more for the young man, he's got a healthy appetite," they say.

"Jesus, Gerald," we laugh. The boy walks away, eyebrows up, eating the dessert in one bite. He did this act another time, but for ginger ale.

The occasion takes an hour. Outside, it is night. The doors are wide open, but with the number of men in the room, we cannot feel the stab of cold air. We sat through a few servings. We drink a hooch made from distilled and fermented salmonberries found on the tundra. A bottle of whiskey made its way to our group. We swig and pass the bottle along in the spirit of sharing. Thank God! Whiskey. I feel the burn of whiskey in my cheeks, my body lighter, happier. Like Sten, I'm determined to find as much drink as possible for the night. Myself, I'd like candy from the store.

The violinist made his way into the center of the room. He started playing 'Oh My Darling, Clementine' and the captains sang, wives sang, whalers sang. We held up our drinks, if we held any, men sway, hold each other's shoulders, and we belt out the song. We sing 'Oh Susannah' and 'My Bonnie Lies Over the Ocean'.

The Elder wife speaks to the wives. "Ladies, let's leave the men to their drinking. Join me for tea."

All the wives stand.

"It is late."

"I need rest."

"Our boys need to let out this energy before returning to sea."

"Don't drink too much, lads. Save your strength for the days ahead."

We thank all the wives and commend their dishes.

"Thank you, ladies, for the wonderful food and delightful company," Merihim says.

"You two are gentlemen. Bring your lovely wife next year."

"We are off in the morning. We have to catch up on our stores."

After the wives depart, we get our leave.

We leave the overheated main hall, leaving the singing captains, out into the crisp cold night, stars shining ahead. We stream outside and head to the tavern or store, to find women, find the church, or find food.

24 | NALUAGMIUT TOWN

WE ARRIVE AT THE NALUAGMIUT TOWN AT NIGHT, driven by the dull lavender glow of the town reflecting against the ocean and night sky, visible from miles away. We watch Herschel from the ocean. The town spurts with gunshots. The island is alive, crawling and infested with Yankees.

The boys stare and speak to each other.

"There it is."

"There are so many ships. I've never seen so many ships or white men."

"You think she's there?"

"She has to be."

"We have to go anyway."

"Do you see her ship?"

"I don't know. We must go anyway."

"Are you scared?"

"Yes."

"Me too."

Nasau spoke. "All of you are brave. Braver than I was at your age."

"No one is braver than you. Boys? Do you want to wait on the beach?" I ask the boys.

"Aaka, no!" They said.

"I don't want you to wait either. Stay with me. Don't say any-thing. Follow everything we do."

"Aaka, is the ship here?"

"I don't know, son. Don't leave my side."

We row passed the anchored ships, away from the heavily peo-pled cove, where the Nalaugmiut men pulled up their little wooden boats. We land, instead, on the south beach, farther from the cove. Across the channel are vast marshes, barely visible from the ocean.

"Leave everything." Nasau says.

We leave everything and start our walk to town.

We smell the town long before arriving.

Baleen dries nearby, in vast quantities. We recognize the smell. We dry baleen for weirs and baskets. All the flesh must be scrapped from the baleen, or it goes bad and the baleen becomes useless. The whalers dry the baleen in barrels, sticking upright like fields of grass. The flesh rots somewhere nearby, putrid, overpowering, and inescapable.

Along with the stench, added to rotting flesh is human excre-ment. The Nalaugmiut foul the outskirts of town, using the tun-dra as an outhouse. We walk through the tundra, watching our footsteps, avoiding human feces. Reminds me of walking in a bog, mud up to the ankles, surrounded by flies and mosquitoes.

"Yuck!"

"This is disgusting."

A white man walks into the tundra, away from the closest tent. He staggers, heaves over, and vomits. We walk around him in a big circle. He wipes his long hair back and then heaves over again. His shirt is many different colors, cranberry, green, yellow, and black, twined together in lines and angles.

The main pathway is a winding river, crawling with a thousand Yankee men and women.

The greying shacks face the road, built close together. White canvas tents fill in the gaps between the wooden shacks, muddy almost all the way to the roof. We walk past a burnt down tent, nothing left but charred bits of canvas and crumbling rotten wood. We see the ships anchored in the bay, the ships looming over the town.

Fires are lit every few feet, it seems, fire pits, chimneys, smoke clouds, lamps, even torches lit in the streets. They shoot guns into the air. Why do they do this?

A hundred years ago, Tikigaq was twice the size of this town. We had six clans. Each clan owned a whaling site, each whaling site marked with the tall, arced jawbones of the bowhead. I've heard stories of houses upon houses, the beach lined with drying racks, and fields of sled dogs.

Nasau pokes her head into the tents. She scowls at any man who stares at her. When men get too close, she pushes them away. Move, she says. We wait on the road for her.

In the tents, we see shadows of men and women. A man and woman roll on a cot, laughing, falling against the tent wall, shaking the whole tent. A man opens the tent door, and we see it's an eskimo woman and Naluagmiut man. Another man in the tent stood up and began undressing. His companions yell, pushing him away but he continues until he's naked. His friends throw ale and beer while others cheer. The naked man stumbles outside the tent, teeters, not focusing, and runs towards the harbor.

In another tent, a small fire starts. Men kick up sand. Outside the tent, a man masturbates.

A man stops. He removed his hat, a strange wide hat, and held it to his chest. He smiles at me. I know this smile, a wanting smile. He asks a question in his language but I ignore him. I give him a look of disgust and shield his expression from the boys with my arm. He scowls. When Nasau arrives, she spits at his feet, and pushes him aside with one arm. Men laugh. He looks around, pretending to laugh with the other men.

Nauraq holds my arm with both hands, shoulders curled downwards.

"It's alright, son. You're fine. Stand up straight. Do not be afraid."

He let go of my hand but stays close behind.

Nasau pushes us onward. "Don't stop. Keep going. Don't try to understand white men. They don't make sense."

A bit further, a bright building shines light from every window. The door is propped open. It is a store. Men stand in line at the counter. The wall is lined with arctic fox, red fox, wolves, wolverines, and polar bear. One worker is a native man wearing a white man's shirt and hair cut like a white man.

There are glasses on the counter, empty, stacked side-by-side. The boys touch the glasses. "What is it?"

"Boys. C'mon." I'm pulling at their arms. "Think of your sister."

A few buildings down, there is a large building with a mass of men. The men sing songs. They stand in groups, drinking.

I hide the boys in the shadows. Nasau pushes through the crowd.

I can't tell how long we've waited. My heart is beating. I watch every man who passes.

She emerged from the large building, unharmed, untouched. She shook her head.

"Nothing but old men and old women. There's a church. Look," She says.

"What?"

"A church." She walks across the street. We follow.

"Nasau, we can't stop."

"I know. We won't."

The door opens as we cross the street, a wooden cross nailed to the door. A man walks outside while another man walks in. It is a small one-room house with a wood stove and six benches facing the front wall. A lantern glows in a small window. They stack firewood under the eave, almost to the roof. They built steps up to the doorway, an elevated entrance.

The wife, I assume his wife, holds the door open for the visitor. She is a tall, muscular woman, like Nasauyaaq, maybe in her late forties, yet still a young face. She wears a long floor-length skirt with tiny pale flowers, and a dark wool scarf over her shoulders. The woman has large healthy arms that could crush a man.

The preacher steps out into the doorway. He is silver-haired and tall but a young face, too. He wears wire-rim glasses and a wool shirt. He smiles. Both husband and wife have the soft, supple skin of youth, unlike the callousness of whalers, the sunspots, wrinkles, and wreckage of booze on their faces.

The wife asks me a question. I shake my head and hurry the boys along. She wants something. What is it? Nasau grabs the cross around her neck, which the woman notices. Nasau grabs the woman's hand and says something in Yankee. I don't know what it is. It is a few words. The couple smiles and shakes their heads. We leave.

"What did you say to them?"

"I said the name of the Lord."

"Why?"

"Intuition."

We leave the husband and wife. They watch, hoping we'll return.

A small group of eskimo children cross the street. I'm trotting. I'm jogging. The children walk off the street, down into the tundra. Nasau and the boys jog after me.

I stop the children. They stop and look up.

"Oh. I thought you were someone else," I say.

They leave, walking towards a group of eskimo tents. We follow the children. We see other Indigenous peoples outside the tents.

"Say nothing about Samaruna. Some of them work for the ships," Nasau says.

The natives camp together. There are different tents from different areas: circular tents of the Inupiaq, birch tents of the Koyukon, octagonal yurts of the Siberian, oblong tents of the Inuit, and a lean-to made of long, skinny spruce poles. Every tent is sagging, rotten, and musty. A few dogs are chained up behind their tents, not enough to make one team. There is something strange in the air around these sullen tents.

A woman sits at the fire with her dog. The boys stop to pet the large dog. Nasau walks further to talk to a group of eskimos.

"Hi. Hi. Hello, relatives. It's a MacKenzie river husky. Pure breed," She says to the boys.

"He's huge," Nauraq says.

The woman seems too comfortable, too much at home. How could any people live this way, living in mold, feet covered in mud, with drunk men buzzing like insects? The boys notice the smell, too. They don't say anything about the smell. I've taught the boys to be polite.

"Where are you from?" I ask.

"My home is gone. Your boys?"

"My sons."

"Take care of your Aaka, you hear?" She speaks loud and murky, as if she's been drunk for a week and now waking up. Or, like an obnoxious child who's never been disciplined, never shown how to speak politely and respectfully. She lights a pipe and offers it to me. I decline, smiling.

"I'm glad to see relatives here. I didn't think I'd see many Inupiaq people," I say.

"More people are working. We need work. Too many problems."

"Are there more camps in town? More eskimos?"

"No. This is the only one. Looking for someone?"

"No. Wondering what's in town. My boys want to go to the store."

"They got peppermint candy. Yummiest candy. Your boys, they'll like peppermint candy." She speaks to the boys like they're infants while she smokes her pipe.

"Are ships looking for workers?"

"Ships always looking for eskimo workers. They'll get you what you want."

"What I want?"

"The vaccine. You looking to work for the vaccine?"

I don't know what to say. We got ours free. I don't want to embarrass her. I'm flustered. "Yes. For all three. Me and the boys. How do we get on the ship?"

"Talk to a captain. Ask any Yankee here. They'll find you a captain."

Nasau returns. Nasau wants to continue through the town.

I stand. "Sorry, we must leave. We can't, we can't lose our friend. Enjoy the evening. Boys."

Nasau whispers. "There's a tavern. Where the Naluagmiut get their drink. Let's see if the crew is there." She looks back at the eskimos. "Cowards. When I was a child, cowards ran away from battles. Now cowards run away from themselves."

In a bend in the street, two women walk by in long, billowy skirts, covered head to toe in fabric. Even their necks are covered in fabric. The boys stare at their clothes. The women smile. I looked at their faces, their eyebrows, and their skin. They smile at me, as well.

The older woman stands with hands clasped together. The younger woman, sun kissed and slender, offers her hand to Nauraq. She wore gloves made of green leather. Green! He smiles and shakes her hand. "Look at her hair. Her hair is yellow, Aaka!"

"Shhh. Be nice," I smile.

The women smile and leave. The boys watch them walk away.

We reach the largest tent, loud with laughter, music, and glass breaking. Men stagger outside into the street.

"Wait here. On the side," Nasau says.

We watch through a slit in the tent. It's smoky. A hundred men squeeze into this tent. An iron stove heats the room and lamps burn at every table. Men line up to buy drinks. Two men guard the casks, taking money, one with a curled-up moustache and black hat. A man serves steaming seal flippers to hungry men.

I search the room for my daughter. She is not here.

White women and native women dance in the center, stomping in unison on a wooden floor. They laugh and push each other, fighting for attention on the dance floor. The women are drunk. All of them. A red-haired white woman dances in a worn skirt, pale breasts overflowing a corset, hair curled and wild, and her cheeks painted with bright red rouge.

I recognize an Inupiaq woman. She swings around the dance floor, laughing, spilling her drink. She is my age, where is her husband? When the music stops, she sits on a white man's lap.

I've admired her since we met. She makes friends quickly, she knows how to speak to other women, not like me, not like my quiet self. Isn't she afraid of the Naluagmiut?

Naluagmiut music plays: A fiddle, Inupiaq drum, and other instruments I don't recognize. Men stand up to the music, place their hands over their heart, singing and swaying. Other men stand up, raise their fists, and yell in their face. I don't know why they'd get angry over a song.

The song ends. Another song begins while the fighting continues.

It took a moment before Nasau pushed through the doorway. She makes her way around the room. Men whistle at her. A bald man offers her a drink. She ignores him.

My hands shake. There he is, the tall lanky captain wearing navy wool cap. I see his face. I finally see his face. A strange light hits him. The dancing women keep getting in the way.

He sits in the chair with no knowledge of my presence. No knowledge of Sam's mother who chases him, standing in a dark alley. He leans against a table, unmoved, stable, like he draws strength from the tavern's chaos.

"Aaka? What's wrong? Is it her?"

"Sam isn't here. Where's Nasau? Where'd she go?"

"I thought I saw her leave."

"She was there. I just saw her. Let's go. If Sam isn't here, then she is on the ship. Or in a tent."

"But we checked all the tents."

We hurry down to the cove. The street ends at the makeshift harbor, where the white men store their little wooden boats, leaning on the sands. Little boats arrive in a hurry to join the festivities while other men stock up their departing boats.

I search through all the ships in the cove. I see her ship. I see it. "That's her ship! She must be on the ship."

"Aaka! Let's wait for Nasauyaaq. Wait!" Nauraq clings my arm.

I see a little wooden boat arrive at Sam's ship. A dark figure climbs her ship.

"Who is it?" Ebrulik asks.

"I can't tell. It's too dark. We'll wait for Nasau. She must know to find us at the harbor. She must know. I didn't see her leave the other way. No, she wouldn't go the other way."

We sit in the shadows, watching all the men arriving and departing. The boys yawn. They've been awake all day, now through the late night.

"Rest your eyes. I'll look out for her," I say.

"Now? I can't sleep," Ebrulik says.

"It's late. It's alright. I'll watch for Nasau. She must be coming."

The boys didn't want to sleep but they listen. As dawn rises, the town quiets. It is peaceful even. When Nauraq was a baby, I'd walk him on my back underneath my parka in the early dawn hours. He was a fussy baby, so I'd walk him to sleep.

Nauraq fell asleep, then Ebrulik. I sat with Nauraq's head on my lap as the sun peeked over the horizon. The horizon burst with coral, blushing pinks, and blooming lavenders against the blackest black. Dawn is another world, another existence, something sacred. Fog rolls in from the sea. Soon the dawn will be overcome with fog.

Where can she be? Damn it! Why would she leave? All this psychotic waiting, an air of lunacy swirling around my head. I sigh again and notice I'm brushing Nauraq's sweaty head over and over. I need to get on the ship. I'll wake the boys and tell them to wait for me by our umiaq. I'll climb the ship. It's still dark enough to sneak onto the ship.

"Boys. Boys. Wake up."

Ebrulik's eyes open. "Did she come? Did you find her?"

"No. Nauraq, wake up."

"Aaka! Aaka!" Ebrulik runs down the beach.

"Wait! Son!" I pull Nauraq to his feet, his eyes opening as he stands, and we run after Ebrulik. What is he doing? I can't see anything.

Ebrulik stops, bends over, and pulls her body up the shore. He pulls Nasau out of the waves. She's drenched.

"She's alive. She's alive," I say.

Her lips are blue. She holds the cross around her neck, clutching it. She holds her torso with the other hand. I pry her hand away. Her torso is sliced open, skin white around the wound, pink and lavender organs bulging outwards. "She was there. I told her to get off the ship. She's there. She's on the ship. I told her to get to land. You'll get her back. Are you listening, Kaya?"

"I'm listening. I'm here." A seal's insides are identical to a person's. I've butchered enough seals to know her liver and stomach will not function. She spits blood.

"I'm sorry. I'm sorry."

"Don't apologize. We couldn't have made it without you."

"She was there. She was on the ship. I went to the ship. I told her to jump. I told her, your Aaka is here."

"What do I do? How do I get her off the ship?"

"Don't give up. She's there. She knows. They're here. They're dancing for me."

"Does she want the holy man, the preacher? From town?" Nauraq asks.

"Yes. You're good boys. Wait. A moment longer."

"Nasauyaaq. Nasauyaaq. I love you, Nasauyaaq. Thank you. Thank you." Her eyes empty. I close her eyes. I hold her to my chest. We sit for a few moments. I know I can't wait any longer to board the ship. "Boys. Get the preacher."

The boys run off to the church.

Sam is on the ship. I must try. She is there. My baby is there. I place Nasau down on the sand and shut her eyes. I grab her knife. I wait until the boys are far out of sight. I find a white man's boat and row out to the harbor. Damn it! What do I do? She went on board. They killed her. They killed her!

I see the ship. I hear arguing. Shouting. Damn it! Is it all the crew?

They stand on guard. I stop. They stop. I row to another ship, an empty ship, a ship with no men on deck. I pass out of their sight.

I hear the crew before I see them. The entire crew returns to Sam's ship. It can't be! It's not true! Please don't let it be true!

They row out to her ship and start boarding. The men on deck point at me. I can't do anything except row.

Ebrulik and Nauraq pace the shore with the reverend and his wife. She clutches a scarf around her body. The boys wave their arms. The husband and wife preacher kneel by Nasau's body.

"Where did you go? Aaka!"

"I'm sorry. I'm sorry! Boys, we must go." I kiss Nasau's forehead again. The wife looks at me. I look at her. I thank her. She nods her head.

We launch, leaving Nasau with the reverend and wife.

"What is happening," Ebrulik asks.

"The ship is leaving! Row, son!" I say.

The ship pulls their boats up on deck. The deck fills with men. Men with guns appear, watching our little boat. Two men aim their guns at our boat. I see the captain's face. He sees mine. He stares, those evil eyes and dark beard.

"What do we do?"

"I don't know. Stop! Boys! Stop!" We're too close to their ship. On other ships, other men watch from their decks. We see them, watching. Crowds of men watch from their ships but do nothing. I'm shaking. I look at their faces.

The anchor pulls up from the water. The engine starts. Water spews underneath the ship. They're leaving! The ship leaves the harbor and we row after them.

"Aaka!" I hear her on deck.

"Sam? Samaruna! Jump into the water! Jump, baby!" We stand up and tell her to jump.

The captain grabs her, kicking and screaming. She kicks and hits. How small she looks against the Yankee captain and how much she's grown in a month. She looks both small and grown at the same time. She's gone. Her screaming disappears.

Our boat rocks in the curls left behind by the ship, a trail of white water, "We lost her."

The ship disappears in the fog. She disappears in the fog.

I collapse.

Where am I? What day is it? My ears ring loud, sharp, and monotone. I'm face down in a wooden boat. My face is wet. I wipe my face. Salt water. I look up without moving. I see my boys. I see foggy sky. My boys cry. My boys clutch each other. They stare into the same direction. I push myself up and look in the same direction. I cry, too.

My husband. My love.

At dawn, on the thirty-seventh day of leaving Tikigaq, outside the white man's town on Herschel Island, we are found by my uncle Ataŋauraq who travels with five umiaqs, two qayaqs, and a total of thirty-four men and women. He yanks me from my seat, along with our sons.

"She wandered too far. I let her wander too far! I wasn't watching!" I cry.

"You're with me now. Shush."

Ataŋauraq opens his sails made of ugruk skins, and we sail west to Siberia, following Samaruna's ship.

25 | Tattooed Man

⌄

M Y UNCLE ATAŊAURAQ HOISTS THE SAILS FROM THE REAR. He
tests his rudder and rests his paddle within reach.

Ataŋauraq is a replica of my dad. He's grown more grey hairs,
now greying on his brow. My dad and Ataŋauraq leg-wrestled,
arm-wrestled, pushed against each other in competition like caribou bulls fighting over a cow. They compared their arms side-by-
side, brothers' camaraderie ending in jokes. They didn't compete in
life, except these innocent amusements. Ataŋauraq carried me on
his shoulders as a child. He propped me on a shoulder and my sister Qiviu on the other, a show of power and gaiety. He took me rabbit hunting in the year of plentiful rabbits. We waited in a bright,
ornate dawn, ready to tug a long twine coiled as a rabbit trap con-
cealed in alder saplings.

"Stay with me. You and your children," he says.

"I will."

He comforts me with a smile and then he looks up at his tanned
sealskin sails. We marvel at his sails together. "Beautiful, aren't
they? I got the sails from Kiŋigin. Your boys grew fast. Look at
them. Tall as me! Tall as their ataata. They are young men. Boyers.
My new boyers!"

I don't look, but I feel my sons smiling. "How far is it to Siberia?" I ask.

"Days. Get some rest. The currents do the work. Sleep, panik." He's called me his daughter since I was born. He bundles me up to the neck in polar bear and seal skins. Ataŋauraq pats my cheek with his calloused hand, his veins thick as blueberry branches. I feel a tinge of peace, a flimsy shard of peace fluttering its way to life. I forget everything for a short moment, semblance of my former peaceful life. He smiles like my dad. I cry. "My panik. Don't cry." I can't stop weeping. A thousand regrets are planted in my heart, spread like spores, growing viscid roots, gnawing my heart like weeds.

Eventually, I close my eyes. I hear calls of beluga in the sea, reverberating under the umiaq's ribbed frame, mixed with the sound of whipping sails. I dream of water creatures swimming on my arms, creatures with oily skin and protruding spines.

I awake to a starry sky. The fog cleared away. Radiant stars illuminate the sky in spiraling and metallic fronds, flowering with silver petals. My love, are you there? Are you listening to me? Do you see me? Do you think of me at every moment of the day like I think of you? Watch over our children.

My mother saw a rock fall from the sky in a plume of fire. She felt the rock hit the earth. Boom. Rock, stones, and earth flew upwards, a circular splash. The smoking rock melted permafrost. Half of the rock was filled with holes, the other half was a strange deep blue, like ice in the water, the turquoise of icebergs. They chipped pieces away from the rock and made them into beads. Where are my mother's beads? I check my neck. No. I left them, another thing lost.

I kneel and take up a paddle. We sail in a gentle current, slower than earlier, but steady. There are five people in this umiaq: my uncle Ataŋauraq, my cousin Nasugluk, and two others I haven't met before. Their names are Ivisaak and Atanik.

Nasugluk is six years younger than me. I chewed his food when he was a baby. I carried him on my back. He was a chubby, happy baby. His mother was Koyukon and Gwich'in. She died giving birth

to him. I met her when I was a baby and have no memory of her. I
know she loved my mother and my father.

Nasugluk's harpooned whales since he was 15 years old. His
lips are pieced with labrets when not all young men pierce with
labrets anymore. This is the Yankee-influence. They see drawings
of young people wearing black and white clothing and wide gowns.
He's not moved by anything from the Yankees except the harpoon
darting guns.

Nasugluk wears his hair long like his Koyukon and Gwich'in
people. When he's not hunting, he wears moosehide clothing. He
doesn't mix land animals with sea animals in clothing, our Inupiaq
way. Nasugluk hardly sleeps, even as a child. He wakes in the early
hours and learned not to wake others. He's stealthy and camou-
flaged as a hunter.

The men lecture the boys about the stars. The boys look up,
pointing.

It is a strange feeling to float in the sea at night, no land in
sight. I search all directions. It smells salty and briny like soggy
salt-laden driftwood. But I see nothing but water.

I listen to men talking. They speak of everything, finding a
wife, hunting, and raising their children. In these moments, I find
glimpses of peace.

"The boys want to know how to read the stars, and they like
the dog."

"Ha! Of course. They're interested in the dog." A dog sat at the
bow, panting at the wind.

"Ebrulik! Look at the dog! Do you see him," Nauraq says.

"That's Kik. She's a good boat dog," Ataŋauraq says. The dog sits
on a pile of packed furs, sitting high in the boat.

"Did it take long to train her like that?" Ebrulik asks.

"I don't know. You'll have to ask Atnatchiaq."

The boys smile. "Aaka! I learned the constellations sikupsikkat
and tuvaurat."

"Yes. It'll be a hard winter," Ataŋauraq says. "There is a great battlefield among the stars. By the sun and moon and stars, our Creator
leads a great war against evil. Your father and aapa fight with them,"

"A war?" Nauraq asks.

"A battle between good and evil. We witness evil spirits on earth. Evil spirits scare away the animals or bring in bad weather. They're creating chaos and mischief. We have great warriors—our Ancestors, our peoples, like your father and aapa. The Creator sometimes takes the strongest young men and women while the decrepit live long lives, because they are needed to fight a bigger battle, an unseen battle. A war spanning generations. Mourn their passing. Remember their good deeds. Pray for their families, but honor their crossing. They're warriors. They fight for you and me on a great battlefield."

The boys smile at the sky, and at Ataŋauraq.

"We looked for you at home," I say.

"We were a few weeks behind you. We first saw your tracks at the mesa. The storm wiped every track."

I pieced their story together over the following days. They traveled on the coastline, first going northeast to Kali, Ulguniq, and Utqiaġvik, traveling on the northern sea, and then south on the Kukpiik river. They believe the sickness began in Port Clarence, but no one could be certain. They were far inland when they heard of Samaruna.

Some camps are nothing but corpses. Men died outside pushing their young ones to the cemetery. They hunted sheep in the mountains, taking a hunter's trail. They found a young girl up there who died by herself. They couldn't tell if it was a girl or boy at first. She curled up and looked like a ball of fur. She wasn't wearing a parka. She was infected. Probably went there to keep her people from getting sick.

She wasn't wearing a parka. I wanted to dress dad in the finest clothes for his burial, but he wanted me to leave him. He bled from his eyes, ears, mouth, crotch, in his vomit and feces. He didn't want his fine parka in death. I burned their bodies dressed in rags while the Yankees bury their dead with riches. I pray Death carries the Yankee secrets to the other world.

"It is not the last days of our people. Sedna fights for Her people in the underworld," Ataŋauraq says.

"How did you know where to find us? How did you know we were at Herschel?" I ask.

"Driggs. The Reverend Driggs. He sent messengers."

The white man, the holy man at Tikigaq sent messengers. Thank you Reverend Driggs.

He gives me a seaglass and points south. I see a glowing arc on the horizon, small and fragile, a lantern glowing on the sea.

"A ship?"

"Yes. There's another in the north. We need to stay out of sight from the ships until we reach her ship."

"Will we see Siberia soon?"

"Siberia is miles away. Let's not lose sight of the ships."

"Yes. Yes. I don't want to lose sight of the ships."

"Will we fight the Siberians?" Ebrulik asks.

"Yupiks, they are called. We fought the Siberians a long time ago. They might be more peaceful towards Inupiaq people now because of the Yankees. We're not equipped to fight with the Siberians now. We're not here to steal. We'll avoid them, if we can. Our aim is Samaruna. Nothing more, but if we do see the Yupiks, we'll find a wife for my son."

"You first, uncle. No more being a bachelor," I say. I didn't mean this as a joke, but everyone laughs, including my uncle. He doesn't mind people poking fun at him. Instead, he laughs with people.

I'm fearful of the ocean. I've known strong young men who've drowned at sea, caught in the strong curling surf, overcome by the stark cold waters.

A few years ago, five men from Kiŋigin drifted away on an ice floe while hunting for seals. They regarded the men as dead, repercussions of unpredictable ice.

The five Kiŋiginmiut survived three weeks on the ocean. They attempted to harness pieces of ice, thinking they could tow the ice and slow their northward movement, but they couldn't get close enough to the icebergs. They managed to save their weapons, including long-staffed hooks, which they decided to use as a rudder. If they could not stop their northward drifting, then they must steer eastward.

When it snowed, they collected snow for fresh water. They later discovered fresh water on their ice floe, where rainwater collected, pooled, and froze over, yielding days of fresh water for all. They salvaged what they could, chiseling fresh water out of the salty sea ice.

They fished daily, without exception, even at night, and when forcible winds brought choppy water.

By the time they saw land, the ice floe eroded into little bigger than a sled.

"We'll have to swim," a Kiŋigin man said.

"We'll freeze! Even if we get to shore, we'll freeze on shore," another said.

"Do you want to die here?" He jumped into the frigid water.

They fought the currents to swim to shore, landing at Imnaqpait, near Tikigaq. They bartered passage to their home on a whaling ship.

Ataŋauraq proposes we find the ship and board at night. I don't protest. This is the best plan. We've got five rifles, two handguns, spears, axes, clubs, knives, and spare bullets. Ataŋauraq takes great care of the rifles, entombing the rifles in waterproof seal intestine hides. If he senses danger, he'll unwrap the hides and drape a tarp over them.

The sea bestows fine weather for the first three days. We're blessed with good, strong northern winds, pushing our umiaqs towards Siberia, the sun glaring against the water's surface. We tan like whalers. We milk every gust of wind, harnessing the wind even as we sleep.

There is water in the boat at every moment. I continue to dump water from a cup. I sit up on a small block of driftwood, positioned on the keel, enough to keep my body dry.

My challenge is keeping my feet from going numb. Without movement or ability to stand, my feet and calves grow numb with cold and inactivity. I switch from wedging my feet under my legs and stretching them straight outwards. Rowing in an umiaq for days is hard work on the knees.

I imagined the open ocean like a desert, void of life, empty, and nothing except waves. We see signs of life everywhere. Even though we cannot see land, gyrfalcons, peregrine falcons, eagles, hawks, murres, gulls, and kittiwakes fly in the southeast, showing the direction of land.

On the third day, we see a floating island of green seaweed, surrounded by circling, swarming seagulls. It is an odd sight, an entire floating forest of seaweed underneath the sea. A raven flies overhead, chasing the seagulls.

"A storm must've torn up the ocean floor somewhere in the south," Uncle says.

"A raven? This far out?"

"Birds have no limits."

"Raven is here, protecting me again," I say.

We adopt a strict routine. As the ships approach, we veer closer to land. We assess each whaling ship by sending the qayaqs, preferably during the night. Better to assess the ships at night as a precaution. The qayaqs ride ahead with our sea glasses, looking for the distinct sea serpent at the bow. They reconnoiter every ship, gathering how many men on board.

To our advantage, Yankees are ignorant about Indigenous peoples. They don't know the difference between Siberian, Yupik, or Inupiaq. If we're spotted, they don't know the difference. They see our boats from their seaglasses, and then ignore our presence.

We sometimes spot up to five ships in one day. I didn't know so many ships traveled through our seas, varying in size and shape. From land, it is easy to see but a fraction of the ships' numbers.

"You think the captain will be looking for me?" I ask.

"I wouldn't look for you. He's got no reason to fear. We pose no threat to them at all. This is good. He didn't see me with you. They won't expect you."

At least once a day we see a ship pulling up a whale. It is a sad sight. We don't like seeing the sacred whale pulled up in chains, sideways, drooping. Ships are like flies, hovering, finding a corpse, sucking up the corpse, eating, feeding, laying eggs, and leaving behind squirming larvae to further infect their presence.

Ataŋauraq teaches the boys how to navigate in an umiaq. Hold the oar with both hands about a forearm apart. Keep your hands light and loose. Thumb curled over. The blade of the paddle enters the water, but little more than the blade. The last part of the stroke is wasted energy, let go before the paddle emerges from the water. If you're going to capsize, level out the umiaq with a slap to the water. When we surf onto the beach, throw your weight forward. Sprint forward. To stabilize the boats over heavy waves, the man at the stern will drag.

Every morning, all day, they check the winds and currents. They obsess about our location, looking for any signs to indicate location.

Ataŋauraq possesses a map of the Siberian coastline, drawn on sealskin. He told me when he was a boy, he heard of a hunter who got lost on the ice. The man drifted away, ended up in Siberia. His wife thought he died. He wintered in Siberia with our enemies. He made friends with them. When the ice opened, the Siberians sent him home in a qayaq and a token of their friendship, a gift. They made sure he could find his way back to them. They tattooed the Siberian coastline on his back, so he knew how to return.

Ataŋauraq found this tattooed man. He's now an old man. No one asked to trace the tattoo until now, the old man said.

This is the moment. This is why the old man got lost at sea, wintered in Siberia, and returned home with a map. I must believe this is the reason.

26 | WHY STAY AWAKE

LEAVING HERSCHEL, THE CAPTAIN RAN THE ENGINES far longer than necessary, even after the little skin boat became a small dot and disappeared over the horizon, he continued to run the engine.

"Captain. The girl's mother." I say on deck. I stand erect. I look straight, stiff as a naval officer.

"Back to work, sailor." He says.

"The mother, sir." I prepare myself. I feel the air moving.

"Shit bastard son of a whore!" He kicks me in the back. I'm on deck. Damn, fucked up my back. My muscles cramp, all I can do is arc my back upwards. I groan through the pain. Remigio and Gerald help me down to the forecastle. Remigio shares a swig of gin, shaking his head. He's impressed but shakes his head.

The girl slept for two days.

"Is she dead?" Gerald asks.

"Nothing is wrong with her. No fever. No chills. Why stay awake? She sees her family in her dreams," I say.

"He can't find a girl in the states? Damn shame. Really damn shame," Remigio says.

"She needs water. Broth. Something."

We wet a cotton linen cloth and drip water into her mouth. She drinks the water but doesn't open her eyes.

The crewmen, all of us, we felt pity for the girl. How could you not? Any man with a heart in his chest felt her sorrow. Yet, we do nothing. Which pains me even more than seeing her sweating brow and motionless body. The men asked me about her condition throughout the day. Any movement yet? She awake?

Not a stir. Not a flutter of an eyelash. Her eyes move in her sleep, the only indication she lived. When the captain walked into the forecastle to check on the girl, we said nothing.

He saw the men's sideways glances. Never have I seen the captain take notice of the men's behavior.

"Well, the child must be growing. Isn't that what they say? A growing child needs rest." Merihim concludes. He struts around the forecastle, daring men to look him in his eyes, and leaves.

27 | STORMY SEAS

ON THE FOURTH DAY, WE BATTLE A STRONG HEADWIND. Because of the winds, we branch out, rowing in a scattered line. We fight to gain a few feet, then get pushed back a few feet. We drag in the troughs to level out. It is a frustrating day.

"Don't get discouraged, panik. We won't gain any miles today, but let's not drift back north!"

I'm elated when the wind softens. It grows warm. The weather could not be more ideal, but Ataŋauraq wants to talk with the other men.

"What are you thinking?" He asks them.

"Birds flying low," they said.

They look upwards to the sky, searching the horizon, and shaking their heads. The warm air is not a good sign. They want to find land in case of a storm.

"If there's a storm, we'll have to land," Ataŋauraq says.

"Away from the ships?"

"If the winds stay this direction, they'll be safest near Siberia. Don't worry, panik. Trust your uncle."

For a time, the winds remain warm and still. Everyone watches the sky. At first, the waves grew choppy. We bounced every few feet, rocking, whipping, and getting seasick, even those men accustomed to the sea. Seafoam spreads over the waves like webbing, dissipating, forming, and embellishing.

We saw the rain approaching.

Everyone gave their waterproof clothing to the boys, a few outercoats and tarps, raingear made from seal intestines. The boys wrapped themselves, but the oars continued to drip seawater down their sleeves.

We hunch over from the rain, paddling, soaked, and battling the waves. The waves, which were short and bumpy, now grew longer and higher, and we sled down into the trenches, the concave, the craters between waves, our stomachs churning. We carve oars into the waves as we descend, ready to counterbalance or correct any tilting.

I'm shivering. I'm drenched from the waist up. I can't hear anything from the other men and women. At times, I lose sight of the farthest umiaq.

My sons are seasick. They've done well on the water until now. They look small against the waves, paddling, and vomiting. They throw up until their stomachs are dry. I wish I could take away all their pains. For whatever reason, I'm unaffected by the motion. Distracted by the ships. Distracted by my sons' seasickness. I'm too absorbed in their pains for my own.

I see a strange sight. Waves standing still. We oared, fighting the waves, and not far away, waves seem to stand still, the current and winds fighting each other.

We hear rumbling in the sky. I've heard thunder, once in my life, long ago, in the far interior. Lightning started a fire in a spruce forest. It was the hottest of summers. We examined the scorched earth, grey, hot, and smoking. "Medicine," my father said. "Go to the forest after a fire. Gather the ashes of a birch. Look for coltsfoot. When coltsfoot is burned, it gives salt." I see flashes of him in the sunlight, smiling, looking back at me, the black skeletons of spruce behind him, and we search for ashes of birch and coltsfoot.

"Aaka?" Nauraq looks at me. The boys have not seen lightning in their lives.

"We're alright, son! Keep paddling," I say, trying to be heard.

"Land!" Ataŋauraq yells. I see the other men and women waving from the other umiaqs. I see the faint line in the distance. It is not far.

Lightning moves between the clouds in long skeleton hands. We cower. Nauraq covers his ears. Lightning strikes in the east. In the distance, I see a crater of water bulging upwards. In the lightning, I see flashes of beluga whales in the waves. Close. So close. They swim so close to our umiaqs, a wave away.

"Aaka! Aaka!"

"Row, son!"

"We can't land here! We're above a reef," Ataŋauraq yells. Coral could rip a hole in our umiaq. He motions to the others, but I don't know if they hear him. They follow, nonetheless.

We fight south along the coastline until dark.

The waves let up, gentle, and more gentleness.

"We're in a bay. Can you feel it?"

"Yes." I can't tell by the waves if we're in a bay, but I'm too exhausted to explain.

"We're here. We're at Siberia."

At first, I see nothing, blackness in more black. Then I hear the surf, a faint rumor, like a tinge in the winds. I see the crest line, shoals of white surf.

All umiaqs reached the bay. We land, one by one, guiding each other, and dragging the umiaqs up on shore.

"Be careful. Not a sound," Ataŋauraq says.

We stand together on the Siberian shoreline, feet submerged in shallow water, standing on a seabed of rounded stones. Even as we stand drenched and shivering on the beach, we don't move. I hold Nauraq around his shoulders.

Up further, slabs of rock cover the beach. We look up to the dark lines of the beach, listening through the winds. I imagined landing in Siberia and hordes of Siberians flooding the beach, ready to fight. For centuries our people have died on Siberian shores or drown in their waters.

Ataŋauraq and two other men walk up the rocky slabs, taking the first sacred steps into Siberia, up the stony beach, and onto dark ridges. We observe them walking from north to south. We wait. They make no sudden movements. They walk down together.

"There is nothing," a man says.

"We'll camp here, up there," Ataŋauraq says.

We prop the umiaqs upside down, propped up on driftwood, and secure tarps for shelters. The boys dig for dry twigs and dry moss underneath hanging crags on the beach. I hang all the boys clothes underneath the umiaq, and I help the men and women hang their clothes.

The boys are now feeling better. They drink water, silently sharing a bag of water. Now I feel sick. I feel the movement of the ocean in my legs. I feel the swaying waves in my body, pulsating, beating like another heart. A few times, I slipped down to the ground.

The boys and I wander up on a tiny, flat knoll covered in stunted spruce trees, over the slabs of rock, on a small hill. I spot a small patch of crowberries and pick a few handfuls for my sons. At home, the women must be picking akpiks, blueberries, and crowberries, spending days on the tundra, muskeg, and bogs. We pick every day, even when it rains. Picking berries during a sunny day is better, but we pick berries anyway. We can use them to make a jelly. Early autumn is a precious season.

"Boys, time for bed," I say. I sit, waiting for the boys to lie down.

Ataŋauraq crouches down, arms on his legs, thoughtful. Just like dad. "Seems like a dream. I've wanted to travel to Siberia since I was a boy," he says.

"Did our aapa come here?" Ebrulik asks.

"No."

"No. We're the first to visit Siberia for many, many generations. You'll tell your children about this night. Me and your aapa talked about coming here. He wanted to hunt for reindeer. Your dad built a tiny paddle raft, but it sank almost as soon as it hit the water. We took it out to the lagoon. I laughed and he ran home crying. Poor brother."

"Will we hunt reindeer?"

"On the way home."

"After we get Samaruna."

"After we get Samaruna."

"Where are they? Looks like no one lives here."

"I don't know. Maybe they got the sickness, too."

"What will we do if we see them?"

"I don't know. We'll decide when we see them. First, we must be friendly. Close your eyes."

"Ataata. Are you afraid?" Nauraq asks Ataŋauraq.

"Yes."

"Me too."

"It's alright to be afraid. I'm afraid of spiders," Ataŋauraq says.

"Spiders?"

"They move too fast."

"I'm not afraid of spiders. I'll get them for you."

"Good."

"Will you watch for Siberians in the night?"

"I'll stay awake for a while. I'm a light sleeper. Sleep, little man," Ataŋauraq leaves, checking on the others.

I listened in my sleep. I heard others stirring, too. We slept light.

I'm the first to wake in the morning. I woke to a fog-laden dawn, misty, drizzling, and wet. This is the foggy season. Fog rolls in and stays for weeks at a time. I walk farther up the beach and see tundra as far as I can see. I see nothing on land. I cannot see far into the ocean, but I hear the creaking ships, their coal engines. I know they are there in the fog.

I start a small cooking fire. I boil water for tea. I cut dried meat and maktak. Ataŋauraq joins me at the cook fire. "I sent my friend Ina to deliver the vaccines to your dad. I don't know why he didn't make it. I didn't know about, well, I didn't find out about my brother until Driggs. I'm sorry. I'm sorry. I could have delivered them myself. Nasugluk won't forgive himself. I told him to trust Ina. I needed him on the trail. It's my fault. It's all my fault."

"Don't blame yourself. There is no one to blame. I could have gone north. I talked about it with my husband. There wasn't enough time."

We cry together.

Afterwards, Nasugluk arrives. He hugs me awkwardly. Nasugluk doesn't know how to comfort people, like me, I don't know how to comfort people. He asks questions like, "Are you thirsty? Are you warm? Are you hungry?" He is like me, in this way. Other people rid their sadness through speaking, giving their grief outwards into the world. We try to make things as normal, the way things were before the sadness. It is our way of coping.

"The ships won't move far in the fog, but we can. Let's see what we can see" Ataŋauraq says.

"Yes," I say.

The men and women in our umiaqs are from all over. Nuataam Kuuŋa, Tikigaq, Kali, Qikiqtaġruk, Utqiaġvik. I thank them all. I draw a serpent in the sand, the serpent on the ship's bow, for all the people to memorize.

Siberia looks like home. Somehow, I thought the sands would be darker and softer, the water sweeter and clearer, the winds gentle and warmer. It's the same, but backwards. It's opposite, a mirror-image, and disorienting.

I imagine the Siberians build weirs in this cove, trapping fish in shallow waters, even driving belugas with their spears. Everyone searches the ground, looking for a small token, a stone, clear rock, a shell, a seal's bleached vertebrae disc. We want to remember this day. It isn't long before we get the umiaqs ready.

"No one volunteered to travel with you to Herschel? Savikmun?" Ataŋauraq asks.

"Savikmun wasn't home, maybe went to find husbands for his daughters. A woman helped us."

"Who? Where is she now?"

I couldn't answer. Not for a few hours.

"The Yankees killed her. She helped us, and they killed her," I say.

"Who was she?"

"Nasauyaaq."

"Nasauyaaq?"

"You knew her?"

"She's older than me? Scar on her neck."

"Yes. Yes."

"How did you find her? Did you know her before?"

"We ran after the ship, and she was on the beach. She got a new net. I think she was getting ready to fish."

"Accidentally ran into her? You didn't know her before this?"

"No. Didn't meet her before."

"She died fighting the Yankees? She fought them?"

"Yes. Yes. They killed her."

"How?"

"Cut her in the gut."

"Not by a gun?"

"I wasn't there. She went alone."

"By herself? Azaa. Did she kill any of the Yankees?"

"Yes. Seven. I mean, we both did."

"You, Kaya?"

"Yes. How did you know her?"

"I first met her when I was young. I won't forget first meeting her. I can't believe you traveled with Nasauyaaq. Nasauyaaq! What was she like?"

"A strong woman. A hunter," I say.

I tell Ataŋauraq how we ran into Nasau on the beach, how she helped trap the Yankees with seals, attack Yankees on the ice, climb their ship, how she traded her dogs for an umiaq, and climbed the ship by herself. It is a long story.

They tell stories of Nasau.

"When she was young, she fought in Siberia. My father was there. He saw it. He fought with her. There were three battles, two in Siberia, one in Qikiqtaġruk. A little south of Qikiqtaġruk, the year before, the Siberians raided a village. They killed men and took women and children. She got the scars on her neck in Siberia, at the last fight. They paddled passed a cape, passed tall cliffs. It was almost winter. The ground was cold already. Fat snowflakes that day. They saw people camped up on the cape. It's not good to fight uphill. They decided to climb up the cliffs, starting from their umiaqs in the sea. A surprise attack from behind, you see? It was hard climbing the cliffs. Nasau climbed with them. Other men, they landed on the beach. While the Siberians got their attention on our men on the beach, they climbed over the cliff. They started fighting. A few men got pushed into the ocean from the cliffs. Falling all the way down into rocks and water. Nasau had a boy on her back. A Siberian tried pulling the boy off her back while another man tried killing her. The boy hung onto her neck, scratching her neck. She killed both those men. They paddled for two days without stopping. By the time they looked at her cuts, they were infected. Green with puss. She fevered for days. My dad told me that story. She was a good woman. Nasauyaaq. A strong woman."

I cry thinking of this story, not in front of anyone, when night comes.

This afternoon, as we row along the Siberian coast, we see a reindeer herd on the beach. My heart stops. My sons perch on the edge of the umiaq. They run like caribou, thundering hooves on the land.

"Aaka! How many are there?"

"I don't know. Hundreds. Hundreds."

"So many."

"Aaka, are we going to get reindeer?"

"Ask your aatata. On our way back home, with your sister."

"We'll get skins for parkas. Skins for all of us."

"I'll sew fancy parkas for all my children."

"Can I hunt the reindeer myself?"

"Yes, by yourself."

Ataŋauraq talks of filling up the umiaqs with reindeer skins. They mark this spot on their map. Autumn is a good time to get skins. The animals' fur is thick and ready for winter.

"We haven't seen any Siberians. Maybe the sickness killed them all, like us. What life is left?"

"They'll be strong again. We'll be strong again."

"You sound like dad."

"He copied me. Trying to be like me. Who could blame him? I'm wise," Ataŋauraq laughs. "I'm going to miss your dad. He was my best friend, and a good man."

After seeing the reindeer, I dreamt the ship sails next to our umiaqs, shadowy, moaning, creaking, and vibrating in a low rumble. "The ship is here! It is here! Wake up!" I yell. I can't move. I hear the awful high pitch noise and I'm not able to move. Paralyzed, my mouth fills with sand, so much sand. I'm drowning in sand. Ataŋauraq shakes my shoulder. He doesn't say anything. I make sure I didn't wake up the boys.

The following day, we smell walrus in the morning. We know they're close. We hear the walrus barking across the water. Before long, we see the walrus herding up onto the beach. The herd is tremendous, hundreds, maybe thousands, I don't know. We row around the herd in a large arc. It is overwhelming.

"This is where the walrus migrate. This is where the walrus go," Ataŋauraq says.

"Aaka! Aaka! Is this all the walrus in the world?" Nauraq asks.

"I don't know. Seems like it."

We keep our distance from the herd. We fear walrus piercing holes in our umiaqs.

I see Siberians. I see a Siberian child, actually. I see a boy wearing a green cloth parka, waving, running on the beach after our umiaqs.

We stop.

Other children join. They're smiling until a woman screams. She scares the children, running and pushing the children along.

"Keep going?" I ask.

"It'll be better to stop. I don't want to keep looking behind for attacks. Better to talk to them," Ataŋauraq says.

"Do they know where we're from?" Ebrulik asks.

"They know," Ataŋauraq says.

"They look so much like Inupiaq people," Nauraq says.

"They do," I say.

"Will we go to them?"

"We can't now, son. On the way home we can. Let your aatata speak to them."

"Their village is right there! Can you imagine? Walrus outside your door," Another man says.

"They're hunting. See them?" I say.

The women butcher walrus on the beach, near our umiaqs, yet

the walrus do not budge on the other side of the herd, barking, snorting, and sunbathing.

We wait.

Two dozen Siberians gather on the beach, men, women, Elders, and children. Women grab their children to their sides. Men stand on the beach, armed with rifles, although they don't aim their rifles towards our boats. They're talking on the beach, gesturing about what to do.

The Siberians don't know how many weapons we carry. We're carrying weapons stashed in every crevasse, hold, and bend of the hull. We carry weapons on our backs, in our belts, and in our kamiks. We row with the spears against the keels, tucked underneath our feet. Within my reach, I've got an axe, knife, spear, and handgun.

"What will happen if they see how many weapons we have?" I ask.

"I don't know. I wouldn't trust them if we were in the same position."

A Yupik man asks questions of his companions. We listen. We watch his oratory.

I start singing my family's song. My sons start singing with me. Everyone joins. The song is well-known. My parents and grandparents dance this song at every annual whaling feast.

The Siberians stop talking while we sing. Afterwards, they sing a song. No one dances or beats a drum. I don't recognize any words, but it is moving. I don't know what to say.

A man rows out to the sea by himself, dressed in a blue cloth shirt and fur leggings. He's about Ataŋauraq's age. He looks like an Inupiaq man, copper skin from hunting on the ice, black reddish hair and brown eyes. It is his eyes that are different.

"They are Yupik or Chukchi. I don't know. Give him some maktak. Something," Ataŋauraq says.

I unwrap food. I give him maktak, a square piece, as big as a man's forearm. He recognizes the gift. He holds up the maktak for his people to see, his arms tattooed in dark, blue, thick symbols. He shouts at his people, smiling.

"I don't understand any of their language," Ataŋauraq says.

Other Siberian hunters row out together in one boat. A few smile. A few men are suspicious. A man in their umiaq bears small-pox scars. They've suffered from the sickness, too. A man presents a walrus heart, intestines, meat, and fat to Ataŋauraq.

Ataŋauraq shows him the map. The man in the blue shirt recognizes the drawing as a map right away. He points. It is choppy interaction.

With his hands, he asks where we are from.

"Tikigaq," Ataŋauraq points. "We follow Yankee ships."

He understands the word Yankee. Ataŋauraq imitated shooting a rifle at a Yankee ship. He understands.

"Yankee," he states. He speaks long sentences to his companions. He asks questions to his companions. We don't understand any words. I understand but two words. Yankee. Smallpox. Nothing else I understood.

"Yes, Yankee ships," Ataŋauraq points south with his entire hand.

Ataŋauraq asks to pass south using gestures. The Siberian nods his head. Ataŋauraq didn't need to ask him permission. We out-number the Siberians. It is an act of diplomacy.

We leave their beach, going south. Their umiaqs stay in the water. We were quiet for a while, watching if they'd follow our boats. They don't. They returned to shore and continue their hunt.

"You didn't ask for a wife," I say.

"Next time. Next time," Ataŋauraq says.

No one said anything more. Their peoples barely survive, like us. So little survived from the sickness.

28 | INTERPRETER OF DREAMS

IT IS NIGHT WHEN THE QAYAQS RETURN WITH THE NEWS about her ship. The night is moonless and starless. Clouds cover the sky from horizon to horizon.

"We will go tonight," Ataŋauraq says. "We'll land. We need to cache everything."

Husband, the time has come.

We land on a long stretch of beach, headlands faraway towards the south. High hillocks, not far up the beach, beyond a berm, will hide our supplies. We unpack our supplies up the berm, rushing, but not frantic.

"Don't tire yourself. Let your boys empty out the umiaqs," Nasugluk says.

We light small fires, heating water for tea and warming cold food. By the firelight, the boys learned how to memorize the land-marks, curves of the land, streams, and other grooves, in order to find our cache. They mark the shape of the land on rabbit skin and plant young saplings on top of the hillock.

The men smoke tobacco, drink coffee, and eat small por-tions of dry meat. A few men rest by the warm fire, shutting their eyes, but not sleeping. Others sharpen blades, load rifles, and fill up bullet bags with bullets.

"You can rest, if you want," Nasugluk says.

I shake my head, smiling, thankful for my cousin.

Uncle mixes a black gritty clay. He paints black lines down my chin over my tattoos and black dots across my cheeks. He paints a black band across my eyes, from my eyes to my forehead. He paints the boys with the same black band across the eyes and forehead, a way to find them, even in the dark. A woman braids my hair in tight braids, braiding hair away from my face. A few men shear down their hair, almost to the scalp.

We strip down to leggings and doe skin tunics, wearing as little as possible, leaving all heavy clothing on the beach. A few men go bare-chested.

I carry the axe on my back, the axe Nasau taught me to carry.

"You are certain you want them in the umiaqs? It is your decision," Ataŋauraq asks.

"Better to be by my side then left alone, wondering if their mother is alive. They'll stay hidden. They listen."

"Apologies, young men. I have to ask."

"They aren't offended. They'll follow directions, and they're good with a needle and thread."

"Good. Good. Whatever you decide, I'll support you. Young men. Come. Let me talk to you. If you want to see your sister by morning, listen to everything I say. Protect the umiaqs. You think protecting umiaqs is a child's errand. What if the umiaqs drifted away? What if they are shot through with holes?"

"We'll watch them," Ebrulik says.

"We have stories of young men like you. They used their wits, skills, and sometimes luck. They are watching over you. Listen with your heart. Spirits whisper to your heart, not your ears."

"Thank you," they say together.

Ataŋauraq leaves. The men and women make last checks of the umiaqs. We're ready to launch. I fasten the axe against my back, hang Nasau's polar bear club from my waist, and secure the handgun—stowed in a holster and slung around my torso.

I talk to my sons. "They want you to stay behind. That is our tradition, but I won't leave you."

"We'll stay quiet," Nauraq says.

"Your father fights to keep clouds in the sky, and to keep you safe. Your dad and I wanted to learn how to build sleds. We'll build a new sled when we get home."

"Alright," They say.

The boys leave to ready the umiaqs, mixing well among the men. I remember my children at the hands of the white men, which seems like a year ago, but not more than two months. I'm haunted at these memories, remembering how the white men circled and taunted my children. I memorized the figures of the Naluagmiut, bent, playful, evil, and towering. How delicate my children seemed. Look how much they've grown.

My husband, my light, my love, my everything. Help me. I'm terrified. I hear the rumbling of the ravine, the sounds of rock breaking against rock. I fight images of ravens pecking away at our flesh or crabs pulling apart our skin in the darkest ocean ravines. What a feast we'd make for the bottom-feeders. How should I be buried? If I burned on the pyre, floated on the sea winds, would we be reunited? No. No, my love. I'll be buried like our Ancestors so our children have a parent to mourn and lament and remember, a burial in which they can visit and heal themselves. You and I didn't speak of death or burials. There was no need.

Our sons do not tremble. If they are afraid, I cannot sense it. They are young but have the courage of men. When asked to stay behind, they weren't offended. They aren't drawn to anger like me, anger as a first response. They are more like you in that way. They left pieces of hair on the beach. They said it is for Sedna, for the Creator, and for their father. What wasn't braided tight against my scalp, I cut off. I give it all to you. Help me bring our daughter off the ship.

Creator, Sedna, Ancestors, spirits from the underworld, above-world, dual world, those old men and old women made young again, help me. Sharpen our eyes. Sharpen our senses. Prepare to fight the Yankee demons as we fight the Yankees possessed by demons.

I ride in an umiaq with Ataŋauraq and cousin. Without our gear, our umiaqs are light, speedy, and maneuverable. Our umiaq seems to leap out of the water with every row. We row over clear, black, marbleized waves, like volcano glass or the black chert from Qiqkiktavik. There are calm swells, the kind of night a fisherman seeks large halibut and bottom-dwellers.

"Nasau traveled these waters," Ataŋauraq says.

"Yes," I say.

"You were with her when she died?"

"She died a brave woman. She said do not accept the Yankee abuses. Do not accept the way we've been treated."

"Wise, brave, she will be missed."

For a time, everyone is quiet.

"We'll be home in time for berry-picking, and the last fish before winter."

"Let's hunt for reindeer on our way home."

"And a wife for Ataŋauraq."

Ataŋauraq laughs. Everyone laughs.

"My sons will join your whaling crew, Ataŋauraq. They are meant to be whaling captains. I'll be Ataŋauraq's age when they become whaling captains."

"You mean old?" he asks.

"Yes. I mean old, old man. My sons Ebrulik and Nauraq. Whaling captains. I'll naluktaaq. I'll throw skins of wolverines and wolves to the old women and give gifts to the old man Ataŋauraq and his many wives." Everyone laughs.

In these early hours, we hear beluga spraying water. We see their distinct backs on the water, surfacing, curling back downwards to dive. There is an ache to hunt the whales, but we continue rowing.

"What did you dream last night, boys," Ataŋauraq asks.

"My uncle is superstitious. Like an old woman. He wants to interpret your dreams," I say.

"I dreamt of a room underneath our house. It went far. All these rooms going way back. The room led to another room, then another," Ebrulik says.

The men and women say it's the Underworld. The spirits showing you their world. Ataŋauraq agrees.

"And you, Nauraq?"

"I lost my kamik. My aapa was helping me find it."

We rally. A good omen, to dream of late relatives.

"Both of you had fortunate dreams. A room underneath your house. A dream about my brother. My brother would be proud. Proud of his daughter. Proud of his grandsons."

"Do you hear it?"

"A hawk?"

"An eagle."

In the night sky, we hear an eagle calling above the clouds. First, we heard the beluga, and now we hear an eagle. Good signs.

We spot the glimmer of a lamp. No one speaks. We ride the hills of ocean, following the lamp, the lamplight disappearing when dipping down into the concave of the waves, the glimmer present, then not present.

Ataŋauraq sees my shaky hands. He holds my hands together. "I've never fought a man while at sea. You beat me to it. Steady your heartbeat and you steady your hands."

I nod, although I don't know if he saw my acknowledgment.

We're the first to arrive at the ship. The other umiaqs wait behind until we've got hold of the ship.

I climb the ship with Ataŋauraq, behind two other men. My second time climbing this ship. The boys tow away our umiaq. I look down at my boys. They look up at me, quiet, scared, but rowing away.

We reach the deck, hiding behind tall wooden boxy frames. We need to make our way towards the stairs.

I can't see my own feet. I can't see upwards. The ropes on deck disappear into the night sky.

I hear male voices nearby and underneath our feet. Light shines from the rooms below. I hear the ship creaking and water sloshing in some distant corner. Whale oil is in the air, fresh, bloody, and ingrained into the deck. They cleaned the deck, but I feel whale oil coated into the wood.

Nasugluk pokes my thigh, then points to the north. I see the Yankees.

The Yankees aren't drinking. There are more men than before. They each hold rifles, slung around their shoulders. A fat and stout man sits with his eyes closed, arms crossed against his chest. Another, blows into his cold hands, coughing, and swaying back and forth for warmth.

A man on deck whispers up to the crow's nest. Two distinct voices answer. I don't understand but I know the man asks a question. He's disappointed with the answer, flopping his hand in dejection, as if not to believe what the two said above.

Ataŋauraq peeks over the wooden boxy equipment on deck. I see his eyes in the lamplight. He hunches over, walking toward the Yankees with his rifle pointed.

Moments pass. Where is he? What's happening?

Ropes creak in the dark sky. Two Yankee men hung by the necks, swaying in long arcs. I see their bodies swaying towards the masts, ready to collide. When the Yankees looked upwards, I heard the first gunshots.

All at once, the Yankees shoot their guns in all directions.

"The stairs" Nasugluk yells.

I'm running after Nasugluk through a cloud of splinters, my cheek burning. My lungs fill with talc air, like sulfur, rotten eggs, and charcoal.

I land on deck, near the stairs, crashing into Nasugluk. Cousin pulls me by my ankle away from the blasts.

His left cheek bleeds. I reach up and feel my cheek. My left cheek bleeds, too. Somewhere I scraped my arm from the wrist to elbow. Hot blood drips from my wrist.

Gunshots continue on the other side of the ship. Bells ring.

Between the gunfire, blasts, and yelling, I hear her voice, a yell, a scream. I'm on my hands and knees, listening, my ear against the deck. I hear her voice, faint, moving, and strong. My love, I heard her voice! I heard her voice!

"Nasugluk! I heard her voice! I heard her voice!" I'm shaking his shoulder, clutching at his tunic.

He's not listening. He's watching the deck. He checks the stairs.

Ataŋauraq arrives, sweating, bloody, and out of breath. "No Yankees on deck. The stairs?"

"Stairs are clear. They're shooting from down the corridor,"

Nasugluk readies to run down the stairs, clutching his rifle with both hands.

We look down the dark stairway, a sudden hole in the deck, bullets piercing the stairs.

"Sounds like one rifle?"

All the men and women agree.

"We have to run through it. I'll shoot. It'll give you time to run." Ataŋauraq positions himself to shoot down the corridor. He won't get a clear shot of the Yankees, but it'll be enough to give time. "Panik. Are you ready?" he asks.

"Yes," I say.

"To the left! Down the stairs to the left! Ready," he yells.

"Yes." I've got the handgun in my hand.

I follow Nasugluk. I almost fall down the stairs. I slip and drop down a few stairs at a time. We went crashing into the room, almost headfirst. I slipped as I ran, stepping on a squishy slimy mess.

It takes a moment to see in the darkness.

We're in a tiny and cramped room, a few paces across, filled to the ceiling with gear. I remember seeing slivers of this room. I thought the room would be large and grand, but it is an angular-shaped storage room, a forgotten corner, nothing more.

"Anything? No doors?" I check the corners. Nothing.

Everything in this tiny room is old, worn, scabbed over in rust, except for soggy coils of rope arranged in symmetry. The wooden panels are blistering with seawater, while algae grows in every corner. I check for signs of a doorway behind canvas bags hung on the walls, swaying with the waves. The stench is overwhelming. Whale oil. Mildew. Smells of feces and the armpit of a sweaty man. I need to find her and get her out of this stinking rotting ship.

I check the bottom of my kamik. It is a squished eyeball with light eyes. How?

Taktuuk and Kimmaqsuuq run down the stairs with Yankee shirts and Yankee hats, trying to disguise themselves as the enemy. We've got seven men squeezed together in this little room.

The Yankees are at least two rooms away. They shoot and yell to each other.

Strange insects crawl on the floor, large and maroon colored.

"What is it?" Someone asks.

Someone pokes at the insect with their kamik. The insect scurries away and we all push ourselves backwards away from the bug.

I pick out a few splinters from my cheek. I check my weapons. Axe. Club. Handgun.

"I heard her. It was her!"

"When?"

"A moment ago."

"Good, good."

"They'll soon have more guns. We can't give them more time."

"Are you ready, panik?" Uncle asks.

I get ready to run. It is the same as before. Ataŋauraq shooting his rifle while we run to the next room.

The men file down the hallway. I don't see where I'm running. I follow their feet. Parts of the floor are slimy and saturated.

We crash into the next room, across the hallway. This time I fall into the room, skidding across the floor on my stomach.

It is a larger room with tables and stools nailed to the floor. We duck behind tables. Farther back, there is a small room with a window. A tiny kitchen. Food burns on a stove. I check under the tables and start circling the room with Nasugluk. There is nothing.

We gather near the doorway where Kimmiqsuuq and Nasugluk shoot their rifles down the hallway.

"What's down the hall? What do you see?" Ataŋauraq asks Kimmiqsuuq and Nasugluk.

"I see a door a few feet away. Yankees with guns further down."

"They've got more guns. It might be too late to cut them off from their weapons."

"We can't wait here. They're digging in."

Ataŋauraq and Taktuuk stand up, aiming their rifles to the kitchen.

I didn't hear anything, but everyone quiets.

I follow them, holding up my handgun.

Two women exit from the little room, holding up their hands. "Don't shoot! We're innocent!" They say.

I check the kitchen again, opening every little door. Nothing but sacks of food.

"You. How many guns do they got?" Ataŋauraq asks the older woman.

"I don't know. We don't know." She shook her head.

The white men yell from down the hall. They yell to each other.

"What are they saying," he asks.

"I don't know. We're prisoners."

"Where's the girl? A little girl, Samaruna?" Ataŋauraq asks.

"I don't know. We don't know," they say.

"You're safe. We've got boats. Stay behind me," he says.

We sit at the doorway, checking the next room. I check my handgun, club, and axe. Good, all set.

"Our numbers are the same. Equal men between us," Nasugluk says.

"Storm in!"

"I don't trust them. Don't trust a Yankee to fight hand to hand! No."

I agree. We argue about the next room while gunshots continue down the corridor.

"Psst. Sssstttt. Is that your dad? Your husband?" The woman asks.

Gunshots. More gunshots.

"What? No. No," I say. It is hard to hear her. The women huddle close together like sisters.

"Is he married?"

"What about the other one?"

"Do they trade with the white men? Are they married? Are they rich? Do they own more guns?" Their questions mixed together.

"What? I don't know!"

They are southern Inupiaq. I love the beauty of southern Inupiaq women: glowing skin, dimpled smiles, and tiny delicate hands. They look too sallow, unkempt, sunken inwards, and speak with voices hoarse and thick with liquor. Whiskey sucked away their youth. I can't tell their age. The older woman wears a parka too big for her. The younger woman wears a drab Yankee shirt.

They styled their hair like the Yankee women, puffed, pulled into a knot on their head, and they wear bright red rouge over their entire cheeks.

I've met women like them. Their confidence doesn't last on its own. They need men's attention to live, like we need water to live. Their confidence rebuilds itself after gaining attention, but crumbles just as fast. They'll suffer great abuses from a man to keep their attentions.

Some women are not even tricked or conned into the Yankee life. They go willingly, happily, and ready to abandon their homes. The Yankees often trade women at the ports, tired of a woman, they'll trade for another.

I hear them speaking Yankee. What is it about them? I look at them again and both look down at the floor. She scratches her neck with blackened fingernails, avoiding my gaze.

They're scared of me.

I do something I can't believe. I yank an arrow from Ataŋauraq's bag and stab the older woman's leg. Even as my hands reach for an arrow and plunge it into her thigh, I can't believe my own actions. She stands up, limping, and screaming with a hoarse voice. She's leaning against a table. The other woman stands up, too. I grab her collar, the ugly itchy Yankee shirt, and headbutt her ugly face. She flings backwards, disappearing in the shadows.

I twist the arrow.

"Lies, lies! You want to be a Yankee? Where is she?" She screams. I punch her face and she flops onto the table by her belly. Blood smears over her teeth. These women know we are looking for Sam. They know I am her mother. Yet they stand there like prisoners. Liars. "Where is she?" I pull out my axe. I'm going to cut off her toes. I'll cut off her foot if I have to. I say this with my whole body.

"With the captain! In the captain's quarters! There's another way! Up on deck!"

"How many guns?" I yell.

"Twelve guns, at least. Twenty! She's with the captain. In the back room. Go up. Go up on deck. There's a door!"

I yank the arrow out. I spit at the ground at her feet. She takes refuge with her companion, hoisting an arm over her shoulder for support.

"Let me out! Let me out," The woman yells, limping.

"Go! Go!" I shove the younger woman towards the door. The younger one helps the older one out the door. "Go be with your own kind!"

The men stare at me in disbelief.

Ataŋauraq gives me a rifle.

The women yell something in Yankee to the white men, something frantic and begging. Still, the Yankees don't answer. I hear shots and the women falling and the women gurgling.

I feel no pity or sorrow. They were responsible for their own deaths. I didn't bring them on board. They boarded themselves, willingly, knowingly.

"Let's get the next room!"

"They've got more guns!"

"Block the entrance. Light up the whole ship!"

"She's in there! She'll burn up! No," I say.

It is Nasugluk that has the idea. "We'll smoke them! They won't know the difference!"

"It's your decision. Kaya," Ataŋauraq says.

"C'mon!" I grab Nasugluk's hand.

In the little kitchen, there is a stove. I open the stove to find it filled with coal. "No, no. We need wood. They must think it is wood that is burning."

I throw cast iron pans across the entire stove, filling with oil and bits of my hair. With my axe, Nasugluk breaks up a wooden crate. Then, starts breaking up a barrel. I pile all the tinder upon the pans. The fire doesn't start right away. Nasugluk pours more oil. We wait until the fire builds into a sizeable blaze.

At the doorway, I grab the rifle with both hands. I'm headed to the deck.

Ataŋauraq and all the men and women load up their guns. They know I'm headed to the captain's quarters.

Three rifles shoot down the hallway. I run up to the deck.

The sun rises on the horizon. I see my sons. Do they know it is me?

I hear Yankees panicking, coughing, pounding against the ship. Too much smoke. My baby. My baby.

I see the outline of a small door. I pull up. It's locked. I axe away at the door, concentrating at the hinges. It takes time. I watch for the Yankees, but none escape from the stairs. The boys circle around to see me axing at the deck. I'm sweating. My arms burning. It's not getting at the hinges. No good. It's no good.

Smoke rises from the deck in dark wisps. This isn't smoke. This is a fire below. I have no time. No time. I need to use the rifle. What if I shoot her? Shoot at an angle. Shoot at the most severe angle. I step back, as far as I can against the ship's railing. Gun against the shoulder. First shot, splinters shoot upwards. Second shot, and the door buckles downwards. It is enough to open the door. I reload my rifle.

I yank up the broken door, smoke escaping, and shoulder my rifle.

29 | HER MOTHER

I WOKE UP TO GUNSHOTS. I HIT MY HEAD AGAINST THE BUNK. What time is it? It's 3 am.

They're here. It's the girl's mother.

I throw off my blanket. The girl looks up to the ceiling, then to the doorway. Already the captain stands at the door, snatches her up, runs down the hallway, slamming doors.

"Shit! Asshole," I say. I'm on my feet.

"Ibai, what do we do?" Gerald yells.

"Get dressed," I tell him.

"Will we have to abandon ship?"

"Grab your shit, Gerald."

We hear deep hurried footsteps running up on deck, right above our bunks. We hear men yelling for help in far-off cries. We hear a man splashing into the sea.

"I can't see. Where's my glasses? Shit! I need my glasses. I can't see shit," A whaler says.

There is a lamp in the room. I can't see anything either. Shadows obscure everything. I grope in my plunder chest for my wool shirt. I put aside my parka because I'm taking it with me. I stuff my sailor's bag with my boots, brogans, and any fur-covered items. I carry my knife.

Whalers yell all at once. Men crowd through the door, piling in the forecastle.

"What the fuck!"

"What's happening?"

Emilio joins the forecastle, panting, sweating, and carrying his knife. "We're under attack!"

Whalers shout.

"Eskimos are on the ship!"

"It's a damn invasion! A mutiny!"

"Who is manning the ship? They'll run the ship into the ground."

"It's the girl's people. Don't you understand?" I yell.

"What?" Remigio says.

"The girl! The little girl! It's the girl's people," I say.

"Bull shit! She's an orphan," Emilio yells.

"They'll leave after they get the girl," I yell back.

"They're savages. You don't know what they want."

Remigio grabs my forearm. He hisses. "Tell the captain. Tell him they want the girl and then they'll leave," Remigio says.

"He grabbed her already," I say.

"Shit! Fuckin asshole," He hisses.

The bow-facing door bursts with gunshots, blown off at the top hinge.

We hit the floor, our faces buried in the wood. Bullets buzz by my ear. We crawl and shuffle to the farthest wall.

"Barricade the door!" Jurek yells.

"He's right. Barricade the door," Emilio says.

Everyone scrambles. We collect all the loose furniture in the room, plunder chests, straw mattresses, stools, water cask, stove, dumping it by the door. Even the damn crap bucket. Someone grabs a broom and props it against the wall. We wince at every bullet piercing the ship. Someone pissed their pants, now the piss zigzags across the floor as we roll in the waves. Anthony prays with both hands. He prays, looking up at the ceiling.

Emilio gives his keys to Jurek for the guns. Jurek leaves for our weapons, exiting the stern door.

We crouch on the floor, half-dressed in fur clothing, a few men holding their sheath knives upright. We watch the doors. Apart from the gunshots, we hear the eskimos yelling in their tongues.

Because of shift change, almost the entire crew is now in the forecastle. The previous shift crew was eating in the mess hall, along with Anthony. Frank ran into the forecastle still holding his plate and fork.

"Who's on deck?"

"Alastor," someone says.

Alastor, Keres, Clayton, and that other new recruit from Herschel. That guy from Maine. Damn.

"What about the stern door," someone asks.

"Locked! Captain shut himself in!"

We cuss.

There are two escape routes on the ship, one towards the stern, the other towards the bow. The eskimos blocked off the door at the bow. The captain blocks off the door at the stern.

"They're commandeering the ship!"

"A mutiny!"

"They're going to rob us blind!"

"Damn assholes. Can't work for themselves. They have to steal. I hate nothing more than thieves. Can't work hard for their own shit so they steal it. They need to be hung. All of them. Not one thief left on earth, if it were up to me," Emilio says.

"What about the damn cutter service? Where's the damn cutter service," a whaler asks.

"Healy's probably looking for ale to dump. Fucking revenue cutters! Where's your precious Healy? Nowhere. Cause he isn't the hero of the seas. I have to do the whaling and cutter service duties as well," Emilio says.

A few whalers wrap their forearms with torn bedding.

"What the hell are they doing?" Emilio asks.

"They've been to war. In their home country. They are getting ready to fight," I say.

"Good. Good men. Be like these fearless men here."

"Are we close to land? Are we close to Alaska? We must be close," a whaler yells.

"Other ships will see us."

"No doubt. Just you see."

"They messed with the wrong ship. Wrong industry," Emilio scoffs.

"We're closer to Russia than Alaska, fools."

"We have to be close to a city by now."

"And what if there isn't?"

"Damned, cursed by the devil!"

"You fall into these waters and you're a dead man. A corpse."

"This is a war ship!"

"With what weapons? A few rifles?"

"There are some explosives on the ship."

"We can't use explosives on our own ship."

"Yeah, but we don't even know how many there are!"

"They'll be hanged. This is treason. This is piracy on the high seas. Loot and pillage!"

"They come to kill. They're savages. They want blood, not loot."

"God is here to collect our souls for our sins."

"Shut that blabber. Quit being so dramatic! Keep it together! Stop, let me think! Throw those bags. We're not retreating. Get ready to fight, you cowards," Emilio yells.

We've heard endless stories of ships sinking at sea, Cleopatra and Anthony's doomed fleet, Viking ships crossing the Atlantic Ocean, whaling ships rammed and sunk by sperm whales, explorers traveling to tropical isles, cargo ships sinking at Cape Horn, slave ships mutinied and destroyed, revenue cutters, pirates crashing into coral reefs, and Confederate ships attacked in the bay.

"Do we evacuate?" someone asks.

"We must evacuate, sir," another yells.

"Evacuate? Cowards! Protect your captain!"

"What do we do? Who's got the manual?"

"I didn't read the manual."

"Me neither."

"Because you can't read, clown. Degenerate."

"I read it!" They know I can read, and they know I read the manual in my first weeks assigned to the ship. "First priority is the ship's men. Then the resources. That's company protocol."

"Shut up! We have a right to defend ourselves and our property," Emilio counters.

"Can you not negotiate with them? The women can translate. They're eskimos. They can translate. Negotiate," I say. The men repeat the word 'negotiate'. Some of them didn't know what the word meant, but they said it anyway.

"You can't negotiate with those tundra niggers! They're hostile! They're here to kill! Not to negotiate. Damn asshole fucks! Exploiting our labors! They waited until we had full barrels! Oppressors and looters! They wait until we're full of oil and vulnerable in the icy seas, then they come down to loot and pillage and strike down every able man for their own vile and perverse nature. They've got no souls! No souls!"

"I'd cut my own fingers and toes for the company, sir, but 'tis better to negotiate first. They're men, aren't they," Remigio states.

"I suppose you're going to slip away in all this commotion. Cowards. Shits. Fight to the death!"

I tried to remember the stories of savage attacks on ships. I hear the fragile newspapers crinkling through my fingers. Reading the heroic stories of whalers who survived attacks by the savage peoples. What did they do? What happened? The ships sank. All their ships sank. And they had to survive on a tropical island eating coconuts and little crabs for food. This isn't the tropics. This is the arctic. Falling into these waters means death.

"Be ready to get into a boat," I tell Gerald.

Jurek arrives with the rifles. He's brought four. Jurek stays at the door, firing the rifle down the hallway. He's a marksman. At least this is what I'm told.

"That's it? Four rifles?"

"I grabbed what I could, sir."

"Might as well hand my ass over to the eskimos. Damn! Four, four! Fucking shit mother fucking assholes. I have to do everything myself."

"What do they do on a naval ship? Jurek, what do they do on a naval ship?"

"Gather arms. Find your squadron. Line up in position."

We straighten out as best we can in the dark, crawling, shuffling. We group together with our boat crews, harpooners, linemen, and whalemen, like our whaling drills in the middle of the Pacific.

Jurek's shooting, reloading, and yelling. "Every man is in charge of their own ammunition. Attack when the commander gives the order."

"Jesus Christ! We knew that. Useless. Load them up. Load 'em."

Niek died in his bed. I see his blood dripping from his back to the floor. Shit.

George squeezes his thigh, hobbling, and groaning. He falls into the wall, headfirst. I thought he was dead for a second, but he crawls away from the barricade towards the bunks.

"Get a ligature, tie it, tie it," Remigio yells.

"Jurek's been shot," Gerald yells.

Jurek holds his wrist, stopping the bleeding. He's shot through the palm, fingers distorted into a claw.

"Find him something," Emilio orders.

Gerald helps bandage his hand. Gerald leans over and vomits, adding to the piss pool rolling across the floor.

We hear the eskimo women yelling from down the hall. "Rich-chard! Rich-chard! Don't shoot! It's us! Don't shoot!"

Emilio shoots. He shoots the eskimo women and reloads.

One of the eskimo women chokes in the hallway. We hear gurgling and spitting. He watches in silence, pointing the rifle down the hall.

"They haven't met a hellion before me. Think they have? No, no sir," Emilio yells. He shoots his rifle.

"We're all going to die," A whaler yells.

"All of you. Shut the fuck up!"

"Jesus, shit! They're in the mess hall."

"Where's the captain?"

"In his cabin. Protect the captain! It's your duty," Emilio screams at them.

"I'm not dying for the company! They want the girl so give them the girl," a whaler states.

"Not your decision," he says.

"Jesus Christ!"

"He's right!"

"Shut up!"

"They got cover in the mess! We don't."

"I can't swim! We'll drown! We'll get sucked in with the ship," Utah says.

"Shut up!"

"Ibai, I'm not a good swimmer," Gerald sounds like a child. I've not felt more pity than in this moment.

"You'll be fine. We'll find a boat. Gerald. Stay with me. We need to get up to deck and find a boat!" I whisper.

No one can swim in arctic waters. You'll go frozen from the cold. Unable to swim. We've heard of it.

When the water comes, it'll be like a river we'll have to fight up the stairs, bursting open all the doors, sending the mattresses, barrels, kitchen tools, and whaling gear crashing around the room. The room would go black, and we'd die floating in this dreary room.

The eskimos yell down the hall.

"They're in the mess hall!"

"Does anyone understand?"

"Shit!"

Rats squeal from their hiding spots. I see their faint orb-like figures run across the crook of the wall and slip underneath the stern-forward door, altogether, scampering away. Cockroaches chittered, clicking up the walls.

Smoke gathers at the ceiling, thin as a wedding veil. The smoke thickens, from opaque to grey.

"Oh shit," I say.

"Shit!"

"They've started a fire."

"We'll suffocate! We'll burn to death!"

"It's the demons of hell. Straight from the hellfire!"

"The Lord threw us down into this hole and gave the key to Satan!"

"We can run for it. We can run for the stairs."

"Shut! Up! Quiet!" Emilio yells. He drinks some concoction from a glass bottle, squinting his eyes.

"We'll suffocate! We'll burn alive!" Someone yells.

"Tell my wife and children I love them," Anthony cries.

"Stop blabbering. Give me the plagues of Egypt! Shut the fuck up, all of you. Fire doesn't live long on the sea!" Emilio loads up his rifle, continues shooting, although his eyes stream down tears. He rubs his eyes against his sleeve.

I taste caustic ashes and the musty odors of the ship, amplified by the smoke. Fresh air. Fresh air. Fresh sea air. I cover my nose and mouth with my shirt.

Men disobey Emilio's orders. He doesn't notice or pretends not to notice. Whalers stuff their canvas bags, bought from the company. They throw their bags over their shoulders, crouching, ready to run for the stairs.

Other men clutch their crosses and rosaries. Another man clutches a vial of holy oil. "Our Mary, Mother of God, watch over your children who praise your name. Keep your children in safety. Hail our Father. You are the Guardian. You are the Rescuer. The Redeemer of souls. Avenge us. Avenge us. Strike down the enemy, in your name Jesus Christ. Smite the enemy!"

Another man speaks in tongues, swaying back and forth, back and forth.

"Let me live and I will go to the woman's feet and beg her forgiveness."

"Driven by the devil themselves! It's the devil's concubines. The devil worshipers."

"Gerald, boy! Take up a rifle. Get over here!" Emilio yells. He shoves a rifle to Gerald.

I shake my head. "He can't shoot a gun, sir! Give it to me."

"Not you, you prick. Gerald! Get your fat ass over here! Load up those bullets. Load it up." Gerald crawls over. He sits snug against Emilio. Gerald doesn't know what he is doing. Gerald tries to push in bullets but two pop out of his hand. He fumbles with his clumsy hands. With much rattling of metal against metal, he loaded the rifle. "Don't point that near me. Down the hallway. Aim the rifle, aim it," Emilio snaps.

"Sorry, sir," Gerald says.

Gerald's going to get killed. Killed. My thumbnail almost breaks the skin against my pointer finger. Damn it! "Sir! I'm experienced," I demand. A few bullets fly by my ear.

Gerald's choking.

"Gerald! Gerald!"

I run to him.

He chokes blood. His eye fills with blood. I see blood staining over his eye, starting from the corner, going upwards, clear as a cup filling with blood.

He can't speak. He's shot through the neck. He's choking on his own blood. I hold his neck. He pleads for help with his eyes. I can't. I don't know how.

I grab his hand, hold it against his chest. Remigio joins me. We both hold his hands.

"Gerald. Gerald. Do you renounce your sins?"

He tries to speak. He nods yes. The other whalers crowd behind me. They lay their hands on him. He's swallowing and choking. I look him in the eye for as long as possible.

We recite together, fast, rambling, ducking, taking cover, and yelling at times. "The Lord is my shepherd; I shall not want. He maketh me to lie down in green pastures: he leadeth me beside the still waters. He restoreth my soul: he leadeth me in the paths of righteousness for his name's sake. Yea, though I walk through the valley of the shadow of Death, I will fear no evil: for thou art with me; thy rod and thy staff they comfort me. Thou preparest a table before me in the presence of mine enemies: thou anointest my head with oil; my cup runneth over. Surely goodness and mercy shall follow me all the days of my life: and I will dwell in the house of the Lord forever. Amen."

Amen, they said.

"Be with God, my brother."

Another gunshot hits him under the armpit.

What will I tell his mother? I failed him. I failed him. His poor mother. He's a child. He was a child.

I yank the rifle from Emilio's hands. I punch him. I want to yank his head off. I punch Emilio over and over. My eyes burn from the smoke as we stand up, but I continue punching him. I taste blood.

My eyes go white from getting punched. A gunshot breaks apart a wooden beam, but we continue punching.

"What the fuck, boy," he yells.

We land on the floor, gripping each other and punching.

He kicks me so hard I end up standing in the doorway. He stops. He's waiting for me to get shot. I grab my parka.

"I'm not dying in this box." I kick over the barricade, pushing aside the plunder chests and debris. The shooting continues but I throw debris aside anyway.

"You, coward fuck," Emilio yells.

I stand in the lightless corridor. Cockroaches crawl away from the smoke. I carry nothing except my parka in one hand.

The shooting stops.

I don't see more than a few feet away in the smoke, but they don't shoot.

I feel the eskimos looking at me. They see me but do nothing. They're wondering what I'm doing.

In all the haze, smoke, and caustic air, I know it is time to get off the ship. This isn't the life for me.

I walk, one foot in front of another, pawing my way down the corridor.

I hear Emilio yelling as I reach the captain's quarters. "Hellion demon son of a bitch!"

Captain locked his door. He shut himself in his quarters.

Underneath his door, I see the captain pacing the floor. Damn snake! What do I do? I knock. "Captain! I'm here to protect the captain! Emilio sent me!"

A second, two seconds. He's thinking. I hear chairs and chests moved away from the door. He unlocks the door. "Good man, Emilio. He's a good man."

I shove open the door which throws him backward. He's partly dressed for an escape. He wears the fur skin pants of the eskimo. He was determined to scurry off in a boat while we fought off the eskimos.

I punch him. He's surprised. He's not processing what's happening. It takes him a second to realize what's happening.

I'm wrestling with the captain. He grunts like a horse. We punch and kick. We got hands around each other's necks, and we whip around the room. I see slivers of images of the room. I see the girl standing against the wall.

"Boy! You goddamn nigger! Damn you sailor! You trader asshole!"

He spits. He's full of fury. His hands dig into my shoulders. I'm blinded by punches. My eye closes up. I can't see out of my left eye. I taste blood. I move too slow and too heavy.

"Get back to where you belong! That's an order!" He bites my forearm. Flops his entire body with his teeth, like a shark frenzied kill. The cheater! The coward! I punch him in the face and he lets go of his bite.

"I quit! I resign from the company. My contract is void! Liquor! Kidnapping children! My contract is void!"

I hear a loud explosion, a blast through the rear hatch. Slivers of wood burst downwards and outwards. The noise. I can't hear for a moment. Smoke escapes the hatch. Daylight shows through the room.

I'm shot. I'm shot. Blood on my stomach. The captain and I both look down. We both realize he's been shot.

I'm not shot.

The mother walks down the tiny, narrow staircase. She's beautiful, stone-faced, and armed. She painted her eyes black, from her forehead to her eyes.

She shot the captain through the abdomen. He squirms up against the wall. I push myself up against the wall. I hold my hands up into the air.

The girl runs.

They hug each other but the mother doesn't drop her rifle.

She speaks in eskimo. I don't know what she says.

The girl covers her ears with both hands and looks away.

To our surprise the mother props her rifle on the staircase. What is she doing? The captain wonders, too. She grabs an axe from her back. She holds the axe with both hands.

"Merihim." Her voice is fluid, steady, and determined. She

studies his face. Not in cruelty. Maybe for remembrance. Maybe she wants him to see her face.

The captain hisses, "You bitch! You damn quim cunt bitch!"

The axe comes down and I shield my face with my arms. The axe twangs against the floor. First, there is no noise from the captain's open mouth, but the scream comes. He brings up an arm missing a hand, spurting blood. He looks frantically around the room. He holds onto his stump, trying to stop the bleeding.

Jesus Christ, his expression. His open mouth. I see his hand on the floor. His fingers twitch.

With her foot, she pushes his severed twitching hand away from him. She watches his reactions. She isn't cruel, but she isn't remorseful.

"You damn bitch! My hand! My hand!" She spits in the captain's face. He tries to spit back but he's got no breath in his lungs. She retrieves the axe by planting a foot against the wall, pulling up. She hoists the axe above her head again, almost to the ceiling. This time he screams, "No, no, no!" Axe twangs against the floor again. No sound from his mouth. She cleaved off his other hand. His mouth is open, gasping.

His breath smells like whiskey and cigar smoke. The woman smells like the sea, salt and fresh air. I feel vibrations on the floor from gunshots, deep, echoing, and distant. The canopy of grey smoke on the ceiling forms like ripples, textured, rolling, and mesmerizing. I can't do anything. It's not sadness. It's not fear. It's the levity of the moment, ineffable and triumph. Yes, triumph.

I stand up, pushing myself up against the wall. She doesn't notice. He looks to me for help. His eyes are red, like a band across both eyes. I don't show him remorse either. I show him nothing. She speaks in eskimo. Before a scream comes again, she axes both of his eyes. She retrieves the axe, all in smooth motions.

When she picks up his severed hands, I notice her tattooed fingers. Rings upon rings upon rings. She grabs his severed hands in one hand and picks up her daughter with the other hand.

She leaves me in the smoky room, sunlight piercing downwards into the captain's quarters. She didn't look at me. Not once.

The captain's body falls over onto the floor. There are no more shooting guns. I hear fire. I can't think. What do I do? I grab my parka and walk up on deck.

For a moment, I'm blinded by the sunlight. I hold up my hands in surrender.

The masts burn in tall slender flames. Smoke billows from the stairs. The smoke blots out the sunrays. The port deck is blackened from the fire below. I see the tips of flames on the side of the ship. The fire eats a giant hole. I see Remigio, Anthony, Jurek, and Frank, and about a dozen other men. All the survivors crowd together. We've got our hands up.

The eskimos aim their rifles, but they allow whalers to untie the boats.

"They're letting us go?" Remigio asks.

"So, it seems," I say. I help lower the boats into the water. "We lost Gerald," He joins the other young boys forced to fight in wars, battles, and meaningless causes. He joins the other young boys forced to fight for men's greed.

"All this for the girl,"

"So, it seems,"

30 | SIVULLIQ: ANCESTOR

NASUGLUK AND ATAŊAURAQ CRAM THE YANKEES against the ship's railing. The Yankees hold up their hands. Their faces are grey, streaked, and blotchy. A few Yankees carry food sacks tucked under their elbows, others carry cloth sacks over their shoulders. The Yankees stand in a line, shuffling, backs against the railing, climbing down the ladder, and even then, when reaching the wooden umiaqs they raise their hands in the air.

"Aaka, I cried for you," my daughter tucks her hands underneath her chin.

I cradle her like a baby. I sit down on the deck with my back against the ship. We cry together. She smells like the ocean and warm skin. I kiss her cheeks, her forehead, and I wipe her tears with my palms. "Come. Let me see you. Did you get taller? You're this much taller. Look at that! My sweet, sweet girl,"

She's shaking. I know she's thinking about the captain.

"I'm sorry I scared you. I scared you. I did it so he could not hurt anyone else in the afterlife. Our people will be safe. You're safe. You're safe with me," I kiss her forehead.

In the afterlife, he will be blind. Without his eyes, he won't be able to distinguish a human form from a doll. Without his hands, he cannot commit cruelty. I won't leave injustices to fate.

I toss the hands of the captain into a flaming pit, a spreading fire taking over the ship. The captain will never find his hands. His hands are ashes, scattered, cleaved, and conquered.

"Aaka! I see Ebrulik. I see Nauraq,"

"I see them,"

"They're here!"

"Yes, they're here. We're all here,"

She touches my bloody cheek. She's checking if it hurts.

"I'm alright. Aaka will be fine. Can you help clean me up?"

"Yes,"

"You're a good helper,"

"Aaka?"

"Yes?"

"Let's go home and be happy,"

Ataŋauraq limps. His hands are streaked with gunpowder, soot, and blood. Blood dries on his hands in branches, waxen, dark as cranberry, ruddy, and flowing outwards. Yet he looks younger than I remember. Had I thought of him as an old man? He's a strong man with many years ahead.

Later, I heard of the fight between Ataŋauraq and the big officer. They fought with guns, bare hands, whatever weapons they could find. The big man bit Ataŋauraq's shoulder, biting through his leather tunic. Ataŋauraq threw the big man through a wall and smashed his hand with a metal pulley.

I'd soon stitch up two long lacerations on uncle's forearm, the flesh peeling upwards like the officer tried to skin meat from the bone. Ataŋauraq's skin is thick as uugruk leather and his bones strong as stone.

"The Yankee wouldn't look me in the eye. Skittish as a mouse. Coward. Yankee cities grow weak and savage men. I pray he's reborn as an Indigenous man and he'll know true happiness,"

Ataŋauraq leans in towards Samaruna's face. "Hi buniin. You remember me?"

"Hi aapa,"

"Good girl," He kisses her forehead with force, holding the back of her head. She squeezes her eyes tight, smiling. "Wait down in the water for aapa. I want to get back to our coast before other ships arrive,"

"I miss my other aapa,"

"Me too. He's up behind the moon with your aaka," He kisses the palm of her hand.

The front of the ship plops downward. We grab the railing. The Yankees scramble off the ship. Rats escape from below deck, now clawing upwards, a few rats lose their holding and fall squealing into the ship's flames.

"Come. Hurry," Ataŋauraq waves.

"Sweet girl. Let's go down to the water. Ready to see Ebrulik and Nauraq?"

Everyone gets to an umiaq, wooden or sealskin.

The boys steady the umiaq against the ship. I climb down first, then Samaruna.

My children form a circle, Samaruna in the middle. In this maddening scene, in the choking oppressive smoke, the ship sinking deeper at the hull, my children form a circle, hugging, weeping, and laughing. The boys promise to watch over her. They traveled hundreds of miles to rescue each other. I see my children together and I cannot recall a purer moment of joy. A mother's love cannot be compared to any other form of love, compassion, or joy.

Ebrulik shivers. He's wet and pale.

"What happened?"

"I'm warming up. I need dry clothes,"

Ebrulik saved two drowning men. The two men fell into the ocean, dragged down by the weight of their parkas. Ebrulik removed his shirt, dove into the ocean, and pulled up both men.

I give him a parka and waterproof pants, then I drape extra fur over him.

I can't help but laugh from happiness. All three of my children in our umiaq. I kiss Sam's forehead over and over and smell her hair. How healthy her skin looks, the freshness of youth.

"Let me look at you. So beautiful. So strong,"

"Aaka, there's a dog,"

"I see it. She's a good dog,"

"Where's my puppy?"

"My girl. My silly girl," I laugh and cry.

Sunshine glows behind the clouds. The ship burns. We watch the ship from a distance. We see the Yankee whalers in their boats, distorted, miraged from the heat of the fire. We let them escape. Flames burst from the sides of the ship. Crates, debris, ropes, and canvas sails float in the water. We leave it all for the Yankees. We salvage nothing. Everywhere, rats swim outwards, searching for land. It takes time for the ship to sink. First it plops, pulled down by the water at the bow. The ship succumbs to the icy water, sinking, and I let my grief sink with the ship. The ship will sink to the seafloor, to the ravines and glens with large eels, crabs, and scavengers ready to devour and clean every inch of the ship.

"We must leave," Ataŋauraq says.

"What will happen to them?" Sam asks.

"Ships come every day. At least three in a day. Land isn't far away. Not even a day to the east. They have their boats,"

"Can he come with us?"

"Who?"

"The taqsipuuk,"

"What is he to you? Tell me,"

"He is my friend,"

"There's lots of ships,"

"He is our Ancestor,"

"Who taught you the word Ancestor?"

"My dad,"

I see him. It is as if the taqsipuuk heard our conversation. He rows with the Yankees, but he watches our umiaqs. "Uncle. Bring me over to the Yankees,"

"Are you certain?" Ataŋauraq asks.

"Yes,"

They stop rowing. They raise their hands, creaking in their little wooden boats. The Yankee boats are stocked with ropes, steel-headed harpoons, lancing tools but they don't risk their lives with any small gestures of defiance. Ataŋauraq keeps them in gun-sight, nonetheless.

How small they look in their small wooden boats. On Herschel Island, they seemed large as giants. They are not fiery or illumi-nated like the drawings in newspapers or books, instead they are bland, drab, flecked with blood, and sour to the tongue. They shirk away, shoulders small, and eyes moving fast as a birds.

I see him. I notice his eyes, dignified, and black as night. I didn't notice his age before, in that dark smoky room of the Yankee ship. He is a man, old enough to have his own whaling crew.

"Ask him to come with us. Yes. Him," I say.

"To come with us?"

"Yes,"

Ataŋauraq waits a moment, and then extends his hand to the dark man.

The Yankees shake their heads. The Yankees ask him ques-tions. The taqsipuuk says nothing. He speaks with his eyes like an Inupiaq.

"They think we'll kill him," Ataŋauraq argues.

"He'll come," I say.

With politeness, he grabs Ataŋauraq's hand. He joins our umiaq and picks up an oar. We leave the burning ship, the Yankees, and the thin line of Siberian shores.

Men and women died on the journey to rescue my daughter. The preacher buried Nasauyaaq in the Naluagmiut way, the Christian way, redeemed and washed of her sins. Our people descend to the ocean floor where they'll live everlasting, and where the all-know-ing and all-seeing Sedna transforms darkness into light. They sail downwards like the sea birds diving from the cliffs, cast on the winds, soaring, suspended, almost motionless, yet fluttering. They live in glory, with Jesus, with Sedna, and our Ancestors. They live in glory beside my husband. He was called into the afterlife to fight for his children.

My dear husband, my love. Our children are safe. We sail back home to Tikigaq. Our sons row with their strong arms and strong hearts. The Creator spared our children from the epidemic. For some months, I was blinded from seeing these gifts. Samaruna says the taqsipuuk is an Ancestor. Perhaps he is. Our children know when they meet an Inupiaq. Our children know when they meet a real human being.

Charles J. Tice

Lɪʟʏ Tᴜᴢʀᴏʏʟᴜᴋᴇ ɪs ᴀɴ ɪɴᴅɪɢᴇɴᴏᴜs ᴡʀɪᴛᴇʀ from Alaska and Canada. She is a graduate student at the University of Alaska Fairbanks and previously served in Tribal Government. Lily now resides in Anchorage, Alaska.